KU-586-202

Award-winning author **Jennifer Faye** pens fun
contemporary romances. Internationally published, with
books translated into more than a dozen languages, she
is a two-time winner of the *RT Book Reviews* Reviewers'
Choice Award and winner of the CataRomance
Reviewers' Choice Award. Now, living her dream, she
resides with her very patient husband and Writer Kitty.
When she's not plotting out her next romance, you can
find her with a mug of tea and a book. Learn more at
jenniferfaye.com.

Hana Sheik falls in love every day, reading her
favourite romances and writing her own happily-ever-
afters. She's worked at various jobs—but never for very
long, because she's always wanted to be a romance
author. Now she gets to happily live that dream. Born in
Somalia, she moved to Ottawa, Canada, at a very young
age, and still resides there with her family.

Llyfrgelloedd Caerdyd
www.caerdydd.gov.uk/llyfrgelloe
Cardiff Libraries
www.cardiff.gov.uk/libraries

ACC. No: 05232281

Also by Jennifer Faye

Falling for Her Convenient Groom

Greek Paradise Escape miniseries

Greek Heir to Claim Her Heart
It Started with a Royal Kiss

Also by Hana Sheik

Second Chance to Wear His Ring
Temptation in Istanbul

Discover more at millsandboon.co.uk.

SECOND CHANCE WITH THE BRIDESMAID

JENNIFER FAYE

FORBIDDEN KISSES WITH HER MILLIONAIRE BOSS

HANA SHEIK

MILLS & BOON

All rights reserved including the right of reproduction
in whole or in part in any form. This edition is published
by arrangement with Harlequin Enterprises ULC.

This is a work of fiction. Names, characters, places, locations
and incidents are purely fictional and bear no relationship to
any real life individuals, living or dead, or to any actual places,
business establishments, locations, events or incidents.
Any resemblance is entirely coincidental.

This book is sold subject to the condition that it
shall not, by way of trade or otherwise, be lent, resold, hired out
or otherwise circulated without the prior consent of the publisher
in any form of binding or cover other than that in which it is published
and without a similar condition including this condition
being imposed on the subsequent purchaser.

® and TM are trademarks owned and used by the trademark owner
and/or its licensee. Trademarks marked with ® are registered with the
United Kingdom Patent Office and/or the Office for Harmonisation
in the Internal Market and in other countries.

First published in Great Britain 2022
by Mills & Boon, an imprint of HarperCollins*Publishers* Ltd,
1 London Bridge Street, London, SE1 9GF

www.harpercollins.co.uk

HarperCollins*Publishers*
1st Floor, Watermarque Building,
Ringsend Road, Dublin 4, Ireland

Second Chance with the Bridesmaid © 2022 Jennifer F. Stroka

Forbidden Kisses with Her Millionaire Boss © 2022 Muna Sheik

ISBN: 978-0-263-30230-1

11/22

This book is produced from independently certified FSC™ paper
to ensure responsible forest management.
For more information visit: www.harpercollins.co.uk/green.

Printed and Bound in Spain using 100% Renewable Electricity
at CPI Black Print, Barcelona

SECOND CHANCE WITH THE BRIDESMAID

JENNIFER FAYE

MILLS & BOON

PROLOGUE

July, Paris, France

PITTER-PATTER. PITTER-PATTER.

Adara Galinis's heartbeat accelerated as the elevator slowly rose in one of the poshest hotels in Paris. That wasn't what was making her nervous. As the concierge of an elite island resort that hosted celebrities and millionaires, she was used to the finest surroundings.

Her racing heart had to do with the fact that she had traveled from Greece to Paris on the spur of the moment. She wasn't normally spontaneous. She liked things neat and orderly. Her job provided all the spontaneity she needed in life.

But she had a long weekend off, and in order to spend time with Krystof, she needed to come to him. Ever since they'd met at Valentine's on Ludus Island, they'd been casually seeing each other.

Krystof was best friends with the island's owner, Atlas Othonos. Earlier that year, when Atlas had briefly considered selling the island, he'd contacted Krystof in hopes that he'd want to buy the place. The sale didn't work out, but Adara had caught Krystof's attention. He'd pursued her in a charming sort of way—requesting concierge service and explaining that he wanted to dance with the most beautiful woman at the resort that evening. She was all prepared to extend an invitation on his behalf to whichever woman he'd chosen when he'd announced that the woman he was interested in was her.

She'd hesitated at first. After all, she made it a rule not to fraternize with the guests, but his warm smile and his enchanting way with words had won her over. They'd danced the night away at the Valentine's ball. It had been a magical evening that didn't end until the sun came up the next morning.

Now whenever Krystof stayed at the Ludus Resort, they made sure to spend as much time together as possible. At the end of each visit, he always asked her to fly away with him to some far-flung country. And though the idea tempted her, she'd always turned him down. She just couldn't imagine picking up and leaving without any planning. How was her assistant supposed to know what needed to be done? What if one of her regular clients arrived and she wasn't there? Part of her success was knowing the regulars and anticipating their wants before they had to ask her. She kept extensive files on their regular guests, from their favorite foods and colors to the names of their children and pets.

However, this weekend Hermione, her boss and best friend, had insisted she use some of her accumulated vacation time. Adara had been so focused on her job recently that she'd let her social life slide, and as for hobbies, well, she didn't have any unless you counted shopping.

So when she heard Krystof would be visiting Paris, the shopping mecca of the world, she took it as a sign. She couldn't wait to see him again. Their visits were so infrequent that it was always a rush to be with him. At least that's what she told herself was the reason for her heart racing every time she laid eyes on him.

She ran her hand down over the short, snug black dress. Her effort was a waste, because there was nowhere for the dress to go. It clung to her body like a second skin. It was a far more daring dress than she was accustomed to wearing. She'd bought it specifically for Krystof. She hoped he'd like her surprise.

As the elevator rose, her gaze focused on the increasing numbers. With each floor she passed, her heart beat faster. All too quickly, the elevator quietly came to a stop on the ninth floor. The door whooshed open.

Adara drew in a deep breath and then exhaled. With her fingers wrapped around the handle of her weekender bag, she stepped out. The door closed behind her.

This plush hotel felt so far away from the privately owned island of Ludus. Of course, it wasn't a fair comparison, as the Ludus Resort had been founded by a former king—King Georgios, an amazing man who'd abdicated the throne of Rydiania. She didn't know all the details of why he'd stepped away from the crown, but once he had, his family had promptly disowned him. He'd moved to Greece and bought Ludus Island, where he would live out his days. It was both a sad and an amazing tale.

As she looked around the spacious foyer, she realized her initial assessment had been misguided. Though the wine-colored carpet was plush, and the fixtures were brass on cream-colored walls, that was where it ended. There was no precious artwork on the walls or greenery throughout the hallway. Whereas the Ludus was always looking to make the resort stand out in both big and small ways, it appeared this hotel excelled at a minimalist approach. Interesting.

There was no one about in the foyer. The only sound as she walked was the soft rumble from the wheels of her case. She couldn't wait to see Krystof. She was so excited. She hoped he'd be just as thrilled to see her.

The gold plaque on the wall showed that his room was to the right. She turned that way. Her footsteps were muffled by the thick carpeting. What would he think about her spontaneity? This presumed he was even in his hotel room. What if he was out at a card game or some other such thing?

She would have to phone him, then, to tell him she was here, and the surprise would be ruined, but she was jumping too far ahead. She lifted her head and noticed a stylishly dressed woman at the end of the hallway. The woman knocked on a door. Was the young woman doing the same as her and being spontaneous? She hoped the woman had as good a weekend as she was about to have with Krystof.

Just then, the door in front of the woman swung open. The woman stood off to the side, giving Adara full view of the person inside the hotel room. She stopped walking. The breath caught in Adara's lungs. Krystof stood there. *Oh, my!* Her heart lodged in her throat at the sight of him.

His dark hair was spiky and going every which way, as though he'd just stepped out of the shower. His broad shoulders led to his bare chest. She was too far away to see if there were beads of water on his tanned skin. As her gaze lowered, her mouth grew dry. No man had a right to look as good as him.

He wore nothing more than a white towel draped around his trim waist. She swallowed hard. The only thing wrong with this picture was that she was supposed to be the one standing at his doorway.

His gaze lingered on the other woman. A smile lit up his face. The woman practically threw herself at him. They hugged as though they knew each other very well.

Adara blinked, willing away the image. But when she focused again, he was still holding the woman. So this was what he did when they were apart. Her heart plummeted down to her new black heels.

She turned away before she was spotted. The only thing that could have made this moment worse was if Krystof were to spot her. Her utter humiliation would then be complete.

Her steps were rapid as she retreated to the elevator. She wanted to disappear as quickly as possible. And lucky for her, one of the two sets of elevator doors swung open immediately. An older couple stepped off.

"Could you hold that for me?" Adara asked.

The gentleman held the door for her until she stepped inside. She thanked him. As the door closed, she recalled the image of a smiling, practically naked Krystof drawing that woman into his arms. Tears stung the backs of her eyes. She blinked them away. She wasn't going to fall apart in the elevator. All the while fury churned within her. Why had she let herself believe they shared something special?

It was quite obvious she was just someone to warm his bed whenever one of his other girlfriends wasn't available. How could she have been so blind? Sure, they had said this arrangement was casual, but that was in the beginning—months ago, on Valentine's. She'd thought they were getting closer—starting something more serious. Obviously she was the only one to think this.

She had been so wrong—about him, about herself, about them. She was done with him. Because his idea of casual and hers were two different things. In the end, she wasn't cut out to do casual—not if it meant him seeing other women while he was still involved with her. But it didn't matter now, because they were over.

CHAPTER ONE

September, Ludus Island, Greece

SHE WAS LATE. Very late…

Adara checked the calendar on her phone again. Her gaze scanned back through the days, one by one. She searched for the X that usually marked the first day of her period.

Day by day her gaze scanned down over her digital tablet. This wasn't the first time she'd been through this exercise, but it didn't keep her from wishing that she'd missed the little mark. *Please be there.* And once again, it was nowhere to be found.

Maybe she'd accidentally deleted it. Yes, that sounded like a legitimate explanation. Right now, she'd agree to any logical explanation—any reason except for her being late. Maybe she should have a backup plan. She would think that over for the future, but it wouldn't help her right now.

How was any of this possible? She hadn't been in Krystof's bed in months. After the episode in Paris, he'd messaged her to arrange for them to spend more time together, and she'd replied, telling him point-blank that it was over. They were finished. And then she'd promptly blocked his number.

Since her fling with Krystof, there had been no one else. Like it or not, she wasn't ready to move on. And she was certain she'd had her monthly since she'd been with Krystof. So what was going on?

She didn't feel any different. Just a little tired, but she credited her busy work schedule for her lack of energy. Not only was the resort hopping, but she had been training a new assistant for the past six months—an assistant who was now almost as good as her.

One pregnancy test later, and it was negative. Just as she'd suspected.

Two and three negative pregnancy tests later, and she was certain something was wrong. Hopefully it was just too little sleep or too much stress—something simple and easily remedied. Yes, that must be it. Ever since she'd seen Krystof with another woman, she'd thrown herself into her work even more so than she normally did.

She had known from the first time she'd met him that he wasn't traditional by any stretch. She was so drawn in by his outgoing personality and the way he could make her laugh that she'd talked herself into stepping outside her norm and taking a risk on him. Maybe deep inside she'd thought she could change him.

In the end, she'd been so wrong about herself. She was a one-man woman not suited to casual dating. She'd also been wrong about trying to change him. Krystof had no intention of changing his ways for anyone. Looking back, she realized that she'd let infatuation sway her decision as she'd agreed to his terms.

And now she was the one paying the price. She'd let herself get too caught up in what might have been. The reality of him with another woman in his arms flashed in her mind. It was immediately followed by the ache in her chest. She refused to acknowledge just how much he'd come to mean to her.

Her missing monthly was the wake-up call she needed. She was in her thirties now. If she wanted a husband and a couple of kids, she couldn't waste her time on guys who didn't share her life goals. And Krystof definitely didn't want the same things that she did. He couldn't even commit to having an apartment. He lived out of his jet and a suitcase as he globetrotted around the world. Who did such a thing?

Her head started to throb. She shoved aside the troubling thoughts. It was so much easier to be distracted by her work than to deal with the gaping crack in her heart and now her missing period. Could things get any worse?

But first she had to get settled into her room at the resort. She was going to be the maid-of-honor for her best friend, Hermione. The wedding was going to be here at the resort in ten days' time. Both Hermione, the resort's manager, and Atlas had offered her accommodations until the wedding to make it more convenient for her. She had the bachelorette party to host and the final details to oversee for the big wedding on top of her usual duties. She planned to make Hermione and Atlas's wedding the most amazing event the island had ever seen.

This was the first time since she'd been hired straight out of the university that she was a guest here. Adara wheeled her suitcase into her temporary room. She couldn't believe she was going to be staying at one of the world's most prestigious resorts! As the lights came on, she stood in place, taking it all in. She wasn't used to living in such extravagance.

She'd grown up in a modest home in a small village north of Athens with her loving parents. They'd raised her to be responsible and sensible. They'd also encouraged her to take the position at the Ludus, even if it meant moving away from home. That's why when they'd suddenly died in a car accident while on a long-awaited vacation in Ireland, it had turned Adara's life upside down.

For the past two years, she'd struggled to come to terms with a life without her parents in it. Their deaths had left a gigantic void in her heart. She'd clung to her familiar life at the Ludus. Her good friends at the resort had filled her days with their warmth and companionship. She didn't know what she'd do without Hermione and Indigo, as well as the other employees at the resort.

As her gaze took in her room, she couldn't help but notice it was so unlike her modest little apartment on the outskirts of Athens. This living room contained two white couches that faced each other with a long glass coffee table in the center. Decorations consisting of a crystal X and a matching ball sat on either side of an arrangement of fresh-cut blush peonies. The room's outer wall consisted of floor-to-ceiling windows with sheers that could be opened or closed remotely. At the moment, they were open, letting in the sunshine from the skylights overlooking the indoor pool area.

Ding.

The sound of an incoming message reminded her that she wasn't truly a guest of the resort but rather an employee with a very important job—the concierge. Her job was to make sure the guests' wishes were met and when possible exceeded.

Adara withdrew her phone from her pocket. She glanced at the screen. There was a message from Hermione.

Can we meet to talk?

It wasn't like Hermione to request an unscheduled meeting first thing in the morning. Something was wrong. Was it something to do with the resort? Or the wedding?

Sure. When and where?

Hermione responded, telling her to meet up in the penthouse apartment as soon as possible.

Adara left her still-packed suitcase sitting in the middle of the room. She would deal with it later. She headed out the door and made her way to the private elevator. You had to either have a key card or press the button to have someone in the penthouse buzz you up. As soon as Adara pressed the button, the elevator door opened. It was though Hermione had been standing there awaiting her appearance. Whatever was going on must be serious.

At the top of the resort sat the owner's apartment. It was huge and had the most amazing panoramic views. It was originally built by King Georgios. Seeing as it had all been designed by royalty, it was no wonder the resort loosely resembled a palace.

As Adara stepped out into the small foyer with a white marble floor and artwork adorning the walls, she had to admit the entire floor was truly suited to housing a king.

Hermione was standing at the open doorway to the suite wearing a frown. "I'm so glad you're here. Come in."

Adara followed Hermione inside to the spacious living room that was now a bit chaotic with wedding stuff all over the place, from favors for the guests to bridal magazines and decorations. But it was the two suitcases in the middle of the room that caught and held her attention.

Adara's gaze moved to her friend. "Are you packing for your honeymoon already?"

"No. We're getting ready to visit Atlas's father."

"Oh." Adara wasn't sure what to say, because the last she knew, Atlas and his father had a very strained relationship—to the point where she didn't think they even spoke anymore.

"His father is in the hospital, and I've finally convinced Atlas that we need to go to him."

"Oh, no. I'm sorry. What can I do?"

Hermione's gaze moved about the room. "Can you stay on top of the wedding? I mean, everything is planned. I know this room looks like a mess, but most of it's under control. I promise."

Adara's gaze moved about the room. Every surface was covered with boxes of stuff. Some decorations were complete. Other decorations still needed put together, not to mention the favors. "No problem. And if you need to push back the wedding until things calm down, I can help you with that, too."

Hermione shook her head. "I mentioned it to Atlas, and he staunchly refused. You know that there's bad history between him and his father." When Adara nodded, Hermione continued. "So he said he wasn't going to let his father ruin his wedding. I'm hoping with all of the time that has passed since they last saw each other that there's a possibility of forgiveness. I know it's a lot to hope for, but I'm worried that if it's not attempted now, Atlas won't get another chance for reconciliation."

Okay. "What else do you need?"

"Just keep everything for the wedding on track. There shouldn't be much to do. But if any questions come up, can you take care of them?"

"Sure. No problem." They really had nailed down all the details already. What could possibly go wrong?

"When will you be back?"

"I'm not sure." Hermione grabbed her purse from the couch. She glanced inside, as though making sure everything she wanted was in there, and then she zipped it. "They were light on details about his father's condition at the hospital. All we know is that it's serious."

Adara could see her friend was worked up. She went to her and placed a hand on her shoulder. "It's going to be okay. Everything will be all right."

Hermione nodded before glancing around, as though worried she was forgetting something. "I guess we have everything." She turned back to Adara. "I'm sorry to just up and leave you with everything. Indigo said she would be around sometime today. She just got back from Rydiania. She can help you if you need anything."

Hermione rolled the suitcases to the elevator. As she stood in front of the open doors, she reached into her pocket and pulled out a key card. "If I'm gone for a while, you might need this to get to the wedding stuff. Make yourself comfortable. Like I said, we don't know how long we'll be away. Atlas thinks it'll just be overnight, but I'm hoping he'll change his mind once we get there."

"It's okay. I'll take care of everything. Don't worry about this place." Adara took one of the suitcases and rolled it onto the elevator for her.

"What would I do without you? You're the best friend I could have ever asked for." Hermione moved to give her a hug.

Adara hugged her back. "You're the best, too."

And then they rode the elevator down to the main floor. All the while, Adara went over the wedding to-do list in her mind. It all seemed doable, even if Hermione didn't make it back right away. No worries. She had this wedding stuff under control.

CHAPTER TWO

HE'D RETURNED TO Ludus Island.

Krystof Mikos had been avoiding the island ever since things had abruptly ended with Adara. No woman had ever treated him in such a dismissive fashion. The memory of her brush-off and subsequent blocking of his number still burned him.

But now that he was the best man in Atlas and Hermione's wedding, he didn't have a choice but to return. Though the wedding was still a couple of weeks away, he'd arrived early to steal away the groom for a long and extravagant bachelor weekend. It was his hope that he'd be gone again before he ran into Adara.

He had nothing to say to her after the way she'd ghosted him. He didn't even understand what had prompted her to act in such an outrageous manner. He could understand it better if they'd argued, but that hadn't happened. The last time he'd seen her on the island, their weekend had ended with a lingering kiss. And their final phone conversation had ended with him pleading with her to fly away with him. The destination could be her decision. She'd promised to think about it. So where had it all gone so wrong?

He longed to know the answer, but there was no way he was going to beg her to come back to him—even if he missed spending time with her. He was better off alone—just as he'd been most of his life.

He shoved aside the troubling thoughts of Adara. Right now, he had a bachelor party to focus on. He couldn't believe the man he considered a brother was tying the knot. He'd always thought they'd both grow old as bachelors, seeing as both of them had had rough childhoods and neither wanted a repeat of family life. But ever since Atlas had laid eyes on Hermione, his tune had changed.

Krystof couldn't help thinking that his friend was making a mistake. Sure, spend time with Hermione, have a great time together, but to pledge forever to each other—why?

There was no such thing as forever. Relationships didn't last. All you had to do was to look at the statistics, which would prove his point.

In Krystof's case, he didn't even have to see the numbers. The story of his childhood in northern Greece was proof enough. He never knew his birth parents. His earliest memories consisted of being shuttled from one foster family to the next. His high IQ had gotten him into lots of trouble, and he'd quickly been labeled a problem child.

His life was littered with short-lived relationships. He'd learned not to let people get too close to him— but there were two exceptions, Atlas and Krystof's foster sister, who had refused to let him disappear from her life.

Atlas had surprised him when he'd proclaimed he was about to be married. When he'd asked Krystof to be his best man, what was Krystof to do—turn down his best friend and tell him he didn't believe in marriage? Even he wasn't that heartless. And so he'd agreed to stand up for Atlas—even if he firmly believed it was a mistake.

And now it was time for them to jet off for a long bachelor weekend in Ibiza, which was one of the Balearic Islands, an archipelago off Spain in the Mediterranean Sea. It was known for its nightlife. They were going to have the most amazing time. He didn't exactly have a plan, because he liked to live life on a whim. However they decided to entertain themselves, it would be memorable.

He'd invited Prince Istvan of Rydiania, who'd said he'd meet them in Ibiza. Krystof had also contacted some of his and Atlas's old classmates from school. It'd be good to catch up with people and find out what had happened with everyone.

Krystof had just flown into Athens on his private jet to pick up Atlas. His hired car whisked him south of the city and onto a ferry that would deliver him to Ludus Island. When the car pulled to a stop beneath the portico of the resort hotel, Krystof made his way inside the lavish lobby with a white marble floor and a large crystal chandelier in the center of the spacious room.

He practically ran straight into Atlas. "Wow. Didn't expect you to be this anxious to leave. I thought we'd head off in the morning, but now works, too." He glanced around. "Where's your suitcase?"

Atlas frowned. "There's been a change of plans."

"Oh." This was news to him. But, hey, he was flexible. "Did you want to go somewhere else? I can call the guys and let them know the new location."

Atlas shook his head. "It's not that. I can't go."

"What?" Surely he couldn't be serious. "Of course you have to go. If this has something to do with Hermione, you can assure her that the partying won't get too out of hand." He sent him a big grin. Of course the partying would get out of hand. It was Atlas's last chance to have a good time before he was married.

Atlas arched an incredulous brow, and then he shook his head. "Do you really think Hermione's going to believe you would ever behave?"

"Why shouldn't she?" He wasn't that wild. He'd gotten most of that out of his system when he was a kid. "I'm a great guy." He planted his hands on his trim waist and straightened his broad shoulders. "Just ask anyone." His thoughts immediately strayed to Adara. "Maybe not quite anyone. But most people who know me love me."

Atlas rolled his eyes. "You definitely don't have an ego problem at all."

"Hey, I might resemble that comment."

Atlas let out a short laugh. "You're making this hard on me, but I can't do the trip to Ibiza. Something happened with my father, and we're heading there now."

That was the last thing Krystof had expected to hear. "Dude, are you sure you want to see him?"

Atlas shrugged. "Hermione thinks it's for the best."

"She doesn't understand. How could she? She wasn't around for all of the bad stuff."

His friend shrugged. "I don't know. It all happened a lot of years ago." He raked his fingers through his hair. "I didn't want to come to the island when my mother willed me this place. I was so angry with her, but while I was here, I found out that what I believed about her wasn't correct."

"But this is different. This is your father. He didn't just walk away. He made every day of your life hell."

"I know. I know."

But still, he was going. Krystof was worried about his friend. Nobody needed to go through that pain again. But it didn't appear anything he said was going to change Atlas's mind about this trip. All he could do was be there for him.

"What can I do?" Krystof asked.

"Hermione suggested delaying the wedding, but I don't want to. My father took a lot of things from me while growing up. I won't let him take this away from me, too." He shifted his weight from one foot to the other. "Would you mind staying here and helping Adara with the wedding details? I know something happened between the two of you, so if it's too much, I understand."

He would be alone with Adara? He wasn't so sure that was a good idea. In fact, he was quite certain it was a very bad idea. Then an intriguing thought came to him. There would be hundreds of guests for Adara to deal with, but he just might be able to pull her away from all that so they could talk privately for a moment— just long enough to appease his curiosity about why she'd brushed him off.

He could accomplish two things by staying: helping out Atlas and perhaps fixing things with Adara. "I'll do it."

Atlas arched a brow. "Are you sure? Did I mention there would be wedding details involved?"

"I heard." He was certain Adara would handle all those. She liked to be in charge and do things her way.

"And what about the problem between you and Adara?"

"I'll talk to her, fix things with her."

Atlas looked taken aback. "Are you sure about that?"

Krystof nodded. "Don't worry about a thing. I've got this."

"Really?" Atlas's dark brows gathered. "Where's

the Krystof I know? What have you done with him? The last I knew you didn't do anything complicated."

"Maybe I'm changing." Had those words really come out of his mouth? The surprise showed on Atlas's face, too. Not wanting to dissect what he'd just said, Krystof rushed on. "I know a thing or two about weddings. Honestly, I can handle this."

"Tell me the last one you attended."

Krystof paused to think. He really gave it serious thought. There were frequent invitations, but he routinely declined them with the excuse that he'd be out of the country, because he was always on the go.

"See. I told you. There's something not right about you agreeing to stay here and help. And I bet I know why—or should I say *who* has you agreeing."

"Atlas, there you are. Did you get the car?" Hermione approached them.

Krystof breathed a sigh of relief that Hermione had interrupted the beginning of Atlas's interrogation. With a smile on his face, he turned to the bride-to-be.

"I was just about to when I ran into Krystof." Atlas moved to Hermione's side and gave her a brief kiss. "I didn't have a chance to call him about the change of plans, so I was just filling him in."

"Hi, Krystof." Hermione hugged him before quickly pulling back. "I'm so sorry that this messes up your bachelor party plans."

"No worries. I understand. I'll message all the guys and explain. I hope your trip goes well. And feel free to take my car. The driver is waiting right out front."

They thanked him and promised to be back as soon as possible. He walked them out so he could retrieve his luggage. He wasn't looking forward to seeing Adara again—at least that's what he told himself.

And yet there was part of him that badly wanted to know where things had gone wrong. Since they'd been apart, he hadn't met anyone else who could garner his attention quite the way she had done. She'd grounded him. She'd actually made staying in one place feel all right for him—at least for a time.

Sometimes she was quiet, and other times she was talkative. She liked to share some of the fascinating details of her work—like the time she'd had to make preparations for a wealthy and influential guest to arrive at the resort via parachute—talk about going out of your way to avoid a traffic delay! She was very gifted in her ability to make people's wishes come true.

He wondered if a guest had turned her head. Did she have another man in her life now? Was that why she'd dumped him without explanation? The thought of her with someone else had his lips settling into a firm line as his gut twisted into a knot.

CHAPTER THREE

EVERYTHING WOULD BE FINE.

Adara should be smiling. After all, she was the maid of honor. And the wedding was going to be the biggest, splashiest affair this island had ever seen. She would make sure of it.

If only she didn't have this cloud of worry hanging over her. She regretted doing an internet search to find a reason for her missing period. Instead of it making her feel better, it made her feel worse. She didn't like the possibilities: hormonal imbalances or serious health conditions. What exactly was wrong with her?

She reached for her phone. She'd put this off long enough. She had to call the doctor. But when she got ahold of them, she found out she'd have to wait to get in. The earliest they could squeeze her in was the following Monday. It seemed so far off, even though it was only five days away. Five very long days of worry.

At least she would see the doctor and get her answer before she had to deal with the next stressful thing in her life—seeing Krystof again. Since he was Atlas's best friend, he was the best man for the wedding. She inwardly groaned.

She hadn't spoken to him for over two months. She was still angry with him for being nothing more than a playboy and upset with herself for reading too much into their relationship. She wouldn't make that mistake again. Krystof was a part of her past—a painful lesson learned.

Thankfully, he wouldn't be here until next week, just before the ceremony. Krystof never spent too much time in one place, and without Atlas being on the island, there would be no reason for him to be here. He would most likely swing in at the last minute and then leave immediately after the reception. She could deal with that brief encounter. At least that's what she kept telling herself.

Lunch had come and gone in a flurry of special requests from guests. With her work under control, it was time to meet up with her friend Indigo, who was still doing a few special requests for drawings and portraits for guests of the resort. But Indigo's life was now quite busy, as she split her time between Athens and jetting off to Rydiania with her handsome prince—soon to be her husband. It just went to prove that happily-ever-afters did exist…for some people.

Adara made her way to her guest room. It was going to be her headquarters for all things pertaining to the wedding. As soon as she reached the room, she picked up her digital tablet. Her fingers moved over the screen, and then her gaze scanned down over the list of things to do.

They had worked hard to put things in order ahead of time. The to-do list was in pretty good shape. A smile pulled at her lips. This wedding was going to go off without a hitch. Then the image of Krystof with that other woman in his arms flashed in her mind. Okay, maybe one small hitch. And then a worrisome thought came to her. Would he bring the other woman to the wedding?

Her stomach soured at the thought. But in the next breath, she realized that bringing a date to the wedding would be tantamount to being in a relationship in Krystof's mind. It was something he would go out of his way to avoid. With that thought in mind, she breathed easier.

Knock-knock.

That must be Indigo. Adara closed her tablet and moved to the door. She swung it open. "Indigo, you're just in time."

The breath hitched in the back of her throat. It was Krystof. She blinked, but he was still there. "What are you doing here?"

His dark eyes stared at her while his expression gave nothing away about what he was thinking. "Aren't you even going to invite me in?"

A refusal teetered on the tip of her tongue. A glance over his shoulder revealed a number of guests in the hallway. She didn't need to create a scene. She opened the door wide. "Come in, if you must."

"Such a warm welcome. I feel like you really missed me." Sarcasm dripped from his voice.

She pushed the door closed. "What are you doing here? The wedding isn't until the end of next week."

He walked farther into the room and glanced around. Then he turned to her. "I want to know what I did for you to refuse to speak to me." His gaze narrowed in on her. The heat of his anger had her resisting the urge to fan herself. "You even went so far as to block my number." His voice vibrated with agitation. "You ghosted me. And I did nothing to deserve it."

Her mouth gaped before she forced it closed. Did

he really think she didn't know she was just one of a number of women who passed through his life? Did he think she would be okay with that?

She crossed her arms. This wasn't the time for this conversation, not with Indigo about to arrive at any moment. "We're not having this conversation."

"You can't ghost me now. I'm not going anywhere until you explain yourself."

"I don't know why you're making a big deal of this." If he wanted to pretend he hadn't been seeing other women, then she could pretend as well. "It was a casual thing, and now it's over."

"It's another man, isn't it?" He studied her as though he could read the answer on her face.

She refused to glance away. He wouldn't intimidate her into confessing that she'd gone to Paris to surprise him and instead she was the one to be unpleasantly surprised. "If there was another man, would that put an end to this conversation?"

"No."

"Too bad. Now I have work to do." She turned to open the door for him.

"Not so fast. Hermione and Atlas sent me."

The mention of her friends' names gave her pause. Her fingers slipped from the door handle as she turned around. "What do you mean, they sent you?"

"They asked me to stick around to help out with the wedding details while they are away."

She couldn't resist a little laugh. "You're going to help with the wedding? You?"

He shrugged. "Sure. Why not?"

His insistence on staying to help made her amusement fizzle out. "Well, Hermione already asked me to stay on top of things. So as you can see, your help is not needed here."

"I'm sure Hermione has everything planned out, down to the table setting for the reception, but with so many details to keep on top of, there are bound to be a few issues that crop up."

"And you feel that you're the best person to deal with those problems?" His unwavering gaze and confident look irritated her. "I don't think so. You don't know the first thing about the wedding plans."

His gaze lowered to her digital notebook on the table next to him. "I bet if I read your notes, I'd get up to speed pretty quickly."

She checked the time on her smart watch. "Well, that will have to wait." She opened the door and gestured for him to leave. "I have another appointment now."

As he walked past her, he said quietly, "You can't avoid me forever."

Maybe not. But it didn't mean she wouldn't try her best. She leveled her shoulders and closed the door firmly behind him. She pulled her phone from her pocket and started running her finger over the screen as she messaged Hermione.

Did you know Krystof is here?

A couple minutes passed with no response. Adara made her way to the other side of the suite. How was she supposed to deal with Krystof without the buffer of Atlas and Hermione?

Ding.

Adara glanced at her phone.

Sorry. I meant to tell you that he arrived early. I hope it's not too awkward.

Her friend had enough on her mind. She didn't need to worry about Adara's dismal love life. It wasn't like she couldn't deal with Krystof. If only there was some way to distract him—like a high-stakes poker game. And yet there were none planned at the resort in the immediate future.

We'll be fine. How are things there?

Adara grabbed her tablet and moved to the couch. She sat down and opened her tablet. She needed to go over the list of things to do again. She didn't want to miss anything, especially with Krystof looking over her shoulder.

Atlas's father had a stroke. No details yet.

Adara closed her tablet. This was far more serious than she'd been imagining.

I'm so sorry.

I'll let you know more after talking to the doctors.

Don't worry about things here. I've got everything under control.

You're the best. Thank you!

Adara set aside her phone. How hard could it be to keep the wedding on track? After all, everything had been ordered and planned. All she had to do was make sure everything was delivered and put together. It would all be fine.

She just wished she could say the same thing about dealing with Krystof.

It shouldn't bother him.

And yet it did.

Krystof sensed that Adara was keeping something from him. It wasn't like her to be secretive, so if she didn't have a new man in her life, what was going on? And why wouldn't she tell him?

Perhaps she felt her reasons for not seeing him anymore were none of his business. He was the one who had insisted on having no strings between them. Now that he'd seen her, he felt as though they still had some unfinished business. And yet Adara had insisted on putting up a wall between them—a wall he kept failing to get around.

He'd been true to her in the months they'd been seeing each other. He hadn't even been tempted to see anyone else, not even in the last two months. Adara made him feel special—like she really cared about what he had to say.

They'd been having such a good time in each other's company that they'd kept it going for months, which was highly unusual for him. He hated to see it end. If he could just figure out the problem, he could fix it and they could keep going with their arrangement. He just had to get her to open up to him. But how?

He rubbed the back of his neck where his muscles had tightened. He was starting to get a headache. However, he wasn't leaving this island until he got some straight answers from her.

Buzz-buzz.

He pulled his phone from his pocket and glanced at the caller ID. It was Atlas. Krystof pressed the phone to his ear. "Hey Atlas, how's it going?"

"We just saw my father. He's not doing great. We stepped out while he was sleeping to get some coffee. While Hermione is placing the order, I thought I'd check in and see how things are going there. Have you straightened out things with Adara?"

Krystof stifled another groan. "About that...ah...we haven't really had much of a chance to talk."

"What are you waiting for? I don't want anything to ruin this wedding. Not my father. And not your messy love life."

"Hey, it's not like that. We aren't a couple. We were just having fun."

"Did Adara know that?"

The question hung heavy in the air. Krystof swallowed hard. "Of course she did. We talked about it in the beginning."

"You mean the whole way back at Valentine's?"

"Yes."

It wasn't like their arrangement had had an expiration date, did it? Was that what Adara thought? Had she grown bored of him? Impossible. She'd enjoyed their time together as much as he had. He was certain of it.

Things had remained the same between them up until he'd texted her a couple of months ago to arrange their next meeting and she'd messaged him back, ending things. He was the one who normally ended an affair. He didn't like being brushed off. He really didn't like it happening with Adara. There was just something special about her, from the way she took great pains to care for those around her to her gentle laugh that warmed a spot in his chest and the way she made him feel like he was the only man in the room.

"Krystof, you do realize that the Valentine's ball was many months ago, don't you? And you've been seeing her pretty regularly ever since then. Maybe she thought there was something growing between the two of you."

He refused to see it Atlas's way. It wasn't like he'd ever said anything to lead her on. He wouldn't do that—he wouldn't intentionally hurt her. "We were becoming better friends."

"Is that all?"

Was it all? As soon as the question crossed his mind, he shoved it away. "Of course that's all. I didn't deserve her ghosting me with no explanation."

"If you say so."

"I do."

"Then keep your distance from her as much as possible."

"What?" Surely his best friend hadn't just warned him away from a woman, had he?

"I'm not messing around, Krystof. You've done something to upset her already. You can't mess up again."

The stubborn part of him countered with, "And what if I don't stay away?"

A tense silence ensued. "Don't make me regret asking you to stand up for me at the wedding. I don't ask you for much. Just don't mess up my wedding."

"I won't." The promise was out of his mouth before he had a chance to think about the implications. Because even now, he was tempted by the memories of pulling Adara into his arms and kissing her long and hard.

"Thank you. I knew I could count on you. I've got to go. Hermione is coming."

The line went dead.

Wow. Atlas had never warned him away from a woman before. It didn't sit well with Krystof, but since Atlas was under so much stress with having to face his father again after so many years and his upcoming wedding, Krystof would abide by his wishes. Once he got some answers from Adara, of course.

CHAPTER FOUR

IT HAD BEEN a crazy, busy day.

Adara finally stopped long enough to take a full breath. Who knew so many people could have so many special requests while on vacation? But her workday was finally over, and the guests had all been taken care of, from needing a rare brand of shampoo and conditioner to providing a sunset helicopter tour of the island. When it came to Ludus guests, no request was denied... well, within reason. She'd been propositioned today— and she'd immediately shot down the advance from an international star who was twice her age.

She had only been propositioned twice in the entire time she'd worked at the resort. It was the first proposition that had been more like an invitation—an alluring invitation that she had been more than willing to accept.

As the memory of that long-ago Valentine's night filtered through her mind, she remembered being swept off her feet. Krystof had been attentive and charming. He'd been everything she'd been looking for in a man— or at least she'd thought so at the time. So when he'd suggested they start something casual, she'd surprised herself when she'd agreed. It was so unlike her, but there was something different about Krystof.

She shoved aside the unwanted memories. She wasn't

going to let her guard down with him again. Fool her once, shame on him. Fool her twice, shame on her.

Her hope was that Krystof would grow bored at the resort without Atlas around and he would leave until the wedding. It wasn't like she couldn't manage things until Hermione and Atlas returned. She did not need him to help her.

Adara had made sure to review the wedding checklist twice. Everything up to and including the two-week mark had been accomplished. They were in great shape. And that's exactly what she'd told Hermione when she'd called not once but twice that day to check in on the resort and the wedding. Hermione really was a bit of a control freak. That's probably why the wedding couple had had the penthouse remodeled so they could live there after the wedding and be close to their business.

Chime.

It was a reminder on Adara's phone letting her know it was time to try on the wedding dresses one last time. They'd been delivered yesterday, but Indigo hadn't been available until now. So they'd decided to wait and try them on together. Even though Hermione was away, they really couldn't delay it any longer.

Adara was anxious to see the dresses again. Hermione had had both Adara and Indigo pick out the style of dress they preferred. They were simple and classic. The bride had chosen an arctic blue for the wedding color.

She texted a reminder to Indigo to meet her in her guest room. With the workday over, they would have a chance to check out their dresses without being rushed. They'd already had their final fittings, but with Adara now being in charge of making sure there were no foulups with the wedding, she wanted to try them on one last time before they put the dresses in storage until the big day. Afterward, she was thinking, they could share a glass of wine and catch up on each other's lives—not that she had much to share.

When she reached her room, she found Indigo pacing outside her door. When Indigo lifted her head and spotted Adara, she sent her a big smile. It was the same smile she'd been wearing ever since Prince Istvan had declared his love for her and placed a ruby-and-diamond ring on her finger.

Adara never asked, but she got the distinct feeling the ring was somehow related to the Ruby Heart on display in the gallery. Hermione swore that gemstone had something to do with her and Atlas finding their way together. Adara didn't believe in legends, but just to be safe, she was keeping her distance from the gallery and the Ruby Heart. She wasn't interested in a love match, especially after the way things had ended with Krystof.

"I hope I didn't keep you waiting too long." Adara opened the door to her room.

"Not at all." Indigo followed her inside. "How's Atlas's father doing?"

Adara placed the files and digital tablet she'd brought with her on the table before turning to her friend. "He's not the best. They're going to stay at the hospital until he's stable."

"That's a shame. I wish there was something I could do."

"There is… We have to try on these dresses one last time, and then I'll put them in storage until the big day." She glanced over, catching Indigo admiring her engagement ring. "Have you two set a wedding date yet?"

Indigo shook her head. "When you marry a prince, a lot of the decisions are taken out of your hands."

"Oh, really? I mean, I just thought with him stepping out of the line of succession that, well, you guys would be pretty much on your own."

Indigo shook her head again. "You would think, but because he did step down from inheriting the crown, the king and queen are even more invested in making a big deal out of our wedding. They want to portray a united front to the world."

"So it's going to be a royal wedding?"

Indigo nodded. Her expression was blank, as though she hadn't made up her mind about how she felt about having the royals involved in her wedding.

"That must be so exciting." And then a thought came to her. "Hey, does this mean you'll be a princess?"

Indigo's eyes widened as she nodded her head. "Can you believe it?"

Adara sent her friend a reassuring smile. "You're going to make the best princess ever."

Indigo let out a laugh. "I highly doubt it, since I have absolutely no idea what a princess is supposed to do. And even when I figure it out, I'm sure I'll do it all wrong."

"Not a chance. You have a big, wonderful heart. You're exactly what the palace needs."

"I'm not sure they'd agree with you, since their son stepped away from the crown for me. Though he would tell you there were other reasons for his decision, I still feel some sort of responsibility."

"But didn't you say before that he's at last getting along with his parents?"

Indigo nodded again. "Yes, they're getting along better than ever. At least, that's what he says. I just hope he never regrets his decision to give up the crown."

"He won't. How could he? After all, he's marrying

you, and you both have such amazing lives. Him with his charities and you with your art."

Knock-knock.

"Looks like it's time to try on the dresses." Adara moved to the door and opened it. One of the staff rolled in the rack with the dresses. After thanking him, Adara moved to the rack with the white garment bags. She checked the tags. "This one is yours."

Indigo took it and moved to the couch, where she laid out the garment bag. She pulled down the zipper and then uttered a loud gasp.

"What's wrong?" Adara asked, alarmed.

"This dress. It's not mine."

"What?"

Indigo held up the fuchsia dress with its many sequins and ruffles. It definitely wasn't the slim-fitting blue gown they'd picked. And when Indigo held it in front of her, it was clear it was both too wide and too long.

Adara turned to the garment bag that was supposed to hold her gown. She pulled down the zipper to find another fuchsia dress. Her stomach knotted up. Where were their dresses?

"Where are our dresses?" Indigo unconsciously echoed her.

"I don't know," Adara said.

With dread, she moved to the last dress bag. It was supposed to be Hermione's wedding gown. After the final fitting, the seamstress promised to fix a couple of the loose pearls and steam out any wrinkles before delivering it.

Please let this be the right dress.

Adara lowered the zipper. All the while her heart was in her throat. This just had to be the right dress, because if worse came to worst, they could find new bridesmaids' dresses, but a wedding gown…it was special. You couldn't just run out and buy a new one—especially with the bride away dealing with a family emergency and the ceremony next week.

She paused for just a second in pulling down the zipper, not sure she wanted to see the dress. Indigo moved to stand next to her. Adara pushed the garment bag back to find an ivory bridal gown with ruffles. Lots and lots of ruffles. Hermione's beloved snow-white gown didn't have a ruffle anywhere on it.

Both Adara and Indigo gasped in horror.

Oh, no! This is a mess.

She told herself not to panic. This could be easily resolved. She would just call the bridal boutique. She was certain whoever owned these gowns wanted them back as much as Adara and her friends wanted their dresses.

"We should tell Hermione."

"No." Adara shook her head. "We aren't going to bother her with this. She has other, more important things to deal with at the moment. I plan to find out where our dresses are. Just leave these ones with me, and I'll contact the boutique to sort this out."

Indigo sent her a worried look. "Can I do anything to help?"

"Not right now. But closer to the wedding, I'll need your help making the favors and some decorations."

"I can do that. Just let me know when you need me."

Indigo returned the dresses to the rack and then left. Adara checked the bags for the name of the boutique, but there was no logo. She retrieved a stack of paperwork for the wedding. Somewhere in there would be the phone number for the boutique. For some reason she thought it would be right on top, but it wasn't. And to her frustration, she couldn't recall the name. She'd only been there a couple of times and hadn't paid attention.

There was a knock at the door. With the stack of papers in hand, she moved to the door and opened it. There stood Krystof. She inwardly groaned. She didn't have time for him at the moment. If she hurried, she might be able to reach the shop before they closed for the day.

"Unless this is an emergency, it's going to have to wait. I've got something important to deal with right now." She resumed thumbing through the pages.

"What's the matter?" Krystof's deep, rich voice was unmistakable.

She wanted to ignore him until he grew bored and went away, but she knew him too well. Krystof thrived on a challenge. And her ignoring him would strike him as a challenge to try and distract her from whatever she was working on. And she couldn't let that happen.

With great reluctance, she paused and looked at him—really looked at him. That was her first mistake, as her gaze hungrily took in his tanned legs clad in a pair of navy shorts and a white polo shirt that hinted at his muscled chest. When she drew her gaze upward past his broad shoulders, she admired his strong jawline and squared chin. And then there were those kissable lips that could make her forget about everything else but getting lost in his arms.

But none of that mattered now. The fling they'd had was over. She'd thought she could do the casual thing with him, but she'd been wrong. She was a one-man woman, and she wanted a man who was only interested in her. The memory of him holding that other woman in her arms cooled her warmed blood.

When her gaze finally met his brown eyes, she found amusement glittering in them. Her back teeth ground together. He'd caught her checking him out. Why had she done that? She was over him. It didn't matter how great a lover he was, he wasn't her man. And he never would be.

"What do you want, Krystof? Can't you see I'm in the middle of something important?"

"It wouldn't happen to have something to do with the wedding, would it?"

She considered lying to him so he'd leave, but what good would that do her? It was easier just to honest with him and send him on his way. "Promise this just stays between us?"

His dark brows arched. "Of course. How bad is it?"

"Well, considering they delivered the wrong dresses for the wedding, it's definitely not the best news."

"The wrong dresses! How did you miss this?"

"How did *I*?" Was he serious? "I didn't miss anything. This is the first chance we had to look at the dresses. Remember, some of us have to work for a living." She glared at him.

His brown eyes grew stormy, but when he spoke, his tone was level. "How wrong are they? Maybe it's still something you can work with."

"Are you kidding me?" Then she realized he was perfectly serious. "No. We can't just swap them for the originals. These dresses are the wrong color, the wrong style and the wrong sizes."

"That does seem to be a problem."

"You think? Now if you'll leave me be, I'm about to call the boutique." She returned her attention to the pages of wedding receipts and forms.

She could feel Krystof's gaze upon her, but she didn't give him the satisfaction of knowing that she was paying him any attention. Her priority was fixing this snafu with the wedding before Hermione found out.

In this particular moment, she didn't want to talk to him. She'd already wasted enough time on him. Now she just wanted to pretend he didn't exist, but he was making that difficult as he stood there with his arms crossed over his broad chest and a frown on his handsome face. And that irritated her, too. No one that annoying should be so good-looking.

CHAPTER FIVE

HE SHOULD WALK AWAY. This was not his problem.

And yet Krystof could see the worry written all over Adara's beautiful face. Her brown hair with its blond highlights was pulled back in a braid that swept past her shoulders. A fringe framed her perfectly made-up face.

It was the stubborn jut of her chin and the firm line of her glossy lips that let him know she wasn't giving up until the dress situation was properly resolved— with the original dresses located and returned to her as soon as possible.

He honestly didn't see the big deal. After all, these were just dresses, weren't they? Surely they could buy other dresses.

But he wasn't so out of the loop that he didn't know some women invested a lot of effort and dreams into weddings. They had a vision, and it upset them greatly when that vision didn't come to fruition. That appeared to be the case here.

Thankfully he didn't have any intention of getting married. He'd already had enough people let him down in life. He wasn't about to open himself up just to be hurt all over again. All those vows about loving each other until death—he wondered how many people really believed the words when they said them. Did they really believe in forever? He categorically did not.

He took in the lines that now bracketed Adara's blue eyes and kissable mouth as she stood there with the phone pressed to her ear. As the silence dragged on, twin lines formed between her brows. It didn't appear the bridal boutique was going to answer.

When she disconnected the call, his curiosity got the best of him. "When do they open again?"

"I don't know. They were supposed to be open now."

"Maybe they're busy with other customers. Try again."

He expected an argument, but instead she once more dialed the boutique. She held the phone to her ear as she began to pace. Eventually she disconnected the call and shook her head.

"I don't understand," she said. "Between the three of us, we've been to the shop numerous times, when you include picking out the dresses and the fittings. They were always open during business hours."

He reached for his phone. "What's the name of the shop?"

She told him, and he typed it into the search engine. It took him a couple of tries until he spelled it correctly. And then at last the shop's website popped up on the screen.

He checked their hours of operation. "It says they should be open today until six."

Adara checked the time. "It's only four."

"Maybe we should go for a ride."

"Good idea. I'll take the dresses with me. I don't want to have to make a second trip." She reached for her purse and grabbed the dresses.

When she started for the door, he fell into step behind

her. He was certain this mix-up could be easily resolved. After all, who would want a dress that didn't fit them?

Adara stopped abruptly in the hallway. He nearly ran into her. When she spun around, he was so close she stumbled. Her hands landed on his chest. He reached out to her. His fingers grasped her waist, and he pulled her close to steady her.

Time seemed to stand still as she leaned into him. He stared deep into her eyes as she stared back at him. His pulse kicked up a notch or two. For weeks and weeks now, he'd envisioned this moment. When he closed his eyes each night, holding her close and claiming her lips with his own was what he envisioned. And now he wanted more than anything to hold on to this moment—to make it last as long as possible.

His gaze dipped to her lips. All he could think about was how much he wanted to kiss her. The months they'd been apart felt like years. He'd really missed her a lot more than he'd been willing to admit to himself. But he couldn't give in to his desires—not with so much still unsettled between them.

His gaze rose to meet hers once more. He'd missed her smile and her laughter. He missed all of it. Still, he wasn't going to beg her to come back to him if she wasn't interested. Not a chance. He didn't beg anyone for anything.

How could she so quickly dismiss their perfect friends-with-benefits arrangement? Maybe Adara simply needed a reminder? Yes, that sounded like a good idea. His gaze lowered to her lips. They were devoid of any lipstick or gloss, as though she'd been caught off guard that morning and forgotten to put it on. Which was strange, because Adara was the most organized, put-together person he knew. He wondered what had distracted her.

He had always loved to be her distraction, but she hadn't given him the time of day since he'd arrived. And as much as he wanted to kiss her, he refused to do that until things were settled between them.

It was with the greatest regret that he released his hold on her and took a step back. It was though that's all it took for Adara to regain her senses.

She frowned fiercely at him. "What are you doing?"

"Keeping you from falling."

"Not that. Why are you following me?"

"Um…" Was this a trick question? "I'm walking with you to the car."

She shook her head. "No, you're not."

"Of course I am. We have to get this dress thing sorted."

"*We* aren't doing anything. I'm going to go take care of this. You…well, you can go sit on the beach or find a card game to play." She turned and continued to walk away.

Cards didn't mean that much to him, at least not these days. Years ago, they'd been a quick way for him to climb his way out of poverty. With a photogenic memory and a high IQ, which had earned him a scholarship to a top university, he'd found he was good at card games. Very good.

These days playing cards just didn't hold a challenge like they used to. He'd never told anyone this. He simply let everyone assume he traveled from one card game to the next. In truth, he just liked to travel. Sometimes he played, but often he worked on his computer programing. Utilizing computer language was like a puzzle to him, and it challenged him in a way that cards never had.

He'd developed a social media platform called My-Post. At first it had been a way to connect card sharks and arrange large tournaments. Then MyPost had started to grow. Now he had a staff that managed the site for him, allowing him to continue his nomadic ways.

He continued to follow Adara. "I'm going with you."

This time when she stopped, he was ready for her and had left enough room between them. She turned to him with an exasperated sigh. "Are you really going to stick around until the wedding?"

"I am."

Adara dramatically rolled her eyes. "Is there anything I can say to dissuade you?"

"No." He made a point of checking his Rolex. "We're wasting time."

Her gaze narrowed as she was silent for a moment. "Fine. But when we get there, I'll do the talking."

"Be my guest." But he planned to do some talking before they arrived at the boutique.

She glared at him. "Has anyone ever told you that you're stubborn?"

"Yes."

With a deep sigh, she held out the dresses to him. "If you insist on coming with me, you can make yourself useful." When he took the dresses from her, she said, "Hold them higher. They can't touch the ground." When he went to drape them over his arm, she frowned. "They'll get wrinkled that way."

Was she serious? They weren't even her dresses. "Why do you care?"

"Because if I was the person that owned those

dresses, I'd hope someone would take good care of them."

He lifted the dresses until she was satisfied. Then she turned and continued walking. She pulled out her phone and made a call. "Demi, an emergency has come up. I need to step out for a bit. Can you handle things here?" Her head bobbed up and down as though she were agreeing with whatever was said on the other end of the phone. "Thank you. I appreciate this."

"Everything okay?" he asked.

"With the resort, yes. As for the wedding, it will be fine as soon as we find the correct dresses."

When they came to the end of the hallway, instead of turning right to head to the lobby, Adara turned to the left. He was confused. "I thought we were leaving."

"We are. My car is parked in the back."

"But why don't we just take one of the resort's sedans?"

"Because those are for guests." She kept walking.

He hurried to keep up with her. "Of which I happen to be one."

"But I'm not."

"Really? Because I'd heard from Atlas that you're staying at the resort until the wedding."

"That's just a matter of convenience. I'm not a true guest." She stopped at the exit and turned to him. "Must we do this?"

"Do what?"

"Talk. It'd be so much easier if I was doing this alone." And then she slipped on her sunglasses and headed outside.

He may have been warned off pursuing Adara by his best friend, but if he could just get her to stop long enough to really listen to him, he was certain he could clear up their misunderstanding. And then they could go back to their friends-with-benefits status. No one would get hurt, because emotions wouldn't be involved.

And this car ride was the perfect opportunity to have a conversation. He refused to let the opportunity slip by him. He was certain that by the time they returned to the resort, he'd know exactly where things had gone wrong between them.

Why was he here?

Not the wedding part. She understood about his best man duties. But why was he in her car? Why was he inserting himself in the preparations when she was fully capable of handling them alone?

Adara had no answers. It certainly wasn't because wedding planning excited him. And it wasn't likely he was still interested in her—not when he could have his pick of so many other women. So was what he said true? He was just looking out for his best friend?

He'd just told her he planned to stick around until the wedding and seemed insistent he should insert himself into the wedding plans. But why? She wanted nothing to do with him. What about that didn't he get?

She needed to tell him point-blank that she didn't want him around. Maybe then he'd move on to his next card game or next beautiful woman. The thought of him with another woman in his arms had her gripping the steering wheel tighter. She refused to let her thoughts go there.

When they reached the ferry to the mainland, he took a phone call. She thought at first it was one of his girlfriends, and once again an uneasy feeling churned in the pit of her stomach. However, when he mentioned assets and liabilities, she breathed easier. A business call. She couldn't deny her curiosity. Was this a new direction in his life? She was dying to ask him questions, but she refused to get drawn into his world again.

With him distracted, she moved to the upper deck and approached the railing. She hoped for a little breathing room. Krystof was starting to feel like her shadow. She couldn't ever remember him being so attentive. In fact, she was quite certain he'd never been this persistent. Was it guilt? Had he spotted her back at the Paris hotel after all?

She'd never know, because she wasn't going to discuss that episode with him. To live through it was enough humiliation for her. She didn't want to rehash the horrible scene.

Was it possible he regretted the other woman? Did he realize what a good thing he'd had with her? It would serve him right if he had regrets. She had her own for thinking he could change.

There had been the briefest moment when she'd first run into him again, when the episode in Paris had vanished from her mind. For a split second, she'd forgotten everything except how good they were together.

When he had gazed into her eyes, her heart had pounded so loud that it'd echoed in her ears. Her body had thoroughly and completely betrayed her. Because there was absolutely no reason she should want him any longer.

She'd been wrong to get involved with him in the first place. He was nothing like her. He acted without thinking. He didn't believe in making plans. He didn't even comprehend the use of a day planner. He liked to live on a whim. She could understand being spontaneous for dinner, but not as a lifestyle choice.

She liked to have everything sorted and arranged on

her digital calendar, with its handy reminders. Every minute of her workday was accounted for, and she took comfort in knowing what to expect from her day. She didn't have to worry about where she should be and what needed doing, because it was already organized.

"I wondered where you'd gone." Krystof's voice came from behind her.

She inwardly groaned. So much for her moment alone to gather her thoughts. She grudgingly turned. "What do you need?"

"You."

Her heart leapt into her throat. His bold answer stood between them like a declaration. What was he trying to say? That he wanted her back? *No. No. No.* That wasn't going to happen.

She turned back to stare out at the sea. She concentrated on the swells of the water, trying to calm herself. Then, hoping her voice didn't betray the way his words had unnerved her, she said, "I'm not in the mood to play word games. Just go."

"No. I'm not going to be dismissed like you've been doing for the last two months." There was a resolute tone to his deep voice. "We're going to talk. It's long overdue."

She turned to him, noticing his arms were crossed and his lips were pressed in a firm line. "You have nothing to say that I want to hear."

"Too bad. I'm going to say it anyway."

She noticed how he'd waited until they were stuck on the ferry between Ludus Island and the mainland. There was absolutely nowhere for her to go to avoid him. She should have known his offer to join her today came with an ulterior motive.

She narrowed her gaze on him and jutted out her

chin. "Once you have your say, will you give me some space?"

"I can't do that. I'm staying until the wedding whether you want me here or not. This isn't about us. It's about Hermione and Atlas."

"Agreed. But it doesn't mean you have to be everywhere I am."

"I'm just keeping my word to Atlas."

She restrained a sigh. She wondered how much longer he was going to use that excuse. There was another reason he was sticking around. "Is that the only reason?"

"Of course."

"Because if you think you and I are going start up again where we left off, it's never going to happen."

A muscle in his jaw twitched. "You make it sound like you were miserable with me. I happen to know different. I know how to turn you on. I know the spot to kiss on your neck that makes you moan—"

"Stop!"

Just then the whistle blew long and loud, letting everyone know they would soon be pulling into the dock. With her face hot, she rushed back to the car. She'd wanted to tell him that he was wrong about knowing such intimate details about her, but she wasn't going to lie. The truth was that he knew far too much about pleasing her—more than anyone had ever known.

She didn't care if he followed her or not. That wasn't quite true. But she told herself that it didn't matter what he did. She was finished speaking to him, because he was utterly impossible.

CHAPTER SIX

SHE'D REJECTED HIM. AGAIN.

At least that was the way it felt after their conversation on the ferry.

Krystof wasn't used to being cast off once, much less twice. In fact, it had never happened before. He was always the one who did the walking away. And now that it had happened, he wasn't quite sure what to do about it.

His pricked ego told him to cut his losses and leave the island. Because Adara was completely and utterly organized. She didn't need anyone, including, apparently, him. The thought didn't sit well with him, but he refused to evaluate why it bothered him.

As for the wedding, what could go wrong? Okay, other than the mix-up with the dresses. But they were almost to the dress shop, and then the dresses would be sorted. In no time, they'd head back to the island with the correct ones.

With the bachelor party canceled, his services weren't needed on the island until the wedding. Between now and then, he could visit Singapore or perhaps head to Paris to work on his tentative plan to buy a tech company. He'd been putting off exploring the option until after the wedding, but why put it off when he could do it now?

And so he decided that, after things were remedied at the dress shop, he would go back to the resort to collect his things and then he'd be on his way. Atlas would understand, since he'd warned him not to stir things up with Adara. Yes, that's exactly what he'd do.

Adara slowed the car before gracefully maneuvering into a parallel parking spot. Krystof glanced around at all the colorful shops with their showroom windows painted with the stores' logos and the colorful awnings. If he liked to shop, which he categorically did not, this would be the area he would frequent. It was welcoming, and he appeared not to be the only one who thought so, because the sidewalks were busy with pedestrians carrying lots of shopping bags.

His gaze took in one side of the street before moving to the other. He searched for their destination. It was easy to spot because of the pink-and-white-striped awning with a wooden sign that read Dora's Wedding Heaven. In the big picture windows were mannequins— naked mannequins.

Where are their clothes? Aren't they supposed by wearing wedding dresses?

He wasn't so sure about this shop. It was an odd display, to say the least. And then he noticed the lights were out. That was strange, too. He checked the time. It was only a few minutes after five. The shop was supposed to be open until six.

"It looks like they've closed early," he said. "And they really should consider clothing their mannequins."

"Leave it to you to notice that." She rolled her eyes before gathering her purse. "I'm going to try the door." She got out of the car.

He'd come this far. He might as well go the rest of the way. And so he followed her across the street.

Adara made it to the door and pulled on the handle. The door didn't budge. She tried again. "I don't understand. Why would they be closed?"

He noticed the sign above her head. It read Out of Business. Well, that certainly wasn't good news.

He nudged Adara and pointed. When she saw the sign, there was a loud gasp. She took a couple of steps back on the sidewalk as though she were stunned by this turn of events.

"That can't be right," she said. "I just talked to them the other day to make arrangements to have the dresses delivered."

He noticed the phone number on the door. He tried it, only to find it was disconnected.

"Why didn't you leave a message?" Adara asked.

"The phone has been disconnected."

"That can't be right." She dialed the number and then held the phone to her ear. A low growl let him know she'd gotten the same response. She ended the call and looked at him. "Now what are we going to do?"

He noticed how she'd said *we* this time, but when he went to point it out to her, the worry reflected in her eyes silenced him. "They can't just hold your dresses hostage."

Adara once more stepped up to the glass door. She pulled out her phone and selected the flashlight app. He stepped up beside her. She held the phone to the door, letting the light reflect through the window onto the empty dress racks. The dresses were all gone. The store was completely deserted.

"No. No. No." Her voice filled with frustration. "This can't be happening. They seemed like such nice people."

"You don't know what happened. They might very

well be nice people. We'll get this sorted." He hoped. "Let's go."

He turned around to find they weren't the only ones peering in the windows of the shop and asking questions. He cleared his throat. "Does anyone know what happened to the owners?"

The six or so people who had stopped in front of the shop shook their heads. No one seemed to know what had happened. This didn't bode well for them finding the correct dresses.

Once back inside the car, he checked the time. "Do you want to grab something to eat?"

She shook her head. "I have no appetite. What I want is to find the dresses for the wedding. How could this have happened?" She turned her head until their gazes met. "How am I going to tell Hermione that her wedding dress is missing?"

"You're not." His words were quick and firm. "She has enough to worry about."

"But I can't keep this from her forever. When she gets back, she's going to learn the truth."

"Unless we can figure out what happened between now and then."

Turmoil shown in her eyes. "Do you think we can do it?"

"I don't know." He couldn't lie to her. He had absolutely no idea what had happened to the dresses. Were they delivered to the wrong people? Or had the owners taken off with them to offload somewhere else? "All I know is that we can try our best to find them."

She nodded as she started the car. "We'll do everything we can."

"Yes, we will." He fastened his seat belt.

In that moment, he realized his plans to escape the

island and the woman who'd rejected him had just been upended. Because somewhere along the way, he'd promised to help her resolve this problem.

And though he'd like to think it would just take a phone call or two to locate the gowns, he had a feeling it wasn't going to be that simple. Just as working with Adara wasn't going to be simple. But he would deal with it all, one way or the other.

This was the worst.

Okay, maybe not quite the worst. But it wasn't good.

Adara tried the phone number for the shop again and again. And then she started a search for the name of the owner. It wasn't as easy to find as she might have thought. Because the owner's name wasn't Dora.

Go figure.

The owner was actually a man. And when she tried to find a phone number for him, she ran into problems. It was a common name, so she had a long list of names and numbers. This was going to take some time, and it was getting late.

Knock-knock.

Krystof stuck his head inside her office. "I thought I'd find you here."

She sighed and leaned back in her chair. "I've been trying to get ahold of anyone involved with the shop."

"And did you find someone?"

"No. And the owner's name isn't Dora. It's Michalis."

"Interesting." He stepped farther into the office.

"I've called a dozen people by that name, and they all say they have nothing to do with the shop." She turned off her computer. She needed a break. "How did things go for you? Were you able to come up with a way to track down the dresses?"

"I'm not sure. I have an idea. I'll let you know if I'm successful."

His words gave her a glimmer of hope when she desperately needed something to cling to. "Don't keep me in suspense. Tell me what you're doing."

"I'd rather not. It might not come to anything."

"Please. I've struck out all evening. I need some hope."

"I'll make you a deal. Come have some dinner with me, and I'll tell you my plan to find the dresses."

She arched a brow. "How can you be sure I haven't already eaten?"

"Because I know you, and you were set on locating the dresses. You wouldn't have stopped to eat. And that's why I'm going to make sure you have something to eat tonight."

"I don't think that's part of your responsibilities. You only promised Atlas that you'd help with the wedding."

"Um, but you're a part of the wedding, so I have to make sure you take care of yourself." This was his chance to dig a little deeper into what had happened between them. "That is, unless you have a date with someone else?"

She shook her head. "No date."

"What about a boyfriend?" He couldn't help himself. He had to know if she'd moved on.

Her eyes widened momentarily. "No boyfriend, either."

"Good." So if it wasn't another man, that meant whatever the problem was between them was likely fixable.

"Good?" She eyed him suspiciously.

That would teach him for letting his thoughts translate into spoken words. "Yes, good, because now you have no excuse not to join me."

She hesitated as though making up her mind, and then she shrugged. "I guess I can't argue about that."

He hadn't expected her to give in so easily. Every now and then she totally surprised him. This was one of those times.

"Then let's go."

She stood and rounded the desk. On her way out the door, she turned off the lights. That was a good sign. He was worried she was going to work all night trying to find the dresses.

"Where are we having dinner?" she asked.

"I thought maybe we'd dine in my suite. I already ordered food. It should be there when we arrive."

She stopped walking. "Krystof, I don't think this is a good idea. I told you we're not going back to the way things used to be."

"I heard you. I just knew that a lot of the resort's restaurants would be booked, and I thought you would be tired and want a chance to kick off your heels and relax. I promise I have no plans beyond that."

She hesitated, as though trying to decide if she should believe him or not. "Okay. Just a quick dinner, and then I'm off. I have an early day tomorrow."

"Sounds like a plan."

As they resumed walking, she asked, "How did you know what to order me?"

"It wasn't hard. We spent quite a few meals together. I know that you prefer fish or vegetarian meals. So I ordered scampi and wild rice with a salad."

Her eyes said what her mouth didn't. She was surprised he knew her so well. "It sounds good. And suddenly I'm hungry."

He liked the idea of them sharing a friendly meal. He held the door of his suite for her. He had been given the gamer-themed suite. There was a super-size flat screen on one wall with all the various gaming consoles, as well as a dedicated internet connection for online role playing. There were a couple of gamer's chairs that were so comfortable he would buy one if he had a place he called home.

The room was painted with graphics from various games. And a 3-D roulette table was on the ceiling. There were vintage pinball tables and early video games. On the other side of the room was a pool table, a Ping-Pong table and a shuffleboard table. And there were more games that he hadn't even gotten to yet, including a dartboard and a basketball hoop.

The best part was that the room had excellent sound-proofing, so you could crank up the stereo system and play games the entire night without bothering the other suites. Not that he was into that these days. He found the idea of staying up all night and sleeping all day not as appealing as it had been in his younger years.

He noticed Adara taking in the room, kind of like a kid in a toy store. "I take it you haven't been in this suite."

"This is a large resort. There are a lot of suites that I have yet to visit. And they redecorate them on a regular basis. Nothing about the resort gets stale or, worse, old. Guests like to be constantly surprised. This suite looks like it was created for an overgrown kid."

"Did you just call me a kid?"

She shrugged. "I didn't say that, but if the title fits…"

He'd wondered how long it would be until she started to complain about his transient lifestyle. He'd told her from the beginning that he wasn't going to change, not for her, not for anyone. He'd always been proud of his easy, breezy lifestyle, without any ties to any one place.

But seeing as how she didn't want to resume their friends-with-benefits arrangement, he didn't feel a need to defend his choices. He did as he pleased. He had no one to answer to except himself. And up until that point, it was the way he liked it. But since meeting Adara, he was finding his lifestyle perhaps a little too freeing and, dare he admit it, lonely.

"I'm sorry," she said. "I shouldn't have said that. After all, you're helping me locate the missing dresses. I'm just tired, and there's so much to worry about."

So much to worry about? He was confused. "I thought the only problem was with the dresses."

"Oh, yes. Right. Don't mind me. I guess the hunger is getting to me, too."

She tried to cover for her slip, but he didn't believe her. There was obviously more going on than she was willing to share with him. He wondered what it could be.

"Why don't we play a game while we wait for the food?" she suggested.

She didn't have to ask him twice. "What would you like to play?"

She turned in a circle, taking in the numerous games. "How about pinball? I haven't played that since I was a kid."

"Pinball it is."

And so they took turns playing. He had to give it to her—she was pretty good for not playing since she was a kid. The more they played, the more the worry lines on her face faded and the more she smiled.

Someone knocked at the door.

"That would be our dinner." He moved to the door

and opened it. A server stood there with a white linen–covered cart.

"Good evening, sir. Where would you like your dinner set up?"

"I think it would be a nice evening to eat out on the patio."

The young man, in black trousers and a white dress shirt, nodded. "Certainly. Just give me a moment."

"Not a problem. We have a round of pinball to finish." He turned back to Adara.

She pushed the ball-launch button. The screen lit up with flashing lights as the machine *ding-ding-dinged*. Krystof enjoyed watching her play. She was very focused on the game. And when she scored an extra ball, she gave out a little cheer.

For the first time ever, Krystof didn't feel the need to win. He'd already won by being in Adara's presence and feeling her happiness. He just hoped his idea to locate the dresses would work out in order to sustain her good mood.

Dinner was waiting for them by the time Adara's last silver ball slipped down the chute. She'd won the round, and her big smile made Krystof grin, too.

They moved out onto the private patio where a table had been set with a linen tablecloth, candles and a red rose in a bud vase. Beneath silver covers was their meal, still warm, and the aroma was divine. For the most part, dinner was quiet as they each made short work of their food.

As they leaned back to sip their coffee, Adara asked, "What is your idea to get back the dresses?"

This was his moment for a confession. It was something he didn't tell many people. "I have posted it to my social media on MyPost."

"MyPost? You're on there?" Surprise was written all over her face. "I just didn't see you as the type to share things on social media."

"I actually developed the platform."

She sat up straighter. "What?"

For the first time, he felt awkward for allowing everyone to think he was nothing more than a card-playing nomad. He cleared his throat. "I write code."

Her mouth gaped. It took her a moment to gather herself. "Why is tonight the first I'm hearing of this?"

He shrugged and shifted his gaze to the moonlight as it played over the darkened sea. "Because I don't talk much about it. I guess I got used to keeping things to myself when I was growing up. Without ever knowing my parents, I learned the only person I could count on was myself."

"I'm sorry. That must have been so tough for you."

He shrugged. "I never really knew any other way to be."

"So you went to school for programming?" When he nodded, she said, "Wow. That's very impressive. And you own MyPost?"

"I do. I've hired a team to do the day-to-day maintenance. It's gotten a lot bigger than I ever imagined." The site had millions of users that spanned the globe, and it was growing every day.

"So you're no longer involved with it?"

That was the thing. He'd had thoughts about ways he could expand it to make it more vital to a larger group of people. "When I started it, it was just a means to bring together card players. A way to plan and organize card games around the world. But I couldn't leave it alone, so I'd work on it in my spare time. It just grew and grew.

And now it's getting so large that I either need to sell it or take a more active role in its processes."

"And what will you do?"

"I'm not sure I'm willing to give up traveling and be locked into one place."

"Oh." The light in her eyes dimmed as she busied herself with reaching for her glass of water. "What does all of this have to do with the dresses?"

"I've put up a post about the dress shop closing and asked if anyone else also received the wrong dress."

She set aside her water glass. "Wait. Are you saying you have that many friends on MyPost that your post would have a chance of reaching the right people?"

He shook his head. "I don't have any friends on the platform. I belong to a private card group. That's it. But I'm the owner. I can make the platform do what I want. And so I constructed a notification that has gone out to each and every user. When they log on, they'll see it. They will have to read it and click through to get to their page."

Adara reached in her pocket and pulled out her phone. Her fingers rapidly moved over the screen, and then there was a gasp. "You really did it."

He smiled. "I did. Now we have to hope it'll be seen by the right people."

She continued staring at her phone as her fingers moved over the touch screen. "And you formed a private group for all of those affected by this issue. There are already people in the group. We aren't the only ones searching for the right dresses."

"Yes, but so far no one has dresses like you're searching for."

Adara's gaze lifted to meet his. "This is wonderful. Thank you."

He shrugged. "It's not a lot. It still hasn't recovered the dresses."

"But it might. This is more than I've been able to do." Then twin lines formed between her brows.

"What's the matter?"

She shook her head. "Nothing."

"It's definitely something, so out with it."

"I was just wondering if Hermione would see it. Maybe I need to call her now and tell her what happened." Her fingers began to move over the phone again.

He reached out and placed his hand over hers, pausing her actions. "Don't phone her. The chances of her being on social media right now would be slim, don't you think?"

Adara paused before nodding.

"And hopefully the dresses will be recovered before she realizes anything happened."

"I hope you're right." She made a point of checking the time on her phone. "It's getting late. I should be going."

He wanted to ask her to stay. He wanted to pull her into his arms once more and kiss her lips. Instead he said, "And I have a card game to get to on the mainland."

A brief frown skittered across her face as she got to her feet. When she faced him, her face was devoid of expression. "I don't want to keep you."

"I'll walk you out." He had to rush to catch up with her quick steps.

She was mad at him *again*. And once more, he didn't understand what he'd done. Was he supposed to work all night trying to recover the dresses? At this point, he didn't know what else he could do.

At the door, she paused and turned to him. "Thank you for the help today."

"You're welcome. I don't know that I did much, but I have a feeling everything will work out." And then he leaned forward. He resisted the urge to place a kiss on her lips and instead pressed his lips to her cheek.

When he pulled back, he noticed that pinkness had bloomed in her cheeks. And as much as he wanted to pull her into his arms and kiss her properly, he knew it wasn't a good idea. She wasn't ready for that.

At least not yet.

CHAPTER SEVEN

HE'D KISSED HER CHEEK, not her lips.

What did that mean?

Adara had wondered about the kiss the rest of the evening and late into the night. She'd gotten to know Krystof fairly well over the last seven months. He was a man who knew what he wanted and wasn't afraid to go after it.

There was nothing in that kiss that spoke of passion or longing. And she couldn't deny that it disappointed her. She knew she should be fine with it, because they both wanted different things in life.

He'd obviously found what he was looking for in that other woman. She tried to tell herself that it didn't matter—he didn't matter to her. So then why was her stomach knotted?

The following day, she was thankfully busy all morning—too busy to have breakfast with Krystof when he stopped by her office. In fact, she'd come to work early today. It was so easy to be early when she was staying at the resort. Before Atlas and Hermione owned the resort, it would have been impossible for her to stay in a suite. There had been rules about the employees not being able to utilize the resort's amenities, from the rooms to the spa. But the new owners had seen fit to relax those rules—within reason.

She had spent the lunch hour in her office making phone calls to track down the owner of the bridal shop. And so far she hadn't had any luck. It was like the owners had just up and disappeared overnight. How was that possible?

Someone rapped their knuckles on the door.

She glanced up to find Krystof standing in the doorway. He sent her a smile that made her stomach dip. She automatically returned his smile. As soon as she realized what she was doing, she pressed her lips into a firm line.

"Hi. What can I do for you?" she asked in her concierge voice.

"It's a matter of what I can do for you."

"For me?" She had absolutely no idea what he was talking about.

"You know how I told you I set up that message on MyPost?" When she nodded, he said, "I've had a response. Someone has the wrong wedding dress. They think it might be the one we're hunting for."

"Did they include a photo?"

He pulled it up on his phone and then held it out for her to see. "I hope it's the right one."

"Me, too." She took the phone from him and stared at the image. It was the correct shade of white. The quality of the photo wasn't good enough to make out the detail of the beadwork. But the neckline was all wrong. Instead of the sweetheart neckline that Hermione had loved, this one had a square neckline.

Her heart sank. "This isn't the right dress."

"Are you sure?"

She nodded. "I'm positive."

"Oh. Okay. We'll keep looking. It'll turn up."

"I hope so."

"We should take pictures of the dresses you have and I'll post them to the group. The more eyes we get on the post in MyPost, the more people will talk about it. The more attention the wedding dress mix-up gets, the better chance of finding the correct dresses."

"Good idea. I've had them moved to my room so they were out of the way." She glanced at her calendar. "We can go now. I have a half hour before I'm supposed to meet with the Carringtons about their cocktail party."

As they walked to her room, the awkwardness between them returned. She had no idea how to make small talk with him, nor did she want to. If she hadn't caught on to the fact that he was seeing other women, would he have even told her?

She told herself that it didn't matter now. It was all behind them. She needed to stay focused on the task at hand—the hunt for the wedding dress.

In the end, Krystof was all wrong for her. Maybe it was the fact that something was possibly going wrong with her body. It had her looking toward the future differently. She wanted a real relationship. Something with strings and words of endearment. Was it so wrong to want someone to say *I love you*? Someone who wanted to stick around through the good and the bad? Was that asking too much?

Krystof had made it clear during their time together that he wasn't that kind of man—the kind who settled down. And for a time she'd thought she was perfectly okay with that—that it would be enough. She'd been wrong.

"Adara, isn't that your room we just passed?" Krystof's voice drew her from her thoughts.

She glanced around and realized he was right. She'd been so deep in thought that she'd walked straight past her room. The heat of embarrassment climbed up her neck and settled in her cheeks, and she retraced her steps.

"I... I'm not used to staying here yet." She let herself into the room.

Compared to his suite, her room was very modest. On the opposite side of the room from her white couches and glass coffee table was a king-size bed with an assortment of pillows in shades of aqua and white.

Although with Krystof in the room with her, it suddenly didn't seem so big—and the bed loomed large. She felt his gaze following her. She tried to ignore him but soon found it was an impossibility.

"I have the dresses over here." She'd had them place the cart into the spacious walk-in closet. She rolled it out. "We can just photograph them hanging on the rack."

"Or you could model all the dresses," he teased.

"Not a chance."

"Why not? I thought you wanted to get married."

"I never said that." Not to him, anyway. She thought some day she might get married and have a family of her own—something like her parents once had. But she didn't want to think of any of that now. "I'll just unzip the garment bag and fluff out the wedding gown."

She did that, and he took a photo. And then they did the same with the bridesmaid dresses. But as she was putting the wedding dress carefully in the garment bag, some of the material got caught in the zipper. As she struggled to free the material without damaging the dress, she pulled too hard on the garment bag, and the rack began to fall on her.

Krystof launched into action and caught the rack before it could touch her. When she straightened, she turned too quickly and bumped into him. She got a brief whiff of his spicy cologne. The scent was enough to take her back in time to a place where it would be so natural for her to just lean forward and press her lips to his.

Her heart started to beat quickly. She tilted her chin upward until their gazes caught and held. She should pull away, and yet her feet wouldn't cooperate.

The breath solidified in her throat. She couldn't remember why she was resisting falling into his arms and picking up where they'd left off. She longed to feel the passionate touch of his kiss. Because in that moment, she missed him so very much.

"Adara, where did things go wrong with us?" he asked gruffly.

It all came rushing back to her. His suggestion that they should have a casual relationship. His repeated requests for her to take time off work to visit him in various parts of the world. Her eye-opening surprise, the one time she'd done that, only to find him with another woman.

She shook her head. "Don't go acting like it matters to you."

"I'd really like to know."

Her gaze narrowed as she tried to decide if he was messing with her. Sincerity reflected in his gaze. He really didn't know that she'd seen him in Paris.

She sighed. "Remember how you kept asking me to meet you for a weekend?" When he nodded, she continued. "Well, I finally did. I flew to Paris in July, and I saw you with another woman."

His brows lifted, and then he stared off into space as though he were trying to recall the specific occasion.

She started to wonder how many women he had on the side. Was she just one of a multitude?

"I don't recall seeing you."

She noticed how he ignored the mention of another woman. "You're right. You didn't see me. I'd just stepped off the elevator on your floor of the hotel. When I turned the corner, I saw a woman at your door."

His eyes widened. "Adara, you got things wrong in Paris."

"So you're saying I imagined you answering the door smiling, wearing nothing more than a bath towel, and the woman rushing into your arms?"

"No. I'm saying you misunderstood the situation."

There was a part of her that wanted to believe him, and it annoyed her that she could still be drawn in by him. "I think I got the gist of it," she said dryly.

"No, you didn't, because the woman was my sister."

"Your sister?" Surely she hadn't heard him correctly.

He nodded his head. "Yes, my sister."

Thank goodness she had the dress rack to hold her up. It took a moment for this information to sink in.

Krystof had a sister? Since when? From everything he'd told her, he was an only child who'd been abandoned by his parents. Had he done one of those DNA tests and found his sister that way?

Or was this just some sort of story he had concocted to try and fix things between them? She studied him for a moment. Krystof might be unconventional in a lot of ways, but she didn't think he'd outright lie to her just to have his way. With that thought in mind, she decided to hear him out.

"Okay," she said. "I'm listening."

For a moment, he stood silent. Was he surprised that

she'd agreed to hear him out? Or was he trying to find a starting point?

He cleared his throat. "When Celeste found out I was going to be in Paris, we made plans to meet up. I had no idea you were going to surprise me with a visit."

And this was exactly why she didn't like to live spontaneously. Sometimes those spur-of-the-moment decisions worked out, but a lot of the time, they didn't. In her case, it most definitely hadn't worked out.

But if that was his sister, did it mean he wasn't seeing anyone else? Her heart leaped with joy, but her mind tamped down the excitement. There was something not quite right with this story.

"I didn't think you had any siblings." She narrowed her gaze on him, hoping to determine the truth of the matter. "I thought you were an orphan who didn't know your parents. Has that changed?"

"Of course it hasn't changed." He raked his fingers through his hair. "Celeste isn't my biological sister. She was another orphan. We shared the same home for years. She was a couple of years younger than me, and I would watch out for her."

The thought of Krystof playing the protective big brother thawed her icy heart toward him. But she wasn't quite ready to forgive and forget. "So you're saying there's nothing between you two?"

His nose immediately scrunched up. "Between me and Celeste? Ooh… No. She's like my sister."

"But she's not your biological sister. And years have passed. Maybe feelings between you two have changed."

Distaste was written all over his face. "Adara, I have no romantic interest in Celeste. She is now and will forever be the closest thing I have to a sister. Don't try to make it out to be something it isn't."

He was right. She was pushing too hard in her earnest attempt to keep the wall up between them. She took a deep breath. "I'm sorry."

"So you see it was all a big misunderstanding." He smiled at her triumphantly, and her heart dipped like she was on a giant roller coaster. He stepped closer to her. "Now can we at last kiss and make up?"

"No." The answer was quick and short.

She knew if she didn't stop this madness right away, he would wear away her resolve and then what? They'd go back to the way things used to be where they only saw each other when he had time to stop by the island. And their phone conversations were intermittent at best. No. She'd already recognized that she needed a more stable relationship.

He reached out to her, his hands caressing her upper arms. "Come on. You know we were good together." He gazed deep into her eyes and lowered his voice. "Adara, I've missed you."

Her heart skipped a beat. It would be so easy to lean into him and claim his lips with her own. There was a part of her that was dying to do exactly that—but there was another part of her that knew a few stolen moments would never be enough for her.

She pulled away from his touch. "Um… I need to get back to work."

"I understand. I'll have these pictures posted online."

"Sounds good. Thank you."

"No problem." And then he let himself out of the room.

Adara stood there watching him walk away. She told herself repeatedly that she couldn't just fall back into his arms—even though that was what every fiber of her body wanted to do.

Still, she couldn't play by his rules. She couldn't do a casual, no-strings-attached relationship. Seeing him with that other woman—even if it had been innocent that time—had taught her that lesson. So why did she feel so disappointed that he seemed to have accepted her refusal so easily?

CHAPTER EIGHT

AT LAST THINGS were getting back on track, Krystof thought with satisfaction as he strode away from Adara's room. She now knew the truth about Celeste.

That was a good thing, because he didn't know how much longer he could resist kissing her.

Krystof knew Adara still wasn't convinced resuming their arrangement was a good thing. He just needed to take a different approach, that was all. One that drew her out of her safe and predictable life—one that showed her she needed to go after what she wanted.

He had no idea how hard it was going to be to resist her, especially when she looked at him with desire burning in her eyes. But he knew to act in those moments would be a mistake, because she was still putting up a wall between them.

If he could just convince her that they were good together, they could go back to the way things used to be. Lots of fun and no strings. After all, she had her career to focus on, and he had…

His thoughts stumbled as he realized he'd handed most of the control over MyPost to his very capable staff. And his interest in playing cards was waning. But there was still the chance to buy that tech firm in Paris. The only thing holding him back from doing just that was the idea of having to set down roots somewhere. There was still a part of him that felt like he needed to be out searching—no, exploring—exploring for the next big adventure and not locked in somewhere. A memory of his childhood being locked in a small room with no windows came rushing back to him. He pushed it away. That was then and this was now.

Later that day, Krystof stood off to the side of Adara's office as she spoke with a mother and daughter who'd brought in a wedding dress for Adara to examine, and in exchange she'd let them see the wedding dress that had been mistakenly delivered for Hermione. It would appear that though the dresses were a fairly close match, neither had the right one. This mix-up was far larger than he'd imagined. And so the search continued.

As the mother and daughter headed off for dinner, Adara turned to him with a worried gaze. "This isn't looking good."

"No worries. We're not giving up. The page I set up for the dresses is just starting to pick up the pace. And now I'll add the pictures of this other wedding dress we've just seen."

"I don't understand how all this happened in the first place. How could they have mixed up so many orders?"

He shrugged. "I have no idea. I don't know if it was intentional, to take the focus off the owners suddenly closing up shop without delivering all of the gowns, because those stories are starting to crop up online, or if someone unintentionally mixed up all of the tickets with the names. I have a feeling we'll never know the answer."

"I feel like I need to tell Hermione now. That way she'll still have time to get another dress."

"A wedding dress? I thought those took months to order."

Adara sighed. "They do. But maybe she could buy one off the rack or find one at a secondhand shop."

"Do you really think that's what she'd want?"

Adara shook her head. "No. She loved that dress. She knew as soon as she saw it that it was the right one for her. And she didn't bother to look at any others after it."

"Then I think we need to keep looking for it."

Adara's gaze searched his for reassurance. "Do you really think we'll find it?"

"I think we're headed in the right direction." He wanted to promise her that they'd find the dresses, but he honestly didn't know if it was possible, especially in the short amount of time they had left until the wedding. But there was nothing more they could do right now. "Let's go get something to eat."

Adara's gaze moved back to her tidy desk. "I still have a lot of work to do."

He glanced at his Rolex. "And it'll wait. It's time to eat. Come on."

"But..."

"Adara, just leave it."

She expelled a sigh. "Okay." She followed him to the door and switched off the lights. "Dinner at your place? Or mine?"

"Actually, I have something different in mind." He presented his arm to her.

Her gaze moved from his eyes to his arm and then back again. After a brief hesitation, she placed her hand in the crook of his arm. "Where are we going?"

"You'll see."

They quietly walked through the resort. Their footsteps were muffled by the lush carpeting. On the walls were fabulous pieces of art. It was like walking through a museum. It gave Krystof an idea. Perhaps he'd start collecting art—finding the next big artist. Speaking of which, he'd already met a rising artist, Indigo Castellanos. He would have to make sure and purchase one of her works. She could be the start of his collection.

He paused to look at a painting of the ocean. "This is very good."

"I didn't know you were into art."

"It's a new passion of mine."

"Have you checked out the gallery yet?"

He shook his head. "I haven't."

"We could see it after dinner."

"Sounds like a plan." He smiled as he led her outside.

Little by little she was letting down her guard with him. In fact, they were almost friends again. His plan was working. That's good, because he'd missed her smile and the way it was so easy to talk to her about anything and everything.

"Where are we going?"

They continued to the other side of the patio and down the steps. He knew with all she'd been doing for not only her job but also the wedding that she needed to slow down and relax. And he had the perfect idea.

"We're going to eat dinner."

"But where? The restaurants are all behind us back in the resort."

"This is a special dinner. Just trust me."

When they reached the beach, they slipped off their shoes and set them aside. Evening had settled in, and the sun was hovering on the horizon, sending a cascade of pinks and purples over the puffy clouds.

"You want to go for a stroll along the beach?" she asked.

"Not exactly. But now that you mentioned it, it's not a bad idea." He tucked the idea aside for later.

He'd asked the staff to place his surprise for Adara just out of sight from the resort for privacy. So as they moved past a dune, he heard Adara gasp. He watched as she pressed a hand to her chest and gaped.

Candles lined a path of red rose petals to a table with a white linen tablecloth. A few torches surrounded the table, granting some light now that the sun was sinking below the horizon. The staff had done an excellent job.

"Krystof, what have you done?"

"I hope you like it."

"I love it." Her gaze briefly flickered from the table to him. "But how did you do it? I'm the one that usually sets up these special moments."

A smile played at the corners of his lips. "I may have sworn your assistant to silence as we devised this evening."

"Remind me to give Demi a raise."

"I'm sure she'll appreciate it."

"If I'm not careful, she'll be replacing me."

"Trust me. You're irreplaceable." He'd come to that startling conclusion in the time they were apart. She was very special.

They walked along the rose petal–adorned path. Adara stopped next to the table and turned to him. She tilted her chin upward and stared into his eyes. "This is beautiful. But why did you do it?"

A gentle breeze blew and swiped a few strands of hair into her face. He reached out, tucking those silken strands behind her ear. And then he gazed into her eyes. "I want to show you how sorry I am about the way things ended between us."

"You didn't have to go to all of this trouble."

"I wanted to."

He longed to pull her close and press a kiss to her lips. By the way she was looking into his eyes, she wouldn't have complained. But he knew it was too soon. She might kiss him now, but later she would change her mind. He had to be patient, and eventually she'd see that they were better off with their friends-with-benefits arrangement.

He mustered his resolve and moved past her to pull out a chair for her. Once they were both seated, she said, "If I didn't know better, I'd think you were trying to seduce me."

He smiled. "Is it working?"

"Wouldn't you like to know," she teased.

It was a pleasant dinner. No, it was better than that. He was captivated by her words and spellbound by her beauty in the candlelight. He didn't want the evening to end.

With soft music playing in the background and the lull of the tide, they enjoyed a candlelit meal. She told him about some of the more interesting aspects of her job, and he shared snippets of what he'd been up to in the last few months. Then the conversation shifted to his interest in art. She seemed genuinely enthusiastic about him starting an art collection.

"So if you were to collect art," she asked, "where would you keep it?"

He went to speak but then hesitated. He realized he didn't have an answer for her question. "I guess that would pose a problem."

"Unless you were to buy a place." Her eyes lit up. "You know, somewhere to keep your treasures and perhaps to call home."

"I'll give it some thought." Settling down wasn't really in his plans.

"You're frowning. I see you don't like that idea." Disappointment reflected in her eyes.

He owed her an explanation. Maybe then she would stop pushing for him to be something he wasn't. "I know you want me to stay put and create a home, but that just isn't me."

"But why? Everyone I know has a home, except you."

He sighed as he lounged back in his chair. He didn't like to dig around in his memories. Most of them were not happy ones. And though he knew he had it better than others, it still wasn't the happy, loving family that people witnessed on television sitcoms. In fact, his past was quite the opposite.

"I keep moving around because I was stuck in an unhappy foster home where I never felt I belonged." He toyed with the hem of the discarded cloth napkin on the table. "It was a place that I couldn't escape—no matter how many times I ran away." He stopped himself there.

He'd said more than he ever intended. He refused to say more. The past needed to stay exactly where it was—in the past. He never spoke of it. It was none of anyone's business. When he glanced at Adara, she was studying him. She was probably wondering about all the bits of his life that he hadn't told her. Even she wouldn't guess how bad it truly had been.

But it was better this way. He didn't want anyone to view him with sympathy. He was strong and successful. Maybe he wasn't the traditional version of a success story, but he'd created his own version of it.

CHAPTER NINE

HER HEART ACHED for him.

Adara quietly ate her tiramisu as Krystof drank a cup of coffee and stared out at the sea. He seemed lost in his thoughts. She wondered if he was thinking of his past.

She felt bad that she'd pushed him about his nomadic life after he'd gone to such effort to show her a good time. And the dinner had been fantastic. It was an evening she'd created for clients but never had the opportunity to enjoy herself.

And now it was almost over, and she felt guilty that she'd ruined it for Krystof. She wanted to make it up to him and put the smile back on his face.

As she took a last bite of the most delicious tiramisu, she considered suggesting they take a moonlight stroll along the beach. However, as she observed him, she changed her mind. She didn't think that was such a good idea. He was already lost in his thoughts of the past. She needed to get him to think about something else—perhaps a possibility for the future. And then she had her plan.

She wiped her mouth, set aside her napkin and then got to her feet. She moved over next to him. "Come with me."

He shook his head. "I don't think so. I'm just going to sit here for a few more minutes."

That was the very last thing he needed to do. The past had already robbed him of so much. It didn't need to steal any more of his happiness.

She reached out and took his hand in hers. She gave a tug. "Come on. It'll be worth it."

He arched a brow. "You aren't going to give up, are you?"

She smiled and shook her head. "Not a chance."

"Okay. You win." He stood. "Where are we going?"

"You'll see."

And so they set off for the spot where they'd left their shoes. Once the sand had been brushed off and the shoes put on, hand in hand they headed inside the resort. Along the way they passed numerous guests dressed in their finest clothes for dining at one of the three Michelin-starred restaurants at the resort.

She kept her fingers laced with his. She told herself she only did it because she didn't want him to slip away. But there was a part of her that enjoyed the feel of her skin against his. There was one thing they'd always had: chemistry. Lots and lots of sizzling, fiery chemistry.

The problem was sex was all they'd had. Sure, they'd had good times together outside the bedroom, but there was never any depth to any of it. Tonight had been totally different. Krystof had let down his guard long enough for her to get a glimpse of the man inside— the man with scars and insecurities. She had a feeling there was a lot more to his story, but what he'd told her was a start.

His admission dug at her heart. It was hard to hold him at a distance when he had showed her his vulnerabilities. She'd witnessed just how alone he was in this world—partly from a tragic childhood and partly from him keeping people out so he wouldn't be hurt again.

She wanted to help him—show him that taking a chance on a relationship was worth the risk. But she didn't know if she was the right person to coax him from his safety zone. After all, she was dealing with her own medical issues at the moment. But maybe she could help him with this small step forward.

She approached the large frosted glass doors of the Ludus Gallery. "We're here."

Krystof glanced up. "It's the gallery." He stared at the sign with the hours of operation. "It's already closed."

Adara held up a key card. "I can get us in."

He shook his head. "I don't think it's a good idea."

"Sure it is." She didn't wait for him to argue. She flashed the card in front of a card reader, and then she had to press her palm to a biometric security device. The light on the reader changed from red to green. There was a click of the lock releasing at the same time the lights automatically turned on. "See. Easy."

She reached for the oversize brass handle and then easily pulled open the glass door. She held the door for him. Once he was inside, she closed the door and locked it.

He slowly walked around, taking in the various exhibits. He moved closer to the wall and lifted his chin to admire the gallery's latest acquisition. "These are really nice."

"I'll be sure to let Indigo know you said so."

"Indigo did these?"

"Yes. She has stopped working at the resort in order to pursue her art full-time."

His gaze moved along the wall, taking in the portraits of people in everyday life, from an older woman watering flowers to people at the beach and then one of children playing ball and lastly a baby. It was though each portrait displayed a different stage in life.

"These are quite impressive, but I'm sure she won't have time to work on her art once she marries the prince."

"She says she's not giving up her art, and Istvan doesn't want her to. He says he wants her to do whatever will make her happy." Adara hoped that someday she'd be so lucky. She wanted to meet a man who respected her love of her work that much.

They moved on to some pottery displays before viewing various pieces of antique jewelry. The gallery was expanding to the point where they'd soon need to build an addition. Krystof stopped to take in a series of seascapes. Each was the same scene but displayed at various times of the day. She stood next to him, taking it all in. She never tired of visiting the gallery. There was always a new display.

But tonight it was the man next to her that held her attention. She longed to show him that he didn't always have to be on the go, that he could stop in one place and not be hurt.

"How often do you get new exhibits?" Krystof's voice drew her from her thoughts.

"They've really been stepping up their exchange program. In fact, only about half of the gallery's pieces are here right now. The rest have been loaned out." She pointed to the left. "Do you see that large portrait with the tie-dye design?" When he nodded, she said, "That was borrowed from a gallery in Rome." Then she turned and pointed to another portrait. "See the portrait of the lion? It's made from thousands and thousands of seeds. I forget where it originated, but it's the most recent piece on loan to us."

"It's quite a collection." He moved nearer to the lion to have a closer look. "I can't believe I haven't been in here sooner." He turned and pointed to another set of closed doors. "What's back there?"

"It's where they have special displays."

"That sounds intriguing. Can we have a look?"

Under other circumstances, she would have made an excuse not to go back there. But since Krystof had emerged from his dark thoughts of the past, she was eager to do whatever it took to keep his thoughts in the present. And so she moved toward the back room.

She swiped her key card to open the door. While the front of the gallery was a large area with tall, white walls, the back room was much smaller, with black walls and spotlights that focused on the gallery's headliner.

This time Krystof pulled the door open for her. "After you."

"Thanks." She had to step close to him—so very close.

It would have been incredibly tempting to stop and turn to him. Kissing him definitely would have distracted him—and her. His kisses were so mesmerizing that they would often cause her to forget her common sense and lose herself in the moment.

But those moments were behind them now.

And with great regret, she continued past him and into the back room. She swallowed, hoping when she spoke that her voice didn't betray the fact that his nearness had gotten to her. "And these displays back here are royal jewels."

"Let me guess—they are on loan from Istvan's family."

"Actually, they belong to Istvan himself. He inherited them from his grandmother. And the Ruby Heart is the highlight."

Krystof approached the glass case. "The ruby is really large. Too big for a piece of jewelry."

She stepped up beside him. She couldn't resist getting another glimpse of the precious jewel. It was the most amazing gem she'd ever seen. With its many precise cuts, it was a work of art. The spotlights danced upon the various cuts, making it seem as though the gem had a power all of its own.

"There's a brass plaque with it. I can't quite make out what it says." He moved closer to try to read it.

She had hoped he'd miss that part. "It's really no big deal. There are more pieces to see out front."

As though he hadn't heard a word she'd said, he started to read aloud. "'The legend of the Ruby Heart. If destined lovers gaze upon the Ruby Heart at the same time, their lives will be forever entwined.'"

When Krystof's gaze moved to meet hers, heat rushed from her chest up her neck and filled her cheeks.

"Do you think the legend is talking about us?" His voice was low and deep.

"Krystof…" She meant to set him straight, but when his gaze met hers, the words clogged in the back of her throat.

He turned to her and pulled her close. It was as though she were having an out-of-body experience as she leaned into him. She tilted her chin upward. The breath hitched in her lungs.

And then he lowered his head, capturing her lips with his own. Oh, how she'd missed him. Her hands moved up over his shoulders and wrapped around the back of his neck.

It didn't matter how many times they kissed—it always felt like the first time. As the kiss deepened, a moan swelled in the back of her throat.

She didn't want this moment to end. She met him move for move. She opened her mouth to him. His tongue touched hers, and a moan escaped. He was amazing.

It would be so easy to fall for him. But she refused to let herself do something that foolish, because he'd made it clear he didn't feel the same way about her. What had he called them? Oh, yes, friends with benefits. He thought it was cute. She didn't. She wanted more—a real relationship with strings, complications and the hope for a future together.

His fingertips worked her blouse loose and touched the bare skin of her back, sending goose bumps cascading down her body. Her thoughts scattered as her heart beat so loud that it echoed in her ears.

And that's why she didn't realize they were no longer alone.

"Oh, Ms. Galinis, it's you."

She jumped out of Krystof's arms. Heat once again filled her cheeks. She drew in a deep breath, hoping it would calm her racing heart. Her hands moved to her hair, smoothing it. Then her fingertips traced her still-tingling lips. She straightened her shoulders and lifted her chin ever so slightly as she turned.

She forced a smile onto her face. "Good evening, Christos. Yes, it's just me. I was showing Mr. Mikos around the gallery."

The night guard's forehead wrinkled. "You do know it's closed?"

"Um, yes. And we were just leaving." She quickly

glanced at Krystof, who was wearing an amused smile at her awkwardness. "Weren't we, Krystof?"

"Yes. That's exactly what we were doing." He let out a laugh as he made his way past her and headed for the door.

The heat in her face amplified. She resisted the urge to fan herself. She turned to the guard. "Shall I lock up, or would you rather take care of it?"

"I'll handle it." He sent her another confused look, as though he still didn't understand why she would be in the gallery after hours. It was a first for her.

She didn't stick around. She walked quickly to the door. She was so anxious to be out of there. In her rush, she practically ran into Krystof in the hallway. "Oops. Sorry."

"I'm not," he teased. "If you'd like to walk into my arms again, I'm all for it."

She shook her head. "It shouldn't have happened. It was a mistake."

"If that was a mistake, I don't mind being wrong."

She lifted her gaze and frowned at him as he looked at her with amusement dancing in his eyes.

"I can't do casual," she said bluntly.

"I happen to think you do a mighty fine job of it." A smile lifted the corners of his mouth. "Commitments don't last. Forever is just a romantic notion. All we have is the here and now."

The image of him with Celeste in his arms came back to her. The searing jealousy that she'd felt when she'd thought he was interested in someone else meant she was in serious danger of falling for him.

She couldn't let that happen. She refused to set herself up for heartache when Krystof walked away. And he would. She was under no illusions about him ever settling down. Maybe not this week or next week, but soon he'd grow bored with her, and then he'd be gone.

She suddenly regretted bringing Krystof to the gallery. Not only had they been caught making out by the security guard, but they'd gazed upon the Ruby Heart together. And though she didn't believe in legends, she couldn't deny that Hermione and Atlas, as well as Indigo and Istvan, had gazed upon that ruby, and both couples were now getting married. She suddenly felt nauseous.

"I... I'm going to call it a night." Her gaze didn't quite reach his. "Thank you for dinner. It was lovely."

And then, without waiting for him to say anything, she turned and walked away. She resisted the urge to glance over her shoulder. If she wanted to survive this wedding with her heart still intact, she had to keep him at arm's length.

The kiss only made him miss her more.

Krystof spent that evening in a high-stakes poker game that ran most of the night. He'd played on the edge with over-the-top bets and lots of bluffs, hoping the high stakes would distract him from his thoughts of Adara. It didn't work.

After sleeping late the next day, he was tempted to seek out Adara. He resisted going to her as long as he could, but eventually he gave in to his desire. There was only one problem—he couldn't find her. Was she avoiding him?

It wasn't like he'd set out to kiss her. It was a spur-of-the-moment thing, and she had been just as involved in that kiss as he'd been. His thoughts strayed to the Ruby Heart's legend, and he wondered if it had something to do with it. He quickly dismissed the idea. He didn't believe in legends. And it wasn't like this thing between him and Adara hadn't been going on for months now.

By that afternoon, he was ready to face whatever Adara threw at him. But before he could go in search of her, he had an alert on his phone that someone thought they had the bridesmaid dresses. Now he had the perfect excuse to see her.

Demi informed him that Adara was working in her suite. When he showed Adara the photo of the dresses, she said they looked like the right ones, but she wouldn't know for sure until she saw them in person.

The only problem was they had to drive into Athens to meet the person at their home. The ride was quiet, as neither of them broached the subject of the kiss. He didn't want to do anything to push her farther away. He was starting to wonder if his plan to put things back to the way they'd been before Paris was going to work out. Even though the chemistry between them was still there, as fierce as ever, Adara was fighting it at every turn.

In a surprise turn of events, the person did have the right bridesmaids' dresses, but not the right wedding gown. Now they only had one more dress to locate— and, of course, the dresses in their possession to return to the appropriate owner.

"Don't worry," he said as he navigated her car toward the ferry. "We'll find the wedding dress."

"I hope you're right." Adara's fingers moved rapidly over her phone as she answered messages.

With a mix-up at the resort to sort out, Krystof had offered to drive so that she would be free to deal with the problem. She was reluctant to hand over her car keys, but with a sigh, she did it.

Buzz-buzz.

"That better not be more bad news," Krystof grouched as he navigated her car through traffic.

She frowned at him. "Did you have to say that?"

He chanced a quick glance at her. "Why?"

"You've probably just jinxed us."

"Jinxed us how?"

"Oh, never mind." She focused back on her phone. "It's the booking agent for the band for the ceremony."

She pressed the phone to her ear. The conversation was brief. When it concluded, she sat there quietly for a moment, as though taking in what she'd learned.

He gave her a brief glance. "Well, don't just sit there. Tell me what they said."

"There's been an accident, and two of the band members have been injured."

"That's awful." He slowed to a stop at an intersection.

"I agree. Thankfully everyone lived, but they will need some time to recover. In the meantime, we don't have any music for the wedding."

"Maybe this is a sign," he said.

"A sign?"

"That the wedding shouldn't happen."

She gasped. "Are you serious? You don't think Hermione and Atlas should get married?"

He shrugged. He should have kept his thoughts to himself. When he glanced over at Adara, he found her staring expectantly at him. He focused back on the road. "What? You have to admit that nothing about this wedding is easy. The bride and groom aren't even here."

"They are where they're needed. And the wedding doesn't have to be easy. It just has to be right for Hermione and Atlas."

"If you say so."

"I do."

"So what are you going to do?"

"Me?" Her voice rose an octave. "Why should I fix this problem? I thought you wanted to help with the wedding plans. Wasn't that what you said?"

She surely didn't think he would know what to do about this latest problem. "Yes, but this is different."

"Different how?"

"Because it's an urgent problem. The wedding isn't far off."

"And why should I fix it instead of you?"

He panicked and reached for the first excuse he could think of. "Because you're a woman and this is a wedding."

When he chanced a glance in her direction, she was sitting there with her arms crossed as she glared at him. "Really? Are you saying a man can't plan a wedding?"

He sighed. "I'm certain a man could do just as good of a job planning a wedding."

"You think so?"

"I do."

"Good. Then you can find a replacement musical group."

He tapped the brakes a little too hard, jerking them in their seats. "What?"

"You heard me. Unless you don't think you're up to it."

He briefly turned to her with an arched brow before focusing back on the road. "Is that a challenge?"

A smile tugged at the corners of her lips as she settled back in her seat. "Why, yes, it is."

He refused to back down. How hard could it be? And maybe this would at last get him back in her good graces so they could pick up where they'd left off. The thought definitely appealed to him.

There was a moment of silence as he pulled the car off on the berm of the road, and then he turned to her. "What exactly do I need to do?"

"The booking agent is going to email us a list of available musical groups."

"And then what?"

"Then you go listen to them. She's going to include where they are each playing. All you have to do it stop by and check them out."

"And that's it?" He stared at her, not believing it was that easy.

"Yes. That's it."

"Fine. I'll do it." He put the car in Drive and eased back out into traffic.

He didn't like it, but he'd do it. It really didn't sound hard. Who didn't like to listen to a bit of music? It'd be even better if Adara was listening to it with him. Hmm. He might have to plan something to get her to accompany him.

CHAPTER TEN

WHAT WAS IT with this wedding?

Adara had been involved with a lot of weddings, and she couldn't recall any having this many setbacks. It was getting so bad that for a moment she wondered if Krystof was right about this being a sign that it shouldn't take place. As soon as the thought came to her, she dismissed it.

This wedding was right for both Hermione and Atlas. They truly loved each other. And no amount of wedding dilemmas would change their devotion to one another.

Adara had just finished making arrangements for a guest's twenty-fifth wedding anniversary. A party planned for the next evening on the patio with silver and white balloons, a live band, and endless champagne. Another wonderful example of how love could endure. She refused to let Krystof's negativity get to her.

She was almost to her office when her phone rang. She glanced at the caller ID and then pressed the phone to her ear. "Hey, Hermione. How are you doing?"

"As well as can be expected. How are things there?"

"Uh…" She entered her office and closed the door. "The resort is doing fine. No problems."

"But there is a problem. I can hear it in your voice. It's Krystof, isn't it?"

Adara sank into her chair. "He's fine. And you don't need to hear this. You have enough going on with Atlas and his father."

"I could use the distraction. So Krystof is pushing for you to get back together, isn't he?"

Adara sighed. "He wants things to go back to the way they were before I mistook his foster sister for his girlfriend in Paris."

"You did what? Oh, dear. How do you feel about that?"

Part of her was eager to feel Krystof's strong arms around her as he trailed kisses down her neck. The other part of her knew that she could easily get in too deep with him. With every detail she learned, it was easier to imagine starting a real relationship with him. And in the end, she'd be left with a broken heart.

Adara swallowed hard. "I don't want to go backward. I want a real relationship. I'm not saying we would have to get married or anything like that, but I want a commitment. I want to matter to him enough that he would go out of his way to see me often and not just when it's convenient for his schedule. I want to know that I'm the only woman in his life. Is that asking for too much?"

"No." The answer was quick and firm. "But I take it that's not what he wants."

"He wants all the fun without any strings. And that was all right for a while, but now I want more."

"I'm surprised he's sticking around and not off to a card game."

"He's been helping with the wedding."

"Helping? This is certainly surprising news. How exactly has he been helping?"

This was her chance to tell Hermione about the nightmare with the dresses. She needed to tell her now so she had time to make decisions in case her dress never showed up. It just broke her heart to pile more bad news on her friend.

"There's something I should tell you," Adara said.

"I knew there was something wrong. What is it?"

"The dresses were delivered."

"And?"

"Well, um…they weren't the right dresses."

"What? But how?"

And so Adara told her about the dress mix-up and the closing of the bridal boutique. "Krystof is helping to get the word out online about the dresses. We weren't the only one to get the wrong ones. It appears the last delivery was all mixed up. We've recovered the bridesmaid dresses and we're hoping yours will turn up soon, but I can't promise we'll get your wedding gown back in time for the ceremony."

Hermione was silent for a moment as though digesting all the information. "This is awful, but this week has shown me that in the grand scheme of things, a dress isn't what's important. In the end, it doesn't matter if I have a wedding dress or not. What matters is Atlas and me promising our hearts to each other."

Things must be bad for Hermione to be so Zen over the loss of her wedding dress. Adara's heart went out to her and Atlas. "Aw…that's so sweet. You two make the perfect couple."

They talked a little more before they ended the call. Adara was more determined than ever to make sure this wedding was the best it could be.

She had been serious.

Krystof glanced at the itinerary on his phone. Adara had forwarded a list of the musical groups and the times they would perform that week. Today he had two groups to listen to. One was performing at a school this evening. Did he even want to know how old the members of the group were?

And the other was at a gallery in the city. The gallery one he didn't mind. It was the school one that he didn't want to attend. It would remind him of his childhood. It was something he didn't want to dwell on. But he refused to let Adara down.

He had to be at the school by seven. He hoped their performance was at the beginning of the show if he hoped to make it to the gallery across the city. Even then he'd be pushing it.

He put on a white button-up. He left the top buttons undone, gave the sleeves a tug and then threw on a deep blue blazer. He wore dark jeans with loafers. It was as dressy as he got—at least without a wedding or funeral involved.

He exited the suite and headed toward the lobby. When he turned the corner, he practically ran into Adara. He reached out, grabbing her arm to help her regain her balance.

In that moment, time slowed down as his gaze met hers. He watched as her blue eyes widened in surprise. When her gaze took him in, he noticed how her pupils dilated ever so slightly. If she was anyone else, he'd say she was interested in him. But she'd made it perfectly clear that she was over him.

What was it about this woman that had him wanting her, even after she'd rejected him? He decided it was best not to delve too deeply into that subject.

"Whoa." He regretted having to let her go as his arm lowered to his side. "Where are you off to in such a hurry?"

"I was actually going to see you." She took a step back and gave his attire a quick once-over.

When her gaze once more met his, he asked, "Do you approve?"

She nodded. "You look very handsome."

A smile pulled at the corners of his lips. "Thanks." He thought of telling her that she looked beautiful but refrained. He didn't want to ruin this peaceful moment. "What did you need? I don't have much time. I have to hurry if I'm going to make it to both performances."

"Well, I was going to tell you that I'm done working for today, and if you wanted, I could tag along with you tonight."

Wait. Had he heard her correctly? She was going to spend time with him—voluntarily? He felt a surge of happiness.

And then another thought came to him. She didn't trust him. She thought he was going to let their friends down without her guidance. Well, that wasn't going to happen. He'd show her.

He decided to turn the situation around. "You can come with me as long as you don't mind a late dinner."

Her eyes widened. "Did you just blackmail me into having dinner with you?"

He let out a laugh. "I wouldn't put it that way. But I was thinking that as long as I was in Athens, I would try one of their newer restaurants."

"Oh. I see." Her gaze lowered as though she were considering whether or not this was worth her time.

"It's okay. I see you're not interested. I'll go alone." He started to walk away.

"No. I'll go."

He paused and turned to her. "Are you sure?"

She hesitated. "I am."

"Then let's be on our way. I don't want to be late and miss the first performance." He didn't wait for her response as he turned and headed for the lobby.

Once they were on the road, he chanced a glance at her with the warm rays of the setting sun lingering on her face. The beauty of the moment stole his breath away. He had to remind himself that they weren't on a date.

The ride into the city was quiet. Adara spent a great deal of that time on her phone. He wondered if something important had happened. Surely it couldn't be another problem with the wedding. Or perhaps she was just using it to avoid him.

When he pulled into a parking space near the school, he asked, "Is everything okay?"

"Um…" She typed a couple more words and pressed Send before she lifted her gaze to meet his. "Yes. Why?"

"Because you've been on your phone since we left the island. I was beginning to think you were avoiding me."

"No. Of course not. It's just with the wedding, my assistant has been filling in a lot for me. And she had some questions about the notes on my calendar."

"You like to plan out every part of your life, don't you?" He couldn't imagine what that must be like. He preferred to live on a whim and a chance.

"Yes. I try to schedule most of it."

"You never do anything spontaneously?"

A frown pulled at her glossy lips. "The last time I did something spontaneous, it didn't work out at all."

He couldn't help but wonder if she was referring to her sudden appearance at his Paris hotel suite. If only she had hung around, he could have cleared things up. He didn't like that she clung to that unfortunate event and used it to reinforce her opinion that spontaneity wasn't for her.

Just like tonight, she wanted him to think that her accompanying him was spontaneous, but he had a feeling she'd had it planned out for some time. He wanted to know what had happened in life to make her so cautious.

"We should go in," she said, drawing him from his thoughts.

"Right." While she gathered her purse, he exited the vehicle and quickly rounded the back end. And then he proceeded to open her door for her. She glanced up at him with a wide-eyed stare.

"What?" he said. "Can't a guy open the door for a lady?"

Her brows furrowed together as she stood. "A lady, huh?"

This was his cue to take things further. He stepped closer. As his gaze held hers, he reached out, gently brushing his thumb down over her cheek. He lowered his voice. "A very beautiful lady."

She didn't say a word, nor did she move away. But there was this place on her neck where her pulse beat rapidly. It matched the rapid thumping of his own heart.

He should turn away. He should focus on why they were standing in that parking lot with the lingering rays of the sun shining down on them. And yet the reason escaped him. All he could think about was kissing her.

His gaze lowered to her mouth. Her plump lower lip shimmered. It beckoned to him, drawing him to her with a force that smothered any sense of logic. Because this kiss…he knew it would change everything.

When he drew her closer, he heard the swift intake of her breath. And then he lowered his head, claiming her lips with his own. Oh, the kiss was so much sweeter than he recalled. And she was so addictive. He couldn't imagine ever getting enough of her. He could hold her in his arms all night long if she'd let him.

She didn't move immediately. In fact, he was pretty certain she was going to slap him or at the very least pull away. He didn't know how she could fight this chemistry burning between them.

As though she suddenly surrendered to the flames of desire, her lips moved beneath his. And when his tongue traced her lips, she opened up to him. A moan swelled in the back of her throat.

Her hands rested on his chest as his wrapped around her waist, pulling her snug to him. Her curves pressed into his hard planes. He wondered if she could feel the pounding of his heart.

No other woman evoked this sort of reaction from him. No other woman had ever been such a challenge. She made him think that for once the catch would be so much better than the chase—especially with those sweet, sweet kisses.

The sound of a loud car pulling into the lot drew his attention, but nothing was going to get him to let Adara go. He worried that once their kiss ended, Adara would put the wall straight back up between them. And this time the wall would be so high he wouldn't be able to scale it.

Honk-honk.

The decision was taken out of his hands when the car wanted the empty parking spot next to his car. With the utmost reluctance, he lifted his head. Adara's eyelids fluttered open. She gazed up at him with a dazed look in her eyes.

Honk.

"We better move," she said.

He nodded and then presented his arm to her. When she glanced down at it and then sent him a questioning look, he said, "Come on. You don't want to keep them waiting."

She huffed but then proceeded to place her hand in the crook of his arm.

They walked in silence across the parking lot. He couldn't help but notice how natural it felt. Sure, he'd had lots of women on his arm, but Adara was different. Not only was she the most beautiful woman he'd ever known, but she was also the greatest challenge. And he did love a challenge. In fact, he thrived on them.

Adara jerked his arm. "Is something wrong?"

"What?" He'd been so lost in his thoughts that he hadn't been following what she'd been saying.

She stopped walking and removed her hand from his arm. "You aren't even listening to me. What's wrong?"

So she'd felt that, huh? Apparently his thoughts had been more jolting than even he had thought. "It's nothing."

"Okay. If you won't answer that question, then answer this one. Why did you kiss me?"

His gaze lowered to her now-rosy lips, thinking how much he wanted to kiss her again. With the greatest of effort, he lifted his gaze to meet hers. "Because I needed to prove something to you."

"And what would that be?"

"That spontaneity isn't a bad thing. In fact, it can be quite enjoyable." He smiled at her. "Would you like me to show you again?"

A slight pause ensued, as though she too were tempted to indulge in another kiss. "No. That can never happen again."

Never again? He was confused. She'd enjoyed it. Of that he was certain. So why was she continuing to put up a wall between them?

He'd explained the mix-up at his Paris hotel room. Was she expecting something more from him? Adara had known from the beginning that he didn't do commitments. But he'd been utterly and completely faithful to her since they'd met on Valentine's Day. The fact that she had been the only woman in his life all this time shocked even him.

"We're going to be late." Her voice drew him from his thoughts.

She turned and walked away. He was left to follow her. He noticed how she didn't say anything about not enjoying the kiss. In fact, he'd have sworn he heard her moan—or perhaps that had been him. The smile on his face broadened. He just might need help with all these musical auditions.

The more he thought of it, the more he liked the idea. And if he were to prove that he was awful at selecting the right music for the wedding, Adara would have no choice but to accompany him to all the performances. And then they could have some more spontaneous moments.

CHAPTER ELEVEN

He'd kissed her.

That wasn't the part that worried Adara. It was the part where she'd wanted more. More kisses. More touching. More of everything from him.

Her traitorous heart had run amok when his lips had touched hers. And logic had totally abandoned her. She'd clung to a man who didn't believe in commitments or putting down roots. What had she been thinking? He was a nomad and proud of it.

So even if the unfortunate incident in Paris with his sister hadn't happened, eventually their relationship would have run its course. Just like all his other relationships. And she didn't want her heart to end up a casualty of his inability to stay in one place.

She wished the wedding was over already, but it was still several days away. They would be very long days with Krystof on the island. And trying to avoid him was not an option, with them both participating in the wedding.

And that's why when Sunday rolled around and it was time to listen to another musical group, she seriously considered skipping it. But this would mean relying on Krystof's judgment to pick the right music for the wedding. From what she'd seen on Friday evening, he didn't take this task very seriously. He was ready to pick the first group they'd heard. And though they were good, she wasn't prepared to go with the first group without doing their due diligence. This was too important to make snap decisions.

It was with the greatest hesitation that she once more pushed off what was left of her duties that day to her assistant, who surprisingly didn't complain. And then Adara headed toward her room at the resort to change into a sundress—something more appropriate for a concert in the park.

She was tempted to go to the park in her business clothes. She didn't want Krystof to think she was making an effort to look nice for him. But she had been wearing a long-sleeved blouse due to the resort's air-conditioning. It would be really warm at the park. If she were to switch into a summer dress and sandals, she'd be a lot more comfortable.

She subdued a sigh now that she'd just talked herself into dressing for their date—erm…their outing. Because there was no way she was going to date him again. She wanted more than he would ever offer.

She wasn't getting any younger. And if she wanted to find someone to build a future with, she couldn't waste her time with a man with commitment phobia. Krystof couldn't even commit to having a home. The closest thing he had to a home was a suite at a Paris hotel. Who lived their life out of a suitcase?

It didn't take her long to change clothes, but then she decided to wear her hair down and to touch up her makeup. After all, it was hard to tell who'd they run into at the park.

Knock-knock.

"Coming." She gave her reflection one last check.

Then, with her purse in hand, she started toward the door. She briefly paused to grab the throw blanket from the end of the bed. After all, they would need something to sit on.

She opened the door, and Krystof was there leaning against the doorjamb. He gave her outfit a quick once-over. "You look beautiful."

The heat started in her chest and then worked its way to her cheeks. "Thank you."

She stepped into the hallway, pulling the door closed behind her. "Shall we go?"

"Lead the way."

She needed to get this evening over as quickly as possible—before she did something she'd later regret, like confusing this outing for a date. Her steps came quicker. She could feel Krystof keeping pace with her.

"Is this a race?" he called out from behind her. "Because I get the feeling you're trying to get away from me. If that's the case, you don't have to go this evening. I can handle it on my own."

She turned to him. "I'm fine."

"Or we could just go with the first group we heard on Friday." He arched a brow, waiting for her response.

"Are you serious?"

"Sure. Why does it matter?"

"Because this wedding has to be perfect, or at least as close to perfect as I can make it. Don't you want Atlas to be happy?"

Krystof shrugged. "I don't think Atlas is going to care about the music."

"But he will care if his bride is happy."

"I just don't get it." He resumed walking.

She fell in step with him. "Get what?"

"Why he'd even want to get married. He was doing

fine on his own. And we all know that most marriages don't last."

"Wow. I knew you weren't into commitments, but I didn't know how far your dislike for them went."

He didn't look in her direction. "I'm just speaking the truth. You can look up the statistics for yourself."

She didn't know how to counter his total disrespect for marriage and love in general. And so she remained quiet as they made their way into the city and to the park.

As Krystof pulled into a parking spot, he said, "So that's it—you're not going to speak to me the rest of the evening because I'm not in favor of marriage?"

She shifted in her seat in order to face him, and only then did she realize her mistake. This car was much too small and Krystof's shoulders were far too broad, bringing her into close contact with him. Her heart pounded so loud that it echoed in her ears.

It was only when a smile lifted the corners of his very tempting lips that it jarred her back to her senses. What she needed right now was some fresh air, preferably very far from him. But since that wasn't possible at the moment, she'd take what little bit of breathing room she could get.

And with that she turned away, opened the car door, and with the blanket draped over her arm, she alighted from the vehicle. There was already a crowd of people in the park near the stage. She wanted a spot where they could clearly see the group but far enough back that they would have space to themselves.

She picked a spot straight back from the stage, under a tree where they could spread out the blanket. "What about sitting here?"

He shrugged. "Works for me."

She meant to spread the blanket by herself, but Krystof set down the insulated bag and insisted on helping her. She didn't want him being nice to her. She wanted to wallow in her frustration with him. First, for him being against this wedding. And second, for him being opposed to commitments of any kind.

When the blanket was spread out, they sat down. Krystof pulled the insulated bag over. "Would you like to eat first?"

She really didn't have an appetite at this point, but if they were eating, it would mean they didn't have to converse with each other. "We can eat. What did you pack?"

"Me? Nothing. But the kitchen was more than willing to help with our expedition."

"Yes, the resort does excel at catering to the guests." She was very proud of the people she worked with. They went above and beyond to make the guests' visits the very best.

And so she wasn't surprised when Krystof withdrew arrangements of cheeses, vegetables and fruits. It was a lot of food. And it looked quite delicious.

Just then the music started. As a local jazz group began to play, the sounds of the keyboard filled the air with a melodious tune. Two violinists, a guitar and drums stood ready for their moment to chime in. The upbeat music immediately drew her attention. Their conversation would have to wait until later.

The concert in the park had been a nice distraction.

Now that it was over and they'd returned to the resort, Adara wasn't ready for the evening to end. They still had to get to the bottom of Krystof thinking Hermione and Atlas's wedding shouldn't take place. That had her worried.

Krystof had walked with her to her room. He hesitated at the open doorway as though not sure if he should enter or not.

Adara placed her purse on the table and then turned to him. "Aren't you coming in?"

He stepped inside and closed the door before moving to the couch to sit down. "Do you think we've found a replacement band?"

"I don't know. We have one more band to hear the day after tomorrow."

"So you aren't going to pick a favorite yet?"

She shrugged before she reached inside the fridge. "Would you like something to drink?"

"Some water."

She grabbed two waters and then joined him on the couch. After she handed him the bottle, she kicked off her shoes and curled up next to him.

She was worried about Krystof. Something from his past had damaged him to the point that she worried he'd never be able to truly let someone in to love him. If he couldn't believe love was possible for Atlas and Hermione, when everyone could see how they felt about each other, how was he supposed to believe it was possible for himself?

She twisted off the cap of her bottle and took a long, slow drink, enjoying the cold water. Ever since they'd arrived at the park, she'd wanted to ask him questions, and yet she hadn't wanted to ruin the afternoon. But she couldn't hold back the questions now. She longed to understand him better.

In a gentle voice, hoping not to evoke an argument but rather to learn why he thought the way he did, she asked, "Why do you think Hermione and Atlas don't belong together?"

He lowered the bottle of water to the table. "I didn't say they don't belong together."

Now he wanted to play word games with her, but she wasn't having any part of it. "You said you thought they shouldn't get married. So if you aren't in favor of the wedding, it means you don't think they should be together."

He turned his head, and their gazes met. "Those two things are not the same. I think they make a great couple. For now."

"For now?" She rolled around the implication of his words in her mind. "So you think they're going to break up?"

He shrugged. "Statistics prove that relationships don't make the long haul."

Irritation pumped through her veins as she sat up straighter. "What is it with you and numbers?"

He lounged back and rested his arm over the back of the couch. "Numbers are reliable. Numbers make sense."

At last, they were getting somewhere. She was starting to understand what made him tick. "And is this why you spend so much time playing cards?"

He nodded. "Cards are based on odds. Odds aren't reliable, but they are understandable."

"So you don't like relationships because they revolve around emotions? And you think emotions aren't predictable?"

He glanced away. "I guess."

It wasn't much of an acknowledgment. She wanted to know more. She felt as though they were just scratching the surface. "Why did you agree to be the best man if you don't believe the marriage will work?"

His gaze darted to her. His brows furrowed together. "Like I'm going to turn Atlas down."

"So emotions between friends do matter to you?"

"I... I didn't say anything about emotions. But Atlas is a friend. I've known him since we were in school together. I'm not going to let him down."

His loyalty to his lifelong friend meant a lot to her. It meant that he was capable of commitment. If only he would let himself take a risk on a relationship. A risk on love.

"What are you thinking?" he asked.

Heat warmed her face as she glanced away. "I was just thinking for a man who makes his living by taking risks with cards, you aren't willing to do the same thing with your life. Why is that?"

"Maybe because my whole life has been full of unknowns and risks. Now I prefer to keep my risks at the card table only."

Her heart ached for him. And now it didn't seem like he was willing to rely on anyone. She wanted him to trust her. She wanted to prove to him that not all people walked away.

Her gaze met and held his. "You can trust me. I'm not going anywhere."

CHAPTER TWELVE

HE WANTED TO trust her.

And he did…as a friend.

Krystof found himself staring into Adara's eyes. He knew she was asking him to trust her with so much more than friendship. The thought sent an arrow of fear through his heart.

He had once staked his fortune on a high-stakes card game, and it had unnerved him much less than letting down his guard with Adara. He knew she had a way about her that could get past all his defenses. And it would be so easy to let himself care about her more than was safe.

"Tell me about it." Adara's voice was soft and coaxing. "Tell me who turned you against relationships."

He resisted the temptation to lay open all his harrowing scars. He'd never felt this compulsion before—not before he'd met Adara. His past was something he didn't share with anyone, including Atlas.

She placed her hand on his thigh. "You can talk to me—about anything. You don't have to keep putting up walls between us."

Was that what she thought he was doing? Because what he was really doing was protecting her from how messed up he really was on the inside. If she knew about his past, she would run for the door and not look back. He was nothing but damaged goods.

He lowered his arms to his sides and rubbed his damp palms over his thighs. "You don't want to know this."

"I do. If you'll share it with me."

Maybe that's exactly what he should do. He should lay it all out there for her to see that he was never going to be the traditional loving husband and devoted father she wanted. Even if he could stop moving, he wouldn't know how to be either of those things. Adara deserved someone so much better than him.

If he told her about his past, he also knew any hope of them resuming their friends-with-benefits relationship would be over. She would see through his outward facade of being successful and instead see how truly broken he was on the inside. He would once again be totally alone in this world.

It was one thing to choose this solitary life without knowing what it'd be like to share it with someone loving and caring, like Adara, but to know that sort of kindness and companionship and then to lose it—well, it might be more than he could bear. The thought of that sort of loss scared him.

And nothing scared him. He had no choice. He had to do whatever he could to dissuade Adara from wanting more from him than he could give her.

Before he could change his mind, the long-buried memories came rushing back to him. The feeling of helplessness he'd felt growing up crashed over him. And when he'd finally become a legal adult—when he was on his own—there was an unrelenting sense of determination that he was never going to feel trapped by his memories. He would tell her, and then he'd cram those haunting thoughts back in the box at the back of his mind.

Adara didn't say anything as he struggled to pull his thoughts together. He'd never stopped long enough for anyone to question his nomad lifestyle or his lack of a place to call home. In fact, he'd been doing it for so long that he'd thought of it as normal...until Adara happened into his life. Now how did he explain any of this to her?

He cleared his throat. "I never knew my parents. To this day, I don't know if they are alive or dead. I don't know their names. I don't know why they abandoned me. I don't even know what my birth name was or if I ever had one. My name was given to me by a social worker."

He chanced a glance at Adara as unshed tears gathered in her eyes. His body stiffened. He didn't want anyone's pity, most especially hers.

He refocused on his bottle of water, now sitting on the table. If he continued to take in her emotional response to his story, he didn't think he'd get through it.

But he must tell it. He had to make it clear to her why they didn't belong together—of why he couldn't transform into the man she deserved. He would do it for her. And then, when he'd bared his soul to her, he would move on, just like he'd been doing his whole life.

His mouth grew dry as his mind conjured up the painful memories. He swallowed hard. "My third, no, my fourth set of foster parents had no patience with me. I got into trouble every day of my childhood. I was curious and far too smart for my own good. By the time I was old enough to think for myself, I knew I had to get away. I didn't belong there. I believed my birth parents were out there waiting for me and I just had to find them. I was certain if that happened, everything would be right in the world."

He paused as he gathered his emotions. He could remember the desperation he felt as a little boy, longing for the love of his parents. He'd felt so lost and alone with people who didn't like him, much less love him.

All this time, Adara sat there quietly taking it all in. He wanted to look at her, but he didn't allow himself. It was all he could do to hold it all together and get through this story—his story.

He cleared his throat. "Each time I ran away, I was returned to the home. I would be locked in a small, windowless room for days at a time. There was nothing in there. No bed. No blanket. Not even so much as a pillow. Sometimes I felt like I was going to lose it in there."

In his mind, he could still see the details of those four walls. No one should ever be treated that way. "My foster sister was the only person in that home that I ever felt close to. She would sneak over to my door when the adults were distracted. We'd play word games. I don't know if I'd have made it through that period without Celeste. I will forever be indebted to her. If she had been caught, she would have paid dearly."

Adara placed her hand on his and squeezed. "I didn't realize."

He shook his head. "Of course you wouldn't. Only Celeste knows what I went through, because she lived it with me. To this day, I still have to deal with episodes of claustrophobia." He turned to her. "Do you understand what I'm saying?"

"I'm sorry all of that happened to you. I can't even begin to understand what you lived through." Her eyes shone with sympathy.

"Don't do that. Don't look at me like that. I didn't tell

you so you'd feel sorry for me. I told you so you would understand that I can never be the man you deserve."

"The man I deserve? I don't understand."

He pulled his hand away from her and stood. He began to pace. "I can't stop moving around. I can't feel trapped in a house—in a traditional life. I… I just can't do it."

He couldn't believe he'd admitted all this to her. It wasn't that he didn't trust her, because he did. He knew she'd keep the skeletons of his past to herself. But he couldn't help but wonder what she thought of him now. Did she think less of him because he wasn't able to overcome a childhood trauma? Or, worse, did she feel sorry for him?

He moved toward the door. He should leave. He'd told her about his pathetic background. He'd told her how broken he was. And now she knew that they would never be together—not in the way she wanted.

And then he felt her hands on his back. She didn't say anything as her arms wrapped around his sides, and then her cheek pressed to his back. For a moment, she held him, and he let her. He went to remove her hands, but once he touched her, his hands stayed there. For that moment, he let himself take comfort in her touch.

As they stood there quietly, moisture dropped onto his hand. Where had it come from? And then there was another drip. He lifted his head to see if there was a leak in the ceiling. He didn't see anything.

He raised his hand to his cheek and found the moisture had come from him. They were the tears he'd never allowed himself to shed. He'd always told himself he was strong—that he didn't need to cry. But being here with Adara, all his suppressed feelings had come erupting to the surface. He was helpless to hold back the tidal wave of emotions.

When Adara let go of him, he thought she was walking away. Instead she came to stand in front of him. She gazed up at him with warmth in her eyes. She reached out and caressed his cheek, wiping away his tears.

And then she did something most unexpected. She lifted up on her tiptoes and pressed her lips to his. He hadn't known how much he needed her touch until she was kissing him.

He felt like a drowning man—a man drowning in his loneliness and self-isolation. And Adara was a life preserver pulling him back to the land of the caring.

He kissed her with a need and hunger that he'd never known before. He wrapped his arms around her waist, drawing her to him. Her soft curves fit perfectly to his hard planes. Oh, how he'd missed her.

In that moment, he didn't think about the implications of what they were about to do. There were no promises of tomorrow. There was only here and now. Living in the moment, he scooped her up in his arms. Her hands slipped around his neck.

Their kiss never stopped. It was as if she were oxygen and without her he would suffocate. He carried her to the king-size bed and gently laid her down. She wouldn't let go of him and instead pulled him down on top of her.

This was going to be a memorable night. If it was their last time together, he wanted the memories of her to carry with him forever.

CHAPTER THIRTEEN

OH, WHAT A NIGHT.

Before her eyes were even open, Adara reached out for Krystof. Her fingers touched nothing but an empty spot. Her hand moved up and down the sheet. The spot was cold.

Her eyes fluttered open. She scanned the room. There was no sign of him. He must have left sometime during the night.

That was something he never would have done before. He was always there in the morning. Granted, he was always the last one up in the morning. He claimed he was a night owl, while she was an early bird. A smile tugged at the corners of her lips at the memory.

But this morning there was no shared coffee in bed or the teasing of how he would groan that it was too early to get out of bed yet. Today he was already gone.

Even though he had slipped away while she was sleeping, she wasn't upset. In fact, she was hopeful. Last night had been a big breakthrough for them. She now understood him in a way she never had before.

People he was supposed to be able to trust the most in the world had let him down in the worst way. First, his birth parents had abandoned him as a toddler. And then his foster parents had abused him. Tears stung her eyes as she took it all in. How could they do such monstrous things to a child?

She was so thankful that Celeste had been there for him. Her feelings toward the woman shifted from jealousy to gratefulness. It's funny sometimes how life worked out. Maybe someday she and Celeste would be friends.

Chime.

She reached for her phone. It was a reminder for her doctor's appointment. She turned it off. Today she would see the doctor about her missing monthly. She was clinging to hope that it was something minor—something that could be fixed with a week's vacation, or at worse with some medicine.

She climbed out of bed, started the coffee machine and headed for the shower. She'd deal with the doctor first, and then she'd find Krystof. She thought he might be feeling vulnerable after his admission last night, and she wanted to assure him that everything was all right between them—in fact, it was so much better than all right.

Forty-five minutes later, showered and dressed, she headed for the door. She had to drive into the city, so she needed to get going. She didn't want to get stuck in Monday-morning traffic and miss her appointment. She opened her door and nearly ran into Krystof. He was pacing outside her door.

She stopped. "How long have you been out here?"

"I… I don't know." There were shadows under his eyes, as though he hadn't slept. "Not that long."

"Why are you pacing out here? You should have come inside."

"I didn't know if you were awake, and I didn't want

to bother you. You looked so peaceful when I got out of bed."

When she went to hug him, he stepped back. She tried to tell herself that it was all right. Last night had been big for him. She knew he wasn't going to take it well in the morning light.

She lifted her phone and checked the time. If she wasn't on the road in five minutes, she was going to be late, and she just couldn't afford to miss this appointment.

"Krystof, we need to talk, but I have an important appointment right now. I can't miss it. Can we talk later?"

His gaze searched hers. And then he nodded.

She lifted up on her tiptoes and pressed a kiss to his unshaven cheek. And then she headed down the hallway. She had no idea what would come of her appointment, but she was hoping for good news. And later they'd talk. Everything was going to work out.

She'd blown him off.

She didn't see him the same way she used to.

Krystof needed something to keep his mind from the ghosts of the past, the mess of the present and the impossibility of the future. His gut reaction was to hop on his plane and jet off to the next big card game. It's what he did when life got too complicated.

And yet he'd promised Adara he'd be here to help her with the wedding. He didn't want to break his word to her, even if staying here and facing the sympathy in her eyes would be one of the hardest things he had ever done.

He had his assistant send over the financials for the tech company he was seriously considering buying. It would give him the ability to expand MyPost into a more varied social media platform—so it could help people the way he'd been using it to help reunite brides with their missing wedding gowns. As of this morning, there were five relieved brides, but there was still no sign of Hermione's wedding dress. But he wasn't giving up hope.

As he pulled up the financial statements and various spreadsheets on his laptop, he started to relax. Numbers were reliable. They never lied. They were always what they appeared. One plus one always equaled two.

Minutes turned to hours as he worked in his suite, closing out the rest of the world. He shoved thoughts of Adara and all that had happened the previous evening to the back of his mind—even memories of their lovemaking. He wasn't sure if she'd spent the night with him because she'd truly wanted to or if she'd done it out of sympathy. He had the feeling it was the latter, and that made him feel even worse.

Come that evening, there was an alert on his phone. Thinking it was from his assistant, he checked it. To his surprise, there was a response to his posting about the wedding dress on MyPost. Someone had Hermione's wedding dress. It wasn't for certain, but this time the pictures looked like it was the right one. In turn, it was believed that Adara had the missing dresses for their wedding party. They would be at the resort the next morning to exchange the dresses.

Krystof tried to phone Adara, but she didn't answer. He got up to get himself a cup of coffee. And then he tried again. It went to voice mail.

A frown pulled at his face. It felt as though she was avoiding him. He now suspected that she'd spent the night in his arms because she felt sorry for him. He never should have said anything to her. Instead of clarifying things, his revelation had only made everything feel so much more complicated.

He set off for her office, but when he reached it, the door was closed and locked. Next he tried her room, but she didn't answer the door. Finally he tracked down Adara's assistant. Demi checked and told him that Adara was in the penthouse. What was she doing there?

With some instructions, he made his way to the private elevator to the penthouse. He pressed the call button and wondered if Atlas and Hermione had returned. But it was Adara's voice on the intercom.

"Yes?"

He cleared his throat. "I have news."

"Come on up."

Immediately the elevator opened, and he stepped inside. He wondered what Adara was doing there. The elevator moved swiftly, and soon the door slid open. He stepped out and found Adara standing there. She looked expectantly at him.

"I've been trying to reach you," he said.

"You have?" She pulled her phone from her pocket, glanced at the screen and then frowned. "It died. I forgot to charge it last night."

He was the reason she'd forgotten. "About last night—"

"Why don't you come in? Indigo is here." She turned and headed for the living room of Hermione and Atlas's home.

He followed her. His gaze moved around, taking in all the wedding supplies. And then his attention focused on Indigo, who was sitting at a table near one of the floor-to-ceiling windows that offered the most amazing view of the sea. Greetings were exchanged.

He turned to Adara. "What's going on?"

She sat down at the table. "We're working on the final details. And you're just in time to help."

He shook his head. "I don't think so."

"Oh, come on." Indigo patted the chair next to her.

He hesitated, but he didn't want to be rude, so he finally sat down. "What are you doing?"

"These are *koufeta*." Adara held up a white tulle pouch of sugar-coated almonds.

He watched as she gave the tulle a twist and added white ribbon with a small printed note with the wedding date as well as the bride and groom's names.

"Why are you wrapping nuts?" He could honestly admit that he knew nothing about wedding traditions.

"The almond symbolizes endurance." Indigo added almonds to a piece of tulle and gave it a twist.

"And the sugar coating symbolizes a sweet life." Adara finished tying a bow and adjusting the note before setting the favor aside. "See, it's easy. Now wash up." When he hesitated, Adara said, "Hurry. We have two hundred favors to make."

"Two hundred?" Surely he hadn't heard her clearly.

She nodded. "They wanted to include as many friends and resort employees as they could, since neither of them have much family. Now go."

He reluctantly got up and moved to the kitchen, where he washed his hands. He did notice that Adara wasn't acting any different than normal with him. Was it possible that she'd gotten over whatever had had her rushing off this morning? He hoped so.

When he returned to the table, he noticed a stack of cut tulle at his spot as well as a bowl of almonds. He supposed he could help for a little bit. After all, two hundred was a lot of favors to put together.

Both Adara and Indigo were busy adding almonds

to their tulle. He spooned some almonds into his piece of material.

He was just about to give the tulle a twist when Adara asked, "Did you count the number of *koufeta*?"

He shook his head. "I didn't know I was supposed to."

"You have to," Indigo said. "The number of *koufeta* needs to be odd, because an odd number is undividable. It symbolizes the bride and groom will remain undivided."

It made sense, he supposed. He did like the part that relied upon numbers. And so he set to work. Adara made a couple of adjustments to his first favor. By his fifth one, he was on his own.

"So why did you need to see me?" Adara asked.

And then he realized he hadn't told her about the reason for him stopping by. "The wedding dress has been found."

"What?" Adara stopped what she was doing to look at him with her mouth gaping. "Really?"

He nodded and smiled. He was so glad he was able to make her happy again. "They're bringing it to the resort tomorrow."

"That's amazing," Indigo said. "You're a lifesaver. Just wait until Hermione hears the news."

"Hermione." Adara jumped up. "I have to call her." She reached for her phone but then put it back on the table. "But my phone is dead."

He pulled his out of his back pocket and held it out to her. "Here. Use mine."

"Thanks. Hermione's going to be so relieved." Adara moved to the balcony to place the call.

With some wine, they continued to work. Dinner was delivered to the penthouse. Krystof eventually gave up on trying to slip away. Because not only did they have favors to assemble, but they also had some table decorations to make. By the time they finished, it was close to midnight, and they were all exhausted.

Tired or not, Krystof was relieved. Things were mostly back to normal with Adara. Granted, she was a little more quiet than usual, but he'd told himself that she was tired. And why wouldn't she be? She was always working. Maybe he should do something about that.

CHAPTER FOURTEEN

SHE DIDN'T DO well with waiting.

Instead she threw herself into her work.

Tuesday morning, Adara sat behind her desk. She had just finished setting up a surprise engagement for one of the resort's regular guests. They were planning to have a plane fly over the beach with a banner that read, Will You Marry Me? Adara smiled at the thought. It was certainly a grand gesture.

Krystof stepped through her open doorway. "Are you ready?"

She blinked and looked at him. "Ready for what?"

"Remember, the dress is being dropped off today." He arched a brow. "I can't believe you'd forget something like that."

"Sorry. I've just had a lot on my mind lately." That was the biggest understatement of her life. In that moment she realized she'd been so caught up in her medical drama, she'd never had that talk with Krystof. "I'm sorry I got distracted and we never got to talk."

"No problem." He sent her a smile that didn't quite reach his eyes. "What has you so worried?"

Could he read her so easily? She hoped not. "The… uh…wedding, of course. There's just so many details.

And we have to confirm a replacement musical group for the ceremony."

"I was thinking about that, and I already have a favorite."

"But you haven't heard the last one yet."

"I don't need to hear them. I already like this one."

She sighed. Normally she'd insist on hearing the final group, but time was short. "Okay. If we agree on the same musical group, then we'll skip the party tonight. Agreed?"

"Agreed."

"Then what group did you like?"

"I liked the string quartet at the school. They were excellent and classy."

Her mouth gaped. They'd just agreed on something. "I was just thinking the same thing. I'll call the booking agent and set it up. One less thing to worry about."

"Now let's go get those dresses," he said.

She glanced down at her desk and the other things that needed her attention. A busy resort meant there were a lot of guests with a lot of requests.

"Come on," Krystof said. "That can all wait."

"Easy for you to say. You don't have to deal with any of it."

With a sigh, she stood. They went to meet the woman and her daughter. The gowns were exchanged and then Hermione's wedding dress was placed in the penthouse for safekeeping. After so much worry, it was such an easy, painless resolution.

"I'm so relieved," Adara said on the elevator ride down to the main floor.

"Now you can stop worrying so much."

"Not yet—there's still a lot to do before they say 'I do.'"

"What you need is a nice, relaxing lunch."

She glanced at the time on her phone. "It's not even noon yet."

"It will be soon. And I have something special in mind."

"Krystof, you don't understand. I have a meeting at one with Mr. Grant. And I have a meeting at two with the Papadopouloses."

"What I have to show you is more important."

Concern came over her. "What is it? What's wrong? Does it have something to do with the wedding?"

"Just come with me." He gave her outfit a once-over. "Do you have something more casual to wear?"

"Not with me. I didn't anticipate needing anything casual."

"No worries. We'll take care of it." He took her hand in his. "Come with me."

"But my appointments—"

"No worries. May I borrow your phone?"

"No." She tightened her hold on her phone. Without it, she'd be lost. It had her calendar and all her contacts. "Why do you want it?"

"Never mind." He turned to the left and walked toward her assistant, Demi.

What in the world had gotten into him? He'd been acting different ever since he'd told her about his past the other night. And he was certainly intent on showing her something today.

Part of her wanted to run off with him. The other part of her said that she had responsibilities here at the resort. She was torn as to what she should do. Finally the curiosity about what had him so excited won over. What was he up to?

Where was the fun in her life?

She worked all the time.

Krystof knew he might not be serious and responsible—at least by other people's estimations of him—

but he had a different outlook on life. If you took it too seriously, it would do you in.

He'd promised himself that he would enjoy his life. He wouldn't get hung up with the normal responsibilities that people sometimes found themselves trapped in. And so when he'd found that he had a knack for cards, he'd used it to his advantage. After all, who could turn down a challenge? Because that's what a poker game came down to—who could outbluff who?

But Adara was so locked into her routine that her life lacked any real moments of fun and spontaneity. Maybe if she were to experience some with him, she would understand him better.

After a stop at the boutique for some casual clothes and swimsuits followed by a visit to the Cabana Café, he took her hand and they set off on their journey. This outing would do them both some good. They'd been too intense about this wedding and other things. They needed to remember how to have fun.

"Where are we going?" she asked. "I thought maybe we were going on a boat ride, but you're leading us away from the water."

The vegetation grew denser. The leafy trees, lush greenery and bright flowers were beautiful, with shades of green and pinks and reds lining the dirt path. He noticed how Adara slowed down to smell the wildflowers.

When the trees grew denser, it provided a canopy. Slices of sunlight made it through here and there, lighting up the ground. He had never been to a more beautiful place. The gentle sea breeze rustled through the trees' leaves and carried with it a light floral scent.

"It's beautiful out here," Adara said.

"You make it sound like you've never been here before."

"I haven't."

"What?" He stopped in front of her. "You mean to tell me you've been working at the resort for years and you never ventured outside?"

She shrugged. "What? Don't look at me like that. It's not like I was a guest. I was hired to work here. And that's what I do."

"And you never wanted to escape your office to go explore the island?"

"I didn't say that. But I can't just run off whenever I feel like it. I have people counting on me to do my job. Not everyone can be like you."

Ouch. Her comment zinged right into his chest with a wallop. Maybe she was right. Maybe he should take on more responsibility. He thought of that tech company in Paris. He'd gone through the financials and didn't see any reason he shouldn't buy it.

"I'm sorry," she said apologetically. "I shouldn't have said that. I know it's the only life you know. The only life you want."

He paused and stared into her eyes. It wasn't the only life he knew. Because of her, he was finding there was more to life than he'd allowed himself to experience. And there were definite benefits to staying in one place.

"Come on. We're almost there." At least he hoped so. He'd heard about this spot from Titus, the front desk clerk.

They continued to walk until the trees grew sparse and the sound of water could be heard in the distance.

Her face lit up. "Is that the waterfall?"

"If my directions are correct, then yes. That's the twin falls."

With her hand still in his, she took off in a rush. They moved quickly over the overgrown path. It didn't appear many of the guests ventured far from the beach to experience this raw beauty.

Adara didn't stop until they had a clear vision of the twin falls—a high waterfall that spilled onto a piece of rock that jutted out and then a much shorter waterfall that ran into a pond down below.

He moved to a clearing, where he spread out a blanket and placed the picnic basket next to it. The bright sunshine rained down on them. This had to be one of the most magnificent places in the world, but its beauty couldn't compare to Adara's.

He watched as she turned around in a circle, taking in the scenery. The smile on her face told him everything he needed to know. His surprise pleased her.

While she looked around, he stepped off to the side and plucked a white orchid. With the bloom held behind his back, he approached Adara. "I take it you've never been here, either?"

"No. Never. It's so peaceful and beautiful."

He stepped closer to her and held out the orchid. "Not nearly as beautiful as you."

Color flooded her cheeks. She accepted the flower. "Thank you."

His gaze met and held hers. His heart started to pound. All he wanted to do in that moment was to draw her into his arms and hold her close, but he resisted the urge.

"I brought you here," he said, "because I wanted to show you that spontaneity can be good, too. Your whole life doesn't have to be planned out. Leave some room for the unexpected."

"I'm starting to think you might have a good point."

A smile pulled at his lips. "I'm glad. Now, let's have some fun."

When he pulled off his polo shirt and tossed it on the ground, her eyes grew round. "Krystof, I like the way you think." She glanced around. "But not here. What if someone saw us?"

He let out a laugh and pulled her to him. He pressed a kiss to her lips. "I like the way *you* think. But you don't have to worry."

Disappointment flickered across her face. "So you didn't bring me out here to seduce me?"

"I didn't say that. But that will have to wait for a moment." He enjoyed the way her cheeks turned pink at the thought of their lovemaking. "I have something else in mind first." He took off his socks and shoes. He glanced over at her. "You might not want to wear all of that."

She arched a brow. "You just want to see me in my new bikini, don't you?"

"Well, of course." He placed his socks in his shoes.

He told himself that he should turn away. If he got distracted, he'd forget the reason he'd brought her out here. But then her gaze met his and she gave him a mischievous grin. She gently placed the orchid on the ground next to her. When she straightened, she pulled out the hem of her blouse from her shorts.

His breathing changed to shallow, rapid breaths. And then she slowly unbuttoned her shirt. His heart beat frantically. This was the sweetest torture he'd even endured. His gaze was glued to her. There was no chance of him turning away. His body simply refused to move.

And then, ever so slowly, the shirt slid off her slim shoulders before fluttering to the ground. The breath caught in his throat. He should do something. Say something. But he continued to stand there as if in a trance.

When she reached for her shorts, he thought his heart was going to beat out of his chest. She undid the button on her waistband. He swallowed hard. She slowly un-zipped them. She wiggled her hips, allowing the shorts to slip down, and then she stepped out of them. His mouth went dry as he took in the little yellow bikini from the resort boutique that showed off her curves.

"Do you like what you see?" Her voice was deep and sultry.

His voice didn't work, so he vigorously nodded.

She stepped up to him, lifted up on her tiptoes and pressed her lips to his. He kissed her back. He'd never tire of having her so close. There was something so very special about her—something he needed in his life.

When he went to pull her closer, she quickly backed away. A smile played upon her lips. "You said you brought me all the way out here for something other than kissing, so what did you have in mind?"

He sighed. "Did you have to throw my words back in my face?"

A big smile lit up her eyes, making them twinkle. "Yes, I did."

He took her hand in his. "Okay. Let's go."

He led her toward the lower waterfall. There was a large space between the two layers of rock. He led her to that protected area. While they were shielded from the rushing water, in front of them the waterfall flowed down from above, hitting the layer of rock they stood on, and then the water spilled down into the pond below.

"This is so amazing." Adara practically had to shout to be heard over the waterfall.

He turned to her. "Almost as amazing as you."

When she looked at him like he was the only man in the world, his resolve crumbled. He drew her into his arms. And as they stood there on the rocks with the water spilling down, he claimed her lips with his own.

He was finding that the more time he spent with her, the more time he wanted to spend with her. And his driving need to keep moving around—to never stay in one place too long—was dissipating.

With the greatest regret, he pulled back. If they were to kiss any longer, his reason for bringing her out here would be lost. He took her hand in his as he made his way to the edge of the rock.

Adara stopped. "What are you doing?"

He turned to her. "Come on."

"Out there?" She pointed to the edge. "I don't think so."

"You can do it."

"And what are we going to do once we get out there?"

"We're going to jump?"

"Jump!" She started shaking her head. "No. Not a chance."

He gave her hand a reassuring squeeze. "It'll be fun."

"You don't even know if it's safe. What if the water down below is too shallow?"

"I'll have you know I asked Titus at the front desk about it. He said this is a popular cliff-jumping spot. Don't you trust me?"

"I… I trust you." Her gaze moved to follow the water down to the pond below.

"Then come on. Do something spontaneous."

"I did. I came here with you."

"Yes, you did." His thumb moved back and forth over the back of her hand. "Now let's go do something daring."

Her skeptical gaze met his. "You're serious, aren't you?"

"Of course I am." He kept a hold on her hand as he continued toward the edge.

She hesitated at first, but then she followed him. "I can't believe you want us to jump off a cliff."

"It's not a very high one."

Her gaze lowered to the water down below. "High enough."

He turned to her. "Will you jump with me?"

"I... I don't know."

She was so close. He just needed to coax her a little more out of her comfort zone. And then he hoped it would be the first of many new experiences for them.

"What will it take to convince you to jump with me?"

She cautiously leaned forward to peer at the water below, and then she pulled back. "I get to pick our next date."

He liked the idea of there being a promise of another date. "I'll do whatever you want."

"Then what are you waiting for?"

Hand in hand, they moved to the edge of the cliff. He turned his head to look at her. She gazed into his eyes. This was a new beginning for them.

Her heart raced as the blood pulsated in her ears. Adara chanced a glance to the side, at the water rushing down to the pond below. He really wanted them to jump? All the way down there?

Krystof squeezed her hand. When she glanced back at him, he said, "You don't have to do this if you really don't want to."

She swallowed hard. "I know."

Part of her wanted to turn and go back to the place where they'd left their picnic lunch. It would be the safe thing to do—the smart thing to do. And yet her feet wouldn't move.

As she stared into his eyes, it calmed her. She instinctively knew he would never do anything to endanger her. All he wanted her to do was to step outside her comfort zone. But could she do it?

It was so far down there. She had never done something like this before. Maybe this wasn't the best way to step out of her comfort zone. Maybe she should find some other thing to do. Yes, that sounded like a good idea.

"Adara, you can do this. You'll be with me." Krystof's voice was deep and soothing.

"Couldn't we go back down and have a picnic lunch?"

"We will, soon. I promise." He held his hand out to her.

She glanced down at the water again. She turned her head back to him. Her attention focused on his outstretched hand. Her heart pounded in her chest as she placed her hand in his. Her fingers laced with his as though it were the most natural thing.

Don't back out. You can do this.

She needed to prove to herself that she could do the daring and unexpected. Maybe since her parents' deaths, she had sought safety and security within her scheduled plans. Maybe now, with so much time having passed, it was finally time to try something different.

Her gaze rose to his. "Let's do this."

He smiled at her and then nodded. "Let's." They both turned to the edge of the cliff. "At the count of three."

By now she was clutching his hand so tight that it must be cutting off his blood flow, but he didn't complain. Had she forgotten to tell him that she didn't like heights?

"One…"

Her heart beat against her ribs.

"Two..."

Why did it look so far down?

"Three..."

The jerk of his hand spurred her into action. And then she felt weightless as she fell.

Splash.

Somewhere along the way, she'd lost hold of Krystof. She sank deep into the water. She felt as though she were never going to stop slipping farther into the dark depths of the pond.

At long last her body stopped dropping. Now she had to get to the surface. She started to kick her legs, hoping she was headed in the right direction. It was hard to tell as the light moved through the water. She hoped she was swimming upward.

She kicked hard. Her lungs began to burn. She kicked harder. Where was the surface? Panic had her swimming with all her might. Was she almost there?

And then she broke the surface. She gulped down oxygen, never so happy to be able to breathe. She coughed, having inhaled a little water.

"Are you okay?" Krystof's voice came from behind her.

She gathered herself and turned in the water to face him. He was smiling at her. "What are you smiling about?"

"You did it. You took a chance and did something out of the ordinary."

And then she realized he was right. She beamed back at him. "I did. Thanks to you."

She swam closer to him and wrapped her arms around his neck. He lowered his head and caught her lips with his own. His skin was chilled from the water, but she didn't mind, because his touch was all she needed to warm her up.

As their kiss intensified, her legs encircled his waist. The temperature of the water was long forgotten. She had other, more urgent matters on her mind now.

With her wrapped in his arms, Krystof swam on his back to the edge of the pond. He released her to heft himself out first, and then he turned back to help her out.

He swept her up into his arms and resumed kissing her. He carried her back to the clearing. He gently laid her down on the blanket. She refused to let him go. She drew him down on top of her. For her, this was the greatest risk of all. Because every time they made love, he made his way deeper into her heart.

CHAPTER FIFTEEN

LIFE COULD CHANGE in the time it took to flip a coin.

Adara should know, since it'd just happened to her.

One moment, she felt as though her feet were floating above the ground. She'd been so proud of herself for cliff jumping. It was something she'd never done before. It showed her that she could accomplish things she hadn't even considered until this point.

Throughout their picnic lunch at the waterfall followed by their dinner in bed, as well as the following two days they'd spent together, she had started to envision her life a bit differently. She'd even considered what she might do if she no longer worked at the Ludus Resort. After all, her assistant, Demi, was a natural. She could take over, and Adara would be free to do something else. The problem was that she liked her work as a concierge. She liked working with people and making their visions come true.

Krystof pushed her to question her life's decisions. Had she settled too soon? Should she have explored the world more to see if there was somewhere else that she fit in? Should she have worried more about her romantic life than her career? If she'd focused on romance, maybe she'd already have a baby and her current medical problem wouldn't feel so enormous.

The doctor's office had called on Friday morning and insisted they couldn't give her the test results over the phone. She had to meet with the doctor. It was at this point that she could no longer pretend this situation wasn't serious. They never called you into the office to give you good news.

It was the worst time, too. Atlas and Hermione had just arrived back on the island. With the wedding taking place tomorrow, they needed to finish up some last-minute wedding details. However, Adara couldn't delay her doctor's visit. She needed to know what was going on with her. She'd quietly slipped away.

The doctor had told her she was having early-onset menopause. She'd replayed his words over and over in her mind. How was this possible? She was only thirty-two. No one she knew went through menopause that early.

When he'd mentioned that sometimes it ran in families, she'd thought of her mother. Adara had been their only child. Whenever she'd asked her mother for a little brother or sister, her mother had said that wasn't going to happen. Maybe now Adara understood why her mother had looked so sad when she'd said those words.

And now Adara's vision for the future was ruined. There would be no happy little family for her. She wouldn't know what it was like to carry a baby in her body. She wouldn't hold her baby in her arms. Each time the thoughts tormented her, the backs of her eyes stung with unshed tears. She blinked them away. They would have to wait. She didn't have time to mourn the future she'd envisioned.

Right now, they'd just finished an elaborate wedding rehearsal dinner. The six members of the wedding party had dined out on the penthouse balcony. She'd love to say the food was delicious, but she hadn't eaten much, and what she had eaten had tasted like cardboard.

While Krystof, Atlas and Istvan were inside getting everyone some more drinks, the women were seated at the table. Hermione was all smiles. She looked like the happiest bride.

"How is Atlas's father doing?" Adara asked her friend.

"He's been moved to physical rehab. I was hoping he could be here for the wedding, but everyone agreed it would be too much for him."

"I'm sorry he couldn't make it," Indigo said. "But we'll take lots of pictures for you to share with him."

"Thank you. I think he'd like that. He's changed a lot since Atlas last saw him," Hermione said. "He's been sober for three years now. He apologized to Atlas. And I think he really meant it."

"How did Atlas feel about that?" Adara asked.

"He's being cautious. And I can't blame him after all he's been through. But I think there's a chance for some sort of relationship going forward. I just don't know what it'll look like. I guess it's just going to be a day-by-day thing." Hermione turned to Adara. "And how are things with you and Krystof? I hear you two have been spending a lot of time together."

Adara hesitated. She wasn't ready to dissect her complicated relationship with Krystof. Yesterday she would have said they were both learning to take risks and they might have a chance at building a lasting relationship. But today, after speaking to the doctor, she felt confused and unsure about what her future would hold.

Hermione didn't need to know any of this at her rehearsal dinner. Adara frantically searched for a more neutral topic of conversation.

Indigo leaned forward. "On Tuesday, they went cliff jumping at the twin falls."

"What?" Hermione's eyes opened wide. "But why?"

Adara shrugged. "Why not?"

Hermione smiled and shook her head. "Looks like Krystof is having an influence on you. If I'm not careful, he'll steal you away from me."

Adara shook her head. "I don't think so. What would I do? I couldn't just follow him around the world watching him play cards."

"I'm sure you could find something much more entertaining to do with him." Indigo laughed.

As Adara's face grew warm, Hermione let out a giggle.

"What's going on out here?" Atlas handed Hermione a drink.

"We were just catching up on things." Hermione thanked her fiancé and then sipped at her drink.

Krystof placed a hand on Adara's bare shoulder. His touch felt good. She resisted the urge to lean her head against his arm. She refused to allow herself even that small bit of comfort. The news from the doctor had her seeing things differently—had her pulling back from Krystof.

With his other hand, Krystof handed her some ice water. They'd cut off the bubbly a while ago, because no one wanted to party too much with the wedding tomorrow.

He crouched down next to her. "Can I get you anything else?"

She shook her head. "I'm good."

He'd never been this sweet and attentive before. He

was changing before her eyes. She didn't know what it meant, but she definitely felt like he was moving in the right direction. The destination was still a bit fuzzy, though.

The wedding day had arrived.

With the sun barely above the horizon, Adara was wide-awake and showered. She was a mixture of excited and relieved. She couldn't believe all the obstacles they'd had to overcome to make it to this point.

Ding.

She reached for her phone resting next to the bed. It was probably Hermione thinking of one last detail for the wedding. But when she read the message, she learned it was the bakery delivering the cake. *This early?*

She texted back that she would be right there. She twisted her hair and clipped it up. Later she would do something more formal for the wedding. Right now, she had to make sure the cake made it safely into the walk-in fridge.

In a pink flowered summer dress and sandals, she rushed to the elevator and down to the main floor. She hurried to the employee entrance and found the catering van. There were two deliverymen.

"Thanks for being here so early," Adara said. "This is one less thing I have to worry about."

"Where do you want these?" The shorter of the two men loaded the cake boxes onto a cart.

She explained the directions to the appropriate kitchen. "You can place the boxes on the large table to the left of the door. I'll make sure they are placed in the fridge."

The shorter man took off for the door. When she

went to follow him, the taller man stopped her. "I just need you to sign off on the delivery."

"Oh. Certainly." She wondered if she should get the bride to do this, but she suspected Hermione was still tired from her journey yesterday. It was best to let her sleep as long as she could. Adara held her hand out for the receipt.

When he handed over the clipboard, she glanced at the name. Nikolaou.

Please don't let this be another mix-up.

"Um…this is the wrong bill. This is the Kappas or Othonos wedding."

The man's bushy brows drew together. "I don't understand. This was the receipt I was given. Let me look up front." He strode to the front of the truck and swung open the door.

It took a few minutes for him to come back with a small stack of receipts. "What did you say the name was?"

She repeated the names. It took him a moment to sort through the papers. And then he pulled out a slip. "Here it is." He held it out to her. "Just sign."

She wasn't going to just sign. After the last mix-up, she didn't trust the receipt was correct. "What about the cakes? Are they the right ones?"

The man's brows scrunched together again. "Of course they're right."

She was understandably having a problem taking it for granted that the cake hadn't been mixed up just like the receipt. "Maybe I should go check."

"Lady, I don't have all day. It's the right cake. Just sign the receipt."

She crossed her arms. "How can you be sure? You mixed up the receipts."

He expelled a frustrated sigh. "Because the cakes were double-checked at the bakery and marked one through five. This is the only five-tier cake we're delivering today. Therefore it's the right cake."

His explanation sounded reasonable. While the man grumbled about falling behind in his schedule, she read down line by line. And when she was satisfied that it was correct, she signed off. He pulled off a yellow carbon copy and handed it to her.

On her way to the kitchen, she passed the shorter man with an empty cart. Now all she had to do was put the layers of cake in the fridge until it was time for the wedding, and then the kitchen crew would see to assembling it for the reception.

She smiled as she made her way through the hotel. She approached an older woman pushing her cleaning supply cart. "Good morning, Irene."

The woman sent her a big, friendly smile. "It's a gorgeous day for a wedding."

"Yes, it is. I hope you're ready to dance the evening away."

"I still can't believe they invited the staff."

"I can. Hermione looks on all of us as her family. And Atlas finally has the family he never had growing up."

Irene placed a hand over her heart as she sighed. "It's so good they found each other."

"Agreed. I have to get going and see to the cake."

"I bet it'll be beautiful."

"It will be. Soon, you'll see for yourself."

"Then I better get my work done early. I don't want to miss this wedding."

"See you later."

And then they continued in opposite directions. Irene

wasn't the only excited member of staff. In fact, there had been a lottery to see which staff got to attend the wedding and which had to work, because without the lottery, it had been chaos with everyone trying to swap shifts. At last, it was settled. Some employees would be wedding guests, and the others would get a bonus in their next paycheck. It wasn't perfect, but Hermione and Atlas had done their best.

Adara entered the kitchen and looked to the left. The table was empty. Her chest tightened in panic. Where was the cake?

Her gaze swung around the kitchen, searching for the pink bakery boxes. And then she spotted them on the table to the right of the door. She blew out a pent-up breath. It appeared the guy wasn't any better with directions than the driver had been with finding the right receipt.

Adara couldn't believe how much cake there was, but Hermione had fallen in love with this design. There were alternating flavors—the bottom tier was chocolate with a cherry ganache filling, and the next layer was vanilla with a lemon curd filling. Adara's mouth watered just thinking about eating it. She wasn't sure which layer she preferred more.

Now she had to get the cake moved into the large walk-in fridge. The wedding wasn't until that afternoon, but the cooking staff would be there shortly to begin the preparations. Adara hoped to be gone before they showed up.

She walked to the fridge and stepped inside. There were mounds of food everywhere. There was a spare shelf here and there, but no group of shelves. Some rearranging was in order.

Minutes later, she had a spot for the cake boxes. She

moved them one by one, starting with the largest. She held the boxes tightly and took slow, measured steps so as not to trip. She had never been so nervous while holding a cake before. But this wasn't just any cake—it was her best friend's wedding cake.

The first four layers were secure in the fridge. This just left the cake top. She couldn't resist taking a peek. She loosened the tape very carefully. She lifted the lid.

Inside was a pale blue cake with an array of pastel flowers. It was beautiful. And it would totally fit the beach theme of the wedding.

She closed the box, resealing the tape. You couldn't even tell that she'd taken a sneak peek. She carefully lifted the box so as not to tip it to one side or the other.

With the box secure in her hands, she started across the kitchen to the fridge. Just as she stepped in front of the kitchen door, it began to open. It was as if time slowed down.

She froze. The door moved. Her voice caught in her throat.

The door hit the box. It jarred her, and she screamed, "Stop!"

CHAPTER SIXTEEN

IT WAS TOO LATE.

The door struck Adara's fingers.

It pushed her hands back. The box hit her chest. Adara gasped.

The cake box tilted. The lid pressed against her. "Oh, no! No! No! No!"

When the door moved back, she lowered the cake box. Her sole focus was on the cake inside. Was it salvageable? She doubted it.

"What's wrong?" Suddenly Krystof appeared in front of her.

"How could you?" Of all the people to be on the other side of the door, why was she not surprised to find it was Krystof? He was always acting first and thinking later.

His dark brows furrowed together. "What did I do?"

"You ruined everything!" She moved to the closest table and placed the box on it.

"Ruined everything? Don't you think that's a little overdramatic?"

"No. I don't." Her fingers shook with nervous energy as she worked to loosen the tape on the lid. "It just can't be ruined."

"What?" Frustration rang out in his voice.

Her gaze met his as she gestured at the cake box. "What do you think?"

"How am I supposed to know? Someone told me they saw you come down here, and I came to see if you needed any help."

She shook her head. "You have the worst timing ever."

His eyes widened. "Why are you so mad at me?"

All her pent-up emotions came bubbling to the surface. Instead of dealing with her infertility issues, her anger and frustration was focused on the fate of the cake.

"It doesn't matter." She didn't have time to get into this with him. "Just go."

"I'm not leaving." He moved up next to her. "What has you so upset?"

At last she managed to loosen the tape. She lifted the lid. And the cake was even worse than she'd imagined. The frosting was smashed against the lid and the side of the box. The fluffy chocolate cake was split open. Now what was she going to do?

Krystof peered over her shoulder. "Wait. Is that the wedding cake?"

"It was."

"Was?"

"You squashed it against me when you came flying through the door. How could you do that?"

"Wait." He pressed his hand to his chest indignantly. "You're blaming me?"

"Of course I am. You're the one who slammed the door into the cake."

"How was I supposed to know you were standing there? It's not like there's a window in the door or anything!"

She hated that he had a good point. Right now, she needed someplace to focus her frustration. And Krystof was the only one in the vicinity. And it might have had something to do with him trying to win her over when she knew that soon he'd be gone on his next adventure, while she'd still be here on Ludus Island. But she refused to think about that now. She had a cake disaster to deal with.

"What are you going to do?" Krystof looked at her expectantly.

She was tired of solving problems. "What are *you* going to do? After all, you are the best man. So what's it going to be? And don't take long, because we don't have much time."

His brows furrowed together. "Why should I fix it?"

"Because you ruined the cake." She sighed. There was no time for him to figure out a solution. "Never mind. I've got this." She withdrew her phone from her pocket and pulled the receipt from her pocket. She dialed the number for the bakery.

"What are you doing?"

As the phone rang, she held up her finger for Krystof to wait. After a much-too-brief conversation with the bakery, she disconnected the call.

"What did they say?" Krystof leaned against the table.

She placed her palms on the cold metal of the table-top and leaned her weight on them as she stared straight ahead. "They can't help us. They said they delivered unblemished cakes and what happened to them after they were delivered is our problem."

"Can't they make us a new cake? I'm willing to pay whatever it'll cost. I'll even throw in a bonus."

She was relieved he was finally comprehending

the severity of this situation. "They said they're fully booked today. And even if they wanted to help, there simply isn't enough time to bake a new cake, cool it, decorate it and deliver it."

Krystof raked his fingers through his hair, scattering the loose curls. "Then there won't be a cake top. There will still be a cake. That's all that's needed."

"What?" Surely she hadn't heard him correctly. "You can't be serious." When he nodded, she said, "How many weddings have you been to where there wasn't a beautifully decorated cake? And the cake top is the showpiece."

"I don't go to many weddings."

"You're avoiding the question."

He sighed. "Fine. What are you going to do?"

"I think you mean what are *we* going to do, because this mess is as much your fault as mine." Her mind raced, searching for a solution. Because she wasn't going to let Hermione down. "Let me get the next smallest cake."

"*I'll* get the cake. We know what happened the last time you carried one of the cakes."

"Hey, that's not fair."

"But true."

She inwardly groaned. "Fine. The cakes are in the walk-in. They're on the left side in pink boxes. Make sure you grab the smallest box, and please be careful. We can't afford to lose another layer."

"Trust me. I'm sure on my feet."

She rolled her eyes as he walked away. Lucky for her, she'd taken some cake-decorating classes with her neighbor. And here she'd thought those craft classes would never be useful. Boy, had she been wrong.

She'd also learned a shortcut to making fondant. She

just had to find some marshmallows, powdered sugar, shortening, food coloring and water.

"I'll be right back!" She ran out the door.

The best part of working at an exclusive resort was that they had a lot of specialty items. It shouldn't be hard to find the ingredients. And she was right.

Ten minutes later, she was back in the kitchen with the necessary ingredients. Krystof was busy scrolling on his phone. She set the box of items on the table.

"Make yourself useful and find me a mixer." She didn't wait for him to answer. She moved to the sink and washed up.

A few minutes later, she had a batch of fondant. She tried to remember what the topping looked like. It was flowers. Flowers were not easy to make. You had to make each petal, and that took tools that she didn't have.

"What's wrong?" Krystof asked. "Why aren't you doing anything?"

"I am doing something. I'm thinking."

"If you don't hurry, this kitchen is going to fill up with the catering staff."

She glared at him. "You don't think I know that, but I can't recreate the delicate flowers the bakery made for the original cake top."

"Then make something else. Something easier."

"But then Hermione will know."

Krystof smiled and shook his head. "Don't you think she'll know no matter how you decorate the cake? There'll be a layer missing."

Though she hated to admit it, he was right. "Fine. How do you think we should decorate it?"

He shrugged. "How should I know? If it were up to me, there wouldn't be any decorations."

Why had she thought he would be any help? If she

couldn't make flowers, what else could she make that would be rather easy and still fit the wedding's beach theme? She stared at the blue cake. And then she realized she'd come up with the answer—beach items.

"I'll make a sand dollar, a starfish and seashells. They can't be that hard, right?"

"I don't know. I guess not," he said dubiously.

And so she set to work dividing the fondant and then coloring it different shades. She left part of it white. She removed a rolling pin from the box as well as the edible markers. Boy, she loved working in this place that had a little bit of everything.

She consulted an image on her phone as she created it. When she'd finished making the sand dollar, she asked, "What do you think?"

Krystof lowered his phone to look at her creation. "Not bad."

She frowned at him. "Not bad? I'd like to see you do better."

"Okay. It's really good. Better?"

"Much." She laid the sand dollar gently on the top of the cake and frowned.

"What's the matter?"

"It just doesn't look right."

They moved it around, and still she was certain they were missing something. She started to make a starfish. It was a lot harder than it looked in the photo. And considering she didn't have the right shaping tools, she had to make do with what she found in the kitchen.

"I've got it." Krystof started for the door.

She paused as she was about to cover the starfish with granulated sugar. "Where are you going?"

"I have an idea. I'll be right back." Without waiting for her to say another word, he dashed out the door.

She had no idea what he found so urgent at this moment. But she didn't have time to worry about him. She had her own issues. Like making the top of the cake look presentable. Her art skills were not the best—at least she didn't think so.

And though she wanted to cry in frustration, she kept working—kept trying to make the best collection of seashells possible from fondant. She'd make as many as she could and then pick the best ones to place on the cake.

She didn't know how long she continued to work while Krystof was off on his errand, but finally he returned. He stepped up next to her at the counter and perused her work. He was very quiet. Was that a bad sign?

With nerves frazzled, she asked, "Are they that bad?"

"Bad? No. I think they're great."

She glanced at him, at the edible seashells and then back at him. He wasn't smiling or laughing. In fact, he looked quite sincere. "Are you being honest?"

His gaze met hers. "Of course I am. You don't agree?"

"I think there's nothing I could create that would replace the beautiful flowers that were on the original cake top, but these will have to do."

"I disagree. This is going to be much better."

"I don't know about that." She stared at the decorations she'd created. "I feel like there's something missing." She was so worried that she was about to mess up her best friend's wedding, and then she'd never forgive herself.

Krystof reached for a bag of brown sugar and the granulated sugar. He mixed them together. And then he carefully sprinkled it on top of the cake.

"What are you doing?" She moved closer to him. "Wait. Is that supposed to be sand?"

He smiled as he turned to her. "You did say it was a beach theme. And what is a beach without sand?"

"You're brilliant." She reached out and hugged him. "It pulls it all together."

The movement had been an automatic response. She turned her head ever so slightly and breathed in the slight scent of soap mixed with his masculine scent. *Mmm...*

CHAPTER SEVENTEEN

THE SENSUOUS TIMBRE of the violins filled the air.

This was it. It was time for the ceremony.

Adara turned to her friend. "Are you ready for this?"

Hermione's face lit up with a brilliant smile. "I definitely am."

"You look beautiful. I hope Atlas knows how lucky he is."

"Almost as lucky as me. Thank you for all you've done."

"You're welcome." She carefully hugged her friend, trying not to mess up her wedding dress or the styled curls that fell down her back.

Hermione pulled back. "Now you and Indigo better get down that aisle, or else I'm going to beat you to the end."

"You wouldn't."

"Don't tempt me. I can't wait to say 'I do.'"

They both laughed. It felt good to lose herself in the moment and not to think about her problems anymore.

"And I think there's a man waiting at the end of the aisle for you, too." Hermione arched a brow. "I've seen the way you two look at each other. It's a lot more than the fling you had going on before. I think Krystof really cares about you."

Heat swirled in Adara's chest and rushed to her face. "This day isn't about me or Krystof. It's all about you and Atlas." At that moment, the music changed. "I think that's our cue to walk down the aisle."

"This is so exciting," Indigo said. "Let's get these two married."

Indigo was the first down the steps to the beach in the artic-blue gown that showed her slim, tanned shoulders and gave a hint of her lower legs and the sandals they'd picked out. Adara waited until her friend turned the corner, and then she started after her.

When she turned the corner, she saw the sea of white chairs and the handsomely dressed guests. Her gaze moved up the center aisle to the flowered arch and then to the right, where the groom stood. Her gaze quickly moved past him to the best man, who was staring back at her. Her heart skipped a beat.

For a second, she let herself imagine what it'd be like if this was their wedding. Would Krystof stare at her like he was doing now? Or would his gaze be warmed with love?

And yet the way he was looking at her now, it made her feel like the most beautiful woman in the world. For a second, she wondered if he'd look at her the same way if he knew she was broken on the inside. And then she pushed aside the bothersome thought. Today was for celebrating her friends' love. Tomorrow she'd deal with her diagnosis.

At the end of the aisle, she felt a gravitational pull in Krystof's direction, but she resisted the urge and instead took her position to the left of the aisle. She turned to watch Hermione approached them. She looked breathtaking. The pure joy on her face was the way every bride should look on their wedding day. In that moment, as Hermione stepped up to Atlas—as they stared lovingly into each other's eyes—Adara realized all the challenges of the past couple of weeks had been totally worth it. Hermione and Atlas got their happily-ever- after.

Hermione turned to her and handed her bouquet over so that she could hold both of Atlas's hands. As Adara took the flowers, her gaze strayed past Hermione and immediately connected with Krystof's. Was he still staring at her?

As they exchanged vows, Adara was utterly distracted by Krystof's presence. Any time her gaze would stray to him, he'd be looking back at her. What was up with him? Why was he being so attentive?

She looked so much like a bride.

He should turn away, but his body refused to co-operate.

Krystof couldn't keep his gaze from Adara. And then her head turned ever so slightly, and their gazes met. His heart started to pound.

She wore the most brilliant smile that filled his chest with warmth. It was as if she were the sun and he a mere planet in her orbit. He could imagine her walking up to him—being there with him.

Whoa! Where had that thought come from?

He reined in his thoughts. Sure, they were having a good time together. But they had a casual thing going. Why ruin it with a bunch of promises that would one day be broken?

After all, when the wedding was over, he would be on to his next adventure. This time it wasn't a card game. This time he was heading back to Paris. He'd made a decision. After his research and speaking with consultants, he'd determined the tech firm would be a worthwhile investment.

He would return to the island regularly to see Adara. And he had hopes of convincing her to go on some adventures with him. They made a good pair. He hoped it would continue after the wedding. But for how long?

As the priest spoke of love and eternity, Krystof knew as sure as he was standing on that white sand with the sea softly lapping at the beach that one day Adara would be standing there in a white dress with flowers in her hair and stars in her eyes. She would be staring into the eyes of the man she loved. She would be staring at him.

Whoa! Where did that come from?

It was this wedding. It had him all out of sorts. When it was over, they could get back to the way things used to be.

And then the ceremony ended. Mr. and Mrs. Othonos started up the aisle. Now it was his turn to walk Adara up the aisle. He stepped forward and presented his arm to her. When she smiled at him, it stirred this unfamiliar sensation in his chest. He assured himself that it was nothing.

With her hand tucked in the crook of his arm, they were headed toward the patio area that had been reserved for the reception. Adara expelled a dreamy sigh. "Wasn't that the most wonderful wedding?"

"All thanks to you." And he meant it. "You worked really hard so that everything was perfect for them."

"Thank you. But this wedding was a team effort. There were a lot of people that helped with the arrangements, especially you."

He shook his head. "I didn't do much at all."

"You did more than you think. You helped me sort

out the dresses and pick out the music. And let's not forget how you helped decorate the cake."

"Huh. I did do a lot, didn't I?" He sent her a teasing smile. "What did you do again?"

She rolled her eyes. "Give a guy a compliment and it goes straight to his head."

He loved this side of Adara. That trip to the waterfall had done them both a lot of good. It had been an amazing afternoon—one he wouldn't mind repeating in the very near future.

She elbowed him lightly. "What are you smiling about?"

Should he tell her? He didn't see what it would hurt. "I was thinking about our day at the waterfall."

"You mean the day you had me playing hooky from work?"

"Oh, come on. You know you enjoyed it." There was no way he was going to believe that she hadn't. It was a day he would never forget. "We should do it again."

He expected her to agree, but instead, she said, "Come on. We need to form a receiving line." She grabbed his hand to lead him to the spot where he needed to stand. "They're waiting for us."

As her fingers laced with his, a jolt zipped up his arm and sent his heart racing. It didn't matter how much time he spent with her—she still had this special effect on him. He was so relieved they'd patched things up between them. And he would show her how much he appreciated her presence in his life later that evening.

Just a little longer...

She could keep it together a little longer.

Adara was indeed happy for her friends, but the doctor's diagnosis continued to linger on the edges of her thoughts. It was so much to take in. In an instant, everything about her life had changed.

She glanced around and spotted Krystof talking to a guest. At that moment, he glanced in her direction. When their gazes met, he smiled. It was a balm on her tattered heart.

She knew there was a lot more to her than whether or not she could give birth. But in this particular moment, it's where her mind wanted to dwell.

And yet when Krystof looked at her like he was doing now, she felt complete and whole. He made her feel like anything was possible even when she knew that wasn't the case.

Krystof was now headed in her direction. He stopped in front of her and held his hand out to her. "May I have this dance?"

"I... I don't think so." She had to start putting some distance between them.

"Come on. Please. I'm going to look awfully silly dancing out there all by myself."

"You wouldn't."

He smiled at her, making her stomach dip. "I'd do anything to make you smile."

And then he held one hand over his chest and held his other hand at his side as though he were dancing with an invisible person. He started swaying to the music. She couldn't believe her eyes. He was really going to dance without her.

People were stopping to watch their exchange. If she didn't dance with him, they were just going to draw even more attention. And she had promised herself that she was going to have a good time tonight—even if that good time was found in Krystof's arms.

And so she stepped up to him. He reached out to her,

and she walked into his arms. It felt so natural to be with him. It was though at last she was exactly where she belonged.

She corrected her thoughts. She didn't belong with Krystof. And he didn't belong with her. All they were having was a good time together. Nothing more. In the morning, he would leave on his next adventure. And she would be left to pick up the pieces of her life.

CHAPTER EIGHTEEN

THE BRIDE AND groom had departed.

The reception was over.

Krystof had just finished talking to Prince Istvan when he noticed Adara across the room. She was at the buffet speaking with one of the staff, who was clearing the serving dishes. Once she finished her talk, instead of heading toward the lingering guests, she turned toward the kitchen.

He followed her. When he stepped in the kitchen, it was abuzz with staff rushing to clean up so they could head home. There was no sign of Adara. Had she slipped out the back way? Was she trying to avoid him?

He knew she'd been a bit quiet and more reserved than normal during the reception, but he wrote that off to exhaustion. She'd worked so hard to make the wedding the best it could be that she'd worn herself out.

He turned and exited the kitchen. He made his way to Adara's room. He told himself that he needed to make sure she was feeling all right, and then he'd let her get some rest.

He raised his hand and knocked on the door. No response. After a moment, he knocked again. "Adara, it's me. I just came to check on you." He knocked one last time. "Adara, please open the door."

He heard the click of the lock, and then the door swung open. Adara stood there with her hair down and her makeup smudged. Wait. Had she been crying?

"What do you want?" she asked.

He stepped past her into the darkened room, where only the large-screen television cast light. He turned back to her. "What's wrong?"

"Nothing's wrong. The wedding was a success. Hermione and Atlas are happy newlyweds."

She was saying all the right things, but he didn't believe her. He stepped up to her and gazed into her bloodshot eyes. "Adara, what's wrong?"

"Why do you keep asking me that? I answered already."

His gaze searched hers. "But did you? Really? Because I think something has been bothering you all evening. No. Make that since yesterday at dinner. You've been doing your best to cover it up, but there's something wrong. If it's about me leaving tomorrow, I've been giving that some thought."

Her brows gathered. "What are you talking about?"

"I'm talking about me starting to put down roots. I have to fly to Paris briefly but I'll return. Then I could stay here for a while and work on expanding MyPost. It was so helpful with finding the dresses that I think with the right leadership, the site could do a lot of good for so many more people."

"And you're going to—what? Live here at the resort?"

He smiled and nodded. "For a while. And while I'm here, I'm hoping we could spend more time together. We can see where things go with us."

"No." The two-letter word had a big crescendo.

Krystof's eyes widened. "Isn't that what you've

wanted all of this time? I thought you wanted a committed relationship. I thought you wanted me staying in one place for more than a week at a time."

"No." She waved him off as though she were frustrated. "I mean, yes, but not now."

If he'd thought there might be a problem before, he was certain of it now. "Adara, talk to me. What's going on?"

Her fine brows drew together as her lips pursed together. For a moment, she stood there silently glaring at him. "Why are you pushing this?"

"Because I care."

Her eyes momentarily widened. "You do?"

He nodded. "You can talk to me."

He'd never let his guard down long enough to admit that he cared about anyone before, but he got the feeling Adara really needed to hear it tonight.

She sighed. Her shoulders drooped as though they were bearing the weight of the world upon them. He couldn't imagine what had her so worked up.

"Why don't we go out on the balcony?" He gestured for her to lead the way.

For once, she didn't put up an argument, but instead she moved to the balcony high above the now-closed pool area. It was a tranquil spot. He filled a glass with water and followed her. She took a seat in one of the cushioned chairs.

He handed her the water. "Thank you." She took a sip before setting it aside. "Maybe I should head back to the kitchen and make sure there are no problems."

"They have everything under control."

"How do you know?"

"Because I went in there looking for you. And they looked like they knew exactly what they were doing.

All you need to do is sit here and tell me what's going on with you."

Adara opened her mouth as though to argue the point but then wordlessly pressed her lips together. "I don't know why you brought me out here. There's really nothing to talk about."

"And I think that is the biggest understatement I've ever heard." He wanted to push her for answers, because he was concerned, but he resisted the urge. The more he pushed, the more she'd shut down on him. And so he sat there quietly staring down at the pool.

After several minutes of silence, she sighed. "You aren't going to move until we talk, are you?"

"I'm not leaving until I'm sure you're okay. If that means we talk a bit, I'm good with that. If you want to sit here quietly and drink your water, I'm fine with that, too."

Her gaze narrowed. "Since when are you so Zen?"

A smile pulled at the corners of his lips. "Zen, huh?"

"Don't let it go to your head." She took another sip. "I can't believe you're holding me hostage."

He arched a brow. "A little melodramatic, don't you think?"

She set aside the water. "You just don't understand."

"I would if you talked to me. Don't you think after all we've shared that you can trust me?"

She hesitated as though she had to actually give the answer to that question some serious thought. His pride was pricked. Because no matter what he had or hadn't done, he had never betrayed her. And he never would.

"Adara?" His voice was filled with disbelief.

"Okay. Yes, I trust you."

"Then talk to me. If I can help, you have to know that I'll do it."

She shook her head. "That's just it. No one can help."

Had there been a wave of emotion in her voice? He turned to look into her eyes, and that's when he saw the gloomy look on her face. Whatever was weighing on her mind was serious.

"I care about you," he said. "And I'll support you through whatever this is."

She got to her feet and moved to the railing. "I can't have children."

Had he heard her correctly? Maybe she'd said she *wanted* to have children. The thought had the breath catching in his lungs. Children were not something he'd ever considered in his life.

Still, this wasn't about him. This was about Adara and her desires. And he needed to keep his promise to be there for her, no matter the subject.

He stood and moved next to her. In a soft voice, he said, "What has you thinking about this?"

Her face grew pale. "Does it matter?"

"Yes. It matters to you, so it matters to me."

"Please stop. Stop being so understanding. So caring." Her voice wavered with emotion.

He reached out to where she had her hand resting on the railing. He placed his hand over hers. "I think life happens, and we have to deal with it as it comes to us."

She struggled to keep her composure.

He was being so nice to her. She didn't know what to think.

Adara didn't dare turn her head to look at Krystof. She knew if she looked into his eyes, she'd lose the little control she had on her emotions. She didn't know he could be so understanding.

"I don't even know where to start," she said.

"At the beginning usually helps."

It felt strange discussing something so distinctively female with a man. And yet she knew that whatever she discussed with Krystof wouldn't go any further. He'd proved that over and over again.

"It started when I missed my monthly."

Krystof remained quiet. Very quiet. But he didn't remove his hand from hers.

"I knew I wasn't pregnant, because you were the only person I'd been with in a really long time. And I'd had it since the last time we were together. But as one month passed without it and then two, I knew something was terribly wrong."

"And I didn't make things easy for you. I'm sorry."

She shook her head. "It wasn't your fault. You had no idea that I had a medical issue."

"Maybe if I had slowed down, I would have realized you were dealing with something."

She glanced at him and saw the serious look on his face. "Don't blame yourself. Even if you had noticed back then, I wouldn't have talked to you about it. Back then I was still in denial about what was happening."

"Which is what?"

"Well, the doctor said it could have been a lot of things. And so they ran a bunch of tests. It took a while for them to all come back. Yesterday, I met with my doctor."

"That's where you went?"

She nodded. "They wouldn't give me the results over the phone. I had to go to the office. I know I probably shouldn't have done it the day before the wedding, but I just couldn't wait any longer."

"Of course you should have gone. I just wish you'd have said something to me. I would have gone with you."

She shook her head. "It was something I needed to do on my own." She drew in a deep brew. "I found out that I have early-onset menopause."

He paused for a moment as though digesting this information. "And this is the reason you can't have children?"

She nodded once more. "I think my mother had it, and now I have it. I... I didn't even know if I wanted to have children." Her voice wavered with emotion. "I mean, I thought maybe someday if I met the right person, I might have a family with them. But now that decision is out of my control." Her vision blurred with unshed tears.

"Can they reverse this menopause?"

She shook her head as the tears spilled onto her cheeks.

Krystof reached out and pulled her into his arms. She didn't want to need his hug, but she longed for the reassurance that everything was going to be all right.

And so she let herself be drawn into his embrace. Her arms wrapped around his trim waist as her cheek landed on his shoulder. Her face nuzzled into the curve of his neck. She inhaled his masculine scent mingled with a whiff of spicy cologne.

In that moment, she was distracted from her sorrow, and instead she lived in the moment. Her heart pitter-pattered quickly. And just as quickly, she remembered that she would never make anyone the perfect partner, because she was only a part of whom she'd once been.

She pulled away. "I'm sorry. I shouldn't have cried on your shoulder."

"My shoulder is there for you any time you need it."

She had to keep her emotions under control. She couldn't let herself fall apart and have him put the pieces back together. He was at last understanding that he had options if he put down roots—he could have a family of his own. Just not with her.

He studied her for a moment. "And now it all makes sense."

"What makes sense?" She had no idea what he was talking about.

"The reason you've been going out of your way to make sure everything was perfect for the wedding."

"And what reason is that?"

He reached up and ever so gently tucked a strand of hair behind her ear. "Your body feels out of control, and so you felt a need to control every aspect of the wedding. I just want you to know that you can relax now, because you've accomplished your goal. This was the best wedding."

She hated how easily he read her. Because if he could figure all that out, he would also know that she felt inadequate and uncertain of what her future would hold. Would she stay at the resort forever because she didn't have any other place she belonged—no other family of her own?

The more the troubling thoughts crowded into her mind, the more her emotions rose. And she couldn't fall apart now. Not when Krystof was prepared to hold her together—to be there like she'd thought she wanted.

But now she couldn't be the person he needed. If they were to stay together, he might one day want a family. She couldn't give it to him. He'd feel compelled to tell her that it didn't matter. But it did matter so much that she felt utterly gutted. And someday it might matter that much to him, too.

"Krystof, you need to go."

"I'm not going anywhere. I'm here for you." He

looked at her like he really cared. And it was making this so incredibly hard.

"I don't need you." She stepped back. "We're not a couple. We never really were. This is my problem to deal with. Not yours."

"Adara, why are you doing this?"

She was doing what was best for both of them. "Are you going to leave?"

"No. I'm not going anywhere."

Of all the times for him not to want to leave at the first chance. She knew if she stayed here, he would wear her down and they'd spend the night together. And in the morning, they'd be right back in this same awful position, because they had no future.

She didn't know why he was trying so hard. It wasn't like they were in love or anything. He felt sorry for her—that was it. And she couldn't keep doing this.

"If you aren't going to leave, then I am." She turned and went back inside the room.

"Adara, where are you going?"

"It doesn't matter." She grabbed her purse and keys before heading for the door.

"Adara, wait. Don't go."

She kept walking.

This time Krystof didn't try to stop her. He must have realized there was nothing that could be done for her. She was broken beyond repair.

CHAPTER NINETEEN

HOME AT LAST.

Her apartment didn't feel warm and comforting like she'd thought it would. It felt cold and empty.

Adara hadn't slept much that night. She already missed Krystof, and he hadn't even left the island yet. But he would soon be jetting off to some card game in a far-off location.

She hoped he wouldn't give up on finding someone special in his life. She wanted him to be happy, and she didn't think his nomadic ways would make him happy the rest of his life.

Knock-knock.

No one knew she was home. It had to be Krystof. Was he there to say goodbye on his way out of town?

She scrambled out of bed. She glanced in the mirror. Her day-old makeup was smeared. She had raccoon eyes. She rubbed them. It only smeared her makeup more.

Knock-knock.

Whoever was on the other side of the door wasn't going away. Adara groaned. She didn't want to see anyone.

"Coming!" In her shorts and T-shirt, she headed for

the door. She swung it open. "Hermione, what are you doing here?"

"Good morning to you, too."

And then Adara remembered her manners and opened the door wide. "Come in. Shouldn't you be on your honeymoon?"

Hermione moved into the living room and sat down on the couch. "We're leaving today to visit Atlas's father, and if he's doing well, we're going on our honeymoon. But first, I wanted to check on you."

"Why?" Adara sat down, too. "What did Krystof tell you?"

Hermione's brows drew together. Concern reflected in her eyes. "Nothing. I haven't seen him this morning. But now I want to know what's going on with you two."

She couldn't hold it all in any longer. She needed her best friend. And so it all came tumbling out about her diagnosis and how Krystof wanted to stay on at the resort.

"So what did you say?"

"I told him we're not a couple. I... I told him we never really were." Her voice cracked with emotion. "I told him... I told him I didn't need him."

Hermione reached out and gave her hand a quick squeeze. "But you do need him, don't you?"

Adara shrugged. And then she gave in to the truth and nodded. "But he's finally figuring out that he doesn't have to be a nomad. He can make a home, have a family, if he wants. But I can't give him that."

"Did you ask him what he wants?"

Adara shook her head. "He would just say what he thought I'd want him to say."

"Would you want him making decisions for you?"

"No. But this is different."

"Is it?" Hermione arched a brow. "Or are you afraid to let yourself admit that you love him?"

"What? No. Of course not. We weren't a couple. It wasn't ever serious."

"And yet you two made sure that no matter how many miles separated you, that you saw each other regularly for months. I've seen the way you both look at each other. If that's not love, I don't know what it is."

It was true. She loved Krystof. She couldn't keep hiding from the truth. "But we're so different. I like to have my life planned out, and he doesn't even know what country he'll be in tomorrow."

"Have you ever considered another life—someplace far from Ludus Island?"

"No."

"Maybe you should give it some thought. I'll miss you, but we can video chat and visit often. The resort will always be home to you."

Could she be happy somewhere else? Could she be happy always moving around? She didn't know the answers.

Krystof had taught her that she needed to take chances and reach for the things she wanted. She had been thinking about starting her own event-planning business. Was now the time for her to be her own boss? Was it time to take a leap with Krystof?

It was time to move on.

And yet his bags weren't packed. He didn't want to leave.

Krystof rode the elevator to the penthouse. He wanted to say goodbye to Atlas before they both left. He had no idea when he'd see his friend again. He had a feeling it would be a long time before he set foot on Ludus Island again.

The elevator stopped, and the door opened. Krystof stepped off and found Atlas standing in the doorway to the penthouse. He waved him inside. "Come on in. Hermione isn't here right now."

Krystof stepped forward, coming to a stop right inside the doorway. "I won't take much of your time. I just wanted to wish you the best. And let you know that I'm getting ready to leave."

"Thanks for all you did. We both really appreciate everything you and Adara did for us and the wedding. So where are you off to? The Riviera? The Orient?"

He shrugged. "I don't know."

"You don't know? I know you like to be spontaneous, but don't you need a destination before you get on your jet?"

"I'll figure something out." There was no place he wanted to go. That had never happened to him before. He wasn't even excited about purchasing the tech company in Paris anymore. He just knew he couldn't stay here, not after learning that Adara didn't want a future with him. "I won't be back for a while."

"What happened with you and Adara? I thought you two were getting along really well."

Krystof blew out a breath as he leaned back against the doorjamb. "I thought so, too. And then when I told her that I was planning to stick around the Ludus so we could figure things out, she told me to leave."

"How did you tell her?"

"Tell her what? That I'm leaving?"

"No. How did you tell her that you love her? Did you include flowers and champagne?"

"What? No. I didn't do any of that."

Atlas waved him in the living room, where he went to the bar and poured them each some scotch. "Here." He held out the glass. "Take this. I think you're going to need it."

Krystof took the glass and took a healthy sip. "I don't know what to do."

"You need to tell Adara how you feel about her."

"Even though she already told me that we're over?"

"What do you have to lose? I don't know too many women who are willing to put up with your idiosyncrasies, but Adara has stuck it out this long without you stating your feelings for her. Maybe she's tired of waiting around. Maybe she thinks you don't love her."

"But I do." It struck him how easy it was to make that confession.

"Good. Tell her that. Don't hold back anything. And one more thing—when you tell her, don't forget the flowers."

"But will any of that sway her?"

Atlas looked at him pointedly. "Do you really love her? Are you willing to change for her?"

Krystof had been giving this a lot of thought. In fact, it's all he'd thought about last night. "Yes. Yes, to it all."

"Then why are you standing there wasting time telling me? You need to go tell Adara all of this before it's too late."

Krystof put down his glass. "I will."

"And by the way, she's at her apartment on the mainland."

"Thanks."

Krystof headed out the door. He wasn't good at romance. He had no experience at it. But he could do flowers. He would buy her all the flowers in the world if she would just give him another chance.

She had changed him. She made him want to stay in one place—to have a place to call home. He wanted someplace that could be their home.

CHAPTER TWENTY

HER HEART RACED.

Her stomach was twisted up in knots. And her thoughts were scattered.

Adara continued to pick out an outfit to wear when she talked to Krystof—if he was still on Ludus Island. For all she knew, he'd listened to her and left last night. And then she recalled Hermione mentioning he was still on the island that morning.

But would he hear her out? Would he give her a chance to apologize? She had no idea, and she couldn't blame him if he didn't want anything to do with her.

She chose a summer dress instead of her usual business attire. Instead of putting her hair up, she left it down. Instead of putting on all her makeup for a polished look, she applied foundation, powder, mascara and lip gloss. It was a very casual appearance. And though all this was a diversion from her usual routine, she looked in the mirror and approved.

Change was scary and unnerving, but she could do it. She could move beyond the routine that she'd found comfort in for so many years. She could be something else, or do something else. It was in that moment she knew—with or without Krystof, she was leaving Ludus

Island and going on an adventure. She had no idea where she'd end up, but the fun would be in the journey.

She wanted Krystof to join her. Not because she couldn't do it on her own, but rather she wanted to share it with him because somewhere along the way he'd become her best friend. He was the person she confided in, the person who inspired her to be more than she was now. And, most of all, she loved him.

She went to put on her high heels but then reconsidered. She dug a pair of beautiful sandals out of the back of her closet. She'd bought them on a whim and never found the right time to wear them because they didn't go with her business attire. But now was the right time. She slipped them on. They were so comfortable and looked adorable.

She searched the closet for a matching purse, because she liked things to be organized and matching. But she decided that not everything had to be perfect. Sometimes things just had to be good enough. She was good enough as she was.

Knock-knock.

Was Hermione back? Had she forgotten something? On her way to the door, Adara glanced around the living room for something that looked out of place, but she didn't notice anything.

She swung the door open and was greeted with a sea of red roses. Her mouth gaped. She'd never seen so many flowers in an arrangement. There had to be hundreds of them.

And she was certain there was a person behind them, but she couldn't see their face. Was it possible it was Krystof? Her pulse raced. He'd never bought her flowers before. But if not him, who else could it be?

The flowers lowered, and there was Krystof. "These are for you."

She'd have taken them from him, but she wasn't sure she could hold so many flowers. When Krystof did something, he definitely went all in. But what did this mean?

She opened the door wide and backed out of the way. "Come in."

He stepped into the living room. "Adara, we need to talk."

"I was just coming to see you."

His eyes widened. "You were?"

She nodded. "I need to apologize for last night. I shouldn't have said those things to you and then walked out."

He went to approach her, but the flowers stopped him.

"Why don't you put those on the table?" She gestured to the small table in her kitchen.

He did as she asked. They took up the entire table. And then he returned to her. "I'm sorry, too. I pushed last night when I should have let you take all of this at your pace. I should have told you that I'd be there for you, no matter how long it took for you to make sense of your diagnosis."

Her gaze met and held his. "You'd really wait for me?"

He stepped closer and took her hands in his. "My life hasn't been the same since you danced into my heart on Valentine's Day. I thought I could ignore what was happening between us. I thought it would just flame out, but none of that has happened. Adara, I love you and I want a future with you—no matter what the future looks like or where it is."

Tears of joy stung the backs of her eyes. "But I can't even give you the family you deserve."

He gently cupped her face. "That would never change my feelings for you. I love you."

"I love you, too." She lifted up on her tiptoes and pressed her lips to his. Her heart filled with love for him. The warmth spread throughout her body.

And before she was ready, he pulled back. His gaze once more met hers. "Stop worrying about everything. I don't even know if I want a family."

"But you might someday, and I don't want to take that opportunity away from you."

"If we did choose to have a family, I would love to adopt. I was an orphan, and I would like to bring a child into our hearts and share a happy, loving home with them."

Adara hadn't even considered that option. She was so caught off guard that he had given this some thought. The idea most definitely appealed to her. "I would like that, too. But there's one more thing..."

"What's that?"

"We have to have someplace to call home—someplace we can return to after an adventure. A place to keep all our treasures."

He pressed his hand to his heart. "This is where I keep the greatest treasure—your love."

Her heart swooned as their lips met. Her life would never be boring again, and she didn't mind that at all. As long as Krystof was by her side, she would always be at home.

EPILOGUE

New Year's Eve, Paris, France

IT WAS ALMOST MIDNIGHT.

Adara sat at the ornate desk in the corner of their spacious living room awaiting Krystof's arrival. The mail was stacked neatly in the center of the desk with a cream-colored envelope from the royal palace of Rydiania on top. Her chest fluttered with anticipation. She knew someone who was royal.

She reached for the silver letter opener. Excitement coursed through her veins. It easily slipped beneath the sealed flap and gently sliced it open. She pulled out the invitation.

She couldn't believe she—well, they'd both, been invited to the palace to witness their friends, Indigo and Prince Istvan, be married. Adara expelled a dreamy sigh. She was so happy that Indigo had found her very own Prince Charming.

And she wasn't alone. Hermione was now happily married. And even Adara had found her own true love. How had they all gotten so lucky?

Since Hermione and Atlas's wedding, there had been a lot of changes. Adara had quit her job at the Ludus Resort. The decision had weighed on her, but if she was going to take chances, most especially with her heart, she also had to take chances with her career. She had to reach for her dreams. Giving up all she'd known, from her comfy apartment to her longtime job, was the scariest thing she'd ever done.

But now she resided in Paris, one of the most beautiful cities in the world. And she'd launched her very own business. She was now an official event planner with her own staff. She planned special events, from conferences to weddings, and the world was her stage. She'd traveled all over the world to some of the most glamorous locations.

Best of all, they'd been able to find a way to make both herself and Krystof happy. She could still have a career that fulfilled her, and Krystof didn't have to curtail his wanderlust, as he traveled with her when his work schedule allowed. And in the end, they had a place to call home—this spacious five-bedroom Paris apartment that was situated along the world's most beautiful avenue, the Champs-élysées.

Adara had taken great pains to take both of their tastes into consideration when she'd decorated it. There was a touch of classic flair mixed with some modern touches. It had been a tough balancing act, but she'd learned that some of the best things in life were worth the extra effort.

And they'd even brought a bit of Ludus Island to their home. Over the fireplace hung a portrait of the twin falls that Krystof had commissioned Indigo to paint. It had turned out perfectly and was a constant reminder of the magical day they'd spent there.

Their life had settled into a comfortable routine of new adventures. Krystof had bought the tech company he'd been eyeing and merged it with his MyPost social media app. The company was taking off with him at the helm, and best of all Krystof enjoyed the new challenges it presented him.

Speaking of Krystof, the apartment door opened and he stepped inside.

"And how was your day?" He crossed the foyer into the living room.

"It was really good. And you're really late. Problems with your meeting?"

"Actually it was just the opposite. We're expanding, and negotiations ran long."

"That's awesome." She smiled at him. "You're really happy, aren't you?"

He slipped off his coat and laid it over the back of a white couch. "I definitely am, with you in my life."

Her heart skipped a beat. "I was beginning to think I'd have to usher in the new year alone."

"The plane got grounded for a bit in Rome due to bad weather. But I would never let you celebrate alone."

She held up the opened envelope with a royal seal on the back. "Look what we got."

"What's that?"

"An invitation to the royal wedding." She beamed. "Isn't it so exciting? We're going to the palace for a royal wedding."

"It's not as exciting as this." He walked over and placed a leisurely kiss on the nape of her neck. A throbbing sensation spread throughout her body. "I've missed you."

"You were only gone overnight."

"It was still too long."

She reached up and caressed his cheek. "Have I told you lately how much I love you?"

"No." He sent her a serious look as he straightened. "You haven't."

She got to her feet. "Are you sure I haven't?"

"Very sure. The last time you told me was on the phone this afternoon. And that was so long ago." He pursed his lips in a pout.

"My apologies. I love you from the bottom of my heart. Am I forgiven?"

"I suppose. Don't let it happen again."

"I won't. Did you get something to eat?"

"They fed me well on the jet." He glanced down at her work clothes. "I thought you'd be ready for bed by now."

"And miss the fireworks? Not a chance."

Krystof checked the time on his Rolex. "It's almost midnight."

"Let's go out on the balcony."

"I'm right behind you."

As they made it to the railing, they could hear the jubilant voices from the street below.

"Ten—nine—eight—"

She gazed up at her husband. *Her husband.* It sounded so nice.

"Seven—six—five—"

She was the luckiest lady in the world.

"Four—three—two—"

Her heart pounded with love—love she hadn't known was possible.

"One!"

"I love you," he said.

"I love you, too."

And then their lips met as the fireworks popped and sparkled overhead. This was going to be the best year ever.

* * * * *

FORBIDDEN KISSES WITH HER MILLIONAIRE BOSS

HANA SHEIK

MILLS & BOON

This one is for all the holidays.
Thanks for the good food and cheering us up.

CHAPTER ONE

Snow in Africa.

Karl Sinclair had thought he'd seen it all. Skydiving nuptials, twelve-foot cakes suspended in midair and a holographic groomsman who couldn't make it to his brother's wedding on time. Nothing extravagant fazed him now.

And yet he froze at the crunch of snow beneath his patent leather sneakers.

The venue was as it should be. A luxury chalet constructed in two months and on schedule. Only instead of the cold climes being outdoors, the wintry theme had been brought inside. Just as he'd envisioned it when his clients approached him with ideas for their big day. Like all his previous events, the venue had come to life the way he knew it would. He never doubted his ability to reproduce the elaborate, memorable occasions his clients expected of his event-management company, Heartbeat Events. Karl hadn't thought he would travel from Canada to Nairobi, Kenya, to see it in person, though. With it being the middle of September, and nearer to the busy holiday season, he'd had one of his top event coordinators, Nadine, take over the project. At least, he had planned for it to be like that. Usually, his plans were foolproof once set on their course.

Only, he hadn't expected Nadine would come down with the flu at the very last moment.

Sending someone else in his place felt wrong. His clients expected a personal touch. *His* touch. And with the sky-high price tag on his service, the least he could do was carry the torch to the finish line. A line that would be crossed tomorrow once the bride and groom exchanged their vows and celebrated their reception with four hundred of their family and closest friends in this lavish venue.

The snow flooded the corridor like fluffy white clouds that had fallen from above. Karl turned his head up to admire the force of the air-conditioning. He stored a mental note to ensure that the building's management team monitored the HVAC system. The last thing anyone needed was costly damage to one of the compressors or refrigerants. Snow inside a Swiss chalet was romantic. Melted snow was another thing. His bride and groom hadn't signed up for an underwater reception. It was his job to coordinate everything and see that the snow remained in its solid state.

He popped up the collar of his overcoat, glad he'd remembered to dress appropriately for his tour.

The snow followed him from the chalet's entrance up a winding flight of stairs to the mezzanine overlooking the main hall. Spanning five thousand square feet, the hall's jet-black floors were covered with sixty-three tables seating eight each, according to the notes from Nadine's detailed report. Security would see to it that no extra plus-ones slipped into the private event. No one crashed his parties. Exclusivity was part of his brand. High-profile clients paid for their privacy as much as the glamour, glitz and romance.

Buttoning his coat, Karl tensed his muscles against

the shiver skittering up and down his spine. Once again, he was relieved to have chosen attire that withstood the frigid blast of the building's top-notch air-conditioning.

It was also how he knew that the woman striding up the striking white aisle runner down below wasn't where she ought to be.

Her endlessly long dark brown legs were what caught his attention first. Easy to admire that part of her when she wore a miniskirt. The striped skirt suited her long-sleeved wrap crop top, as did her red-soled Louboutin pumps. She hadn't noticed him watching from above. She walked purposefully down the aisle created for the central moment when the newlyweds joined their guests at the reception and climbed the short set of steps to the wedding-party table. The table was set with florid centerpieces. Gold candelabra with pearl-encrusted handles, exquisite Wedgwood tableware and gold-wire vases he could only describe as unique in design. They were empty now, but tomorrow they would be brimming with frost-resistant floral arrangements: camellias, winterberries, evergreen sprigs and a few other hardy perennials he couldn't recall from Nadine's report. And he wasn't making a real effort to remember.

The woman down below had his full attention.

She carried a vase that she set down on the table. Then plucking up an identical one, she eyed it shrewdly, turning it this way and that, her chin-length sleek black bob swinging briskly with her movements. Seemingly having made a decision, she traded the one vase for the other.

What's she up to?

He narrowed his eyes and gripped the railing, his jaw full of unyielding steel and his curiosity overriding the goal to survey the venue for any minute missing details. Keyed up, he stalked toward the stairs. Taking them two at a time, he reached the ground floor and headed to intercept the mystery woman.

She gasped when he was halfway to her, her body going rigid, hands stilling on the vase that she'd swapped out.

"W-where did you come from?" she said.

Karl stopped below the dais with the wedding table and looked up at her. "I could ask you the same question." Because whoever she was, she clearly didn't belong here. She had come in from the dry heat outdoors, unsuspecting of what the wedding venue held in store. Snow. Lots of it. If she were a wedding crasher, she was twenty-four hours too early to the party. And he frowned when he thought of the alternative. A thief under his nose.

A very alluring thief…

But a thief, nevertheless, he thought firmly, scowling.

"This is private property," he said. "I'm not sure how you passed building security, but your adventure ends here."

"My *adventure*?" she sputtered, somehow managing to sound indignant. As though she had the right to be offended.

Despite his best effort to be unaffected, a smile twitched at his lips. It was hard to clamp down on the sudden humor she provoked in him. But it would be harder for him to remain stern if he laughed now.

"Trespassing has to be a crime in Kenya too."

"I'm not trespassing!" She gripped the vase tighter. "I have a reason to be here."

He hadn't noticed her African accent, but it was more pronounced now. Possibly because a thread of wariness had crept into her voice. Studying her carefully, he realized he liked the way she looked. Even more than he had when he'd been observing from above, unnoticed. She had a lovely face. Soft in some areas, sharper and more defined in others. It wasn't long before he cataloged her wide-set eyes, a darker shade of brown that deceptively looked soul-piercingly black. Then there was her wide-tipped nose, low cheekbones, round lips and short, smooth chin, each part of her forever slotted in his memory. Normally he wouldn't be a stickler for those kinds of details. People didn't interest him the way event management did. Unlike coordinating events of any scale, people were…unpredictable. Untrustworthy. *Disruptive.*

If he had a greater understanding of people, he'd have a better relationship with those he should've cared most about and who should care about him: his family.

But that was neither here nor there. Snapping his attention up to her eyes again, Karl stoically confronted her glare.

"What could that reason be?" he asked, unfazed by her withering look.

She opened her mouth but snapped it shut when voices sounded from farther behind them.

Karl guessed the noise was coming from the building's entrance. Her widening eyes and startled expression told him that it could be security hunting for their intruder. With nowhere to run and hide, they'd find her soon enough. Unless he stepped aside and aided her escape. Something which he wouldn't do. No matter how panicked she appeared to be.

He scoffed. "I thought you had a reason to be here."

"I do," she said breathily. "I-I can explain. Really. But not now. Not *here*."

The voices were closing in, getting louder and more

distinct. He could almost make out what they were saying.

"Please, let me go," she begged, a frantic air to her words.

Her plea wrenched sharply at his heart, surprising a grunt from him. It wasn't the words, exactly. Rather the emotion behind them. The way her brows pinched together, and her eyes grew round and unblinking with panic. It was a look he recognized subconsciously from his past. Without needing to ask her for clarification, he knew that she felt cornered and helpless.

Not helpless, he amended. She'd asked for his help. And he hadn't decided whether he was up to aiding and abetting her escape when he had been the one that had caught her.

Karl clenched his teeth, mulling over her request and his sudden indecision. He'd been certain that he wouldn't cave.

Yet that was what he was going to do.

"Hide." He spat the one word out before he regretted it.

Heeding his command, she scurried around the bridal party table, still carrying the vase, and ducked between the white opera chairs, out of sight.

Just in time too. They weren't alone anymore.

Turning to their new arrivals, Karl headed them off. The farther they were away from the head table, the better. He didn't even know her name or what her motive was, and here he was, covering for her.

I can explain, she'd said.

Her words felt honest. He chose to rely on them, and he never backtracked on a decision. He hadn't for a long time. Pushing away the memories of his unhappy childhood, he focused on the present.

On the people who had chased his mystery woman into hiding.

When did she become your *woman?*

Banishing that thought someplace dark and unvisited, he greeted the newcomers.

Istarlin cowered on the other side of the table, one hand securing the vase while the other clawed into the long silken gold tablecloth. She strained to hear the conversation happening only a few feet away. To think she'd been saved and spared by the gorgeous stranger even after he'd rudely accused her of being an intruder!

She wasn't breaking any law. Not when the vase belonged to her. Her intent hadn't been to steal anything at all. The vase wasn't perfect, and it had bugged her to know that it could be. Replacing it had been her sole goal. A quick in-and-out mission, but she hadn't anticipated being caught and questioned—and now cornered.

Though, to be fair, the stranger didn't know better. And she would have set him straight, but then she had heard her grandfather, and nothing else mattered except the urge to retreat.

Now her grandfather's booming voice spoke.

"You're the wedding planner?"

"No, I'm not, but the event coordinator sent me in her place."

That voice she knew instantly too. How could she not, when he'd practically interrogated and scolded her like a child caught with her hand in a cookie jar? It was her handsome stranger.

Her stomach swooped at the thought of him, her face warming pleasantly and a dopey smile pulling her lips wide. After his rude insinuation and the haughty manner in which he had summarily chalked her up as a thief, she hadn't expected him to play chivalrous knight. Not that she'd been swooning. Nor had she been in any real danger. She had just not wanted to confront her grandfather, and she had the oddest sensation that the handsome stranger had known and commiserated with her reasoning.

Lin crouched lower with her vase, her attention vaulting back to the discussion on the other side of the table.

"You must be the bride." Her gorgeous stranger's smooth, dulcet voice had the same effect on her as a big mug of hot cocoa would after a cold day. She shivered from the rush of pleasure.

"Yes, I had hoped for a tour today. One last time before the big day tomorrow."

Lin smiled at the sound of her childhood friend, Machelle. The blushing bride-to-be.

Machelle's parents and Lin's grandfather were longtime friends and neighbors. Though Machelle's family were well-off, Lin's grandfather had generously offered to help pay for the wedding. She suspected that he knew what Machelle's friendship meant to her, and it was his way of showing he cared.

Still, when Machelle and her family had invited her to be part of today's tour of the venue and Lin had learned her grandfather would be going as well, the decision to decline the bride's invitation had been both easy and difficult. Easy because she hadn't wanted her grandfather to ply her with an endless stream of questions about her career plans, and Machelle had understood that. But difficult because she knew what this moment meant to her friend. They had been there for each other for almost their whole lives. Through all the highs and lows and heartbreaks and triumphs. They had attended university together too. Growing even closer over the past few years when they'd left their families behind to study abroad in Switzerland. It was there, while on a study break in the Swiss Alps at picturesque Zermatt, that Lin had watched Machelle fall in love with her husband-to-be.

And now they'd recreated that first meeting in a snow-capped mountain resort with this Swiss chalet–inspired venue. It was beautiful…but also very cold.

Another shiver raced through her, her teeth chattering lightly and her poor toes curling against the glacial air circulating in the building. She should have known to dress better. But stopping by her apartment for a change of clothes had felt like a waste of time. In hindsight, she'd have liked something big and warm like the Burberry woolen coat her good-looking stranger was wearing. She'd have recognized the designer label's check pattern on his upturned collar anywhere. Meaning he wasn't a broke stranger.

A wealthy wedding planner. Business had to be booming at his workplace.

Envy cut coldly through her warm, fluttery attraction to him. She couldn't help it. She'd been working her tail off to build the beginnings of her own business. The thought of someone else attaining a similar dream left her mouth tasting sour and her heart bitter.

She knew it was irrational to be jealous. She didn't want to be an event planner.

Her aspiration was in her arms and cradled close to her chest.

So why does it feel like it's slipping out of my grasp?

She had hit a metaphoric wall and stalled in her business plan.

And all because she didn't have the courage to face her grandfather.

Not entirely true.

She had faced him somewhat, but it was obvious to her that he wasn't serious about listening to her entrepreneurial planning. *He* was the wall she'd run head-long into and was finding hard to surmount.

The problem was that he had always been the no-nonsense type. He didn't see her renting a studio to produce her work as anything meriting recognition. In his eyes, she was dabbling at a hobby. He hadn't said it aloud, but she heard it nevertheless in the way he shut her out quietly whenever she broached the subject of becoming a business owner.

Now, if Lin worked at a reputable, successful place like where her handsome stranger worked, maybe she'd have avoided all this.

Wait!

She held still as her brain fired off a sudden plan.

What if she *did* work with him?

Lin perked up. Suddenly she bounded with energy. She could almost forget that her legs were beginning to cramp. Almost. She wasn't superhuman. Her calves burned, and her knees wobbled. If they didn't get going soon, she might just have to face the music and come out from hiding…

"I would be happy to host the tour. Let's begin with the ice sculptures in the freezer. They'll be displayed right before the reception begins," the stranger said, coming to her rescue for a second time.

She heard them leaving. Knew when it was the right time to peek over the table and stand and stretch her legs. Blissfully alone, Lin marched toward the exit, and before anyone could stop her, she escaped out of the snowy venue into the early-evening heat of Nairobi.

For a moment she soaked in the warmth, sighing happily as the cold entombing her limbs thawed. It was so nice to be outdoors again. She'd been freezing her buns off in there. Free of the chill holding her hostage, she raced away from the imposing building which occupied the larger part of the parking lot that it had been constructed on. She didn't stop until she crossed the street and slipped into the idling taxi that she had instructed to wait for her.

The cabbie beamed when she handed him the extra dollar bills for his trouble.

"Where to next, ma'am?"

Lin thought of several places she could go next. Looking down at her vase and then gazing at the sloping roof of the stone and wood building across the street, she settled on the place she wanted to be most right then.

"We'll stay here for a little longer. There's someone I'm waiting for."

She didn't elaborate, holding the image of the stranger's face in her mind. His very good-looking face. She had to be crazy. Drooling over the guy when he had been ready to assume the worst about her character. As far as first impressions went, it sucked.

Memorable, she conceded bitterly. Yet still awful. But she couldn't turn her back on the idea of working with his event-management company. Surely his boss would be willing to consider her business proposal…

She also was stumped as to why he had changed his mind and helped hide her.

The man was a conundrum. A coldly curt and very gorgeous enigma.

The meter ran for another hour before she sat up and gave the cab driver her next instruction.

"Follow that car." She pointed out the vehicle the stranger had gotten into when he'd walked out of the venue, unaccompanied by Lin's grandfather, Machelle or anyone else.

With a dip of his chin, the cabbie proceeded to shadow the shining black Lamborghini that roared out onto the street ahead of them. Wishing she'd sat up front with the driver, Lin flung off her seat belt and sat forward to keep her eyes on the car they were trailing closely. She wouldn't lose sight of him. Whoever he was. After all, she still owed him an explanation. More so now that he'd spared her an embarrassing moment with her grandfather.

She had plenty to say. And she'd start by thanking him.

CHAPTER TWO

RETURNING TO HIS hotel suite, he was left with a strong taste of defeat in his mouth.

Perplexed by the restlessness still pressing down on his shoulders, Karl tapped the passcode into the lighted keypad and opened the door to his rooms. His first stop was obvious: the bathroom. A splash of cold water over his face did nothing to clear his mind. Stripping off his coat, he tossed it over the bed and did something he normally never did: he left a trail of clothing to the shower. Sloppiness wasn't his MO. The only thing that kept him from falling apart was his persistent need to keep his life organized. Everything he did had purpose. Every task he set his mind to accomplish was a stepping-stone to greater things for him and his company. Every person in his life had a place and reason to matter to him. And he knew when it was the right time to cut off a relationship that wasn't going anywhere, be it romantic, platonic or business.

The problem was he couldn't fully control other people. Didn't know what they were thinking or planning. In his line of work, he could create a masterpiece of an event and still have a client suddenly decide that nothing he had done for them lived up to their expectations.

It didn't happen often, but when it did, it almost always ruined his mood.

He couldn't manage some aspects of his personal life either. His family came to mind, his parents more specifically.

Karl curled his lip into a sneer at the thought of his mom and dad. Serenity and Charles Sinclair. He didn't think he'd ever meet anyone like them. And that wasn't a compliment. His parents had hearts colder and as unforgiving as a winter in the Arctic Circle. They hadn't ever tried to understand him, instead asserting their authority over him. They had attempted and failed to govern his life. When they had realized he wouldn't do as they said, they'd thrown him out of the family home. It had been the end of a string of unpleasant incidents that marked his childhood as unhappy and made him into the grudging adult he was today. He hated that they still provoked strong emotion in him. That was what he wished he could control most whenever he considered them.

With a grumble, he set the controls of the shower panel to his preferred temperature and flow rate and turned the water on.

He couldn't control people…but he *could* dampen the effect they had on him. One tactic he used was to push inconsequential encounters out of his mind. Strangers shouldn't warrant his time and effort.

Strangers like the pretty woman from the wedding venue.

He snapped his teeth together hard. Why had he suddenly thought of her?

Even as he berated himself silently, he thought of her again when he stepped under the showerhead. Water pelted over his knotted muscles, ridding him of most

of his tension but not washing away the underlying unease that had grafted onto him at the venue. It started
right about the time he had left the bride and her tour
party behind and found the wedding hall empty. The
only trace his mystery woman had been there was the
swapped vase.

She is a thief, then. Report her and be done with it.

Easier said than done. It was too simple a solution,
and one that didn't appease his jitteriness.

He exited the shower, a towel covering him, and felt
as anxious as he did when he'd walked into his room.
Spotting the crystal decanter on the sideboard in the sitting room, he turned in that direction. Perhaps a drink
would blow the fog from his mind. Karl poured himself
two fingers of brandy and leaned into the burn sliding
smoothly down his throat. Another glass almost had
him believing he was all right.

Dropping his towel from his waist, he dressed me-
thodically, his mind absent and his heart troubled by
the questions he'd likely never have answered now. He
forced himself to concentrate on what mattered most:
seeing that everything went uninterrupted tomorrow.
Today's mistake wouldn't be repeated. He had seen to
that by briefing security to buff up their surveillance
with round-the-clock monitoring, more muscle and a
no-tolerance policy on any other party-crashers.

Even a certain pretty one if she were to show her
face again.

Taking a breath, he battled the instinct to think of
her anymore. What he needed was a distraction. A suit-
able one that would get his mind onto business that was
far more productive.

A glance at his laptop gave him an idea of what he
could occupy himself with. His godmother, Carrie, had

hired him to plan an event for her that would take place in a few months, at the end of December. As she was important to him, he'd poured himself into the project personally. But it had become that much more crucial when Karl had learned Carrie had invited his parents to the event. Since they'd tossed him out of the house, his mother and father hadn't made any effort to speak with him, least of all inquire about his business. What they had wanted was for him and his four siblings to join Sinclair Corp., the family conglomerate in the real estate and construction industries. Only his older brother, Cyrus, had eventually done as their parents had envisioned for their children. His younger sister, Cherelle, lived as a Canadian expat with her husband and children in Qatar. Meanwhile, his younger twin brothers, Solomon and Simon, had moved out for college and managed a thriving social-media presence as lifestyle influencers.

His parents had been less than thrilled. In their eyes, most of their children had grown to be failures. All but Cyrus, who had followed along with their plans like the good little sheep that he was.

They'd cut Karl off from his trust fund—like he had cared. And it had been the same for his siblings.

Although these days he barely kept in touch with his sister and brothers, Karl had known that their mom and dad hadn't been kind to them either, financially. Not that they'd ever displayed any kindness in their lives apart from their annual corporate charity gala and the occasional philanthropic business venture. But he knew that was more for press politics than out of the milk of human kindness.

It was that lack of compassion he blamed for the lack of closeness to his siblings.

On top of training them to be little drones, their parents had gone out of their way to ensure their children knew who their closest competition was in life: each other. All their lives they'd been pitted against one another, from excelling in school grades to being the top in their approved extracurricular activities. More times it was Cyrus, their golden Sinclair heir, that had been raised to be the eyes, ears and mouthpiece of their mom and dad. Tattling, taunting, spying—none of it was out-of-bounds to Cyrus so long as he did as their parents said and reported back any insurgence that Karl and his other siblings might have in mind.

Cyrus had also turned his back on him when their parents had ousted him from the house.

Karl had never forgiven him for it.

I probably won't ever, he thought darkly of his older brother.

He didn't know if Cyrus would be present at their godmother's party, but if he were, he'd be treated as coolly as their parents. There was no love lost between them. Just anger and questions, starting with how Cyrus could be so disloyal to the younger siblings he should have instead protected.

Karl dismissed his useless thinking, knowing he'd get no peace or answers, and considered what his godmother's event could be for him. He was planning it primarily as a labor of love. Carrie had been the parental figure he'd wished he had instead of his own cold, loveless parents. She had encouraged him to move in with her when he'd been tossed out on his ear. He had been a confused, heartbroken twenty-year-old with no home suddenly. She'd paid for his plane ticket from his home in Toronto to Calgary. There, she had opened the door to her warm home and seen that he finished his last two years of college. It was also Carrie who had opened his eyes to his passion in event planning and coordinating. One Christmas, she'd asked him to help her plan a large holiday gathering, and he had found it a real joy to put together the event and oversee its ultimate success. And it was Carrie who had pushed him to open the doors on Heartbeat Events when he'd first confided in her about his initial idea. Without her, he might have turned out to be exactly who his parents had hoped he would become without their support: a nobody and a failure.

He owed Carrie more than one party. He owed her the devotion he'd wished he had gotten from his mom and dad and Cyrus.

Naturally, besides being a gift for his godmother, it was also the perfect chance to finally exact his brand of vengeance on his parents. He would show his mom and dad that he had thrived without their confidence and support. Once they saw he was living well, he'd have the best kind of revenge.

With that thinking in mind, falling into work was easy. He didn't move from the desk even when he placed a call for room service. Finally, a knock on the door turned his attention away from reading his high-priority emails.

Room service was quicker than he'd anticipated.

Relieved that he wouldn't be disturbed again for the evening, Karl answered the door before the second knock came, fully expecting to have his dinner dropped off and to be left alone.

"You," was the first word that forced its way out of his mouth.

The pretty thief from the wedding venue stood outside his suite, and she looked perfectly comfortable disrupting his privacy. His hand gripped the door tighter, his lower jaw rock-hard, and his heart—to his great annoyance—racing faster with what he swore was exhilaration. Pure, unfiltered, lust-ridden *excitement*.

What was wrong with him? He should have been calling Reception and asking for security to be brought up to escort her away. Instead, he was standing there like a statue, watching as she sized him up from head to toe. A strange, hot anticipation pinched at his skin, and his mouth grew dry as he fought for words.

"Who are you?" he all but growled, demanding an answer.

A smile danced over her glossed lips, her loveliness becoming more…lovely.

He nearly rolled his eyes at his cheesy thinking.

Clearly my brain's turning to mush.

Still smiling, she said, "Oh, that's right. We never introduced ourselves. I'm Istarlin Mohamed. Nobody calls me by my full name, though. It's just Lin, normally."

There was nothing normal about this.

He forced composure into his voice—and pushed away thoughts of how delectable her mouth looked when she pursed her lips just so. Biting the words out, he asked, "How did you find me?"

Her smile grew wider. "That part was surprisingly easy."

"Oh, really?" He clenched his teeth, confused as to whether he should be amused or annoyed. First the security at the venue had failed, and now his hotel was seriously flunking in privacy measures too. He was beginning to suspect she had a knack for showing up in places she shouldn't be. Like his hotel room.

"Let me rephrase my question. Why are you here?"

She looked him over, and he wondered what he saw;

her poker face would kill him. "I promised you an explanation, didn't I?"

She had, but he hadn't really expected one. That was his error in judgment.

Feeling her eyes rake over him once again, he stood taller and recalled that not too long ago he'd been strutting around his suite in nothing but a Turkish-cotton towel. Oddly the thought of her catching him in the buff didn't displease him. Even more strangely, he felt disappointed that their second meeting hadn't unfolded in that way.

"Aren't you going to invite me in?"

He pointedly stared at the decorative vessel she was hugging to her chest. "I'd rather just take the vase you stole."

"I told you I'm not a thief. Nothing was stolen."

Karl raised an eyebrow.

She rolled her eyes, something he wasn't used to others doing around him. When he talked, people often listened intently. Maybe he'd been surrounding himself with sycophants. Or maybe this woman marched to her own drum. Again, instead of it upsetting him, the notion intrigued him. Made her that much more interesting.

"What I have to say can be said in the hall too, you know. I have nothing to be embarrassed about." She looked over her shoulder, smiling brightly suddenly. "Did you order room service?"

A hotel staff member pushed a fully stocked meal-service cart toward his suite.

"Is that pilau?" She licked her lips, the slow drag of her pink tongue more enticing than the tantalizing scents wafting from the service cart.

Tipping the hotel employee, Karl said, "That'll be all, thank you."

Once they were alone, he rolled the cart into his room and wasn't surprised when Lin trailed him inside. Uninvited. Realizing that he wouldn't be rid of her *or* his insistent fascination for her, he threw in the towel and gave her what she wanted. An audience.

"Fine. Let's hear this explanation."

Lin paced, not because it helped calm her strung-out nerves but rather because it gave her something to focus on. And this way she wasn't sitting across from him at the dining table and under his intense scrutiny. She didn't think anyone had a right to have such a powerfully commanding aura to them. Well, outside her grandfather.

"Like I said earlier, I was never an intruder. I couldn't be because I know the bride. She's a close friend of mine."

"Why hide from her, then?" He seared her with his implacable gaze.

The mercy he had shown her in the wedding venue was gone in that moment. It was obvious he wanted it all. Every detail that would clear her name in his eyes. She shouldn't have cared what he thought. If she hadn't followed him, would they ever see each other again? Even at the wedding tomorrow, the odds they'd run into each other with Machelle's crazy-long guest list were slim. Yet here she was, invading his private space, with the sole intent of rectifying their first impression of each other.

Mostly his impression of her.

It wouldn't do for him to think she was a thief or an interloper. Not if they would be working together…but she hadn't gotten to that part yet. Also, if she were being honest with herself, she sensed he was a good person.

Despite all his scowling, and the little bit of growling he'd done when he had opened the door to find her there, Lin just knew that under his gruff, coldly smart exterior beat a good heart. With that stout certainty backing her, she had even indulged in looking at him like a woman might her lover. She openly eyed all his yumminess but stopped at outright flirting with him. Because if he didn't flirt back, it'd sink her chances at repairing his opinion of her *and* she could kiss good-bye any chance of working with him.

She gulped quietly and remembered he had asked a question.

"I wasn't hiding from her. It was my grandfather that I was avoiding." Just as she avoided direct eye contact with her wondrously hot stranger and now host. Swallowing nervously, she explained, "It's complicated, but I have my reasons for doing what I did."

"Your grandfather is Salim Mohamed?"

She nodded, knowing what was coming.

"The cement and sugar tycoon of Kenya."

She bobbed her head again, wincing but adding, "Actually, it's the cement and sugar *lord* of Kenya. A subtle difference, *tycoon* and *lord*."

Talking about her grandfather was difficult these days. Though her favorite person in the world, he had been a large part of her distressing soul-searching journey of late.

"So the bride is your friend." Gesturing to the vase she'd placed on the table, he said, "I'm sure the vase has a story too."

"I made it. It's one of my 3D-printed designs." Machelle had been the biggest supporter of her 3D art when Lin had stumbled into the world of printed materials a year ago. Lin had been hooked instantly. So much so that she had sunk a pretty penny into buying studio space for her printers far from her grandfather's luxurious mansion. It was also the studio that had saved her from spending awkward nights at home after arguments with him.

Not that they *had* to argue. All she wanted from him was to hear her out. Why was it so hard for him to understand she wasn't as passionate about cement and sugar as he was? That had to be a qualification for becoming the new chairperson and president of his multimillion-dollar company.

"You created it?" The first note of interest edged his tone as he grasped the vase and considered it with furrowed eyebrows. Tracing his fingers over the thin gold metal strands forming the ornamental container, he asked, "This was made with a printer?"

"A very expensive printer with very pricey material, yes."

"And the bride requested you to make them for her wedding?"

"She's my friend, and I wanted to do something for her."

"Why take your gift away, then?"

"It hadn't printed perfectly." She pointed to the base where the printer had missed a small space in the net of thin, sticklike strands. Hardly noticeable to the untrained eye, but it bugged her to know the mistake existed. Made her feel like the possibility of selling her 3D designs was a stupid fantasy. "I wanted to replace it before anyone noticed the mistake."

"But I caught you," he finished and placed the creation back down. "It also doesn't explain why you're here."

She stopped pacing and exhaled slowly. "You work for the wedding-planning company, right?"

"We do all events, not just weddings."

Lin smiled meekly, the shyness creeping on her faster. This part would be the hardest to say.

I have to try, though.

"You wouldn't happen to be looking for designers to collaborate with, would you? A contractual basis would be fine. It's not like I need worker benefits or anything." Gee. Did she sound shrill and desperate? Yes, and yes.

Tossing shame aside, she continued her rambling. "I can assure you my 3D art works well for other event decor. Table numbering, photo-booth props, cake toppers, name tags and hanging decorations. Even jewelry. I've done a few pieces. Earrings, a necklace and an anklet."

"An anklet," he murmured after her, sliding his hands off the table and standing.

Worrying that she was losing his interest, Lin babbled on. "If that's your thing, yes. But I could see bigger, more important pieces like tiaras for the brides and bow ties and cuff links for the grooms." She looked at him, awed again by the body-slamming desire she experienced the first time she'd seen him—and each time after that. Bald men normally didn't do it for her, outside of the droolworthy god that was Shemar Moore.

But there was a sexy edge to the sharpness of his dark slanted eyebrows and piercing black-brown eyes, the set of his Roman nose, the rosiness of his Cupid's-bow mouth and well-defined, angular cheekbones and clean-shaven jawline. What did it for her best, though, was the thick but well-trimmed black mustache that made her envision kissing him and feeling the rough tickling brush of his facial hair along her upper lip—

Her mouth tingled as if touched.

"I-I hoped you could give me your boss's contact information."

"For a job," he clarified.

Nodding, she held her breath and waited.

He didn't leave her in suspense for long. Following a slight pause, he moved for the serving cart holding his dinner. "I'll admit, I'm intrigued. I would have to hear more, though."

Had she heard him correctly? "Wait. You're the boss?"

"I am."

That...wasn't what she expected at all. But it suited his authoritative attitude. And it explained why he'd been so presumptive and bossy with her, and why he had cared that she might be a gate-crasher at the venue.

"Is that a problem?" He faced her now, his plate in hand and a brow raised in challenge.

"No." But her stomach churned from the news. From delight or mortification, she didn't know.

"As I said, I'd want to know more of what this partnership would look like. Seeing as your friend's wedding is tomorrow, I'll be busy. My only free slot would be the day after tomorrow. It'd have to be the morning, as I have a flight home later in the day."

Lin bobbed her head, processing his flurry of instructions slowly and quietly.

"Is that all?" he asked, his tone matching his neutral expression.

Understanding she'd outstayed her welcome, and not wanting to irritate him to the point of canceling their business meeting, she hurried for the exit. But she whirled back to him in the hall, feeling him close behind her. "I didn't catch your name."

"It's Karl," he told her before handing her the vase she'd almost left behind in her haste.

"Karl." She tested his name on her tongue and liked the feel of it. "It's a pleasure to meet you, and hopefully it'll be a pleasure to work with you too." She sounded as nervous as she felt. And the nerves continued to assail her as she left the hotel and caught a taxi. She wondered if it would be like this all the time, and if so, whether she'd taken on a greater challenge where Karl was concerned.

CHAPTER THREE

It was an unusual and frustrating sensation for him to be nervous, but Karl couldn't deny that he was a little on edge about this meeting with Istarlin Mohamed.

Lin, he corrected in his mind, recalling that she'd seemed to prefer the nickname. He found it irritating too that he liked the sound of it. That he found her name as beautiful as she was.

He had to stop thinking that way, though. If this meeting panned out well, she could be working with him. What she didn't need was her boss secretly lusting after her. He wouldn't make her uncomfortable.

Or complicate my own life, for that matter, he thought with stony finality.

All he had to do was remind himself that she wasn't any different from the countless people he met in his line of work. Through Heartbeat Events, he'd had the pleasure of planning and coordinating events of elite caliber for individuals from loftier walks of life: popular celebrities and star athletes, dignitaries from the world over and inspirational activists. Lin was no different than the well-heeled heiresses he'd met before. They had been stunning in looks and dress too.

But he hadn't wanted to haul any of those other heiresses up against his chest and kiss them on their prettily glossed lips, now, had he?

Karl blew out a slow, strained breath full of his frustration. Fine. He was attracted to her more fiercely than he had felt about anyone in a long while. He could remember only one other time that he'd experienced a similar force of physical desire for another.

Isaiah.

The name passed through his mind more easily than it had before. Soon as he thought of his past lover, he pushed the comparison aside. Lin wasn't Isaiah. And this wasn't the same attraction—at least he wouldn't allow it to flourish in the way that it had with his college ex-boyfriend.

Cooling his nerves and his heated lustful thinking for the woman he was meeting, Karl concentrated on his surroundings.

Nairobi had the same hyped-up energy as his home in Calgary. The East African city was alive in its own right. The buildings breathing and the paved roads thumping with life force. The sky was mostly blue again, and the weather temperate for September. It helped calm him knowing that he didn't have to worry about the weather on his short trip there. Even if he did, he wouldn't be able to control the climate like the other factors in his life. Although, he wasn't doing any better there.

Like the climate, I can't seem to control what I feel for Lin.

Ignoring the confused desperation in that thought, he realized he was closing in on the meeting place.

"Right there," he instructed the driver, the GPS on his phone pinging with the alert that he was close to his destination. When the cabbie told him that he couldn't get any closer, Karl paid his fare and exited the car, figuring a short walk wouldn't hurt. But almost as soon as he opened the car door, he had to slam it shut when an auto rickshaw roared past dangerously close. The cab driver had a chuckle at his expense, leaving Karl even more irate than how he'd woken up. Crossing the street more carefully, he made it to the overly populated sidewalk and steeled himself for the squeeze through pedestrians thronging all corners of the bustling neighborhood.

Reading again the text Lin had sent him, he followed her guideposts to a two-story building with faded signage and an empty commercial space for lease on the first level. The front entrance was locked. He tried the buzzer, his impatience heightening the uncomfortable and odd anxiety he'd been battling all the way here.

"Yes?" Lin's voice rang like birdsong through the small, stuffy enclosure. He hadn't noticed how pleasing her voice was.

Gritting his teeth and clenching his fists, he barked, "It's Karl. I'm here for our meeting."

She didn't reply, but a second later a tonal buzz indicated that she'd unlocked the entrance for him.

The stairs were the only option. It was a short flight to the second level, his path barred by a door. He rapped his knuckles on the door sharply and rattled the metal frame.

Lin's flushed face was the first thing he saw when she threw open the door, her brown cheeks rosier, and her eyes bright and lively, her smile shining as hot as the early September morning. "Oops, I lost track of the time. I hope you haven't had trouble with directions."

She gestured for him to come through, talking a mile

a minute and with a chirpiness that no amount of coffee could give him, not even on his best of days.

He hadn't seen her since yesterday when he'd glimpsed her briefly at her friend's wedding. They both had been busy: Lin celebrating with her friend, while he ensured that the reception started and ended on the same high note. He'd indicated they wouldn't have a chance to speak all night, and it had been true. But now, with the wedding and their commitments out of the way, they had nothing but the rest of the morning with each other. No interruptions in sight. And later he'd catch his long first-class flight back home.

"Let me just grab my purse, and we can head out." She cast him another sunny smile and then flitted off to do as she said, leaving him in the large, open space to explore and get a feel for who she was. Boxy industrial windows allowed a generous amount of sunlight into the unit and lit up the darker cement walls. The lightly varnished hardwood flooring shone like new. Large machines were neatly arranged behind a workbench. He walked over to what he assumed were the 3D printers. They had all sorts of nuts and bolts and looked more complicated than he'd thought printers ought to be. He recalled how impassioned she'd looked discussing her 3D art two days ago in his hotel room. Now he envisioned her toiling away in the space and with nothing but her craft to keep her company. The feeling felt familiar. It had been that familiarity that had him curious enough to venture out to meet her rather than canceling on her at the very last minute.

Before he delved into the reasoning behind that thought, he spun away from her printers at the sound of clicking heels on the wood floors.

Lin emerged out of the only other room in the space,

her face still flushed and a purse in her hands. Hooking a thumb over her shoulder, she asked, "Did you want to see some of the pieces I have stored away?"

He followed her into what she was using as a storage space…and a bedroom, apparently. A pillow and a blanket lay on a leather recliner squeezed into a corner of the room. It almost appeared as if she'd just woken up. She hadn't even had the time to fold her blanket.

Reading his thoughts, she said, "I work late sometimes. Too late for me to travel home and worry about waking my grandfather. So I just stay here."

Karl supposed it explained the makeshift sleeping quarters. He'd had his bouts of working late into the night, so he spared his judgment on her.

Casting his gaze from the sofa to the metal shelves lining the other side of the room, he was awed by all the items she'd produced. The shelves were laden with all sorts of different pieces in varying sizes, colors and even textures.

"Silver?" He picked up a palm-sized owl figurine that had caught his eye. The detailing work on the figure was precise and exquisite.

"Yes. It's a paperweight. It was my first attempt at printing and casting a mold for sterling silver." She glanced away shyly and said, "I don't think it turned out that great."

Karl stared at her, sensing that she wasn't fishing for compliments but that she truly believed that she'd fallen short of excellence when nothing could be further from the truth. Without thinking, he ventured an opinion.

"I've never been big on beginner's luck. That's just a lazy way of saying you're good at what you're doing. And, clearly, you have a strong talent for what you do."

Their eyes met, and a spasm of electrified lust shot

through him. He stiffened from head to toe and clutched onto her well-made silver paperweight like it was a life-line. It was hard to tell what she was thinking or feel-ing: her face gave nothing away.

Then she blinked, smiled and moved for the door. "We can talk more outside. I don't want to keep you any longer than I have already."

The momentary respite he'd found in Lin's studio van-ished when he set foot outside with her by his side.

"Is it always like this, or have we hit the tourist patch of the city?" Karl hadn't made it a point to research Nairobi beyond its temperature and climate. He had wanted to dress practically. Tourism hadn't been a con-sideration.

Lin grinned at him. "Eastleigh is always like this. Open day and night, business at all hours, and business brings people."

He grunted, figuring he'd have to get used to the jos-tling bodies all around them as he kept up with her pace. She walked with purpose. And he had no doubt that he could rest easy and let her lead him to their next desti-nation. It was strange for him to allow someone else to take control. He always preferred remaining in charge, knowing what could happen when power and control had been used against him. His parents had abused his trust enough times to brand the lesson into him. When-ever Karl wanted to do anything for himself, they were always there to remind him that not only should he lis-ten to them but that without them he would amount to nothing. That he'd *be* nothing.

Tucking aside the unpleasant thoughts about his mom and dad before they fully resurfaced, he concentrated on his surroundings and on the gorgeous woman who was walking alongside him. What he didn't want to think about was the contradictions in his behavior. Didn't want to contemplate what Lin had to do with the uncharacteristic changes he'd been dealing with when he was around her.

It didn't stop him from sneaking glances at her.

She sensed his stare and locked eyes with him. "Did you want a quick walking tour before we head to the restaurant? I know you're leaving Nairobi by the end of the day, but it'd be a shame to miss the city."

They'd decided their meeting could happen over breakfast. The idea of using his time efficiently always appealed to him. He appreciated that Lin felt the same way.

"A walking tour sounds good."

She beamed at that, falling into her role of impromptu tour guide with a graceful ease. He followed her closely as she pointed to the places they passed. To his immediate right, the gated sandy-stoned building with large open doors and a blue domed spire was a well-visited mosque in the area. The row of shops to her left were largely owned by Somali immigrants and locals who formed an overwhelmingly large part of the population in Eastleigh.

"And up ahead we'll catch the *matatu* out of Eastleigh and to the restaurant."

Dust swirled up from the corners of the sidewalk and flooded his lungs with a grainy sensation. He coughed, and she pulled a plastic baggie full of masks from her purse. She handed him one. "Newcomers might be irritated by the dust. It's harder on your lungs than it is on ours."

"It's everywhere," he remarked from behind the

safety of his mask, his eyes still stinging from the sandy grains in the air.

"Eastleigh wasn't like this always. My grandfather tells me it was much greener when he was a young boy." Her accent was soft but pronounced, and her voice lyrical and sweet to his ears. He could close his eyes and listen to her talk all day—

Karl pulled the brake on his thinking. They had come together for business. He wasn't in the market for romantic entanglements. Certainly not with a woman he'd not only just met but whose services he was considering hiring for his company. She couldn't be more off-limits right then.

If a forbidden workplace romance didn't put him off, all he had to do was recall that he'd compared his instant and powerful attraction to her to what he'd had with his only serious lover, Isaiah.

And it hadn't ended well with Isaiah.

No, it hadn't, and though his heartbreak had passed when his ex-boyfriend had dumped him, the scar of it rested atop the emotional wounds his parents had left him with as well. All solid reminders that he couldn't control anyone—not the people he loved and not love itself from inflicting its damage on him.

He wouldn't add Lin to that mess, out of regard for her and as protection for himself.

Unaware of his inner turmoil, she continued with her tour. "Eventually Eastleigh became a business center, and with that the original residents of this enclave were pushed out, as were the trees and any greenery. All of that replaced by buildings, buildings and more buildings." She gestured to the infrastructure crammed into every available space in the area. If there had been green pastures here once, there was no indication of them now. "But the people are friendly and hardworking, and I couldn't have found a better place or price for my studio."

Just as she said that, a young man called to her from one of the shops they were passing.

"Lin, how have you been?"

Lin stopped to chat with him in another language. Karl gave them space and seized the chance to study her undisturbed. She had changed her hair yesterday for the wedding. Her sleek bob had become a wealth of silken raven-black coils she'd tempered with a large butterfly clip at the back of her head. She had on a simple white T-shirt with designer straight crop jeans and slip-on leather sandals that had him admiring her nude-colored toenails. When she laid her hand on the man's arm, a sourness flavored Karl's mouth. He recognized it as jealousy—which was wildly off base. He didn't know her. Had no claim to her. And if she were flirting with the other man, it had nothing to do with him.

But that rationality didn't erase the jealousy. It lingered like the dust riding the air. An irritant that perturbed him more deeply than he thought possible. He folded his arms, clenched his jaws and shifted his weight from foot to foot. The more he watched them, the more his bitterness became apparent.

Pleasantries exchanged, Lin gave the man a wave and fell back into line with Karl.

"As I was saying, the neighbors are a huge appeal to the area. Everyone's just trying to make a living here, and sometimes a little help along the way can make a difference."

"You seemed close," he observed, irked that he was still recalling her hand on the other man's arm.

"He helped find my studio."

"You weren't speaking Swahili." He'd been listening to the locals enough to recognize that she wasn't speaking the language.

"I'm ethnically Somali, but my family's lived in Kenya for decades, and it's the only home I've known."

They reached the end of the road, and Lin guided him to a white-hooded, colorfully painted bus. Political and social logos splashed the bus's exterior in harmonious graffiti art. He'd seen nothing like it before. "The *matatu*," she said, climbing the steps into it ahead of him. She paid the driver and grabbed a seat. He followed, realizing that she'd footed his fare as well. Squeezing into the bus seat with her had them shoulder to shoulder and closer than ever. The option of snagging the empty bench seat across from them had struck him, but his feet had carried him to her, and now that he was seated it would have been too awkward to move away.

At first, he looked everywhere but at her. The interior of the vehicle was painted as artfully inside as it was outside. TV screens were mounted above the seats, and the lights and sound system were in sync with the music that thumped out of the speakers. When he'd had his fill of gawking at the newness of his environment, he had nothing else to do but to strike up a conversation.

"Why 3D printing?"

A thoughtful look crossed her face before she answered, "I fell into it, and it makes me happy."

"You're good at it, too." That was no empty compliment either. From what he had seen of her finished products in her studio, she had talent and the skills to match. And there was no doubt in his mind she had the enthusiasm if she were willing to sleep rough in her studio. It led him to the question he'd been turning over in his mind since she had come to him in his hotel the day before yesterday. "You seem to have everything you need to make this work right here. Why are you looking for a job elsewhere?"

A pensive look crossed her face. "It's a long story better told over a meal."

CHAPTER FOUR

THE RESTAURANT WASN'T any different than it had been the last time Lin had visited—which wasn't too long ago. The menu had the same offerings, and the items she usually ordered were all priced similarly. Same four walls and wooden tables with plastic-covered chairs. The exact same view of Kenyatta Avenue, the central business district's main street, from where they sat under the canopy of the restaurant's patio.

Yes, everything's the same...except him. Karl.

Being close to him and having that intense personality of his homed in on her had her stomach in knots. She blushed furiously under his scrutinizing gaze. And though the dry autumn breeze hit her cheeks more coolly under the shade, it didn't quell the bubbling heat of her nerves entirely. And the anxiousness and physical awareness of their proximity became worse after she and Karl placed their orders with the waiter.

He sipped at his ice water, his eyes holding her gaze the whole time. "I've been trying a lot of Kenyan dishes."

She happily glommed on to the small talk, encouraging him with a smile and a nod. This she could do. Food was a safer topic. Less personal. "Have you found a favorite dish yet?"

"The pilau is something I'd like to recreate in my kitchen."

"It's a staple. I've tried it both with and without the meat and potatoes, with plenty of spices and very little seasoning, and it's always tasty. You can't go wrong with it."

"I would've ordered it if you hadn't influenced me to try something new." Then the corners of his mouth kicked up into the briefest but sexiest smile. There and gone by the time she blinked. She couldn't even be certain he had smiled.

She discreetly swiped her clammy palms down her legs. Taking a gulp of her glass of water, she worked around the lump in her throat to speak. "You'll like the meat stew, *mukimo*, and chapatis."

"I'll take your word for it." Again, she swore he flashed her a smile, but his face switched back to his default stoic expression too quickly.

When their order arrived, Lin had thought they were in the clear. She didn't relish the idea of speaking around a full mouth. But Karl seemed only to have gotten started.

"You never answered my question," he said, his fork scooping up the traditional green side dish of *mukimo* on his plate. He didn't blink when he popped the mixture of potato, peas and corn into his mouth. Just as fluidly, he tore off a piece of the chapati as she'd done and scooped up the meat stew on his plate with it. She sat and watched him eat, his stare never leaving her face.

Tearing her gaze away, she grasped her water glass and drank before replying. "What did you want to know again?"

"Just why you're looking to work someplace else.

From what I've seen of your studio, you could start your own business."

"That's the goal." Though, she wished it were as simple as that.

In theory, she should have had no problem leaping into being a business owner. She had the passion, the plan she'd been working on for over the last six months, and money wasn't an issue either. She was an heiress to her grandfather's fortune. His only grandchild. And she'd known most her life that she would inherit his wealth, properties and other assets. She also knew she was the only choice her grandfather had ever had in mind to lead his company. That kind of pressure put a lot of weight on her shoulders.

A ton of weight on my heart, too, she thought sadly.

"But it's complicated," she added.

"You've said that before," he reminded her.

She recalled that she had, in his hotel suite. "I…have expectations on me. You met my grandfather."

The thought of her grandfather's powerful personality sharing a space with Karl's same level of energy and intensity made her a little dizzy. Luckily she didn't have to worry about that with Karl on his way home, and her grandfather busy planning out the rest of her life for her. At least careerwise. He hadn't shown too much interest in her romantic life. Not that he had to when there was an assumption she would marry well. And there wasn't a lack of men who fit that tall bill working for her grandfather.

"This isn't a public thing, so I hope you'll keep it between us," she began.

He soaked another piece of chapati, the unleavened flatbread passing his thick dusky-brown lips and mesmerizing her with the simple action. She gave her head a quick shake, patted her mouth with a napkin to be sure she hadn't dribbled anything and picked up her train of thought.

"My grandfather's planning his retirement." He hadn't announced it yet. And it wouldn't happen overnight by any means. But she understood his retirement was in the near future. In two or three years, her life could change drastically. With him stepping down, she was expected to take over, and it scared her because it wasn't what she wanted.

"And you're his heir," said Karl, unsurprisingly connecting the dots and saving her the trouble of explaining that part.

She leaped into the rest of it with an ease that should have startled her. At least, it gave her pause to wonder who he was for her to feel so comfortable confiding in him. "My grandfather set his mind on it when he adopted me."

"Your parents?" he asked.

"My dad passed away, and my mom had filed for divorce and left us before he got sick." It popped out of her mouth, almost as easily as everything else had. She didn't talk about it often. Not because she hated to but because she didn't know what to make of it. She hadn't been in control of either her father dying when she'd been eight or her mother walking out on them when she'd been only two years old. If it hadn't been for her grandfather, she'd have been an orphan. Her dad had no siblings. She hadn't met any distant cousins, uncles or aunts. Only her grandfather. Though he hadn't ever showed how hard it had been on him to lose his son and suddenly be caring for his young granddaughter, Lin could only imagine the difficulties he'd had to bear quietly and stoically. He hadn't had the luxury of falling apart on her. She'd have been too young to understand and was grieving the loss of her dad.

As she grew older, she'd learned that her grandfather had lost his wife to childbirth a long time ago. So not only had he been handling the tragic passing of his wife but he had also shouldered the burden all parents feared in the premature death of his son.

Sometimes, when he thought she wasn't watching, she'd notice a distant, sorrowful look in his eyes. She noticed it happened more whenever she mentioned her dad. Without needing to ask explicitly, she knew he had to be mourning both her late grandmother and father.

Even with all her understanding and compassion, Lin couldn't know fully what he was feeling. She hadn't felt the love that he had once had and lost, especially his love for his wife.

She hadn't fallen in love yet. She'd dated, sure. But had she loved any of her dates? No. Some had been pleasant enough for her to want to see again, but she hadn't ever felt that spark, that bone-deep, soul-charging connection that fairy tales were all about, and it had steered her from many relationships that might have turned out to be...decent. Maybe not romances that were mindlessly passionate, but she could have had a companionable partnership with someone by now.

Deep down, if she were being more open with herself, she was a bit scared of falling in love. She'd seen how love had brought misery to her grandfather, and to herself when she'd lost her dad.

She hadn't wondered too much about her mom, but a small, secret part of her questioned whether her mother had stopped loving her all these years—or had it been that she had never loved her from the start? Lin knew she could go see her and ask. After Lin's dad passed away, her mom hadn't shown up for the funeral, but she would keep in touch with Lin's grandfather. For what? Lin hadn't ever asked or pursued the subject. She'd been just as fearful then to confirm that her mom might not want her. Being twenty-five now hadn't changed that. In some ways, she was still that sad, confused eight-year-old standing by her stern-faced grandfather as she said goodbye to her dad one last time.

She blinked sharply, the stark image of her dad's burial mound vanishing, and the restaurant and Karl calling her back from her reverie.

"Sorry for your loss," he said deeply and clearly.

Reflex kicked in, and she painted on a smile. "It was a long time ago."

"Still. Losing family is a challenge whose effects can ripple through the rest of our lives." Karl's response was unique. It fit his whole look and attitude, or what she'd experienced of him thus far. He looked at ease in his dove-gray polo shirt and slim-fit chinos, like she hadn't added her hectic past to their menu. Leaning back in his chair, he steepled his hands over his flat stomach and quietly assessed her.

He did that for a while before he remarked, "You have something to prove."

A blush stole over her cheeks again. It was hard not to be embarrassed when he had read her correctly. It was also a relief that she didn't have to explain herself. She'd been doing enough of that lately with her grandfather, trying to make him see her perspective. Having Karl understand her so readily was nice.

More than nice, she thought warmly.

Also, it got them to the heart of why she'd offered her 3D designing and printing services to his event-management company. "I love doing what I do in my studio.

But if I were to open a business someday, I wouldn't be able to run my grandfather's company."

"Where does my company fit into your plan?"

"I want to see if I could do this professionally. I've had a few orders from friends, and then there was Machelle's wedding, but I haven't done anything large-scale beyond that. Your company's well-established, and it caters to clients who have the pockets to host big parties. That means plenty of network opportunities and a chance to showcase my designs."

"You've given it a lot of thought," he drawled.

Cheeks still flushed and hot, Lin murmured, "Consider it my pitch."

He lapsed into a thoughtful silence and then said, "I do have an upcoming project that could work."

She sat up in her chair, pushed aside her plate and bobbed her head eagerly for him to continue.

"My godmother is renewing her marriage vows to her husband. The event is Kwanzaa-themed, so it's scheduled for the end of December."

"Kwanzaa?"

"I'm not surprised you haven't heard of it. It's a seven-day, pan-African celebration that's almost exclusively observed in North America. It's supposed to uplift the African culture and community over the weeklong festivities. It also happens to be my godmother's favorite holiday besides Christmas.

"I'd require a quick turnaround and a guarantee of quality from you. Also, the winter holiday season is our busiest, so we'll need to time-manage accordingly."

"Okay," she agreed, prepared to work around a tighter schedule. This was all a part of doing business. Working under all sorts of pressure and time constraints to deliver high-caliber and uniform goods.

"One more thing. You'd have to move offices."

She jerked back. "What?"

"I prefer my team work closely, side by side, and so I would need you to temporarily join us in Calgary. That is, you'd be agreeing to move to Canada for a short while to complete the work."

She sucked in her lips, her brows knitting together. In all her planning, Lin hadn't factored in relocation. What he said made sense. He'd likely want to oversee what she was creating and have a say in her designs for his godmother's event. Though she did have in mind negotiating wiggle room for her creative license, she didn't think that mattered right then.

"Canada," she echoed softly.

"Canada," he repeated with his usual blank expression. Familiar but not reassuring.

"I'd have to think about it…" She trailed off when her phone buzzed in her purse. Pulling it out, she stood with the phone in hand and muttered, "Sorry, I have to take this. It's my grandfather."

The call was quick. Her grandfather wanted to know whether she'd be willing to host a last-minute business dinner for some of his colleagues. It was why she had hesitated to agree to Karl's parameters. Going to Canada meant leaving her grandfather behind to fend for himself. He was pushing eighty, and though he was fit as a fiddle, he was slowing down. Not to mention he'd long since relied on her for day-to-day tasks from housekeeping duties to hosting dinner parties. Who would tell the chef to prepare his pilau the way he liked it? Who would cohost his work dinners when she left for Canada?

She rubbed her temples as she walked back to their

table. Losing her appetite, she picked at her food before pushing her plate away for good.

"If I agree, I will need a week to prepare, at the very least," she said, firm about not budging that deadline. If he thought she was being unreasonable, then she didn't want to work with him.

It was a relief when he agreed. "That's fine. Take two weeks, even. I'll need to file for a rush work permit and prepare a space for you at my office."

His office. It sounded so official already. A skitter of pleasure raced through her as she beamed at him. Some of that pleasure had to do with the rogue twinkle in his darkly mysterious eyes.

She couldn't help teasing him. "Guess I should be glad you accused me of stealing." Awkward though it had been, without it they wouldn't have had the opportunity to meet like this.

Lin didn't expect the atmosphere to change.

She saw him frown, and she frowned too. "What is it?" Was he having second thoughts about working with her already?

"I shouldn't have accused you of stealing." A muscle in his jaw leaped, once, twice. "I'm sorry," he said gruffly, though she inferred the roughness to his tone had more to do with the fact that he wasn't used to apologizing. He didn't seem the sort to admit he'd made a mistake. *Alpha* she'd label him, but not to the point that he had her wanting to hurl a drink into his face. His apology rang as genuine and heartfelt. He was sorry. And she had already figured he'd suffered through some embarrassment for leaping to conclusions.

"You were trying to protect my friend's wedding."

"I could have handled the…*situation* better."

She grinned and leaned in. "I won't disagree there."

He really did smile then. Shocking her into a breathless state from one heartbeat to the next. He was hot as his intense, brooding self, but he was something else entirely when his lips pulled back and his teeth gleamed brilliantly at her. The only thing that stopped her from drooling madly and babbling incoherently was the waiter choosing that perfect moment to save her with their bill.

But then the universe wrenched the save out of her hands when she and Karl reached for the bill at the same time. Her palm stilled atop his hand, her eyes growing large, and her face hotter than Nairobi's dry seasonal climate. Belatedly she yanked her hand away. By then it was too late. Judging by the way he slowly lifted the bill and plucked his wallet out to pay for their meal and tip the waitstaff and then some, he'd felt the same arresting spark that she had.

Her heart thumped faster in reaction to his heavy look, and her mouth went dry. She was attracted to him, but attraction hadn't ever left her feeling so vulnerable before. Then again, none of her previous boyfriends or dates could ever replicate Karl's naturally hooded eyes, sculpted facial structure, slightly bent nose and pouty brown lips. None of them would have dared to accuse her of stealing a vase, one that belonged to her or otherwise. And not one of them would've inspired her to blush several times in their presence.

She shouldn't indulge her crush on him.

Karl was a good-looking man. Perfect eye candy. But she didn't know him. And if she got to know him, it would be as business partners. She was doing this so she could prove to herself and to her grandfather that forging her own career path was viable. It was the least she could do before he decided to step down and name her as his successor.

Besides, attraction led to attachment, and from there a natural progression to affection...

And love, she thought.

She wasn't ready to fall in love. Not with anyone. More than that, Lin didn't want to tempt love into existence with what felt like a harmless crush on Karl now. She'd have to fight this attraction for him. Snap a lid on it before she signed up to work with him.

Outside the restaurant, Karl flagged a taxi that was parked nearby.

"When's your flight?"

"I have a couple of hours before I have to check out, but there are a few work-related tasks I have to complete before then." He stared down at her, pensively she might even say if she could read his facial expression more easily. "We should exchange numbers. Keep in touch, so I know what your decision will be."

"I know what my decision is," she said, biting back a sigh and punching her number into his phone. "I just have some things to tie up, and then I'm coming to Canada."

"Then, I'll see you in Canada." With a final look, he swiveled on his heels and caught his cab. She watched him until the traffic swallowed him up and he was out of sight. Alone, she walked a few blocks, deep in thought, before her phone buzzed. She perked up when she saw the message was from Karl.

Just making sure you save my number.

Giddier than she ought to feel, she messaged him back.

It's saved now. Have a safe flight.

She sent the text before she could overthink its simplicity.

When her phone vibrated a second time, she nearly dropped it from the hurry to check her messages.

It should be interesting to work with you.

Karl's reply wasn't anything special. He was being polite. She got that. Did it stop her heart from knocking more wildly against her ribs? Nope. Lin pressed the phone to her chest, forcing calming breaths in and out through her nose before giving a little victorious squeal. Then spying a free taxi ahead, she hailed it and gave the driver her home address. She had to speak to her grandfather. The sooner she caught him up to speed about the plan she'd hatched with Karl, the quicker she could book a flight to Canada.

CHAPTER FIVE

Two weeks later

THE SOUND OF rain pelting his office windows melded with the noise of his fingers clacking the keyboard. Karl sent the email to a client and opened another one sitting in his drafts folder. *Only ten more things on my to-do list.* That was what he'd thought an hour ago. Then an hour had passed. And another. Finally, when he looked up from his dual computer monitors and stretched the kinks out of his neck and shoulders, he realized the rain had stopped and the sky had darkened not from a storm but in nightfall.

Dusk had quietly slipped through his office. He hadn't even known when he'd flicked on his desk lamp to compensate for the loss of gray daylight. Standing, he took a moment to gaze out the wide picture window behind his desk. Snow had fallen intermittently the past few days with the cold rains he'd grown accustomed to this time of year. The city had one foot in autumn and the other toeing into winter already. But snowstorms were common in October, and there were a couple of days left of September.

He filled his lungs and sighed slowly, as much needing something to do as occupying his mind.

Because tonight wasn't like any other night. In approximately an hour, Lin's flight would be arriving from Europe.

It was tough to admit, but she'd been on his mind since he had last seen her. He accepted the strong attraction he felt for her. On top of that, he noted some similarities between them. He empathized with her plight when it was obvious that she wanted to break free of her grandfather's hold on her. She clearly loved the old man, but she'd have to decide for herself if that love was holding her back. He'd been forced to make a similar decision after his parents had left him with no choice. If they hadn't pushed him out of the proverbial nest, he might never have realized how unhappy he'd been.

She was talented. He'd seen it for himself. It had been enough to impress him into hiring her. It'd be a waste if Lin couldn't see it or do anything about it. But it was neither his journey to take nor his decision to make. The choice was her own.

No matter how much he suddenly wanted to intervene.

On a grudging note, he supposed it was hard to turn one's back on family. At least it appeared that way for her. He was the last person to understand what that felt like. Severing ties with his family had been exactly the thing he'd needed to do to discover himself.

He cleared his mind and then turned to clear his desk. Normally he'd work for long stretches well into the evening, but he'd planned to meet Lin at the airport. She had kept him posted via texts, which was how he knew she'd be arriving shortly, and that cut his time at the office. Karl found he wasn't bothered by the disruption to his schedule. He didn't know what to make of it. Even after he'd had some distance, whenever he thought of Lin his skin seemed to grow all hot and tense. His attraction to her was obvious. But what he couldn't understand was why he was allowing it to affect him as much as it did. It wasn't even like he wanted to date her. He absolutely couldn't, now that she'd be working with him.

That didn't stop his body from reacting so intensely to the merest thought of her.

He'd considered scratching the itch that was building inside him. Dating seriously wasn't something he had done since college.

Since Isaiah.

Isaiah had been his first and only serious lover. They had dated through college after meeting in one of their first-year courses. It had started as a quickly formed friendship. They'd just clicked so perfectly, their values and goals aligning. And then one night in Karl's cramped dorm as they crammed for a final together, Isaiah had kissed him, and he'd found that it felt right. That *they* felt right together. They'd dated through college and even made plans for their future. Plans that included buying their first home together, living out their dreams, supporting each other through good times and bad. Marriage had been mentioned a few times, but they'd been two hopelessly in-love kids. Karl had been happy. He'd met Isaiah's family, and they were exactly the opposite of what he thought families were like. He had only known what *his* parents had been like, what his relationship with *his* siblings had devolved into: bitterness, rivalry, jealousy. With Isaiah and his family, he'd finally gotten to see just how unnaturally cold and loveless his upbringing had been at the hands of his parents.

Just when he thought he could escape it all, when his parents had kicked him out, and he could be with

Isaiah just as he had envisioned through their college years, Isaiah pulled the rug out from under him by suggesting they break up.

He'd been gutted then. Torn up about what he'd done wrong.

Isaiah had said he couldn't handle the gloomy person Karl had apparently become after his parents had turned him out of the house.

He closed his eyes and conjured his ex-lover's grim face as he'd said, "You're not the same person I fell in love with. I can't seem to make you happy, and I don't know what will."

Karl snapped his eyes open and gnashed his teeth at the memory and the pain it still caused him.

That was behind him now. The takeaway being that he couldn't be bothered to give love another chance, not when all it had done was hurt him. Moreover, he didn't *need* love. He was a grown man, well into his thirties. He'd gotten used to casual hookups with trusted lovers. Women and men who weren't looking for anything serious, but who also wouldn't use him for his money and business prestige. The last thing he desired was his company's name and his reputation being dragged through the mud for an indiscretion.

He'd been lucky that all his past lovers had been discreet.

He should call one of them soon. But every time he went to, he would stop shy of going through with it. Something was clearly wrong with him. And he'd remedy it soon as he knew exactly what it was. Karl jutted his jaw as he packed his embossed leather briefcase.

A knock on his office door grabbed his attention.

When he called out for the person to come in, the door opened and his godmother sashayed in, looking as vibrant as the vase of flowers sitting atop his glass-topped coffee table in the seating area of his office. She wore a sunshine-yellow pantsuit under her tangerine wrap coat, her string of polished pearls the only thing that was understated. Even her Moschino purse was loud and cartoonish. Patting her braided updo, she shrugged her shoulders at him and gave the most innocent smile.

"I thought I'd check in on my favorite godson."

"Auntie Carrie," he greeted her, with his jaw just a little harder and that knot of muscles between his shoulder blades more bound up.

He channeled his exasperation into something productive, like walking over to hang up her coat. He knew his godmother too well to relax and treat this like any normal visit. It was never that simple when Carrie dropped in unannounced. She was busy running her own thriving business. Her gift shop kept her preoccupied. It didn't hold her back from nosing into his personal life. If they didn't have the close relationship they did, Karl would have been more exasperated than he was.

If he didn't know he loved her like a mother, he'd have turned her out of his office.

"I'm surprised to see you." He led her to the creamy white leather sofa and grabbed one of the two black velvet barrel chairs across from her.

"Stefon is watching over the shop in my place," she explained breezily. Her retired husband was holding down the fort for them. "I told him he should be resting, but he insists that staying cooped up indoors is doing him in." She threw up her hands and blew a huffy breath. "Men. Stubborn when they're young, and impossible when they're old and graying."

But even as she said it, her eyes softened, and her words held none of the irritation they should. It was how Karl knew she didn't mean anything she said about the love of her life.

Eight months ago, Stefon had had triple bypass surgery to ward off a second heart attack after the first one had nearly stolen his life. Karl had been there for his godmother. Watched the horror of a near death suck the color and vibrancy out of her. He'd had trouble recognizing her during that time. Trouble understanding how anyone could take that risk with love and then pick up and continue on like it was nothing when the terror passed, and all was right as rain again.

On the one hand, Carrie and her husband were exactly what he'd thought he had once wanted. A marriage, a family and the kind of happiness that was a simple extension of loving and being loved in return. But then he thought of his parents: their marriage was so unlike what Carrie and Stefon had. Charles and Serenity had married as part of a business arrangement. It had been a union of convenience on both sides. A vow of commerce rather than of love. Charles Sinclair was the heir and CEO of a multimillion-dollar construction company; Serenity was the chairperson of her own family legacy in real estate. They were both rare Black business moguls in their respective industries, so it made sense for them to marry and unite their powerful backgrounds.

From the outside it sounded practical. In practice it had been a disaster. They hadn't grown to love each other over that time. Decades together and they still were frosty to one another. In fact, the only time he could recall his parents ever agreeing on something was how they chose to raise their children. Unfortunately his parents believed it was enough putting them into expensive private schools, hiring nannies and tutors, and using their money and public standing to open what they considered were the so-called right doors for Karl and his siblings when they moved onto college and, later, the workforce. Demonstrating concepts to their kids like kindness, decency and love were extraneous to his parents.

He'd known that he didn't want their loveless relationship—not for all the money in the world.

But he also now knew—after all he'd gone through with Isaiah—that he didn't want the kind of love that Carrie and Stefon had either. It was just as equally terrifying to be in a passionless romance as it was to fall so deeply and devastatingly in love that the loss of that love could ruin him forever.

He didn't know how his godmother endured it.

Carrie jarred him back into the present with a little cough and a sly smile. "I believe we have our special guest arriving."

He'd briefed Carrie about Lin. Once his godmother had heard about the unique three- dimensional art Lin could create, she had shown interest in working with her. Just as he'd suspected she would. But even with the excitement she'd displayed, Karl hadn't expected that alone had brought Carrie around to his office, and so late when his team were likely heading out for the day.

"She's flying in, yes." He hoped that would be all. Sorely mistaken, he settled back in his seat when he noted a spark of interest lighting his godmother's eyes. The first sign that she'd only just begun and that his plan to head to the airport to pick Lin up was in danger of being delayed.

"You've been talking on and on about her, it's almost as if I've met her already."

"Considering she'll be here soon, you'll get the opportunity."

Carrie sucked her teeth, cutting his sass off. "That's not what I meant, and you know it."

He curbed an eye roll, knowing that his godmother would only torture him more if he tried it. It left him with no other option than to let her speak her mind and hope that he wasn't affected by whatever it was she had to say.

"You're interested in this Lin."

"I *admire* her designs, and I know they'll be an asset to your event," he stressed the difference, sweating a little more under the collar when his thoughts strayed to Lin and his heart picked up its pace. This was why he didn't want to have this conversation with Carrie, of all people. She was perceptive; she had an uncanny ability to know exactly what he was thinking and feeling.

It had been helpful to him when he had been abandoned by his parents and he was hurting from the breakup with Isaiah. Back then he'd appreciated not having to spell out his pain for Carrie to know how he was feeling. She just did, and she quietly supported him in whatever way he needed. Emotionally and financially, until he'd gotten on his own two feet and his business had taken off.

"You like her," Carrie deadpanned.

"She'll be working with me." It was a moot point. And even if she weren't…

If she weren't, I'd still keep away.

The force of his attraction was enough cause for worry.

So it didn't matter if he had an instant crush on Lin

or not. His gut was flashing warning signs, and he had no reason to ignore them. Because love was a door he'd closed and sealed tightly, and no one would get him to open it and try again.

It didn't deter his godmother, though.

"Work romances are a thing, aren't they?" Carrie smirked knowingly.

Karl wasn't winning this, so he stood and tried another tactic. "I should hit the road now if I want to beat traffic."

And before he could hustle her out of his office, she gently tapped a finger to one of the golden-rayed lilies in the floral arrangement decorating his coffee table. They were the only spot of color besides his godmother's attire in his monochromatic workspace. "Flowers. I can't think of anything that could be more welcoming. Imagine what she'll think when you greet her with a beautiful bouquet."

Flowers, he noted subconsciously, liking the idea more than he likely should. Now the question was what kind of flowers were best.

Lin couldn't believe he'd gotten her flowers. She sniffed the spherical yellow and orange flower heads, the thistlelike shape of the petals like nothing she'd ever seen before. Karl opened the door to her apartment and rolled in the last of her bulky designer suitcases. He had told her to wait while he made the return trip and ignored her offer of help. Somehow she found it difficult to disobey him when he spoke so authoritatively.

A frisson of desire crackled through her center, making her more highly aware of him than she'd thought was possible, even when he'd been in Kenya with her. She didn't remember being *this* attracted to him. It was a little more than daunting. And she had enough on her mind as it was. Leaving her grandfather behind had been harder than she'd believed it would be. He hadn't been supportive of her coming to Canada to work with Karl. Then there was the guilt she felt knowing that he'd have to cope without her when he was so used to having her around. She fought the misery off tirelessly through her flight, but now that she had landed safely at her destination, she didn't have the same store of energy to push back against the melancholy breaching her defenses.

"Do you like the flowers?" Karl was looking at her. His question gave her sadness pause.

She loosened the chokehold she had on the bouquet, took another sniff that calmed her frazzled emotions and sighed, smiling. "They're lovely. What are they called?"

"Safflowers. The florist picked them out."

Her smile drooped a little at that, but she perked up, remembering that he'd still made the effort to welcome her to his country and city. It was slowly dawning on her that she had traveled thousands of miles and most of a day to begin this new chapter in her life. And a little more than two weeks after she'd met him. He was taking a chance on her, and she was still a virtual stranger to him.

At least someone believes I can do this.

"Is something the matter?" Karl's deep voice husked over to her from where he was arranging her luggage neatly by the front door. He was staring with such intensity she felt a blush unspool through her body, the heat making her breasts heavier and concentrating between her thighs.

"Nothing. I'm just a little tired from the long flight."

She'd flown commercial—first-class, but commercial, nevertheless. Despite knowing that she had free access to her grandfather's jet, she didn't feel right using it after they'd argued their way into a stalemate over her traveling to Canada.

"You're frowning. Is the apartment not to your liking?"

He'd been kind enough to lease a place for the duration of her stay. The luxury apartment was fully furnished, and from what she'd seen of the professional-grade kitchen and the spacious, modern living space, he had her comfort in mind.

"It's perfect. Like the flowers," she said with another whiff of the pleasant display cradled in her arm.

But she sensed that he was still curious, so she divulged some of the truth. In hope that he'd rest easier knowing that she was comfortable in her new home.

"I'm reliving my arguments with my grandfather. He wasn't happy that I was coming here." She didn't mention that he'd also questioned Karl's intentions. Her grandfather wasn't a suspicious man by nature. She knew he was trying to protect her, just as he'd shielded her from feeling the loss of her dad when he'd passed away, and how he didn't mention her mother to her unless she asked. Which she didn't often do because she worried it'd open up buried trauma from having been abandoned by her mom.

"Did you want me to speak to him?" Karl moved closer, a frown that probably matched hers crossing his face. "I could explain to him what you'd be doing here for my company."

As thoughtful as his offer was, it wouldn't do any good. Once her grandfather got an idea into his head, he could be mulish about surrendering it. And he'd long planned for her to take over the family company. As far as he was concerned, nothing should stop that from happening—not even if Lin had told him she had no desire to run his company after he retired.

Shaking her head, she sighed. "It'll only make him dig his heels in more. He can be stubborn—" She winced, hating to talk behind his back. She'd been brought up to respect her elders, but it was hard to do when her grandfather showed little respect for what she loved to do. "Anyways, you won't change his mind about how he views my 3D designing."

"What does he think of it?"

Seeing that Karl seemed to care, she said, "To him, I'm doing a hobby. Something that can't possibly provide for me in the future. He tried to get me to compromise and do my *hobby*—" she said with air quotes "—on the side while he showed me the ropes of taking over his company."

"Does this change our arrangement?"

Blinking in confusion, she frowned anew. "I'm still fully committed to seeing this through, if that's what you're asking."

"Good. Because it'd be a shame to lose your talent. My godmother's excited to meet you too."

Hearing that almost made it worth traveling far from home without the support of the one person she wanted most to back her endeavor. She didn't realize her eyes were watering until her vision blurred.

Quietly, Karl walked away and returned with a tissue in hand.

"Thanks," she mumbled, wiping at her eyes and careful not to jostle the pretty flowers he'd gifted her. "It's just nice *someone* on this end believes in me." She had Machelle, but her best friend hadn't raised her. Her grandfather would always hold a special place in Lin's heart for all the sacrifices he'd made to provide for her when her dad had died and her mom had walked out. He was her only family. And she was worried to death that he'd suddenly stop loving her because of the choice she'd made to come to Canada to work with Karl.

Embarrassment careered through her once she dried her eyes.

Rather than scoffing at her or staring with pity in his intense gaze, Karl said, "Show him what he can't see. The talent and hard work that brought you this far."

"I'll try." She didn't say it with much conviction, though.

He heard it and shook his head. "Make me believe that you mean it."

She breathed slowly and thoughtfully through her nose and then gave it another go.

"I can do it."

"A little better. But it won't cut it because I don't believe it."

Her frustration had been simmering for nearly a day now. All during her flight she'd been wringing her hands, oscillating between being angry at her grandfather and wanting to please him and giving in to his demands. He'd sacrificed for her. Wasn't it time for her to do the same for him, even if it meant her happiness was on the line?

"Make me *believe* you," he stressed, those dark eyes of his cutting through her.

A switch flipped in her, and when she opened her mouth, she didn't recognize the words coming out or the emotion thrumming through her.

"Damn it, I *can* do this! I'm the only one who can do this, and that should be enough."

Lin hadn't felt the quiver in her hands until the bouquet trembled slightly. Somehow Karl had dragged out the fear of losing her grandfather's love and of being abandoned by him and channeled it into strength. She burned with the power of belief in herself. Her head rushed with the sensation, and her heart was fuller for it.

She needn't look to Karl to see his approval.

Though his face barely dropped its cool guard, he was smiling and nodding, and she didn't think that anything else could have made her feel better at that moment. The swooping in her stomach and the breathless tightening in her chest were just products of the outburst she'd just had...or so she told herself. It wasn't because Karl looked sexier smiling, or that she suddenly noticed how close he was to her, his cologne in the air she breathed, and his body heat so enticingly near.

She just had to remember that he was now *technically* her boss...

Making him very forbidden fruit.

CHAPTER SIX

LIN WOKE AND dressed earlier than usual with a fresh confidence the next day.

She had Karl to thank for her good mood.

He'd left her with her hope renewed. She would need the positive thinking if she stood any chance at turning her grandfather on to the idea of her starting a business in 3D designing and printing.

She had a big day ahead, and she didn't want to arrive late. That much she could control. How Karl's staff would react to her was a whole other problem.

I hope they like me.

Otherwise, she was in for a few long months in Canada.

She left her apartment when she received an alert that her ride was waiting downstairs. Karl had told her before leaving yesterday that he'd send a company car to pick her up. The drive itself was short. She was surprised to discover that she didn't live that far from the headquarters.

Once she stepped out of the car, Lin gawked up at the building from the curb. She steeled her spine and focused on the revolving glass doors into the towering monolith of offices. The elevator ride up was quiet and unintrusive. Everyone seemed to have already started their day, which only made her skin feel tighter and itchier and caused her anxiety to spike up again. Her newfound confidence had left the building temporarily, and she hated that it stranded her. She wrapped her arms around her swooping middle, her chest weighty and her mouth drying as she tipped her head up and watched the floors close in on Karl's offices.

His company occupied three whole floors from what the building's security had told her at the front desk when she'd stopped to ask for directions.

It should have comforted her to know that his business was doing just as well as she had hoped. Good for her, because she'd have plenty of work to do and a chance to prove that she could seriously make a profitable career out of her 3D printing. And the best part of it was that she'd have something to show her grandfather by the end of it.

Assuming he was still on speaking terms with her by then.

She sighed and pushed any doubts out of her mind.

The elevator stopped, and the doors opened onto a spacious and welcoming reception center. Its waiting area had a kitchenette, complete with a well-equipped coffee machine and a minifridge that she imagined stored an assortment of beverage options for guests. Eyeing one of the plush chairs when she saw the reception desk was unattended, she picked up one of the tablets stacked neatly in a varnished wooden tray, a note on the side inviting guests to surf freely with Wi-Fi-ready technology while they waited.

She'd barely gotten one of the gaming apps open when a familiar voice came from behind her.

"You arrived," Karl said.

She shot up and beamed, hopefully compensating for

her nerves. He'd read her easily the last time she spoke to him. She didn't want him thinking that she was wavering in her decision to stay and work with him.

If he noticed her clamoring anxiousness to get her first day started, his expression gave no hint of it. As always he was calm and unperturbed.

He also wasn't alone.

Two women flanked him. Looks-wise, they were opposites. But their smiles were matched in warmth and friendliness.

Karl made the introductions. "This is Nadine, a senior coordinator and event planner with Heartbeat."

The name was familiar…

Reading her thoughts, Nadine shook her hand and said, "I was the planner working with your friend, Machelle. Unfortunately I couldn't make it to the party in Kenya, but Karl was able to take my place."

Right. That was where she remembered her name from. Machelle had mentioned her before. Nadine was a short and curvy green-eyed red-haired beauty, and her skin was such a fair beige that the brown freckles smattering her cheeks stood out even more. She seemed as sweet as she looked, and Lin felt the anxiety of meeting a new face ease a little.

"Miranda's our capable receptionist. She helps us run this place," Karl said of the other woman.

"You forgot *personal assistant*," Miranda sassed, her perfect teeth flashing as bright as her rich umber skin glowed blemish-free and healthfully. She had her dark brown hair with its honeyed highlights in soft waves, her edges perfectly laid, and her makeup as flawless as her silver jumpsuit, black heels and big hoop earrings.

"Are you volunteering?" Karl snorted, but he didn't sound or look upset by what she'd said. Lin was surprised. If any of her grandfather's employees had spoken like that to him, they'd have been tossed out on their ear in a flash. The easy camaraderie that obviously existed between Karl and his staff was new to her and nothing she'd ever experience in Kenya. The way she'd been raised, elders in the personal and work spheres were always respected, never talked back to and not treated like they were friends.

It was nice to see that she would be working in a less strict environment. Refreshing, really. She wondered how much of that had to do with wanting to get to know Karl more.

When she'd first met him, she had thought she had gotten a fix on him. He'd seemed cold, unreachable, but intelligent and perceptive. All the traits that likely paved a path to his successful business. In that way he reminded her of her grandfather.

But then he showed glimpses into a more caring nature. And last night he had done plenty for her that she hadn't expected. The flowers, the apartment... It wasn't enough that he'd hired her services and taken a chance on her, he was showing himself to be much kinder than she'd pegged him.

Again, so much like her headstrong grandfather.

With both men, it appeared there was more than met the eye. More beneath their hard, crusty exteriors.

"We should start the tour." Karl extracted himself from the banter with his friendly staff and moved to call the elevator. "Your workspace is on the floor below these offices."

She wouldn't be working near him. Why did that knowledge deflate her mood?

Nadine and Miranda waved goodbye as Lin joined Karl in the elevator. She didn't have long to fidget by his side in the thick, unnerving silence. The ride was short, and before long she was too distracted by her new view to be entranced by the spiced fragrance of his cologne and the minty smell of his aftershave or body wash.

"Wow," she heard herself say breathily.

She was speechless when Karl led her off the elevator into a vast, open-spaced studio. Tall concrete pillars, exposed brick walls and bright, shiny hardwood flooring popped out at her first. Then she noticed the work benches, six of them evenly dispersed. A lounge and kitchenette area that were glassed off. She spied a large flat-screen TV in the lounge, along with a comfy-looking seating space to kick back and relax.

But what really had her jaw dropping to the point she worried she'd have to pick it up from the floor with both her hands was the printers.

She counted six in total, one for each workbench.

Two were large-scale printers that she knew for a fact had to have cost tens of thousands each. All printers were fully assembled, and she figured ready to begin printing if a file were extruded and delivered to them.

She finally managed an awe-filled "Wow!"

"We can rework any areas you're unhappy with. Feel free to let us know what you'd like and need to complete your designs."

Lin goggled at him, trying to gauge whether he was for real. When she realized that he was being dead serious, she snorted, slapped a hand over her mouth and then released the laughter that had quickly built up. She muffled most of it with her hand, but she saw his brows snap up at the noise that slipped free.

"I'm sorry. It's just I can't see how this—" she waved her hands around them at the studio space he'd recreated for her purposes "—could get any better."

"You're pleased," he commented, his thicker, darker eyebrows lowering from their defensive posturing.

"More than pleased," she said a little too hurriedly, and for a moment she didn't recognize who she was, because it sounded like she was flirting. Her voice pitched higher, and the playful note in her response was as clear as the bright day shining through the expansive row of sash windows that took up an entire wall of the floor.

Karl moved nearer to a window, his hands slipping into his trouser pockets, and his back briefly to her before she trailed him to where he stood. She was taken aback when the natural lighting to the room draped him. He was droolworthy standing in the shaft of white sunlight. His bald head gleaming, his shirtsleeves rolled up, forearms taut with lean, clean muscle, his dark brown skin contrasting against his soft-looking cotton oxford shirt and his top buttons undone so casually it had her mouth dry and her heart rate picking up concerningly.

He turned his face to the light, the squint to his eyes adding a realness to his otherwise ethereal beauty. He could be on a magazine cover. With his height and slim but trim build, a fashion-runway model. But his job was still glamorous. Heartbeat Events wasn't a struggling event company in a saturated market with plenty of competition. The clients Karl and his staff worked with and created unforgettable events and experiences for were the crème de la crème of society. Multimillionaire moguls, A-list actors, top-charting musicians, popular politicians—she could probably name just about anyone wealthy and well-known, and he'd likely have had the chance to provide them with his company's services.

There was a reason she'd decided to work with him. If she was going to put everything on the line, it would be because she'd bargained on the power of his success rubbing off on her.

"Are you good to continue?"

She nodded and followed him as he walked her through her new workspace. It was hard to believe that he'd done all of this to make her feel comfortable. And in so short a time. Only two weeks had passed since he'd requested she work alongside his team in Canada. He'd managed all of this in that time and with what little input he had asked of her. He no doubt had done his share of research in what she needed to complete her 3D projects.

He must have also been paying attention back in my studio.

She recalled him observing her workspace in Kenya and showing interest that had her sparkling all over even now as she reminisced.

Concluding the tour, Karl guided her back to the elevator. "I have your work permit and some paperwork for you to fill out in my office. After that, I thought it'd be a good idea to introduce you to my godmother. She's expecting us."

"She is?" Anxiety gripped her. This was it. She was doing this work for him to please his godmother. If she failed to do that, she'd have wasted her time and effort, and her dream to be her own boss would be that much more out of reach.

"I mentioned yesterday that she's been looking forward to meeting you. She owns a gift shop not too far from here."

A fellow entrepreneur. Lin didn't know why that was a bit calming. At least she now knew she was in good company. Maybe they'd even have something to talk about besides the event Karl was planning for his godmother. She could only hope.

Karl had been thinking about how to mitigate the effect Carrie might have on Lin when they first meet. It didn't help that his godmother had gotten it into her mind that there was something going on between him and Lin. When in fact what Carrie had sensed was his desire for Lin and his hyperawareness of her whenever she was in his thoughts or in physical proximity.

He wasn't about to confess to his attraction.

It would give Carrie a strong reason to play at matchmaker. And *that* wasn't something he could have happen.

This partnership with Lin wasn't about that. He had closed his heart off to anything more than no-string flings with partners who were of the same noncommitment mindset. And even if he entertained asking Lin if she were interested in hooking up, what mattered now was they were working together. Pleasure and business never mixed very well. He'd seen it with his parents. They were so busy running and managing their real estate and construction business that they never considered what their loveless marriage had done to their family, to their children.

To me, he thought grimly.

It was all the more reason not to fall for the lure of his lustful thoughts and emotions and to strictly draw a professional line where Lin was concerned.

The charming silver bell above the shop's front door dinged when he strolled in with Lin.

Her eyes went round, her head turning this way and that.

Karl tried to see it from her perspective. There was

an old-timey appeal to his godmother's shop, The Gift Goddess. Gleaming wood-paneled walls and hardwood flooring that was varnished dark and polished to perfection. Handmade shelves and a long glass display case beside the front service desk.

Lin picked up a ceramic ashtray with a silhouette of a beaver painted inside and on the back. She paused to read the small note where she'd lifted the ashtray from and looked adorable with her brows knitted together in concentration.

"Local artisans made everything you see. They use locally sourced material and sell to my godmother." It had been an ingenious business idea when his godmother opened the store more than fifteen years ago. Calgary was a lively metropolis, and in recent years it had become a hot spot for tourists from all over the country and the world. Though, it hadn't always been a sprawling concrete jungle. Like most other places in Canada, it had history, and that history had appealed to his godmother enough for her to connect her vision of business with her love of art.

That clever merger was what had opened the doors of The Gift Goddess. A gift shop that allowed tourists to take a piece of their memories of Calgary with them in the form of locally made pieces. And there was something for everyone. Postcards and key chains, T-shirts and caps, belt buckles, cowboy boots, photography and oil paintings. Carrie was always outsourcing, discovering new artists and new art mediums. One time she'd sold handmade traditional wooden snowshoes. It was her zeal and penchant for business that had kept the shop running all these years.

It's why Carrie had inspired him to kick-start his own business.

She believed that his parents played a role too, but he wasn't anything like them. If they had given him one thing, it might have been his business savvy. Not that he was rushing to concede that fact. The less he thought of his parents and the less he had to do with them, the happier he was.

Lin set down the ashtray and moved around the store with riveted attention, checking out as many items as she could.

Her fascination came to an end when Stefon and Carrie walked out from the backroom. They were arguing about Stefon carrying a hefty-looking box. Carrie sounded as worried as she was annoyed that her husband was ignoring her and doing all the heavy lifting.

"The doctor warned you to take it easy." She swatted Stefon's back, grumbling, "Why are you being so pigheaded?"

"Yeah, well, what the doc doesn't know won't hurt."

She huffed at his response, unamused.

Stefon set down the box and then turned to bundle his wife into his arms. He was short and stout, and his short curly hair was entirely gray, but he cleaned up nicely with his typical sweater-and-jeans combo.

"Forgive me," he said after a kiss to her forehead.

She swatted his shoulder this time, but without the same vehemence, the smile on her face softer, more loving.

Before they continued, Karl coughed to grab their attention.

They pulled apart at the sight of them. His godmother patted the sides of her African-print headscarf, looking resplendent in a dress that matched the scarf's print. She was uniquely vibrant as usual, but he imagined that Lin might be taken aback by Carrie's style.

So it was surprising when Lin sprung in with a question. "Do you sell Ankara dresses?"

They struck up conversation like that. No formal introductions. Just straight into an appreciation of African fashion and design.

At one point, Stefon sidled up beside him.

"Is that her? The woman Carrie says you've been talking on and on about?"

"Yeah, that's her." Karl didn't correct him about the rest of it. He was too mesmerized by Lin's smiles and laughter at whatever Carrie was telling her. She hadn't smiled or laughed that openly around him yet. It had him wondering what it would take to get her to smile at him like that.

He didn't have to wait long to find out.

When they left Carrie's gift shop, Karl decided not to head back to the office and suggested that they visit a nearby park. He'd sold it as a good place to see the city skyline. But Lin appeared on board whether that was true or not.

Though it was true, and Calgary's downtown skyline was more alluring today with a cloudless blue sky as the backdrop of its skyscrapers. She gasped at the colorful autumn leaves on the trees in the park, exclaiming with a smile, "They're gorgeous! Like something out of a painting or a dream."

The smile was what got him. He warmed all over, the mild chill in the air blasted away at the first blush of pride. He'd put that happy expression on her face. And there was this primal urge in him to beat his chest about it. An action he had never thought about doing before.

He had been doing and saying a lot of uncharacteristic things. Like when he spied a perfectly shaped leaf on their path and Lin continued ahead of him, clueless when he stooped to pick it up for her.

"It's got all the colors mixed together," she said of the leaf when he handed it to her.

She was right. The red, yellow and orange blended harmoniously in the leaf. It was a good sign that he'd chosen right and followed his instinct to prolong their time together. Bringing her to enjoy the colours was a good cover for what he'd actually wanted: time alone with her.

Time that he shouldn't really desire.

It was like he was tempting fate, and fate would hit back any moment and make him do something stupid to ruin their work relationship before it had even truly begun.

Just as he thought it, his hand bumped hers and her eyes sprung up to him at the same time as he looked at her. They paused in the middle of the path, gazing at each other. For the first time, he experienced close to the same level of yearning he felt for her mirrored in her eyes.

He opened his mouth, unsure of what he'd say, only knowing that he had to say something. Anything. Because it didn't feel real to him.

"Lin…"

He'd barely said her name when a bike bell chimed ahead in warning, and the moment was lost when they stepped aside out of harm's way.

"Were you saying something?" she asked him a short while later when they continued walking.

He pressed his lips together and shook his head. It didn't feel right taking them back there now.

Lin shrugged and moved on. "I'll have to come to this park again. Maybe jog here or just go for a walk."

She lowered her phone, having snapped a photo of the skyline from their hilltop vantage point.

"You better get it in soon. We've had our first snowfall of the season already, and even though it's melted now, the snow will be back soon." It wasn't rare in Calgary to see snow this early. They hadn't gotten through many Octobers without seeing some of the white stuff. They'd even had the occasional drearily white Thanksgiving. Not that it had deterred the leaves from taking their time changing colors. She'd arrived at a good time to see the full glow of oranges, yellows and reds melding together in perfect harmony. Sometimes together on one tree, and sometimes all on one leaf. Like the special leaf she was holding.

"I liked meeting Carrie and Stefon. They seem really sweet."

Lin grabbed an empty bench that faced the pleasant view of his city below.

"That's because they were showing you their best side." He smothered the full effect of his teasing grin. It felt unfamiliar on his face. He was used to acting more reserved around people he didn't know, and he hadn't known Lin for long. But she made him want to laugh and smile almost as much as she had done with his godmother.

Having grown used to bottling his emotions, it wasn't an altogether easy feeling…

But it's not unpleasant either.

A part of him could even see himself getting used to and growing to find comfort in it.

She stroked the leaf he'd given her and sighed. "It's sad what happened to Stefon. Carrie must have had it rough while he was sick."

Karl was still shocked his godmother had told Lin

about Stefon's heart attack and subsequent emergency surgery, not to mention the year-long battle of his physical recovery. Every day Stefon looked and sounded more like himself, but it had been a long and tough road Carrie had endured with her husband and family. If Karl hadn't watched it unfold, he wouldn't have known just how challenging it had been on their family and their long-standing love.

Even someone like him who trod carefully around the subject knew what love was when he saw it, and Carrie and Stefon loved each other deeply.

It didn't change his mind about it. Facts were just facts.

Love could heal and empower—and it could just as easily weaken and destroy.

"They had family support."

"You helped them too." She didn't phrase it as a question, assuming that he had been there.

The assumption was correct. "Yes, I helped whenever I could. As did their grown children." He'd run errands whenever one of Carrie and Stefon's kids couldn't do it themselves. Unlike their adult children who had families, Karl was a bachelor with no ties. He didn't have the same family demands that pressed his time. So he had worked particularly hard to free his schedule and delegate more tasks to his staff in order to be there for Carrie and Stefon if and when they needed him.

"It must have been especially tough on Carrie. Their love was clearly strong enough to withstand it."

He grunted by way of agreement, suddenly cagier now that they were discussing love and relationships.

"Have you ever wondered what a love that powerful could feel like?" she asked, her eyes searching ahead, gaze distant.

Karl stared at her, first because the question caught him off guard, and then to take in the way a coil of her hair had slipped free of the butterfly clip she'd used to hold it back from her face. Sunlight highlighted the warmer brown tones in her hair and the red undertone of her brown skin and brightened the glow of her full, sleekly polished lips. Lips he wanted to taste so desperately in that instant, he'd have done it if she didn't blink and look at him with widened eyes.

"I'm sorry! You don't have to answer that. I was thinking aloud."

She *had* asked a personal question that he normally would've evaded. But there was something about talking to her that made it impossible to refuse her. It could have been his reptilian brain doing the talking. Her pretty face making him into an idiot. Yet he knew it wasn't that, but more like a fast and easy trust in her to protect whatever he told her.

She had also been admirably vulnerable with him. Sharing her struggle in differences with her grandfather and seeming to be open to his advice about how to cope.

He couldn't see any harm in replying. "I haven't."

The silence that came after that was charged. They stared at each other for who knew how long before one of them blinked.

But she spoke first. "Should we head back?"

Reluctantly he agreed. He'd had enough alone time with her to last him.

So why do I feel like I want more?

More than they'd had already… Maybe even more than the few months that were left until Carrie's vow renewal and Lin's departure to her home in Nairobi.

CHAPTER SEVEN

LIN'S FIRST WEEK passed by in a blur of activity. She was thinking further ahead than what was in front of her. One she finished rendering one design, she was designing and prepping the printers to print another. Before long she had the stockroom filled with designs that were ready for his godmother's vow-renewal ceremony in a couple of months. But she still had more to do.

By the time she left the office and reached her temporary home in the swanky apartment Karl had leased for her, her whole body was mush, but her spirit and mind were active with ideas for the next day. There was even an evening or two where she'd pulled a near all-nighter to get the ideas she had in her head down on the page so she wouldn't forget them.

Karl expected updates every start of the week at his staffwide brief meetings. She'd kept him abreast of all the work she'd completed during these meetings. But the Monday of the second week was Canadian Thanksgiving, a holiday she had heard of in passing. Still a holiday meant the whole office was closed. Everyone at home celebrating with family or enjoying the free time off work.

Everyone but her.

She had gotten permission from Karl to work. It had

happened over a short series of texts. She hadn't missed the fact that they hadn't spoken outside of work since the day they'd visited Carrie's gift shop and the downtown park nearby. Lin hadn't been able to free herself of the niggling sense that he was avoiding her. And if he wasn't avoiding her, then maybe he was treating her as she ought to treat him. Coolly, professionally, and with none of the heat she'd feel whenever he was close to her.

Sighing, she focused on the latest design on her computer screen. It was for a seven-branched candelabra. She'd gotten the idea after doing research on Kwanzaa on her own time. What she learned was that seven candles were lit to represent the seven days of the holiday. A candle for each day until all candles were glowing on the final night of Kwanzaa. Lin had fiddled with the design of the traditional wooden candleholder, or *kinara* as it was called in Swahili. She'd found it interesting that one of her first languages was the language used in Kwanzaa. It seemed fated that she should work on this project and that she should help Karl bring his godmother's vision to life for her event.

Thinking of it that way made her decision feel like it was destined. But it didn't erode her guilt entirely. She hadn't wanted to leave her grandfather, and she hated that he was too stubborn to see that she was happy doing what she was doing.

Lin wiped at her eyes hastily, feeling the tears before they blurred her vision completely.

She walked away from her computer and prepared coffee for herself in the break room. The coffee would jolt new life into her. She wanted to work as long as possible and avoid going home with her sullen thoughts for company.

Lin wasn't paying attention. She'd drifted off waiting for the coffee, the sound of her printers drowning out all other noise.

The noisy printers were why she missed the sound of the elevator pinging open.

And how she didn't notice she was no longer alone in the spacious workroom.

"Lin."

She startled and spun to answer to her name, her heart rate still through the roof when she saw it was Karl. When her nerves faded, though, all she felt was a giddiness to have him close after she'd been thinking of him.

Despite feeling as though he were avoiding her, she didn't feel any less of the usual heat that engulfed her whole body whenever he was nearby. She blushed from head to toe, her skin hot and achy with a deep primal need. She desired him, and if she weren't careful she'd make it obvious to him now.

Like when she breathed his name, "Karl," and it came out all low and bedroom sexy. With a cough, she raised her voice and added, "What are you doing here?"

He was also the last person she would've expected.

"Sorry if I frightened you." He held up the reusable bags in his hands. "Gifts from Carrie. She insisted I bring them to you. I tried calling."

Lin glanced over at where her phone lay hooked up to a portable charger and on mute as she'd wanted no distractions.

"If you're taking a break, why not break for a quick meal? I can have some of this reheated for you in a flash."

She was still too shocked to see him to argue. It was as though her thoughts had conjured him. Either way, it was hard to look any place else while he navigated the dishes Carrie had given him and set up the microwave to reheat all of it.

When he turned, their eyes locked.

He looked good in his dress shirt and black slacks. His long overcoat hung open, and he had his hands tucked in his coat pockets. He could have stepped out of a magazine or off a runaway. If she weren't careful, she'd be salivating…and she could use the food as an excuse, but deep down she would know the real reason.

Stop before he thinks you're over the top.

The warning came right as he said, "I still don't understand why you didn't take the day off. Carrie thought I left you behind. She wouldn't believe that you'd declined her offer to dinner."

She had thought it was too generous of his godmother to have invited her in the first place. Lin knew that Carrie had only worried like any mother might have. But she hadn't wanted to latch onto her sympathy and intrude on a private family gathering.

Besides, Karl would've been there, and nothing would have been more awkward than spending the holiday with her boss.

Her *very handsome* boss.

She swallowed thickly and moved the conversation along. "Did you enjoy dinner at Carrie's?"

When she'd asked if she could come in to work over the holiday and he'd approved, he had also told her that she could reach him if she needed him at any time. It was thoughtful of him to think of her when he'd been busy celebrating the turkey-focused holiday with Carrie and her family.

"It was eventful." He paused and eyed the cup of coffee in her hands. "Have you been working the whole time?"

"I lost track of how long I've been here." But she'd gotten a lot more work completed because of it. Getting her head down and forgetting her problems and worries had worked for her. Now that her head was raised, and she wasn't alone, she was back to being concerned about the factors in her plan she couldn't control. Like her grandfather...*and* her confusing but exciting feelings for Karl.

The microwave pinged.

Karl grabbed plates from the top cabinets. He'd stocked the break room with everything he could possibly need. Again, his thoughtfulness was at odds with his sometimes-brusque personality.

She helped carry the dinner Carrie had sent over with him to an empty workbench and drooled for real at the mouthwatering spread. Baked mac and cheese, glazed turkey slices, candied yams and buttermilk biscuits. There was even dessert, chocolate pecan pie. Just as she was about to dig in, she noticed Karl standing and watching her.

"I can't eat this all on my own."

He shrugged. "Believe me when I say that Carrie made sure I was as stuffed as her turkey before I left her place. She was also explicitly clear when she said all of this was yours."

Lin gawped at the food that could feed her for days and maybe all of next week.

"At least sit with me while I'm eating." It was a compromise.

He grabbed the stool beside her and continued staring at her.

If she weren't so hungry, she'd have squirmed under his watchful eyes.

"Please tell me you've been eating properly."

"I had lunch earlier."

Much earlier.

"Why do I find that hard to believe?" He breathed deeply through his nose, his eyebrows dipping down. "So why don't you show me what had you so preoccupied that you forgot to eat."

He'd seen right through her. Blushing, she tipped her chin toward her laptop, and he brought it back to his stool, scrolling through the files she had open. They were designs she hadn't gotten to yet. Designs she'd wanted to have him approve. It was another good reason he was here.

"Is this a *kinara*?" He was on the file she'd been tweaking with the Kwanzaa candleholder. Without prompting, he nodded satisfyingly. "It looks good. Carrie will like it." He continued scrolling, the same affirming nod given to each file. Her chest puffed out, and her face was hurting from how big she was smiling.

While he perused her designs, he asked, "Why work today of all days?"

"Why not?" She grabbed a warm biscuit, the scent of it calling to her. "Besides, I'm new to the city."

"My point exactly. I know most retail spots are closed for the day, but you could have explored."

"Are you judging me? I thought you'd be the first person to appreciate my display of strong work ethic. Miranda says you work odd hours all the time." She mumbled the last part around a mouthful of the baked good.

"Should I be worried you two are thick as thieves now?"

Lin laughed, and Karl surprised her when he chuckled low, roughly and sexily. She pressed her thighs together, suddenly feeling a little hotter and wondering whether it'd be too obvious to get up and adjust the thermostat.

Nervous that he'd notice the change in her, she blurted, "Do you go to Carrie's often?"

"Most major holidays. Thanksgiving. Christmas. New Year's. Unless I have plans of my own."

Of course. He was too good-looking to be alone. Women probably threw themselves at him. And maybe one of those women were lucky enough to be his girl-friend. Miranda had said he was private about his life and that no one knew whether he was single or not, but it didn't mean that he was a bachelor. She didn't know why that made her so strangely sad.

She had a crush on him; it didn't mean she planned to do anything about it.

He was her boss. And even when she did complete her job and they went their separate ways, from her experience she hadn't found anything special or worth truly pursuing with any of the people she'd dated. She was too busy to be chasing after a crush and the exqui-site high that it gave her being near him. What happened when she came crashing down to reality? There was too much on the line for her to risk. Her grandfather was al-ready upset with her. If she returned home having made Karl's godmother happy, at least she'd feel good about one thing. There was also still hope that her grandfa-ther would give her plan to start a business a chance.

Then there was the fact that Karl might see her dif-ferently if they became more than work colleagues. Up till now he'd been unexpectedly kind to her.

That could change if they got all hot and personal…
And he might not be so kind after.

Lin thought of how her mom had stopped loving them and how that had left her dad to raise her alone—

until he'd passed away. The tightness in her throat and the flash of watery heat around her eyes reminded her where she was and with whom. Crying in front of Karl wasn't an option. He'd ask her questions, and she wasn't sure she'd be able to keep her face straight while she lied about the parts of herself she wasn't ready to share with anyone.

"So you usually stay in the city for the holidays. What about your family? Do they live here too?"

He kept his face neutral in spite of his heart beating faster. Talking about his family always had the same effect on him. He felt restless. Like he needed to jog a mile or two.

Or ten, he thought grumpily.

"They live in Toronto," he said.

She tipped her head. "Isn't that far?"

What he wished to say was that it wasn't far enough sometimes. It was like he could still feel them breathing down his neck. The odd sensation only intensified when he'd understood that Carrie had invited his parents to her vow renewal. It would be pointless to deny that he had repressed his feelings about what had happened.

"They'll be here for Carrie and Stefon's event." They hadn't RSVPed officially, but he'd be prepared if they showed up. This time he would be wielding power and controlling their fate. He'd promised Carrie he'd behave. But if his parents so much as stepped a toe out of line with him…

I'll happily walk them out of the party myself.

He ground his teeth, eager to stop thinking about his family as soon as possible.

Lin must have sensed he didn't want to talk about

them. She ate in silence for a while before she spoke again.

"I didn't answer you honestly before."

Karl rose above his own thoughts and feelings when he heard her. "About?"

"Why I've chosen to work rather than taking time off on a holiday." She patted her mouth with a napkin, sighed and faced him. "I was feeling lonely, and work helped take my mind off the fact that I'm here alone. Something about it being a holiday and knowing that everyone else is with their family."

She was lonely? Why hadn't she said anything to him about it?

Keeping his voice calm, he asked, "Is there something I can do to help?"

Lin smiled so brilliantly then. "You already have." She gestured to the food, teasing, "Saved me from loneliness and hunger."

He blushed…and the sensation was oddly new but familiar. He hadn't felt like this in a long while, again not since Isaiah broke up with him. Every one of his previous lovers since then hadn't roused this carnal hunger to be closer to someone. To know them so intimately. To feel with the whole of his being that he could trust them with every part of him.

Lin had accomplished that in, what, three weeks of knowing her?

Her hand alighted on his arm. "Thanks for coming to visit and for staying with me."

"It was my pleasure," he answered gruffly, his emotion betraying him.

But if she noticed, her smile posed no judgment of him.

"I was being serious when I said you could call me

if you need anything." He'd said it just as nervously the first time too. "If you're ever feeling alone again…"

She squeezed and patted his arm. "I'll call you," she said, completing his thought.

Silently he added, *I promise you won't feel lonely again.*

He didn't want to unpack why it was important to him that she felt like she had someone in her corner— only that he wanted her to know that he was here for her while she worked with him. As a colleague. As a confidant.

Never a lover.

But maybe…maybe he could be a friend to her too.

CHAPTER EIGHT

KARL KEPT HIS WORD.

Five more weeks passed, and Lin hadn't felt lonely again. She hadn't even needed to call him. He was just always there, checking in on her, dropping in unannounced on top of the office's weekly meetings. She'd almost say that he was giving her extra-special treatment, and instead of feeling embarrassed that she was being singled out she was touched by his kindness. It also wasn't helping cure her of her crush on him. Discovering all his good traits was making him more attractive to her.

But she was determined to keep from shaking up their cheerful dynamic. They were working together, but these days he almost felt like a friend to her.

When she'd initially met him, Lin didn't think she'd ever call Karl a friend.

He was so unlike her at first glance. *Coolly distant and impersonal* wasn't how she would describe herself. But it had taken a short time to get to see that he had a warmly sensitive center beneath the bland expression he wore too often. Why else would he have been trying to get to know her outside the office?

On top of checking on her, he'd gone above and beyond by showing her the places he liked best in his home city. Almost every evening that she wasn't spending time with Miranda and Nadine, she was with Karl.

It had become such a habit to go out with him that she began showing up to his office when he worked later than the time they were supposed to meet up. This happened rarely, but it was beginning to happen more often in the last week alone, and Lin suspected the reason had to do with it being nearly mid-November and his godmother's Kwanzaa-themed vow renewal gaining on them.

Once she had him out of the office and it was just the two of them, Lin didn't hesitate to ask.

"You're working late again. Is it for your godmother's event?"

He nodded, the weariness in his face intensifying. "Carrie's thinking of changing venues. Of course she asks for it at the last minute to drive me crazy…" He mumbled the last part.

She had to hide her smile and smother her giggle.

"Why doesn't the current venue work for her?" Carrie and Stefon had chosen a lovely heritage home right in the heart of Calgary. Apparently, it had been where they had gone for their first date decades ago, and they'd wanted to relive the experience. Lin had thought it romantic.

"I'll show you what changed her mind." He pulled out his phone and scrolled through photos on his event company's official website. "A couple had a wedding this past summer at a lake resort."

Lin gaped at the image of the picturesque mountain lake that he showed her. She didn't think a lake could be so blue. The snow-capped mountains in the backdrop were majestic. She knew the Rockies were a unique geological formation, but… "They remind me of the mountains of Switzerland. I can see why Carrie would want to change venues."

"I grudgingly agree. But I still had to actually do the work, and I reached out to a friend who manages the resort. Thankfully, they can squeeze us in. I don't think everyone will want to travel the two hours to the location, but that's a hurdle for tomorrow."

She nodded in agreement. He looked too wiped out to do any more work. Selfishly she also didn't want him breaking their plans.

They were eating dinner together. She didn't have a clue where exactly they were headed, but she figured it had to be within walking distance as he hadn't suggested taking his truck. There had been a few times where he'd taken her to places farther than downtown. Mini golf in a quiet and quaint suburb outside Calgary. A bar and grill off the highway with a view of the city like the one in the park all those weeks ago. Her favorite had been the downhill-karting not too far from where she lived. She hadn't thought she was competitive until she was behind the wheel, ramming Karl off-course. Lin smiled at all the memories he'd given her. She'd have a piece of him always, even when she'd completed her work here and returned home.

"So are you going to tell me where we're going tonight?"

He shook his head, his bald head hidden under a brown knit hat that he'd told her was a gift from Carrie. His black scarf was tied loosely, and his coat was undone, revealing the three-piece suit he'd worn to the office today. Each of his tailored suits had her drooling over him even more, if that were even possible. The luxurious fabrics always molded to his body and showcased his lean, muscled frame. The long coat and winter gear hid some of that, but oodles of snow on the ground made the air they breathed mist before their faces and sting the tip of her nose and her cheeks.

She curled her fingers together beneath the faux-fur muff that Karl had bought her. The gift had been a surprise. He'd explained that she wasn't dressed to withstand the bitter Canadian cold. She had thought he was exaggerating until she'd gotten a taste of the first snowfall. One day it was autumn, the leaves on the trees a stunning array of golden yellows to ruby reds, and then the next a blizzard dumped several feet of snow over the whole city. Even the trees hadn't been given notice, the fall foliage clinging on stubbornly.

As they walked the streets, she craned her head up slightly to admire the contrast of the damp and browning autumn leaves against the stark colorless snow.

Her attention shifted to the sky-high building they were approaching. The Calgary Tower. Lin had seen it plenty of times from outside, and she wondered when she'd get the time to visit the landmark.

A thought struck her.

"Wait. Are we going up there?"

Karl's small secretive smile told her what she suspected.

"Why didn't you tell me?" She swatted his arm before giving him a squeeze and the biggest grin. "I told you I wanted to visit the Tower."

"They have the restaurant *and* the view up there, so I was being practical."

Practical was one thing; being sweet was another. Flutters of excitement rippled through her. She looked up at the ginormous building ahead of them, the kaleidoscope of colors lighting the solid spire, a beacon beckoning them closer. She was thrilled to get to see it finally.

Or am I just happy because Karl's with me?

She conceded that it was a bit of both. Lin liked spending time with him. Even if she shouldn't be indulging this crush that she had on him. Giving in to her desire would be disastrous. They still had a professional relationship, and she didn't want to jeopardize the opportunity he'd given her. It didn't matter that she still doubted that any of this would warm her grandfather to the idea of letting her pursue her dream to run her own business.

She pushed aside her troubles and gave in to the experience of visiting the Calgary Tower. The ride up to the restaurant was as quiet as the lobby and gift shop had been. Given how busy the city could be in the evening—even on a weeknight—she was taken aback.

"Is it always this empty?" She looked up at him, the lights of the elevator and the glow of the touchscreen elevator panel illuminating his gorgeous face. Her heart fluttered again.

"It's off-season for tourists, but yes, you'll have noticed that we almost have the place to ourselves."

Almost included the waitstaff that seated them once they entered the impressive restaurant with its panoramic view of the city.

"Where is everyone?"

The restaurant was eerily empty. No other guests were present, and she knew that it couldn't be some coincidence that they were dining alone together. Just the two of them.

She steadfastly ignored her skipping delight at the thought.

Without batting an eye, he said, "I rented the building out for the evening."

She knew that he was flush with money—millions

if she factored the success of his business. But it was extravagant and a little unlike him to use his wealth to separate them from the masses. He didn't seem the sort to flash his cash. Sure, she'd noted his designer clothing, his platinum, crystal and gold watches, and his leather shoes and flashy kicks, but he wore them in an understated way that had never looked ostentatious. And she was positive that he lived in some McMansion that rivaled her grandfather's gated sprawling manor, yet he hadn't once made it obvious that he was a millionaire. Several times over.

Those zeros in his net worth hadn't inflated his head. She liked that he was as sensible as she'd been raised to be. The money wouldn't have attracted her to him, anyways. She had plenty of it. Lin liked what she saw, and she liked who he was even more.

Still, she couldn't help but tease him about it. "Did you want me all to yourself?"

"That's a perk too." She heard the mirth in his voice and grasped that he was joking too, but the flame in his hooded eyes arrested her. A desire she recognized as her own mirrored back to her from his side of the table. Under the table, his foot brushed hers, and that small touch ignited a harrowing heat in her lower belly. The flutters she'd been feeling were full-on waves of sensation. She buzzed with the headiness of her yearning for him by the time their first course arrived.

And even when his face reverted to its usual inscrutable mask, she knew what she saw was real.

He wanted her too.

What was he doing?

Karl berated himself through the whole of their meal. He'd been doing well—*fantastic* when he considered that he hadn't made a move on her or made an ass out of himself yet. They had gone out together a few times. All platonic, friendly dates. And all in an effort to keep her from feeling the loneliness that she'd admitted to back at Thanksgiving. He hadn't wanted her to feel the absence of her home while she was doing him a favor. Sure, he was paying her to do the work. He also planned to give her any referrals and help boost her through his own network of clients. Lin and her three-dimensional designs would be popular with a lot of them. She could easily open a business right in the city and do well. But he could indulge the thought no more than he could fantasize about what it'd be like if they were on a romantic date instead.

He hid his scowl behind a glass of red wine.

She sipped at her own nonalcoholic beverage. Since she was Muslim, he had been mindful of her dietary choices. All a part of making her comfortable in his world. He hoped that his efforts hadn't been in vain.

"Would you accompany me to the observation deck?" He stood and held a hand down to her at the culmination of their meal.

She followed his lead, her hand steady in the crook of his elbow.

They took the stairs down to the deck below. She marveled at the golden string of lights circling the whole perimeter. Wordlessly, she looked up at him with a question in her eyes as to whether the presentation of lights was his doing.

He didn't answer her, but he had asked that the place be decorated prettily. This was her first time seeing Calgary from this height. He wanted it to be special for her. Doubly so because he still recalled how nervous and uncertain she'd been when she had first arrived. To think that he might have lost her to her doubt. Things would be different if she'd chosen to turn around and hop on the next flight back to Kenya.

It occurred to Karl that he hadn't told her that it mattered to him that she hadn't left.

Once he found a good spot for her by the only table and stools, he spoke up.

"I'm happy you're here."

"I am too," she said with a quick glance at him before looking away, utterly absorbed by the view. It had been the same revolving nighttime panorama of the city during the whole of their meal, but Lin looked out at the slowly changing vista as though she were seeing it through a brand-new perspective. And though he had *definitely* been to the Calgary Tower before and hosted a few events right there on the observation deck, it had been a refreshing experience to live vicariously through her for the evening.

"That's not what I meant. I'm glad you decided to stay with us."

Lin spared him more than a glance now. "You helped make the decision easier."

He had? "How?" he blurted, intrigued.

"You believed in me being able to do this before I believed in myself."

Karl was surprised that she'd ever doubted herself. He didn't think that he'd played a role, but she was looking at him with such openness, he knew that she wasn't gassing him up just because he was her boss, temporarily or otherwise.

"It's been hard, though, I'll admit. I've had days where I can't stop thinking about what awaits me back home, particularly where my grandfather's concerned.

I'd be lying if I said I was confident that he's going to change."

"Have you spoken to him?"

She sighed despondently and looked back at the view in front of them. City lights as bright as the observation deck with the display of fairy lights brightening the space. The sparkle of those lights twinkled in her eyes even while her tone was more somber.

"Machelle—you met her—she's been keeping an eye on him for me. But, no, he hasn't been picking up my calls. It's the same thing with my texts."

"I'm sorry." He grasped that she valued her relationship with her grandfather. Allowing his own broken ties with his family to color his impression of Lin's familial bond was erroneous. It also wouldn't bring him any closer to her. Not that he should want that. His concern now was purely based on the fact that they were work colleagues and friends.

He tucked aside his own confused emotions and focused on comforting her. "The distance could give you both space and time to think. *Absence makes the heart grow fonder* does actually apply sometimes."

Just not where my parents are concerned.

He couldn't say the same for her grandfather.

Lin tucked some of her faux locks behind her ear. The perfect blood-red strands matched the bold, red-tinged blush to the apples of her cheekbones and the eyeshadow framed by black mascara and the longest, most alluring lashes he'd ever seen. But then again, everything about her seemed to grab him more than anyone he knew.

She had left her coat back in the restaurant as he'd done. In her off-shoulder silky emerald wrap dress, she looked like a temptress who had been specially sent to drive him insane. It wasn't her fault she was so beautiful. Or that he was having this crazed reaction to her since he'd first laid eyes on her. This wasn't her problem, but entirely something that he had to own up to—*and put to bed*, he thought, and a fraction later he considered that maybe that wasn't the best choice of words.

The deck was rotating more slowly now, the evening winding down to a quicker close than he'd have liked.

Soon he was escorting her back upstairs, her hand resting like a branding iron on his arm.

Helping her into her coat, he slowed his hands to savor the feel of her under the thin peacoat she'd thought would protect her from the cold. At least her hands would be shielded from the winter elements in the hand warmer he'd given her.

She turned when he was done, her face tilted up to him, her lips a softer caramel red. Her mouth parted, and her eyes flickered over him, searching for something—he didn't know what.

Not until she said, "Can I kiss you?"

Karl's whole system went into shock. Very still for a long time, he finally regained the ability to move his head.

And he damned himself by nodding slowly and firmly.

Lin pulled up, watching him, and asher eyes closed, their lips touched.

The kiss was quiet but revelatory. His joy made up most of it, but her enthusiasm was the missing half. She kissed with her whole body, her hands gripping his arms and her soft chest pressing to his much harder one. He felt her breasts against him, her warmth through the coat that he'd have to keep her from wearing again, and almost naturally his arms circled around her waist and drew her closer to him.

They ended the kiss in a bittersweet way that reminded him of where they were and why they couldn't do it again.

Especially when Lin breathlessly apologized. "I'm sorry. I just had to be sure."

"Of?" he rasped back, just as winded from the lip-lock.

"I thought I was imagining our chemistry." She blinked up at him, long lashes fluttering temptingly. "I wasn't. Was I?"

"You weren't," he said.

"But we can't. I-I mean, we shouldn't be doing this."

"I know." Did it mean that he wanted to be reasonable? Not one bit. But she was right. They both had work to consider. And even if they were consenting adults, he knew that he couldn't offer her more than she might desire one day. It could be a kiss now; tomorrow, she could want love from him.

Karl should be relieved that she agreed they should stop now that they'd proved the connection they had.

"Does this change anything?" she asked when he released her and she backed far enough away.

"No. Nothing's changed," he lied. The lie was worth it when she smiled shyly.

"Thanks for…not freaking out about…you know."

If he wasn't still a mess from their kiss, he might have joined in her nervous laughter. However, he *was* a mess, and he didn't think that anything would be the same for him again. Somehow a kiss had changed a lot more than he was comfortable with, and he didn't know what to do about it.

CHAPTER NINE

CHRISTMAS SNUCK UP on him.

One moment they were shoveling the first heavy snowfall right after Thanksgiving, then he was kissing Lin atop the Calgary Tower, and then December swung in with brutal weather and an equally taxing work schedule.

"Four Christmas parties should be our limit." Miranda kicked up her feet on his desk, either ignoring or unaware of the frown he swung her direction. "Seriously, I'm exhausted just watching you all work."

Nadine smiled benevolently. "Be thankful you weren't born to a large family. I'm flying out to my parents' this year, and I'm not looking forward to the possible flight delays."

Karl could foresee it. They'd been having inclement weather even for the hardy West.

"I have a couple big family gatherings. Also, I'm meeting Darius's parents and sisters and I told him I'm cool with it, but I'm low-key stressing at the same time." Miranda grinned nervously. It was unlike her to be anxious about anything. But she'd been dating her boyfriend for a year now, and not only did she seem to like him but it also sounded like the relationship was serious. Otherwise she wouldn't be meeting his family.

Karl thought of Isaiah. He'd kept his ex-boyfriend from meeting his parents. He had known that sweet and artsy Isaiah wouldn't ever be able to hold his own against Serenity and Charles Sinclair. His parents would have burned him with their icy attitudes. No matter how much Isaiah had asked to meet them, Karl had resolutely refused. Admittedly, he'd also been ashamed of his family after having met Isaiah's.

Of course, I shouldn't have to worry about that now.

Though, he had been doing his own low-key stressing. For the first time in years, he'd have his parents in the same room as him. He'd also be raising the stakes by confronting them in full view of his staff.

He'd have to be careful what he said in public around them. Controlling his emotions was imperative. He wouldn't let his parents get under his skin. Never again. Certainly not when he'd come so far without them supporting him.

Lin would get to meet them too.

His stomach did an extra, nauseating swoop at that fact, particularly as it was followed by the crystalline memory of having her in his arms, their lips touching and sliding against each other, his hands stroking her back and backside. She was a perfect fit in his arms. He'd loved holding her. Loved kissing her.

But he couldn't *love* her.

He couldn't love anyone. He'd been burned once by his parents, and then again by Isaiah. Moreover, Carrie was relying on him to come through for her during her special day with Stefon. He couldn't let either of them down by losing his focus now or distracting Lin from her work.

He'd just box away his feelings for her and hope that they died quietly, unacknowledged and unfulfilled.

"Just be yourself," he advised Miranda. It was all that he could tell her, as inexperienced as he was.

Nadine and Miranda eventually finished updating him. At the end, they had discussed the upcoming office Christmas party. It didn't matter that he'd avoided attending for so long. In the past, he'd flit in, make his rounds greeting everyone and then leave as quietly as he'd entered. He loved creating parties for other people; he didn't so much enjoy participating in them.

But with Christmas Eve right around the corner, they had some planning to do, and like always, Nadine and Miranda were in charge. He just signed off on whatever they suggested, fully trusting in their ability to do their best for the staff.

Karl had delved into his work after the two women left him.

He didn't glance up, not even when a knock sounded at his closed office door. "Come in."

"Am I interrupting you?" Lin's sweet, sexy voice drifted from the doorway. She had one foot in and one still out in the hallway, looking as though she wasn't sure whether to fully enter. Shyness overtaking her, she softly said, "I was hoping you could have lunch with me. I packed extra." She had a lunch bag in her hands, and it did look big enough to feed them both.

Karl's heart did what it was wont to do ever since they had kissed. It pumped faster and harder.

"Yeah. Lunch is good."

Her smile was brilliant, and she slipped into his office now more comfortably. He was curious as to how she did it. As he helped her clear his desk for their meal, he sneaked furtive glances at her. Was she not affected at all by what had happened between them? Because he'd been dreaming about it, and during the day, he found his mind meandering to that special moment. And it *had been* special. He could fight falling in love with her. What he couldn't deny was he'd liked kissing her and wanted desperately to do it again.

But she'd drawn a line there, and he would respect it.

"Are you working on the office party too?" Lin hovered closer to him, considering his dual monitors. He had the files open for Nadine's sketches on the party layout. They were hosting it in a trendy nightclub. The whole space would be cleared out for their staff party. "Miranda and Nadine have been talking about it nonstop."

"I'm not surprised," he mumbled.

She heard his tone and snapped her head to him. "Are you not going?"

"I'll show up. I always do. But I don't stay."

"Why not?" She handed him one of the club sandwiches she'd made. He smelled the smoked turkey and grilled cheese and stifled a ravenous groan.

Realizing they needed coffee, he held off from answering her to grab some cups, and when he was seated again, he finally said, "I'm not a partying kind of person."

She snorted. "You plan parties for a living."

"Ironic, I know," he said dryly. "You should look forward to it, though. The club's a hot spot in the city right now. Gives you a chance to check out the nightlife the city has to offer, even if most of the guests will be people you've met around the office." Everyone could bring a plus-one. Miranda was bringing her boyfriend, Darius. Nadine said she was dragging an old school friend along. He hadn't considered it because he wouldn't be hanging around the party for longer than was necessary for the boss to show his face.

"I've seen a few clubs already. It's not much different from what's available in Nairobi."

"Still, an opportunity to soak in Calgary while you have time."

She hummed in agreement around a mouthful of her sandwich.

"Of course, it's nice that you get to bring a plus-one." As he said it, he felt his heart rebel against him and jerk in protest. He clenched his jaws at the heavy oppression of jealousy squatting on his chest. The envy was, unfortunately, another side effect of kissing her. The thought of another person touching Lin, holding her and kissing her made him want to punch a wall in retaliation. Not that he'd ever behave inappropriately around her. She could bring anyone she wanted, and he wouldn't say or do a damn thing to stop her.

She's not mine to control.

She didn't belong to him, full stop.

He just had to get it through his thick skull.

"Any plans for Christmas besides the office party?" Lin asked when she finished her lunch. She sipped at her cooling coffee and watched him over the rim of her cup.

"Dinner at Carrie's." It was a standing tradition. Every Christmas Eve, Karl spent the evening with Carrie, Stefon and their grown kids and grandkids. Although he didn't like parties, he had to admit that he looked forward to the family gathering. It replaced the thought of what he hadn't had in his parents' cold home.

"Sounds familiar," she said with a warm smile.

"Actually, she's invited you again." Karl had nearly forgotten about it. "You should come." He tried for nonchalance, but his chest tightened in anticipation.

"I shouldn't intrude…" It had been what she'd said the first time.

"I'd love the company," he urged, voice hoarse with a rising need. It burgeoned out of nowhere and drilled him below the belt.

She shrugged lightly but smilingly. "All right." She turned away then to clean his desk of her lunch.

Karl freed a low, shaky breath, realizing the degree to which he'd been invested in her response. And now that he knew she was coming, he privately indulged in a smile of his own.

"Call me over the holidays," shouted Miranda across the parking lot. She waved and blew kisses enthusiastically while her good-natured, less drunk boyfriend escorted her gently into the back of a cab. Lin and Nadine waved back until they were gone.

Turning to her, Nadine said, "I should go too. I have a red-eye to catch, and I still have to wrap presents and pack and—" She broke off with a moan and then winked at something…or someone behind Lin.

"Have a good Christmas," Karl's deep, rumbling and sexy voice washed over her.

Half turning, she saw that he'd come up behind her and was far closer than she thought. And his eyes were on her. She tamped down the urge to shiver from the onslaught of pleasure in response to him.

"Merry Christmas to you both." Nadine walked away to her car.

"Truck's warmed and ready to go. Are you?" He had been busy heating the truck for her, insisting that she remain inside the club. She was glad he had. It was freezing outside. Temperatures had dropped drastically as the sun descended through the sky. But their night was far from over. They had a dinner at Carrie's ahead of them, and it had made sense for her to hitch a ride with Karl.

It also meant that he hadn't been able to leave the office party like he'd told her he usually did.

Not that he'd appeared to mind. He'd said that he didn't like parties, but he had been singing with her on a karaoke duet and cutting up the dance floor when Miranda and Nadine had asked the DJ to play some late-nineties R & B hits. What he hadn't done was drink a drop of alcohol. He was driving them to Carrie's, and he was taking his job seriously.

"Did you have fun?" she asked.

"It was…entertaining."

She laughed. "In other words, you had *fun*."

He chuckled at that, surprising her by the warmth and breadth of his grin.

Lin liked the silence that dispersed through the cabin. It was peaceful. She spent it admiring the holiday lights strung up all over the city. On the black branches of trees, on shop fronts and on the balconies of residential buildings. She cracked open the window and breathed in the refreshing wintry air. Now that she wasn't standing out in the cold, she liked how it brushed over her flushed face.

"Do you mind if I make a detour to my place?"

She looked back at him over her shoulder and shook her head. "Detour away." She was curious to see his place, and she tried to pretend she wasn't getting giddy as she peeled her eyes for the first sight of his home. Soon they had left behind the clustered buildings of downtown, and Karl was driving them past big, beautiful homes in a wealthy suburb.

Some of the houses were clearly historic buildings, their architecture still regal.

Quietly, he turned into the drive of the only unlit home on this side of the road.

"You don't have any lights up," she said, leaning

forward and peeking up at his home through the snow gathering on the windshield.

He unbuckled his seat belt and opened his door, glancing back at the last moment. "You can come in."

When she followed him into his home, the first thing she noticed was the hush. And how cold it was. Shuddering, she willed her teeth to stop chattering and failed. Karl gestured her to trail after him once they both shucked their boots. He guided her to his family room. She should have known that it would be magnificent. She'd gotten a glimpse of the foyer when she'd entered and marveled at the vaulted ceiling with its impressive skylight and curved staircase with glossy wooden handrail and balustrades.

The family room was a mix of contemporary and traditional decor, with half the room covered in dark wood bookshelves, a home bar installed opposite the shelves, a pair of bold blue club chairs positioned in front of a gas fireplace. The earthy red brick of the fireplace surround and the emptiness of its wooden mantel was jarring. She'd have thought it a good place to put framed photos of his family.

He ushered her to the sofa and flicked on the dark fireplace.

In an instant the warmth of the hearth flickered to life and poured through her. Her jaws loosened and her whole body floated in bliss. She soon yawned and blinked blearily when the heat closed around her.

She hadn't been aware Karl had left her until he was with her again and holding out a mug.

Lin tasted it without asking and moaned when she recognized it was hot chocolate.

"I'll just be a second," he said before vanishing again.

He was gone for a while, but when he was back, her fatigue ripped away and she sat up alert. He had a cream-colored thin rectangular box in his hands. The box was elegantly wrapped with gold ribbon. It was definitely a present by the way he held it gently. But for whom, she didn't know.

She'd have sworn he was blushing, but he schooled his features into calm by the time he was close enough to the light of the fire to tell.

Karl sat by her with the box held out halfway.

"I know you don't celebrate Christmas, but I wanted to give this to you…"

"It's for me?" Heat spooled through her. Now she was blushing. "I didn't get anything for you." At his encouragement, she took the box and unwrapped it carefully. She gasped softly when she saw what lay inside.

She lifted the gold chain with its African pendant charm and fought the tears stabbing tiny knives into her eyes. "This is so sweet."

"I thought of you when I saw it." He evaded her eyes and nervously traced his mustache. She knew he was blushing now, and she was leaning in to give him more of a reason to be embarrassed. Before she reconsidered it, she kissed his cheek quickly and drew back, hearing his sharp inhale.

"What was that for?" he asked raspingly.

"I just wasn't expecting a gift." Not from him. He'd been incredibly generous to her, and he hadn't freaked out when she had kissed him that one time. Lin hadn't cast her mind there since it had happened. She'd initiated the kiss, sure. But she hadn't really thought he desired her back. Then he'd clutched her and returned her kiss with equal hunger and admitted that he felt the chemistry she had been feeling between them the whole time.

He brushed the spot she'd kissed on his cheek and lowered his hand, frowning.

Lin's chest rose and fell faster as he stared at her.

His eyes dropped to her mouth. She licked her lips.

Slowly, he pulled into her, giving her plenty of time to push him back by the time his breath mingled with hers. She should have stopped them. The risk of endangering their unlikely but growing friendship was a very real thing that scared her. She was already facing the possibility of never having the same relationship with her grandfather again. He hadn't spoken to her since she'd left. She didn't want the same happening with Karl.

Was losing Karl worth another of his forbidden kisses?

Yes, she decided. And without another thought, she pressed her lips to his like she had before.

He recovered much quicker this time. Lifting her up, he settled her in his lap, her legs wrapping around him instinctually. Karl scorched her mouth with his fiery kisses, his lips expertly stroking hers, his tongue coaxing hers to play, and his hands smoothing over her back and drawing her nearer to his loving.

"Stay with me," he panted, his eyes unfocused, glazed with his longing—an echo of everything she was feeling right then.

She cupped his strong jaw and kissed him slow and long.

It was all the answer he needed.

Lifting her up with him and chuckling low and huskily when she yelped in his ear, he carried her upstairs, and a moment later she was sprawled atop his massive, comfortable bed with him on top of her and their dinner plans forgotten to their passion.

CHAPTER TEN

LIN DIDN'T KNOW how her mom had done it.

All those years ago when she had packed up and called it quits, leaving her daughter and husband behind. She'd eventually sent along the request for a divorce, and Lin knew from her grandfather that she had since remarried and had other children. She still couldn't grasp how easy it had seemed in her mind for her mother to walk away. It had been a selfish thing to do…but maybe it had made her happier.

And maybe it had been selfish of Lin to sleep with Karl. She could certainly say she'd been happy in the moment. She was still floating on cloud nine from the bliss of being with him.

Beside her, he stirred, his eyes cracking open, and his smile indicating he felt as replete as she did.

"Rise and shine," she teased, looking up to where a shaft of moonlight spilled through his half-turned bedroom blinds. "Well, then again, maybe not."

She stroked along his chest, fingers skimming between his flexing pecs, his abs clenched in response to her touch, and his breath quickened. He caught her by the wrist right as she reached the waistband of his black boxer shorts. She didn't remember him pulling them on. But she'd been so boneless by the time he'd been done with her that she wasn't shocked her memory had some holes in it. All she knew perfectly well was that he'd satisfied her thoroughly. And judging by the way he gazed at her adoringly, kissed her tender inner wrist and stroked his thumb where his lips touched her, he had been no less affected by her.

"Too soon," he murmured at her.

There they'd have to disagree. She descended, and he met her kiss halfway. She draped herself over him and gasped into their tangled mouths when he flipped her over with a rumbling growl.

He reached between them, and a second later the hot, heavy and very thick evidence of his desire yielded against her naked quivering flesh.

She arched her back with an eagerness to unite them again.

His phone rang from somewhere across the room. They both groaned at the interruption.

"Ignore it," she moaned and locked her heels behind his back.

Karl seemed happy to oblige, but then it rang again. And again. And finally she loosened her legs and moaned, "On second thought, answer it and then put it on silent."

He laughed gruffly; the sound as pleasant as the sex had been. "It's my godmother," he reported and returned to bed.

She sat up at that. "Oh, no! Carrie's dinner."

Karl gripped her hand and pulled her back onto the bed before she scampered away from him. He wrapped his arms and caged her to him.

Lin gently pushed at his chest. "We're going to be late," she rushed breathlessly, more from the fact that his face was close to hers, and she could feel his rigid erection under her.

"No, we're not. Dinner is over by now, and I already let Carrie know that we would be…indisposed."

She stared at him with a new mortification. "You didn't tell her…" She couldn't complete the sentence, her face on fire from the thought of it alone.

His laughter frothed up around her and matched the way he cuddled her closer.

"Give me more credit than that. If Carrie knew you were here with me right now, she'd switch her event to my wedding." He stiffened suddenly, his muscles tauter, and his voice more strained when he added hastily, "Not that anyone's getting married."

"Of course not," she murmured.

She didn't know what else to say. He knew his godmother better. But it sounded about right. If she'd told her grandfather that she and Karl had… She blushed more furiously.

Let's just say that it's not something I want happening. Ever.

"It's late. Do you want to stay?"

She had her head resting on his shoulder and her naked body curled up to the warmth of him. There was enough natural lighting to see, but even without it she could hear the longing threaded in his voice and the heat spilling through his shadowed eyes.

Not for the first time, she questioned whether she was being selfish like her mother had been. She wanted to stay with him, but she knew realistically that this—whatever this forbidden fling was—would not last. She had a home in Kenya; he had one right here in Calgary. She worked with him, and she would be relying on his strong networking connections once she opened the doors of her own company.

She'd tossed aside her usual selflessness once already when she'd left her grandfather to pursue her dream. She would be gambling her newfound friendship with Karl for another incomparably perfect moment with him.

He dropped a kiss on her forehead, and she angled her head back, knowing exactly what she was going to do.

"I'll stay," she whispered and closed her eyes as he kissed her again.

Two nights.

He'd had Lin in his arms and his bed for two whole nights before they had to resurface out of his home on the day after Christmas. It hadn't been how he planned to spend his holidays, but they had been the best few days, that he'd had in a long while.

It was why his heart sank a little on the morning that she was leaving.

"I can't believe it's the first day of Kwanzaa already," she chirped beside him at his breakfast table. She was cheery for the early morning. Something he'd gotten used to in a short amount of time.

To think that he would have to recall what it had been like without her.

His thinking grew gloomier as the morning whizzed by and it came time for her to leave. She had suffered without her wardrobe and toiletries for two days, just to make him happy. But now she needed to drop by her apartment before they had to go back to work. He hadn't forgotten that the first day of Kwanzaa was also the beginning of Carrie's weeklong events leading up to her vow renewal.

Right before they walked out the front door, he looked around his home, at the lights and tinsel she'd looped around his staircase banister and the Christmas tree she'd had him rummage out of his storage in the basement so they could decorate together, and he sniffed the air that faintly smelled of their copious baking last night. Sugar cookies and a Kenyan fried-dough dish she had called *mandazi*. They'd been more delicious than the sugar cookies.

The lump in his throat had nothing to do with him missing her already.

"It's so sparkly." Lin looked back at him with her hand tossed up to shield her eyes from the bright white snow, but her lovely eyes squinched, anyways.

Okay, maybe he was moping a bit more than he thought he would.

Just like he knew he'd miss her more than he ever believed possible.

Checking another item off the list, Karl trekked from the food truck supplying their dinner for the evening to the big white tent on the white lawn. Snow tumbled lightly from the gray skies. He had to take bigger steps to keep from tripping and falling face first.

Inside, the tent was bustling. The earliest guests had arrived and more were trickling in in a steady stream. Miranda was positioned at the entrance to the tent, clipboard in hand, matching names and guiding Carrie and Stefon's guests to their seats on the seating chart. Nadine was going around checking on the heaters once again, moving them so that the tent was evenly heated and none of the guests were aware of the decline in temperature outdoors. The head table was empty for now, but his godmother would be making her grand entrance later on, once everyone else had arrived.

The tent flaps opened, and in walked Lin.

His heart stuttered.

She saw him immediately and veered in his direction. He took in her hair, her bright red faux locks bundled high on the middle of her head. She wore a colorfully geometric dress that made her rosy-brown skin lovelier, and the strappy black heels winding up her smooth calves had his mind slipping into gutter territory. She looked like an African goddess. The best part was the familiar gold necklace sitting right above the soft swell of her cleavage.

"It looks amazing," she said as soon as she was within earshot of him. She clutched the African charm pendant and looked around with that innocent expression of awe he'd grown used to. He knew that she was used to luxury and it wasn't the splendor of his events that threw her, rather the sentimental touches that were specific to Carrie's Kwanzaa-themed romantic event. "This place was empty when you sent me photos this morning."

He'd come here right after dropping Lin off at her apartment to shower and change. She had lived with him for two days without complaint that she was missing her home. He figured she'd been happy to get a little privacy back. Inexplicable bitterness flavored his tongue as he looked away and tried to see the tent through her eyes.

The decor was African in style. Rustically elegant wood-framed low sofas. Colorful print fabric interspersed with softer, muted shades of browns, beiges and greens. Found objects like feathers, horns and vividly bright African flora were gathered together in hand-crafted wooden jars at each table. The plate settings were copper chargers and rich and earth-toned reds, oranges and greens for the tablecloths and napkins. The place cards were simply the names of the guests in elegant calligraphy in Lin's own hand. She'd done them for the event without asking, but he liked how they'd turned out.

The head table was even more special.

A sparkling swath of fabrics in red, green and black swept down in arches and was pinned above a chandelier that dangled in the middle. The lighting fixture floated right above the special *kinara* that Lin had designed and printed for Carrie and Stefon. He peeked at Lin and noted that she saw it, her wide, joy-filled smile giving her away. Similar decor and color theme adorned the long table along with two gold thronelike chairs for the happy couple renewing their vows. It was coming together nicely…and hopefully quickly, as he blinked and noticed the tent was filling up.

"You should grab your seat." He didn't want her getting caught waiting as a line was beginning to form between the tables.

Lin hesitated, just staring up at him for a moment, but then she squeezed his hand and turned away. It looked like she'd wanted to say something. Whatever it was, he would have to wait to ask her. He had a party to manage.

Carrie and Stefon made a touching speech thanking the guests who'd attended the first of their many scheduled events for the last week of the year. At the end, they lit the central black candle on the *kinara* and spoke the opening phrase to any Kwanzaa festivity: *"Habari gani?" How are you?* The greeting in Lin's native tongue was familiar and comforting. As was the returning chorus of *"Habari gani?"* from other guests.

Dinner came after, and Lin chatted easily with Nadine and Miranda on one side. The chair on her other side was empty, though. Karl had left again to monitor the caterers this time. He'd done it in lieu of Nadine because Lin knew he wanted everything to run smoothly for his godmother.

"Don't look now, but I think that means trouble," Miranda leaned in to whisper, her eyes glued to the tent's entrance.

Lin lowered her fork and knife, the perfectly seasoned salmon and asparagus on her plate left to wait while she observed the newcomers. An older man and woman standing stiffly side by side but decked in head-to-toe designer clothing. The woman wore a gray fur stole and a figure-hugging sparkling dress the color of red wine. The man had gold cufflinks and a brilliant gold Rolex. Their brown skin shone like they'd spent hours in a spa, but their furrowed brows and pruned lips implied otherwise. They appeared wound-up about something, and they only got worse when Karl returned from minding the caterers and approached them.

"His parents," Miranda hissed right into her ear.

Lin startled. She'd been so absorbed by the family drama that she had forgotten she wasn't alone in spectating. She would've guessed they were his parents just by the way Karl had met them. Even from this distance, he looked like he was preparing for war.

"Are they not close?" Lin had wanted to ask him but missed her chance during Thanksgiving. Besides, she didn't think he would've answered her then. They hadn't been as close as they were now. A lot had transpired between them since…

Like having sex.

She blushed at that.

"We don't know." Nadine shrugged her one bare shoulder, her asymmetrical dress shimmering under the dazzling lighting overhead. "He doesn't discuss his family all that much. I know he has a lot of siblings. Three…or maybe it was four. Karl's always been pretty private about his personal life."

"But you're probably right, Lin. It doesn't look like a cozy family reunion, does it?" Miranda clicked her tongue and shook her head, but her glossy updo remained undisturbed. She must have had hundreds of bobby pins to hold all her hair up like that.

"Poor Karl," Nadine murmured in agreement.

"Yeah," Lin added forlornly.

She wasn't exactly in the best place with her grandfather either. It was hard watching Karl interact with his parents when it was obvious that there weren't any warm feelings between the two parties. She clamped her teeth into her bottom lip and realized she wouldn't be able to eat another bite until he was sitting next to her. Just as Lin envisioned herself standing and walking over to intervene, she saw Carrie and Stefon heading in the same direction, and she hoped it was to Karl's rescue.

Sure enough, Karl stepped away when his godmother patted his arm, and he stalked off—in the opposite direction of where Lin sat. He disappeared past a tent flap in the back of the tent where the caterers and waitstaff were coming in and out.

Lin's spirit deflated. She'd thought he would come over to her.

Why would he? Nothing's changed.

That wasn't true. Plenty had changed in a couple of days. She had gone beyond fantasizing about him to experiencing what it would be like waking up draped in his scent and wrapped by his body. She knew she was catching feelings, yet she couldn't stop herself from liking him. It wasn't an on-and-off switch she could easily flip when convenient to her. She shouldn't want to like him either. Shouldn't desire anything more. Not even another of his tasty kisses...

He also didn't seem interested in continuing how they'd spent the past two days.

It's for the best, Lin chided herself.

This way she could finish working without distractions. It just also happened to be the best way to protect her heart from the disappointment of a rejection.

CHAPTER ELEVEN

A CHORUS OF *"Habari gani?"* rose up from the workshop.

More and more of Carrie's guests were filtering into the space, and soon all the workstations were at full capacity. It was the day after the dinner in the tent, and they were enjoying the next event on the list that would culminate in Carrie and Stefon's vow-renewal ceremony. But there were still a few days until it was New Year's and the end of Kwanzaa.

Lin saw Karl. She paused, hesitating about whether to go to him.

Nadine and Miranda were already sharing a table with two other people. There wouldn't be room for her there.

But a cursory look around the room showed her that there were other tables with space for her. It would save her an awkward conversation with him. Since he'd disappeared from the tent yesterday, she'd only briefly glimpsed him when she had been on her way home. But Karl hadn't shown signs that he had seen her leaving. And she wasn't confident that she wouldn't be disturbing him had she gone up to say good-night.

Now here she was, deciding whether to avoid him again or not.

She wasn't any closer to a decision when Miranda hollered her name and caught the attention of everyone in the room. Heads turned toward her. Lin blushed, embarrassed at being in the spotlight. She waved shyly at Miranda and intended to walk over to greet her and Nadine, only her eyes locked onto Karl's.

He watched her, his mouth a long, even line, his face calm. None of the frustration he'd barely restrained around his parents yesterday marred his beautifully perfect face right now. Lin was staring at the man who had made sweetly explosive love to her.

She lowered her hand slowly and took a step toward Karl.

He nodded at her imperceptibly.

Lin smiled back, her doubt vanishing for now.

"Hey," she greeted him warmly, her face steadily growing hotter the longer the two other people at their station stared at her.

"Hey," he echoed. There was a small lift on one side of his mouth. A barely-there smile that was just for her.

She opened her mouth to ask him if everything was all right with his parents but stopped herself at the last second. He might not like her prying into his life. The last thing she wanted was to put a wedge between them. They had a short time left together, and even if she couldn't kiss him again, she didn't want to ruin whatever it was their relationship had become.

I'll miss him.

A sadness rolled through her at the thought. It had happened more often now as she crossed the final days off her mental calendar. Her plane ticket was booked for a week after New Year's Day. She had gone into this knowing she'd be leaving behind the friends and the happy memories she had created in Canada. Still, it was hard to psych herself up for it.

Harder now that she had someone she was going to miss a whole lot.

Casting Karl a sidelong glance, she felt another heart-wrenching pang.

The workshop starting was a good excuse for a distraction.

They were taking a pottery class. Carrie was good friends with the black business owners of the workshop. As part of her Kwanzaa event, she'd wanted as many of her guests as possible to experience African culture, modern and historical. Lin understood the owners were siblings, and they were leading the beginner-level workshop for the day.

A quick look around and she counted nearly two dozen eager workshop participants. It was a good turn-out for a weekday evening. Lin had worried that a week-long event might deter some of the guests, and it had some, just not as many as she'd thought. Clearly Carrie and Stefon had strong friendships in the city and the kind of support an upstanding couple like them deserved. Sadly, there was no sign of Karl's parents.

He'd looked so wound-up after the encounter with them. She commiserated with his plight and the difficulty of having hard-to-deal-with family. It couldn't be easy for him. To add to his problems, he was probably avoiding confrontation for Carrie's and Stefon's sakes.

Lin spotted his godmother.

Carrie saw her too and waved to them from one of the front tables. She nudged Stefon, and he raised a hand in greeting as well. Their enthusiasm was infectious. Lin only hoped it was a good omen for how the rest of the day would be. Or at least how the workshop would pan out.

Once the general introductions and explanations were made by the hosts and the workshop owners, she felt Karl's eyes on her. She looked up and confirmed he was staring at her.

That small smile briefly brushed his lips. "First time throwing on a wheel?"

"First time, period," she confessed, wincing. She loved trying new things, but she didn't want to outright embarrass herself in front of Karl. And throwing mud on a wheel could get messy. She knew that much.

Aprons and protective eyewear were passed around. Karl offered to help her tie the stays of her apron, and then he turned his back for reciprocation. As she tied a double knot, he said, "It's not hard. I'll help teach you."

Before she had a chance to question him, the workshop instructors called for their attention and began a demonstration of how to wedge the clay and prepare it for centering on the wheel head. She watched the same demonstration as everyone else, but when it came time to try her hand at pottery making for the first time, she couldn't recreate what she'd just seen demonstrated.

"It won't stay centered. Why won't it stay centered?" she grumbled under her breath.

She felt Karl's reassuring presence at her side, and she all too naturally leaned in to him, forgetting where they were until she heard Carrie's sparkling laughter from the other side of the room. Cheeks flushed hot, she gave him space and muttered, "Sorry." Little slips like that would land them in the kind of trouble she understood he wouldn't desire. Fielding questions from his staff and from Carrie weren't high on her priority list either. Not when it was general knowledge that she'd be leaving for home once she was done here.

"You're not applying even pressure from the top and side." He came up behind her then and sealed the personal space she'd just given him. With his hands on top of hers, he guided her palms and fingertips to coax cooperation from the red clay on her wheel. "More water. Your hands have to be wet, but not too wet."

He was all around her, his hard chest to her back, and his arms cocooning her closer to him. The scent of his cologne infiltrating her senses and making her brain chemically respond. The smoothness and bigness of his hands engulfing hers. Physically, she was turning to mush. Instead of feeling crowded by him, she wanted to snuggle into him more.

"Just like that. Not too hard, and none too gentle. You're the master. The clay will do what you want it to, but you can't force it either. Lean in, hold firm and gently steer it into doing what you want it to do."

"Got it," she croaked, biting her lip to stop from whimpering when his fingers caressed the back of her hands.

It was a more intimate demonstration than the one the workshop instructors had given.

When Karl moved away to his station, leaving her to practice what he'd taught her in his very hands-on demo, she couldn't help but wonder what might have happened had they been in the workshop alone, just the two of them.

She was having more fantasies of the same ilk.

It wasn't good that she was forming the attachment that she should be avoiding. She could have all the fun she wanted, but she didn't want to leave any piece of her behind with him. Worse for her if that piece turned out to be her heart.

The end of the workshop came too swiftly for her taste. She'd been enjoying herself a little too much. Not that her clay would tell you that. It was…not anything that she would want anyone to fire and glaze.

Case in point, Carrie walked over with a tray to collect Lin's piece for firing. Karl's godmother stopped by her wheel, and her mouth formed a little *O*.

"Is it a mug or a bowl?" she asked.

"I wish I knew." Lin snorted with laughter. Carrie laughed too, but she still insisted on glazing her masterpiece for her.

Carrie whistled when she paused behind her godson, finally bringing Lin's attention to Karl's wheel. She nearly whistled her appreciation as well. Stunned didn't begin to describe what she felt when she saw his finished piece.

He'd crafted a small teapot: stem, lid and all.

She wasn't alone in admiring what he had produced in the short allotted time of the workshop.

The other two guests at their workstation circled his space too, complimenting him.

Some other participants and guests of Carrie and Stefon gathered to praise the teapot—easily the best piece crafted there that evening.

"Show off," Carrie joked, taking his teapot for the baking and glazing that would be done in the back room.

"I should have known you were a pro at this when you were helping me," said Lin as soon as they were alone, the other guests drifting off to a break room in the back that had been converted to a small snacking area with refreshments and even music as entertainment. She shook her head laughingly. "But I'll admit you surprised me. Pottery as a talent."

"I can juggle too," he said with a lopsided smile.

She laughed harder, wiping at the tears pricking her eyes and gasped, "I don't even know who you are." Laughter slowing, she realized just how true that was, yet she still didn't find it a fault. If they had more time left, she would use it unwrapping the mysteries that shrouded him and peeling back the many layers to his heart.

Stopping herself before she started dwelling on it, she tipped her head to the exit.

"It'll take time before our art has baked. Did you want to go for a walk?"

It would give them time together. She only wished she had more of it to spend with him.

Calgary was beautiful at night. Somehow the winter nights right after a decent snowfall were the best. City lights glowing better off the white snow that hadn't browned yet. The air crisp with a chill that took your breath away. The city quieter under the blanket of fresh snow. Karl would almost say it was romantic if he believed in romance and love. Not wanting to ruin the moment with pointless thoughts, he concentrated on what he did have.

Right now it was this nascent but transient bond with Lin.

She was leaving: that was inevitable. He'd known it when he'd hired her services, and he understood it when they had agreed to start a physical relationship. Yet as that time inched closer and closer, he had begun to acknowledge it more with every day that passed—every day that was one day less with Lin.

"I'll need to seriously warm up after this with a cup of tea." Beside him, Lin huddled into her coat, another thin peacoat that wasn't made to withstand the cold.

They had walked far enough from the pottery workshop for him to be all right with risking putting an arm over her shoulders and drawing her closer to the warmth he could provide. She sagged under his embrace, curling into his side, and wrapping her own arm around his waist for support.

Reflexively, he pressed a kiss to her temple, smiling when she hummed her pleasure.

That was how they entered the café he had in mind.

Once they had their orders, they grabbed a table with a view of the street and the snow that had piled there over the day in massive drifts. He was partly glad it wasn't snowing anymore. It would make driving Lin to his home safer. *See? Even that.* Before her, he hadn't had thoughts like that. Somehow her safety was paramount now, and he was too tired to argue or silence the instinct.

"So...pottery. What's up with that?" she asked, her cup of black tea warming her hands, her eyes brighter and her skin looking less chaffed by the cold weather they'd walked through for their prize of caffeine.

"When I was in school, I took a course, and then I did a few months of apprenticeship with a local ceramist." He had thought he'd forgotten the skills of the trade, but the workshop today was a reminder that he still possessed a talent for and interest in it.

"You wanted to work with ceramics," she said, sounding less shocked and more engaged in his past dream.

"It was a long time ago, but yes. It was a career path I'd seriously considered."

She seemed to have forgotten her tea, and he couldn't help but notice she was a little too engaged for his comfort. Especially when she asked, "What happened to change your mind? How did you go from training ceramist to event planner extraordinaire?"

Karl gazed into his cup and felt the scowl tipping his mouth down. He should have seen this coming. Should have known that he wasn't ready to talk about it, let alone to relive the memories tied to his old career dream.

But Lin was waiting on his reply, and he'd dug this hole, so he had to see it through wherever it led him. "My parents didn't approve." It was a simple answer. The plain, ugly truth too. His parents hadn't wanted a son of theirs doing anything that wouldn't directly benefit the family businesses. They'd berated him until it was too much to bear and he had caved in to their wish to see him doing something else with his life. Something *they* approved of.

Of course, that hadn't turned out the way they wanted either.

"They didn't like my ceramics, so I quit." It had just been one more thing that his parents had controlled in his life. "I was lucky that I found something else I enjoy equally and I'm good at. It just wasn't working on a potter's wheel with muddy fingers."

He didn't have to give Lin the playback or go into in-depth explanation. She had a sympathetic look ready for him.

"They were trying to control you," she surmised sadly, and he realized that this hit home for her too. She had done all of this—paused her life in Kenya and worked with him because she wanted to prove her ability to her grandfather. He knew family could be toxic. He knew they could be good but still find ways to hurt you.

His parents hadn't done him any good. Except maybe instill in him the drive to be his own boss.

"They still try. If I let them, they'd be happy."

"Your answer was to stop everything." Her bottom lip actually trembled.

Karl balled his hand into a fist so he wouldn't lose the battle to reach out and comfort her. It was one thing for him to loathe reliving his past but another to see her torn up about it on his behalf. He didn't like to see her upset. "I was young, impressionable. At the time I really believed them when they said that I'd be fine without it. I didn't realize that they were trying to change me to suit their tastes." They'd played the same game with his siblings. Cyrus had been the only one who had jumped at their command. They had done everything possible to suppress their individuality. In the end, all they'd accomplished was pushing their children away.

"You shouldn't have stopped. You shouldn't let them win now. You're so good at pottery."

He snorted humorlessly, one dry note that was half bark, half laugh. "That may be so, Lin, but I'm not quitting what I do or closing my company."

"I didn't say that you should. As a hobby, maybe?"

He hadn't thought of that before. After his parents had crushed his dream, he'd packed it away with the intent never to revisit it. Lin hadn't known that he used to do ceramics, so she couldn't have known that it would dredge up this old grudge he had against his parents. Maybe it was the universe's way of giving him another chance.

A chance he wouldn't have considered if he hadn't had this talk with Lin.

"A hobby perhaps," he agreed.

She rewarded him with a smile. A smile that he wanted pressed to his mouth. Before he talked himself out of it, he leaned over the table separating them, and he touched his lips to hers. He melted when she sighed into their connected mouths, her mewl coiling around his pounding heart like her hands clinging to his shoulders and pulling him closer.

This, he thought, *is why it'll be hard to let her go.*

In that instant, he knew he would trade all the ceramic talent he had for an extra day or two with her. He just didn't know what to do about it.

CHAPTER TWELVE

THE NEXT FEW days blended together for Karl. It was as though he had taken the longest blink of his life, and he'd jumped three, four days into the future, and now it was all that much closer to counting down to the New Year and the end of Kwanzaa.

It also meant Carrie's vow renewal with her husband was fast approaching.

And that means Lin's leaving soon.

He didn't want to worry about that now, though. He had plenty of time to do it *after* Carrie's celebration. The festive mood was in full swing today as Carrie, Stefon, her family and guests were skating. Not everyone was wearing skates, however. A few guests had braved trying the ice bikes that the city park had made available to borrow. Miranda whizzed by on one of them, narrowly missing him. Nadine was hot on her trail. Apparently, they were racing around the perimeter of the wide pond. Karl shook his head, smiling, but he lost that smile when he looked around the people sharing the patch of blue ice with him on that frosty winter afternoon, and he saw that Lin wasn't among them.

She was still nowhere to be seen.

He'd dropped her off at her place to change out of last night's outfit. They had been to another event yesterday and gone back to his home together. If she showed up wearing the same outfit, someone would suspect something. He had wanted to pick her up, but she'd insisted that she could find her way to the park, reminding him that he'd brought her here before when they had been enjoying the leaves together there. It was hard to think that had only been a couple of months ago.

He had always been attracted to her. From the moment he had set eyes on her, there had been this chemical pull she had on him. Then he had learned she felt the same, and they'd embarked on an affair.

An affair that was ending soon.

He didn't need the reminder. What he needed was for Lin to get here so he could stop worrying and wondering whether he should go and fetch her himself. But he understood that space was healthy. They'd spent so much time together in the last week she needed her own time to do her own things. All healthy relationships shared this foundation—

But he wasn't in a relationship with her, not in that sense of the word.

They were lovers. This thing between them was purely physical, sexual.

Romance and love had never been part of the equation. He wasn't sending her flowers, or lighting candles aside from the ones they had for Kwanzaa every night. He sure as heck wasn't falling for her...

Had he fallen for her?

It would explain this nostalgia he'd been struggling with every time he thought of her and replayed their time spent together. He had felt something like this with Isaiah. That was when he'd lost his head and heart to his boyfriend. When he had loved him. Karl froze on the ice rink. He'd been gliding slowly on his skates the whole while, the pace reflecting his deep thinking. Moving aside out of respect for the other skaters, he stood on the bank, hands on his hips, and his face turned up to the gray clouds blotting the blue sky.

He knew he'd felt this way before. Done this dance before. Sung this same song.

No, it's different with Lin than it was with Isaiah.

With Isaiah it had been a roller-coaster. All wild, hot, with flimsy restraints and no quick way to stop. The crash-and-burn of his heartbreak should have been expected. Isaiah hadn't wanted to be saddled with the mess he'd become after his parents had kicked him out. In all fairness, he had been confused and angry and hurt.

With Lin it hadn't been a four-alarm fire. Their time together was less volatile but still so passionate she'd left an indelible impression on him. So not the exact same shade or flavor that he'd once had with Isaiah but adjacent. More addicting, that was for certain. Part nostalgia, the other part was just frighteningly new.

But I loved Isaiah...

Following that logic, he loved Lin. Had fallen in love with her sometime in the span of meeting her and carrying her to his bed.

Karl had scratched the surface of his realization when he heard Lin's name.

Miranda and Nadine were calling out to her from the pond's icy surface.

Breathlessly, he sought her out with his eyes and then breathed easier when he saw it was her. She looked perfectly fine too, which eased his concern that she had somehow been delayed by disaster, and then he saw who was walking with her.

The blood in his veins chilled and congealed. But

the iciness that gripped him didn't root his skates to the frozen lake. He skated forward, gliding choppily in his haste to reach where Lin was with his brother, Cyrus. Behind them, his parents looking as foreboding as they always had.

As they always will.

The only thing keeping him from charging faster to them was that Lin looked comfortable. She was gesturing with her hands and smiling, and Cyrus looked down at her like a big grinning fool.

Karl ground his teeth when his older brother threw back his head and laughed loudly and obnoxiously. God. It was the same annoying sound he'd had to deal with when they'd been children and Cyrus had gotten the upper hand by having their parents take his side in their squabbles. That laughter had haunted him once. Now it just grated badly.

But his blood boiled when Cyrus touched Lin's shoulder and beamed that stupid grin of his down at her.

Enough.

With an angry boost in energy, he leaped onto the embankment and stopped before them.

His parents, Cyrus and Lin all came to a halt, eyes widening at the sight of him.

"Karl," his mom said and smiled, but it rang as forced and tight.

His dad just grumbled under his breath. He didn't catch any of it, but he knew it wasn't anything that could be said in decent company.

Ignoring them, he drilled his focus on Lin. "What took you so long?"

Her eyes doubled in size, and she darted a look from him to his parents before saying softly, "I lost the key to my luggage, so I couldn't grab my favorite jeans."

Then, after a beat of silence, she added, "I hope you weren't worried."

He realized he was acting a fool over a wardrobe mishap. It would have been embarrassing if it had been the two of them, but he'd done it in front of his family. Clenching his teeth, he avoided the press of their stares—and in Cyrus's case, that smarmy grin of his— just knowing that if he looked their way, he would feel worse than he already did.

Lin was frowning lightly, her eyes reflecting the same unease he'd experienced when she had been away from him.

"I wanted to go over a few of your latest designs and prints." He was lying through his teeth. He trusted whatever she had produced for Carrie's events so far. She hadn't disappointed him, not once, and he didn't see the point in looking over her shoulder. Not when she'd started, and not now. But he had to say something to backtrack this humiliation.

"Right now?" she asked.

He jerked his head affirmatively and whirled back to the ice, knowing that she would follow.

Lin stared at the top of Karl's bald head. He had guided her to a bench near the skate-rental place. He had come back with a pair, and it wasn't until he started lacing her up that she realized that she hadn't, in fact, told him her size. Still, he had somehow gotten it right. She had no complaints about pinched toes or poor blood circulation in her feet. Standing with a little wobble, she smiled gratefully when he grasped her hands and helped her onto the ice.

She hadn't forgotten how she'd ended up skating with him.

"What's this about my latest prints?"

"Nothing. They're perfect," he said.

She squeezed his hands and struggled to concentrate on where her feet were on the ice. She wanted to look into his eyes when she asked this next part.

"Were you luring me away from your parents and brother?"

"I hadn't expected they'd show up." A valid answer, yet she heard something in his voice that had her suspecting there was more he wasn't saying.

She let his answer be what it was for a while, focusing on his hands holding hers, his skates expertly sliding backward despite every jerk forward by her. Once they'd done a full circuit of the ice and avoided any mishaps along the way, she trailed back to what they had been discussing. His family's unexpected arrival and his tense reaction to them.

"Aren't you going to ask why I showed up with them?" she asked.

Karl helped her transition off the ice back onto less slippery ground. He stayed standing when she dropped onto a bench and peered up at him.

"I figured there was a good reason." That might be so, but his closed-off expression suggested otherwise.

"We bumped into each other in the parking lot. They asked for directions, and I told them I was part of Carrie's party too."

"See," he said gruffly, looking more satisfied than he had a second earlier, "a perfectly sound reason."

Lin desperately wished she could let him off with that comment, but she needed to know if having his family so near was hurting him.

Why? Because I think he wants comfort.

She knew Karl presented himself as this strong, emo-

tionally resistant person, but she also understood it had
to be tough on him, dealing with whatever bad blood
existed between him and his parents and brother, and
keeping his head on straight to make Carrie and Stefon's celebratory events as amazing as they were as individuals and a couple.

That was why she had to talk to him.

Patting the space on the bench beside her, she said,
"I think there's more to what you're not saying. I don't
want you holding it in."

"I don't know what you mean."

"Pushing it down and pretending it doesn't exist
might make you feel better now, but it doesn't make
the problem go away."

He jutted his jaw out and clenched it. "There isn't
a problem."

"If that were true, you'd have been able to look them
in the eyes. Instead, you ignored them and walked off
with me." She threw up her hands. "I don't know what
you'd call that, but I'd say it was a problem."

She watched his shoulders draw back and his thick
black brows slam down. That dense wall of defense was
sliding into place.

"They're Carrie's guests. Not mine."

Lin was losing him. Any second now he'd tell her
off and walk away. She didn't want that happening. Not
when all she wanted was to help ease the burden he was
shouldering. A burden that had to do with his family
and whatever had driven him to be at odds with them.

"Okay. I know when to back off."

Karl's frown didn't look as scary as it had a second
earlier. "It's not your fault." He locked his hands between his legs and looked out at the frozen pond. His
scowl stormed over his face when she saw his line of

sight aligned with his parents and brother. She knew who he was blaming, but she didn't understand how it had gotten to be this bad.

"Why are you angry with them?" she coaxed softly, in hopes that he would open up to her.

"They kicked me out."

It was said bluntly, so that she didn't miss any of the bitterness roughening his voice.

"Why?" she choked after the shock passed.

"Simple. My parents decided I wasn't ever going to fit that perfect mold they had in their minds of what their children should be like."

She reached for him instinctively, her hand on his leg offering a comforting squeeze.

He didn't seem to register her touch, his gaze focused on the distance and his voice growing harder and angrier. "It was the same with my other siblings too. All except Cyrus." He sneered his brother's name, and she didn't recognize him at that moment. The mask fully stripped, the pain and rage fighting for a place to control him. "Cyrus was their golden boy. He tattled on us. Bullied us. All because he didn't want to *be* us. He had their favor, and he wanted it more than he wanted a relationship with his brothers and sister."

"What about your other siblings?" Surely they'd have bonded over Cyrus's ill treatment of them.

But she guessed she was wrong when Karl pried his jaws apart to grit out, "You'd think we would be closer, but no. Our parents pushed us to compete our whole lives. It was always about one-upping each other. Cyrus did it best, but we all played the game when we were younger, when it was easier to believe that we were fighting for our parents' attention and love instead. It took a long while to realize they didn't have any love to give us. They never had."

"Karl…" She didn't know what else to say to him.

"We never fully healed from that trauma. I can't remember the last time I spoke to or saw my brothers and sister."

"And your parents? How long has it been since…" She couldn't bring herself to say it again, her heart breaking for him.

"Long enough to know that they'd done the best thing for me when they pushed me away." He pushed to his feet and swung that gloomy scowl on her. "I'm better without them in every regard. I just need them to see that I never needed them."

She was on her shaky feet as well, the skates not deterring her from pressing a hand to his chest and peering up at him with solidarity in her every fiber. "I know you're hurting, but wouldn't it help to talk to them? To tell them and *show* them what you're showing me right now?"

Lin hadn't heard anything good about his family, and from what she had sensed from them they weren't the most approachable people, yet it didn't change the fact they'd always have ties to Karl. She was raised differently. She got that. Culturally, children didn't disown their parents—or even elder figures who were *like* parents. As much as she butted heads with her grandfather's mulish personality and narrow perception of the world, she still loved and respected him, and she'd have struggled to envision a world where she didn't need him in her life.

She just wanted to see Karl happy. And she didn't know if making his parents and Cyrus see the pain they had caused him would do that, but she wanted to try whatever would work.

"You're unhappy. Wouldn't talking to them help?"

For a second she believed she'd gotten through to him.

The angry fog reddening his vision cleared, and his brows weren't pinched with the fury he'd been leashing this whole while. But then his face darkened, and she knew she'd lost him even before he stepped back from her and covered his emotions with that impenetrable mask of his.

He turned from her, but not before he grumbled, "I have to go. But you should stay."

Lin watched him alight on the pond's surface with the same ease he'd used to craft his ceramic masterpiece a few days ago. He glided away from her, not looking back once, and when he reached the other side of the ice, he worked quickly to untie his skates and pull them off. Finally, she couldn't look anymore, and she ducked her head, her vision swimming, and her heart paining her awfully.

She'd only wanted to help him, but it seemed she had done more harm than good.

She would've sulked for the rest of the day, but Miranda and Nadine rode over on their ice bikes and encouraged her to join them for some fun. For a while she *did* forget her worries. Eventually, though, it wasn't enough to ignore the memory of Karl's embittered expression. She fretted about him. He was alone someplace and probably believing that no one cared about him.

I care!

She did, and that was why it hurt so much to know he was hurting somewhere without her. Lin had to go to him. It didn't matter if he pushed her away again or shut her out, she had to know that she'd tried.

Getting off the ice, she hurried to unlace her skates.

"Need help with those?" Carrie kneeled to assist before she could protest.

Meekly, Lin admitted, "Karl helped tie them on."

"I noticed." The older woman peeked up at her, a sly twinkle in those sharp eyes of hers. "I also saw and sensed a bit of tension."

She wanted to lie, tell Carrie she'd seen wrong, but she couldn't do it and instead babbled, "He was upset to see his parents and brother, and I tried to cheer him up, but I think he's angry with me now too." She squelched the sob that burned her throat, her eyes watering again, and Carrie's kind face blurring.

Freeing her of her skates first, Carrie sat by her on the bench and draped her arm over her shoulder. Lin turned to her naturally and sunk into the maternal comfort Karl's godmother was offering with no qualms.

"He won't talk to me ever again," she said against Carrie's shoulder.

"Hush. I know my godson, and that's the last thing he'd do."

Lin wanted to seek solace in her words, but her guilt at having pushed Karl to try to make up with his parents was greater. Why had she been so intent? She knew why. She was looking at it through her experience. She'd had her mother walk out on her, and the knowledge had stung for years. Even if she knew that rationally she couldn't have done anything as it had happened when she'd been so young, Lin had still felt *responsible*. Perhaps she hadn't been the easiest child to raise? Maybe she'd driven her mom to the point of no return?

Either way, she didn't love me enough to stay.

And Karl's parents hadn't loved him enough just the way he was.

Lin's heart throbbed painfully for them both. Knowing all that she knew now she had still pushed and pushed and *pushed*—until she'd sent him off to who knew where.

"He hates me," she groused, hopelessly stuck to that belief. "I can't see in what universe he'd want to talk to me again."

"Trust me. He'll do some talking. I've been cooking up this scheme far longer than you've known Karl." Carrie's wicked grin softened after she pulled Lin back by her shoulders and asked her sweetly, "Now, my dear, will you do me the honor of attending a dinner I'll be hosting tonight? I know you missed a couple already, but I don't think you'll want to miss this one."

CHAPTER THIRTEEN

KARL SHOULD HAVE known something was up when Carrie called to ask him over for dinner. He hadn't ever had an unplanned evening at his godmother's. She was nearly as meticulous about time as he was. But he'd put aside his suspicion and give her the benefit of the doubt.

Now he knew he shouldn't have.

His first clue that she had something up her sleeve was that her driveway held two cars he didn't recognize. One a forest-green Jeep and the other a gleaming white Escalade that blended in with the fresh snowfall. He narrowed his eyes at the inconvenience of having to park his truck on the curb.

Carrie's home was one of many older houses in the historic neighborhood overlooking the Bow River and the skyline of downtown Calgary. The home was a charming one-and-a-half-story Craftsman build, its siding painted a mellow blue, and its wide sash windows bordered by bone-white windowpanes. The low-pitched roof sloped over a covered front porch. He stood on that porch and rapped the brass knocker beneath an ornate Christmas wreath, his gaze passing over the holiday lights twinkling from many neighboring homes. Carrie had fully decorated her home as usual. Lights hanging on her rafters spilled over the snow on her front lawn. He knew it was even brighter inside her home.

The door opened and he turned to it—stopping short and losing his ability to breathe for a split second.

Cyrus stood in the doorway. He'd opened the door for Karl, his face plastered with that maddening grin of his. "Hey, little bro." He leaned on the doorjamb and blocked his path. "We have some catching up to do."

As Karl ground his teeth down to nubs, he finally realized what Carrie had been up to...and he didn't like it one bit.

Lin heard the doorbell and knew it had to be Karl.

Everyone else had arrived; he was the only dinner guest that was missing. She'd fretted that he wouldn't show up and wished that she had called him. But after the way they'd left things at the pond yesterday, she didn't think that he'd want to talk to her so soon. It was an irrational thought to think he was upset enough not to speak to her again, but she still worried.

She dried her hands quickly and turned to answer the door.

Cyrus leaped up from his spot on the sofa in the family room and called out, "I'll grab it."

Behind her she felt the comforting press of Carrie's hand on her shoulder. Seeing that she had no choice, she whirled back to continue finishing up in the kitchen with Karl's godmother. At least cooking was keeping her mind off the tense showdown that was likely unfolding in the front entrance between Karl and his older brother.

As she set the dining table, she peeled her ears for any hint as to how it was going with Karl. She didn't know if it was a good thing that she heard nothing other than the low rumble of voices.

Her hands shook lightly as she set cutlery down. Unsurprisingly, she dropped a fork and stooped to pick it up from the earth-toned carpet beneath the dining table. Lin stood and choked a gasp when she saw Karl standing across the table from her. He had the same forbidding scowl in place. Obviously, nothing had changed for him. And he wasn't happy that Carrie had invited his family to dinner as well.

"She invited you too." He said it in a coldly matter-of-fact way that made her flinch.

Clutching the fork she'd have to change out between her suddenly sweaty hands, she gulped and said, "I couldn't refuse Carrie's invitation for the third time."

He didn't smile.

It was awful timing then that Cyrus walked into the dining room and cut a glance at them both. "Looks like I'm interrupting—"

"Absolutely nothing," Karl snapped and stalked in the opposite direction.

A moment later, she heard the front door slam, and she knew he'd left. Lin's eyes stung. She couldn't move either as her vision swam, her chest so tight that her breaths sawed out of her lungs noisily. She wasn't even aware of Cyrus's presence anymore. The dinner itself was meaningless now that Karl had walked out. She'd hoped that it would give him the chance to hash it out with his family. Not forgive them necessarily but move past the hurt he still clearly hauled along everywhere.

A hand brushed her arm, and she looked up, right into Carrie's soft, knowing eyes.

Lin whispered, "He's gone."

Carrie nodded and rubbed her arm soothingly.

Cyrus had vanished, and she would bet Carrie had something to do with it. After a little sob, Lin took herself down the hall to the powder room that Karl's godmother had showed her earlier. Along the way she heard the front door opening again. Looking back hopefully, she deflated when she saw it was Stefon and Karl's father, Charles, strolling in, their dark cheeks ruddier from their walk out in the cold. They didn't look as though they'd seen Karl, their conversation about sports continuing normally.

She dried her eyes, careful not to smudge her makeup and ruin the effort she had made to look good for dinner. The pastel blouse she wore was one of her favorite tops. She'd paired it with palazzo pants and ankle boots. Her fingers clasped the shiny gold charm that Karl had given her, her thumb caressing the warm metal surface, and her eyes burning with the threat of tears once more.

When she left the washroom, it wasn't with an easier heart: she was as burdened as ever before.

"We have to talk."

Lin nearly jumped out of her skin as she turned the corner and dodged running headlong into Karl. He'd come from nowhere. But she forgot all about the near collision at the sight of him. Even his brooding frown was welcome to her right then. Fighting against the tears cresting at her eyes, she squeaked, "You're back!"

"To my questionable judgment," he growled.

She shivered at the sound of it, not knowing if it was from concern or because it was the sexiest sound he could make. She supposed it was a bit of both. Which made her a terrible person.

Now's not the time to drool over him. Focus, girl. Focus!

"Why did you come back, then?"

"There's something I need to say to you."

"Now?" she asked, breathless with anxiety all of a sudden. Her stomach cramped with her rising nerves. What did he want to tell her? And was it anything that would make her worry more than she had for him?

"Dinner," Carrie said behind them, popping into the hallway and looking at them with a mischievous sparkle in her smiling features. "You'll have plenty of time to chat after we've had our meal."

As desperately as Lin wanted to know what Karl had to say, she followed his lead when he nodded at his godmother and turned to walk back into the dining room he'd stormed out of not too long ago.

But not before she heard him whisper back a promise to her, "After dinner, we talk."

Dinner unfolded as normally as Lin hoped it would.

No arguments broke out in the middle of breaking bread. No one lobbed Carrie's delicious mac and cheese at anyone's head. Karl remained in his seat throughout, even if he avoided making eye contact with his parents and brother. There was a moment where her heart felt like it had stopped when Karl ignored Cyrus who was closer and he asked Stefon to pass the salt. Cyrus had curled his lips back into a teasing grin, but one look from Carrie ended whatever he might have said to his brother.

They made it to dessert walking on eggshells but without any incident.

And that was when any quiet truce was blown to smithereens.

It started with Cyrus vaulting out of his seat and striding over to where Karl stood by the festively arrayed fireplace. He leaned on the other side of the mantel and grinned widely at his brother.

"So did Mom and Dad tell you I'm leaving the company?"

Of course he said it loudly and in the already-cozy family room it carried over to everyone's ears. Stefon had been chatting with Charles when the other man went silent and darted narrowed eyes to his coldly statuesque wife. Serenity Sinclair was a gorgeous woman, but she would've looked more approachable if she eased up on her tight-lipped frown. She had looked like she was swallowing something sour all night, and now that look only magnified at what her eldest son had said.

For his part Karl appeared unaffected by Cyrus's news. Taking a swig of his amber drink, he walked over to a side bar and poured more of the golden liquid from a decanter. His brother shadowed him and filled a glass of his own.

"You know why they're here, don't you? I step down, and naturally they're looking for a replacement." It was obvious what he meant, but Cyrus nudged him. He stopped abruptly when Karl growled low.

"Is that why you've come?" Karl's eyes flashed to his parents.

Lin revised her earlier observation of him being unfazed. She snapped her eyes between the two sides, Karl and his parents, her heart in her throat and her anxiety making her slide down the sofa. She was nonconfrontational by nature. If she'd been anything like Karl, she'd have already started her business long ago and would have had no trouble making her grandfather see that she was perfectly capable of pursuing her own goals and dreams.

But she wasn't, and she didn't care to be caught in the

crossfire, no matter how much she wanted to rush over to Karl's side and be supportive of him. This wasn't her battle to help him fight. He had to do this on his own. She just hoped it would free him of his troubling past with his parents.

"Because if it is, I'll stop you right now and save you the time. I'm not interested in anything that has to do with this family."

"I told you he won't listen," Cyrus said, his tone matching his smug smirk. He drained his tumbler and set it on the mantel, the back of his hand swiping over his mouth, and his swagger full of the kind of trouble that would only increase the friction in the room. "Karl's still hurt that you kicked him out, Mom and Dad."

Lin cringed and sneaked a peek at Stefon. He looked as uncomfortable as she felt.

"It's been a while, though. A long time to hold onto that chip on your shoulder." Cyrus looped his arm around Karl's shoulder and grunted when it was whacked away. He clutched his hand and chuckled. "Guess you're pissed at me too, little brother."

Karl glowered back at Cyrus, but he didn't add fuel to the fire.

Just as Lin thought it might be over, she shrank back in her seat when Serenity sucked her teeth. "Enough. Cyrus, you're embarrassing yourself."

Cyrus scoffed and stroked his beard. It was thick and dark and as wild as his eyes were in that moment. Flexing his bulkier frame, he crossed his arms and looked twice as big as he'd done a moment earlier. Where Karl was lean and tall, his brother was of stockier build. Cyrus had the kind of muscles that could only be developed with a regular weight-resistance regimen. Lin didn't like the odds of him fighting Karl at all. The instinct to protect the man who'd supported her and loved her body so thoroughly was rearing up again.

Before she attempted to defuse the drama, Lin watched as Serenity rose to her feet, her willowy frame in a slinky patterned silk suit. She had her hair elaborately pinned to the back of her head with wispy tendrils curling from her temples. In short, she looked every part the boss that she sounded when she snipped, "Haven't we raised you both with manners?"

Karl bared his teeth. "You barely raised us."

"He has a point," Cyrus piped in.

Charles stood as well and bristled. "Don't talk back to your mother."

"She stopped *being* my mother the instant she kicked me out," Karl snarled, his chest heaving and his glare slicing through his parents. They both looked aghast at the outburst. He'd stunned them into silence.

Lin grimaced and resisted covering her eyes to see what would happen next. It could only get worse from here…

She sighed when Carrie emerged from the kitchen with a tray of cookies and a pot of tea. Lin didn't think she could be more relieved to see Karl's godmother. Carrie took one look around the room, scowled and snapped, "What's going on? You boys better not be thinking of tearing up my home."

"No one's tearing up anything," Charles said emphatically and pinned a strong look at his sons as if they weren't grown men who were beyond parental censuring. "This isn't a polite topic. We'll discuss this privately later."

"No. I'm done talking." Karl regarded Lin, the fury that had painted his features still present in the brackets around his mouth and the steel in his eyes. "I'll wait for you outside."

Awkwardly, she looked around the room and ducked her head, muttering a quick excuse for leaving so quickly before trailing after him. Karl was waiting at the foot of the porch. He looked up, his shoulders and bald head slick from the snow drifting down from the darkened sky. She slipped her coat on and hurried to catch up when he stalked toward his truck. When they were ensconced inside, he gripped the steering wheel, bowed his head, and strained to say, "Give me a second."

She gave him as much time as he needed to regain his composure.

He hadn't been himself at all in there. It was like she'd witnessed a whole new side to him. When she had first met him, Lin had thought he'd just been cold and unfeeling. Then Karl had shown her the gentle, warm side to him by doing a number of kind things for her. More recently she'd discovered he was also the perfect lover.

But now she'd seen him angry, and it had been like an icy fire, a full mix of his hot-and-cold personality. Now he was trying to retrieve the mask he'd lost when he had confronted his family, and Lin wasn't sure she wanted him hiding away.

"Sorry that you had to witness that." He didn't turn his head, but she could tell from his profile that he was still fighting for control of his emotions.

"It wasn't your fault." His brother had been baiting him. Anyone who had been weaker than Karl would have already started a brawl in there. It was commendable that he'd had enough restraint to simply walk out when he had. She had to admit that dinner hadn't panned out the way she or Carrie had hoped. Looking up at his godmother's cozy-looking home, Lin wondered how Carrie and Stefon were faring in there with Karl's parents and Cyrus.

"It is my fault."

Lin snapped her head to him. "How?"

"I should have left when I figured out what Carrie was trying to do."

"What do you think she was trying to do?" She bit her lip nervously. She'd known what was awaiting him, and she had avoided giving him a warning, believing that it would be for the best. She hadn't thought it was *this* bad with his family. Guilt snapped at her heels as she sat frozen, waiting with bated breath to hear what he had to say.

Karl wrung his hands over the wheel. He hadn't started the engine yet. And it didn't seem like he was in a rush to leave anymore. She didn't blame him. It felt like they were trapped in their own little world. The hush around them was peaceful and a far cry from what it had been like inside Carrie's home just then.

"Carrie is caught up in her own happiness. She can't accept that not everyone has to be happy around her."

"Is it a bad thing for her to want you to be happy?"

He drummed his thumbs over the wheel. "I wasn't happy in there. I don't think I ever will be happy near my parents." Expelling a sigh then, he grumbled, "Again, I don't mean to dump my problems in your lap. What happened in there…shouldn't have happened. I'm sorry if it ruined your evening. I'll have to call Carrie and Stefon and apologize later."

Lin's guilt manifested with a lump in her throat that kept her from saying anything.

She could only nod stiffly when Karl asked, sweet again as always, "Want a ride home?"

"Do you want me to walk you up?" Karl looked over at Lin as he pulled to a stop in front of her apartment's entrance. The well-lit foyer kept him from fearing for her safety.

After tonight, he wouldn't be surprised if she refused to see him again.

He had given in to his anger, and the volatile emotion had chewed him up and spit him out. It had been an awful feeling having so little control over himself. His family had brought out the worst in him, as usual. When he'd been young, it had been a helpless feeling, knowing that he had nowhere else to go. For the longest time, and really up to the point they'd kicked him out, Karl had believed what they had said about him not being able to amount to anything without their help. His mom and dad had him relying on them completely. Then they had snipped the umbilical cord and pushed him out of the carefully cultivated world he'd known.

If it hadn't been for Carrie, he didn't know where he would be now—whether his life would be as good as it was now, or whether he would have proven his parents right about accomplishing nothing.

He looked at Lin, realizing most of all that he might not have met her under any other circumstances.

Still, it didn't change the fact that he probably would be smart to avoid close quarters with his parents and Cyrus. Carrie's final event, the vow renewal itself, was closing in fast, and there would be plenty of room in the big reception hall that he'd booked to keep himself far away from his family.

He couldn't say the same about Lin. It wouldn't be as easy to avoid her.

Particularly when she gazed at him so adorably and softly said, "I would like if you did walk me up."

Karl couldn't refuse her.

It wasn't the longest walk. Before long, they were standing in front of her door, and Lin paused to tap the key code into her apartment. She looked at him curiously. "Back at Carrie's you said you had something to tell me. What was it?"

He hadn't forgotten, but he wasn't sure if the window of opportunity had passed.

Studying her, he realized that he couldn't let it go now that she'd brought it up and that he had to try. It had been weighing on him for a while now. And he was sick and tired of kicking it around his head.

"It's about your work."

"What about it?" She fully turned to him, her eyes rounder, and fear surfacing in her dark irises. "Is something wrong with one of my prints?"

He silently cursed his lack of forethought. Naturally her mind had leaped to the worst-case scenario, and he couldn't fault her when he hadn't given her an indication of what type of news he had for her. She had just imagined it was bad.

But he hoped that what he had to ask her would be met positively.

"I could see us working together on future projects. Some of my clients have shown interest in your pieces, and I can confirm that they'd like to meet and see how you'd incorporate your unique designs into their visions for their parties. Of course, there's no pressure in working out of our headquarters anymore. Remote collaborations would suit as well."

"Karl, that's…"

"A lot to take in," he supplied, nodding. "I know. That's why I wanted to tell you early and let you take your time deciding. The offer is open-ended, and I don't need a response until after New Year's. That's when the first interested client has scheduled an appointment."

"I don't need to think about it. I'd love to work with you. It's just… I'm a little surprised." She smiled slowly past the shock, and then more fully. A heavenly sounding laugh bubbled out of her. She clapped her hands together before her smiling mouth and shook her head, disbelief flowing off her. "Do you really want to work with me?"

He laughed breathily, relief of his own mingling through his voice. "I wouldn't have asked, otherwise."

Lin tossed her arms around him, taking him by surprise with the embrace.

Even so he still recovered quickly and snaked his arms around her, holding her as close as possible, and wishing with all his thundering heart that he didn't have to let her go. If they worked together, though, he would have to stop seeing her as anything more than a colleague. He'd abused his power already. How would her grandfather ever take her seriously if he thought she'd slept her way to her success?

"Thank you," she whispered into his ear, kissing his cheek.

He turned his head and looked into her eyes. Pulling in, he swore it would be for the last time, right before their mouths touched. As always, the sensual reward was mind-blowingly pleasant. He could've kissed her until they both ran out of air. Just as he was contemplating it, he felt resistance from her.

Baffled and breathless, he let her go.

She pulled back abruptly and brushed her hair away from her face, the butterfly clip no longer doing its job as well as it had before he'd mussed her hair. Lin's eyes had gone back to their widened state.

"What's the matter?" he asked, not liking the panicked look on her face. His stomach hollowed. Maybe she hadn't wanted to kiss him. Perhaps he had read the situation wrong...

"I can't lie to you. I have something to tell you too." Her voice pitched and dropped into a croak at the end, a shy little smile curling her lips, and her eyes lowering and avoiding his own. It didn't give him confidence any more than her words had.

Clamping his jaws together, he set his expression to neutral and steeled himself for whatever she had to say.

"I...knew that Carrie was going to invite you and your parents to dinner." Lin covered her face with her hands and continued. "We were just trying to help you. We thought that maybe you needed a little push to confront them, hash it out, and move on and be happy."

He had been preparing himself for everything but that apparently, because he felt her words strike him like a whip. The pain in his heart was devastating. He stopped himself from clutching his chest and grunting. With gritted teeth, he filtered what she said, heard her genuine regret and knew that he shouldn't feel the angry betrayal that was simmering in him. But he *was* betrayed. And by the one person he wasn't expecting.

Then it struck that this wasn't any different from Isaiah.

His ex-boyfriend hadn't been able to stand Karl's anger toward his parents either. Lin was the same: she had been scheming to change him. Even if her heart had been in the right place, her actions had been invasive and wrong. He didn't need anyone interfering in his life. Not his parents. Not his godmother. And certainly not Lin.

"I'm sorry," she sobbed once, looking up from her hands and reaching out with her fingers. "I didn't want you to feel hurt, but I *did* hurt you."

At least she knew what she'd done. Too bad that he was finally understanding that he'd let this go on too long with her. He liked her and had opened up to her, and all he'd gotten was a broken heart.

In a rough voice, he said, "No, I should apologize. I shouldn't have kissed you."

"I wanted you to!" She wrapped her arms around her middle as though she were warding off the same pain carving out his heart.

Maybe she was. Maybe he had so much more to ask her forgiveness for…

"I told you that my mom walked out on me. Well, I never knew what to feel about it. I thought I should hate her, but then I didn't know her, and I started to wonder if she had been right to leave. I could have been a difficult child to raise. I might have been too much for her to handle. I didn't realize that I cared what her answer was until I saw you with your parents yesterday. You looked like you were in such pain, and I recognized that pain. I feel it right now." She hugged her arms tighter around herself and sobbed. "I don't want you to hate me."

"I don't hate you," he heard himself say, his voice roughened and raw with emotion.

I could never hate you streaked through his mind.

Because he loved her.

It was so obvious now, he almost wanted to bang his head against the wall.

He was in love with her. Foolishly so, and now…now he was hurting himself by ending whatever they had begun. But it was for the best. Isaiah had been right to walk away from him all those years ago. He had been someone different when he let his parents crawl under his skin. Someone he didn't recognize.

Someone I don't like.

Someone who could hurt Lin, just like he was hurting her right now.

"You do," Lin choked. "I can see it. You're looking at me differently."

He was looking at her like a man in love. A man who knew that he was going to break his own heart just to save her from tying herself to someone who was capable of hurting her.

"I don't hate you, Lin. I…just don't want to do this anymore."

She understood. He knew she did, because she flinched back from him.

Cowardly, he rasped, "We'll talk when we both have had time to think about this. It doesn't change the job offer." He wouldn't take that away from her. She had earned working with his well-heeled clients.

Lin turned her back to him, unlocked her door and looked back, teary-eyed. "I don't want the job anymore. Not with us like this now."

She closed the door in his face, and the fact that he had lost her doubly sank in.

He held back his roar of frustration until he was sitting back in his truck. After all his effort to keep love at bay, it had found him again, made his heart skip and then stopped it dead with the pain of losing the woman he loved. And the only person he had to blame was himself.

CHAPTER FOURTEEN

"HOME SWEET CABIN!"

Miranda flung open the door to their cabin with an enthusiasm Lin wished she could muster. The most she could give was a forced smile as she trailed Miranda inside. As quaint and comfortable as its exterior, the cabin's interior was all rustic wood and country charm. Miranda claimed the bed in the loft and climbed the pine ladder up to the space. That left Lin to check out her bedroom.

She dropped back onto the bed and wished the cedary aroma in the room was enough to sweep her away from her troubled thoughts. Instead, she closed her eyes and forced her mind clear. The technique had worked so far. She felt deceptively unburdened already. At least, she did…and then reality came knocking—literally.

Lin's eyes sprung open, and she sat up on the bed.

Miranda said, "I'm heading out to help with the setup. Did you want to tag along?"

Did she want to risk seeing Karl? would be the better question.

They hadn't spoken for a couple of days. The last thing she'd told him was that she wouldn't work with him. Which was crazy, because his offer had been more than generous—it had made perfect sense for her to accept and have access to his network of clients. But then she'd have to deal with working with him and not being able to be with him…

And it would hurt too much.

She analyzed why it had stung to think that he might be angry with her. For two nights she racked her brain, and she'd only come to one conclusion. She had fallen in love with him accidentally. She hadn't wanted to. It hadn't been a part of her plan. But it had happened, and it would explain why it felt as though her heart had been torn out.

Like it wouldn't ever be healed and whole again.

"Is that your brother?" Nadine stopped midsentence and pointed across the long hall.

They had most of the tables installed for the reception, and the decor was coming together quickly. Red, green and black were the main color choices for Carrie's Kwanzaa-themed vow renewal, but he'd included earthy tones of brown and beige as well to soften the bolder palette. Lin's three-dimensional contributions stood out to him the most. There were also ornate name cards, vases for the floral arrangements, and candelabra that towered over the guests at each table. She had gone above and beyond in a short amount of time, and all on her own.

It would be hard to walk into her studio under his offices and find it empty without her.

But it was expected.

She hadn't ever planned to stay longer, and after how he had left things with her, there wasn't a chance of that changing now.

So seeing Cyrus was the last thing he wanted. One

look at his brother and he recalled the events that had led up to him letting Lin go.

"I'll just go over there and continue monitoring the setup," Nadine said, walking off with one last curious look over her shoulder.

He was grateful that she wouldn't be within earshot of what he had to say to his brother. He didn't need one other person looking at him as strangely as Lin had last night.

"Reception is off-limits until tonight." He growled the words, the warning in them implicit.

"Easy." Cyrus tossed up his hands in a placating gesture. "I just wanted to check up on you."

Since when had he and Cyrus been close enough for his brother to ever want to check up on him? Karl didn't know what he was up to now, but he didn't want any part of it.

"I have work to do."

Cyrus rolled his eyes and flapped a hand at the venue. "I can see that. You're doing a helluva job, by the way." He whistled long and low, his eyes casting over the whole space. All eight thousand square feet of vaulted ceiling and exposed wooden beams, shiny hardwood floor and picturesque views of the Rockies from where the resort stood perched atop a lakeside valley. "If I'd known you were this good, I would have had you throw some of the companies' parties."

Softening him with compliments wouldn't work. Karl stood imperviously in the face of it. "Just tell me what you want and go."

He expected more of a struggle. But Cyrus rubbed his beard with both hands, blew a big breath and said, "Okay. I get it. I'll get out of your hair—uh, well, you know what I mean." He broke off with a laugh and a wave at Karl's bald head.

"Cyrus..." he warned, his anger barely leashed.

"Yeah, anyways, I'll go. I wanted you to give me five minutes—"

"You have them," Karl interjected and he was starting the timer now.

"Fine. Since you're not giving me a whole lot of time, I'll start by saying I'm sorry."

Surely he hadn't heard his brother correctly. Had Cyrus apologized to him just now? If he'd thought he knew what was going on, he wasn't as sure any longer.

"The dinner at Carrie's got a little out of hand." Cyrus snorted and amended, "Actually, it got more than out of hand. I shouldn't have riled Mom and Dad up the way that I did."

"Why did you?" He wasn't about to let the opportunity slip by, no matter how uneasy Cyrus appeared. His brother had tormented him growing up, and all for the sake of pleasing their unpleasant parents. Had it been worth it? Because Karl and his siblings weren't close the way they probably should be. And Cyrus had helped create the rift when they'd all been younger.

"Old habits," his brother said, nervously palming the nape of his neck. He then ran that big hand over the top of his thick afro. "I was a jerk. I still am, but now I'm a jerk with more of a conscience. I realize you have no reason to believe that I'm being genuine right now, but I *am* sorry, Karl. It's part of why I'm here."

Paint him cynical, but he wasn't buying it.

"If you're done," he said while pointedly looking to the exit and hoping that Cyrus got the message.

Instead of arguing and pushing back, Cyrus heaved a big sigh, and his too-broad shoulders sagged. He looked weaker suddenly. "Cool. I appreciate you listening, anyways."

He was walking off when Karl, out of sheer curiosity and *not* sympathy, asked, "Have you really quit?" Soon as he had been able, Cyrus worked his way through the company and eventually sat in the VP of Operations chair at both their parents' companies. He had sacrificed a relationship with his siblings for it, so Karl had always assumed his brother would never have left working for their parents, and that one day he'd inherit the companies for his loyalty.

"I've given them a month to find my replacement. I figure it's the least I could do—not that Mom and Dad are making it easy for me."

That he could see. Their parents had to be seeing red. Cyrus had always been their first choice as the heir apparent, and when it was obvious that none of their other children cut it, they'd put all their eggs in one basket with their eldest son. Of course now Cyrus was leaving, they had no one else to fall back on in the family. Karl might not be close to his sister and younger brothers, but he knew that they'd been like him and fled the clutches of their parents as soon as they possibly could. He couldn't see any of them returning to the fold just to be micromanaged by their parents.

"Why leave now?" he asked.

Cyrus shrugged and hooked his thumbs in the pockets of his faded jeans. "The truth is that we haven't seen eye to eye in a long while, and my leaving the company has become the best thing for me."

"How?" Karl should have been pushing him out the door. He didn't know why he cared why Cyrus was doing whatever he was doing, or what he had planned that had brought that serene smile to his brother's face. It was unlike his usual smugly grinning mug.

He actually looked at peace with his decision to leave their parents.

"I found someone, and she's opened my eyes to how unhappy I've been."

A woman. Of course. It made sense.

Cyrus seemed to read his mind as he shook his head and laughed. "It's not what you're thinking. I'm not ready to marry her, but we've been dating for a few months, and she's just moved to Toronto to open her restaurant."

Why did that sound familiar? He thought of Lin, and his heart throbbed oddly.

"I'm thinking of helping her run it. But it's still early days, and I have job interviews lined up with companies—"

"What do Mom and Dad think of you job-hunting?"

Cyrus snorted laughter and raised an eyebrow. "What do you think? They aren't coping well, let's just say that. I think they thought I'd never move on."

"To be fair, none of us thought you would."

His brother stared at him quietly and unblinkingly for a while, and then he said, "After you left all those years ago—"

"I didn't *choose* to leave," Karl cut in with clenched teeth.

Cyrus nodded, correcting himself. "After Mom and Dad forced you out, I always wondered whether you were happier for it, in the end." He cocked his head, his gaze assessing before he smiled. "You *look* like you're doing all right. Are you?"

If he'd asked him two days ago, before he had proven that he hadn't grown past the scars their parents had left him with, and prior to showing Lin how messed up he was, Karl would easily have said he was doing well for himself. Better than their parents had ever thought he would do. He couldn't answer with the same confidence right now.

And he didn't have to linger to see pity in his brother's eyes.

Nadine returned and she looked pressed for time. "Sorry to interrupt, but I need your opinion on this."

Karl seized the excuse and turned away from Cyrus. But throughout the day, he returned to their conversation and to the question of whether he was happy or not. And if he wasn't, he had to ask himself what it would take to *be* happy.

Lin walked to the rehearsal dinner on her own from the cabin she shared with Miranda. It was a short distance, but she wished she'd thought better than to wear fancy heels en route. She also wished that she'd invested in a better winter coat, like Karl had told her to do earlier on. Shivering, she hurried along the path through the parking lot into the long log building that would host tomorrow's reception.

She was in such a hurry to get indoors, Lin narrowly missed ramming into someone.

"Karl," she yelped.

His brows vaulted up, genuine surprise breaking up his emotionless mask. "Lin." His voice was deep and soft, and she'd missed hearing it. He looked amazing in his silk black suit. Too good for her to not admire him and suffer her heart's pain a little while longer in his company.

"Am I late?" she asked, looking around at the nearly full room.

"No, grab a seat. We're about to start."

He would've passed her after another curiously long and ponderous look at her, but Lin snagged his arm, and she kept hold of him even when his eyes zipped down to where her fingers alighted on him.

She opened her mouth, thinking that she knew what she wanted to say but blanking on words.

"I should go," he said and slipped free of her hold.

She watched his long, fast strides carry him away from her.

The rehearsal dinner flew by smoothly. Lin glimpsed Karl's parents at one table and Cyrus at another. Carrie must have had something to do with the seating arrangement. Judging by the daggers Karl's parents threw Cyrus's way, she confirmed it had been a good call on Carrie's part. Lin searched for Karl throughout the two-hour event. He had made himself scarce, though. By the time everyone was leaving, she'd given up looking for him.

At least she had, until Carrie stopped her on her way out of the reception hall.

"He's in the kitchen."

Lin was about to head that way, not knowing what she would say, only that she wanted to see him. The only thing that stood in her way was her ringing phone. She was surprised to see her grandfather's name appear on the screen. He hadn't been returning her calls or messages. Now he was calling her out of the blue, and her first thought was concern that something was wrong.

She looked toward the double doors leading into the kitchen longingly, the phone pressed to her ear.

One thing at a time.

Her grandfather first, and then…

Then, she hoped, Karl.

CHAPTER FIFTEEN

CARRIE AND STEFON were glowing with smiles when they were saying their vows to each other the next day. His godmother hadn't ever looked more radiant in a floor-length silver gown that sparkled with crystals embedded in the bodice and long train. Stefon stared at her like a man in love should, and Carrie gazed back with the same answering love.

They spoke their heartfelt promises to each other under a floral arch and, with the still, blue mountain lake behind them, lit six of the seven candles on Lin's specially made *kinara* and faced the riotous ovation from their guests when they turned, with matching smiles, to face them.

Karl clapped and watched from the sidelines, his heart full for them, but his head scrambled by another concern.

Lin had excused herself from the service, the news coming directly from her cabinmate. Apparently she hadn't been feeling well enough to attend the renewal ceremony.

He had thought to apprise Carrie of that fact. He didn't want his godmother thinking Lin had snubbed her, even though he didn't know why that mattered. So he saw to it that Carrie knew, only to have his godmother surprise him by explaining that Lin had dropped by for an early breakfast in the morning and informed her and Stefon on her own. This had unfolded before the ceremony, and he was left fretting through the whole half-hour service about how Lin was feeling right then.

I should go check on her.

Karl was overseeing the caterer, but he pulled Nadine aside and asked her to step in for him. She hadn't complained. In fact, she shot him a knowing look and patted his arm as if she knew *exactly* why he was in such a hurry to leave.

It was the same look that Carrie and Miranda also flung his way as he passed them.

And it was a different look from the scalding glares his parents were lasering from their chairs.

He reached Lin's cabin in record time, but when he knocked, hard enough to rattle the oak door in its frame, he realized that she wasn't in.

Or she's ignoring me.

But he didn't notice the curtains rustling or hear any sounds from inside.

Racking his brain for other ideas as to where to find her, he tried the reception hall. All the finishing touches had been put in the room earlier, and now it awaited the hosts and their guests, but it was devoid of Lin. Frantic now, he searched the trails connecting to a dozen other cabins and didn't run into her. His heart was in his throat by the time he dialed her number shakily.

It rang six torturous times before the call passed to her voice mail.

He followed the instructions of her chirpy prompt and in a strangled voice left her a message. "Call me."

Then, because he didn't like staring at his phone, he texted her too.

Dragging a hand down his face, he swallowed hard and evaluated his behavior. He'd been acting irrationally since he had walked off on her a few days ago. Nothing had felt the same since then. It was a miracle that he'd been able to concentrate and pull off Carrie's event without a hitch. But now that he was almost through working, he didn't have anything else to keep him occupied, and it amplified his desire to find Lin, ensure she was all right, and then…

And then, what?

He had to walk away again, didn't he? That would be the noble thing to do. He couldn't afford to be selfish, not if in the long run he'd be hurt, and she would be hurt, and the love he now knew he had for her transformed into disinterest. Or, worse, *hate*.

He slid his back down a tree and sat crouched on the side of the trail, his eyes glued to his phone, his body ready to wait on her for however long it took for her to get back to him. He just needed to know that she was okay.

Then he swore he'd be okay.

She wasn't all right at all.

Lin had bitten her nails to the quick, nervously waiting on Machelle's call. She sat back in the sleigh and turned her heated cheeks to the wind whipping through her curls. Her hair was probably a mess by now. Two laps in the sleigh and she was looking at a third. Luckily the driver was accommodating and simply shrugged when she paid him for another quick whirl through the wooded trails.

She pulled the woolen blanket that had fallen to her feet up over her legs. It wasn't enough to keep the cold from stinging at her, but it would have to do. She wasn't ready to get off the sleigh. Not until she heard from Machelle about how her grandfather was doing.

Lin was clutching her phone and gazing at it when it rang.

Karl's name confronted her, demanding to be picked up, and she almost gave in, but she stopped herself from tapping on the button to accept the call. What could she say to him? What did he have to say to her? She wasn't ready either way, and it was better to conserve her energy for her grandfather. She hadn't slept since she'd answered his call yesterday and discovered it was her grandfather's new housekeeper who had called to tell her that he'd had a tumble down the stairs. It had been bad enough for him to go to the hospital for immediate surgery.

She had called Machelle, and her friend had dropped everything when she'd heard and gone to check on him. Machelle had promised to call once she had information, but that had been hours ago, and still no call.

All she'd been able to think was that this could've been prevented if she had never left his side. Instead, she'd been selfish and thought only of her own happiness. Now her grandfather was suffering the consequences of her being a bad granddaughter.

This was the thinking that had kept her up all night.

She hadn't slept a wink, and she'd risen early to visit Carrie and excuse herself from what she knew would surely be a lovely celebration. She just didn't have the heart to sit through that touching display when her heart was miles away in an operating room.

Her grandfather was all she had left. She couldn't lose him, and now more than ever with Karl angry at her.

Lin's eyes smarted, and she closed them tight, wiping at the tears that had pinched free.

She slid down the bench and drew the blanket up around her shoulders, her hands still gripping her phone when it buzzed with a message. When she checked, she saw that Karl had not only called but had also left her a voice mail *and* sent a short text.

The text simply read Call me.

The voice message was longer.

"Lin, I heard you're not feeling well. Just call me when you get this. I'm…worried."

She listened to him a couple more times, and it did sound like he was genuinely concerned for her wellbeing. After hearing what had happened to her grandfather, she'd only thought of Karl more and how lonely she was feeling. He was still running through her mind. She hadn't wanted to leave Canada thinking that she had destroyed the relationship they'd had.

She loved him. And it was the first time she'd loved anyone, so she didn't know if she was doing this right, or what words and action would do her feelings for him justice. What she *did* know was she didn't have to be alone.

The horse-drawn sleigh was waiting for him where Lin said it would be.

Karl still had doubts that she'd be waiting for him until he climbed up and saw that she was huddled under a scratchy-looking thick blanket on the other side of the vehicle. Once Karl was ensconced in the sleigh as well, the driver tipped his top hat back at them and signaled for the horses to move. The sleigh rides were available to the guests after the ceremony and all during the reception once it began. He just didn't think anyone had taken opportunity to use it yet. That was why he hadn't gone looking for her there.

Looking her over, he saw the usual healthful color in her cheeks. A little red tinged the tip of her nose, and her lips looked rosier, but her eyes were bright and alert and…perhaps a tad wary of him.

He sighed quietly, realizing that he had a lot of damage to undo.

"I heard you weren't feeling too hot." He frowned when she shivered and noted that she was dressed for the party in a thin-strapped dress. Her coat wasn't buttoned up. And if she wasn't sick, she'd be asking to come down with something miserable soon enough. Without thinking too much on it, he shrugged out of his jacket and draped it over her shoulders. He had to slide over on the bench to do it, and it brought him closer to where her softly floral perfume draped over him. Karl bit down on an appreciative groan. What mattered was that she stopped shivering. Once she did, he breathed easier, and he felt strong enough to control his desire for her from ruining everything as it had before.

If she was leaving him, he wanted closure for them both. The kind that they could eventually move past one day.

Do you want to end things, though?

He packed that thought away. This wasn't about him and what he wanted or even needed.

"I'm not sick in the traditional sense." She gripped his coat and pulled it around her shoulders tighter, her eyes scanning his face, her expression guarded. "What are you doing here?"

"I was concerned." He'd made that obvious, hadn't he?

"That's nice of you. But I'm okay."

Karl didn't know how, but he knew that she was lying. "You're not okay." He didn't care if she got angry.

He'd meant it about being worried for her. His unease wouldn't quit until he knew why she looked like she'd been crying. The puffiness around her eyes were a tell. And she sniffed every now and again, and he didn't think she was getting a cold.

Rather than snapping at him to mind his own business, Lin looked away and sniffed again, which made him dead certain that she was crying.

He reached for her and then curled his fingers into a clenched fist that he dropped at the last moment. It killed him to just sit there. The heart that he'd believed irreparably broken had started beating harder and faster, the pressure over his chest intensifying, and the helplessness he felt debilitating. But he knew he'd be doing more harm if he interrupted her now. She had to work through her emotion on her own. He waited quietly until she composed herself, discreetly wiping at her face with a hand, and turning back to him only when she felt ready.

"It's my grandfather. He…slipped and fell down the stairs at home. The housekeeper was home, luckily, and he received care immediately, but—" She choked off at this point and looked away again.

This time Karl sought her hand to give her as much comfort as she was willing to take.

Lin squeezed him back. "He's in surgery, and I'm waiting on Machelle to call with a report."

Now he understood why she'd left. It all made sense. He was conflicted. In a sense, he was happy that *she* was feeling well, but he knew just how close she was to her grandfather, and it must have been eating away at her to know that she was thousands of miles away from her family and friends and everything she knew and loved because he'd given her a chance to work with him.

It's my fault she's feeling this way right now.

"I don't know what I'll do if he…if he…" She sniffed a few more times, and her shoulders shuddered with silent sobs.

Deciding to let instinct reign, he pulled her into his chest and felt easier with her head buried against him and her tears pressed into him. She cried for a while, and he soothed her as best as he could, quietly stroking her soft, honey-colored hair. The driver was slowing as they neared the end of their circuit, but a quick jut of his chin cued him to continue pulling through another short lap. All around them, looped through bare black branches, were thousands of strung lights. Their multicolored glow brightened as the storm clouds gathered and thick, fat snowflakes began swirling from the sky. A concealed sound system played slow Christmassy jazz, and the holograms of a group of cheery carolers that he'd had installed for the sleigh ride waved at them as they passed. It might have been romantic, but all he cared about was the woman in his arms.

Lin cried through all of it, her sorrow muffled into him.

She was breaking his heart. He didn't know how to help her. All the money in the world couldn't magically take her sadness away. Not that she needed his money; he just wanted to help. Desperately. Maddeningly so.

He gauged the time by the density of snowflakes that had come to rest on the driver's top hat.

By the time Lin pushed off his chest and looked up at him, the driver had a thick brimful of snow.

"I soaked your shirt." She trailed her fingers over the wetness that now adorned his shirtfront. Face crumpling, she appeared on the verge of crying once more.

"It's fine," he murmured soothingly.

She shook her head, but he ignored her protest and held her. Lin allowed him, her tears sparser now. The next time she lifted her head, she had a watery smile for him. She wiped at her face and laughed hoarsely. "I'll have to fix my makeup," she groused.

"You look beautiful." He wasn't gassing her up either. She would always look gorgeous to him.

The sleigh had long stopped, and he hadn't asked the driver to continue. Instead, Karl coaxed Lin out and guided her down the trail that would take her back to her cabin. As they walked, he sensed she wanted to say something when she squeezed his hand.

"Thanks for caring enough to find me."

"You'd have done the same for me, I'm sure," he replied.

"You should go back to the reception. It should be starting right now. Carrie will want you there."

He seriously doubted Carrie would want him to abandon Lin in her time of need. He didn't say this to her, of course. "I'm not missing anything. I'll pop back in when I know you've heard from your friend."

"What if…what if it takes all night?"

"I'll stay with you for however long it takes."

It was the relief, subtle and sweet, on Lin's face that made him realize he'd said the right thing and made the right choice.

Lin hadn't thought Karl would actually stay with her as he said he would. She wouldn't have been cross with him either if he'd had to leave. His godmother's big party was happening, and she was keeping him from celebrating with everyone. Lin's guilt had been real and ugly in the first hour. She'd tried to get him to go, even though it was the very last thing she wanted at the moment.

But each and every time Karl rebuffed her suggestions for him to leave.

He made himself cozy in her shared cabin. At one point he made hot chocolate for them to drink before the woodstove.

Maybe it was the belly full of warmed cocoa, or the heat of the fire when the snow only thickened and fell faster outside...

Or maybe I like the way Karl's sitting so close.

His arm tossed casually over the back of the sofa they were leaning against, and his fingers brushed her shoulder every so often, the brief caress setting off a dizzying need through her. She hadn't forgotten why they were sitting there, isolated in a cabin, just the two of them—but it was also hard to erase the memories of how good it had been with him.

How good he was for her.

Her head slumped forward, eyes drifting shut. She jerked them open and snapped her head back. But a second later she was doing it again. Listing to the side and then catching herself before she leaned against him. Her head had just touched his shoulder when she backed away quickly, muttering an embarrassed apology.

When it happened yet again, Karl simply curled his hand around the back of her neck and held her to him. "Sleep," he instructed in that bossy way of his.

Lin blushed profusely, but sure enough, her eyes closed, and she slipped into a dreamless sleep.

She didn't know how long she slept, only that when she awoke, it was to the discovery that night had fallen, the snow brighter and illuminating the interior of the cabin. She saw that she'd been lying half-sprawled over

Karl, her head on his chest, her hand over his heart, and one of her legs resting atop both of his. He had stuffed a sofa cushion behind his head, and she felt a little better knowing he hadn't completely sacrificed his comfort to see to hers. She was careful in moving up to stare at his peaceful face as he slumbered. It was a rare moment when he wasn't actively masking his emotions.

Lin studied him for a long while. By the time she had to pull away to go to the bathroom, she was confident she could count the number of his eyelashes.

Karl was awake and sitting up when she'd finished freshening up.

He had her phone in his hand. "Your friend called. I told her you'd call right back."

Lin could have kissed him. It wasn't a call she'd have wanted to miss. She took the phone and saw that he was standing to leave, likely wanting to give her some privacy. She grabbed hold of his hand as he passed her.

He looked down to where she was sitting, staring up at him, half his face shrouded in shadow, the other half in the dying embers' light from the stove.

"Stay," she begged.

Karl stared hard at his and Lin's interlaced fingers. He concentrated on their hands while he listened to her one-sided conversation with her friend. He couldn't make out anything that was being said, and she wore a good poker face, except when she gasped and squeezed his hand tightly near the end.

He stroked his thumb over the back of her hand, willing his strength into her.

When she finally ended the call, he was on pins and needles for the news, and it took all his willpower to keep from rushing her to tell him what she'd been told.

Lin didn't leave him in suspense. "He's going to be all right." The smile that glowed through the whole of her face wiped clear all his worries on the matter. Lin went on to explain that her grandfather had had surgery to fix a hip fracture and that he'd need to recover for a while. Her friend had already offered to move in temporarily, and the hospital was also sending a nurse home with him for the first week. Long enough until Lin could get home and take over his care.

She collapsed into his open arms by the end of it, her eyes watering, and her sniffles back in full force.

He hugged her closely and whispered soothing words to her. She'd handled herself well, given how concerned she'd been for her grandfather. Meanwhile, he'd been concerned out of his mind for her. Now he could rest easy knowing that she would spend her last few days in Canada with a lighter heart before she left for her home where she would help her grandfather recover.

Not wanting to think about her departure, he tucked her into an embrace.

The sound of fireworks was what pulled them apart.

"Is that what I think it is?" Lin wiped at her eyes.

"Yes, they were a surprise for Carrie. A little early until we start counting down to the New Year, but would you like to go watch the show with me?"

They walked out of her cabin, hand in hand, in search of the fireworks. They had just cleared the snaking forest trail when they saw the first burst of pyrotechnics light up the sky in a wash of gold, purple and red. Lin gasped when another went off, this one bright enough to illuminate the forest and the lake. He had to admit that it was quite a sight, a stark contrast to the shadowed mountains in the background with the colorful light display entertaining them much closer.

He spied a few people coming out of the forest. Other guests who weren't part of Carrie's party but who were there to enjoy the fireworks he'd had prepared for his godmother on her special day.

Looking down at Lin, he wondered what he'd do without her. He couldn't remember what his life was like before she came into it.

She glanced up and caught him staring, her eyes reflecting some of the electric colors of the fireworks. Her mouth moved, but he couldn't catch anything over the explosive noise of the fireworks.

Lowering his head, he leveled his ear closer to those glossy, tempting lips of hers.

"Are you still upset with me?" she implored.

She would think that, after he had exhausted his energy avoiding her for the past few days. But he knew that it wasn't because he was angry with her. On the contrary, he knew that he loved her, and it was alarming and exciting all at once. He just didn't want to hurt her. Didn't want this to end badly, as it had with Isaiah. His parents had once again shown him how damaged they'd made him. He wasn't sure whether to thank them for saving Lin from him—or whether he should hate them anew for taking yet another chance at happiness from him.

"I'm not angry," he said firmly.

As soon as the words were out of his mouth, Lin hugged him. It was her lips touching his that shocked him. He'd have melted into her if he didn't feel her moving away already. Too soon for his liking.

Fresh tears shone in her eyes.

God, he'd made her cry again. Before he could thumb away the tears that trailed down her cheeks, she kissed him again. A saltiness flavored her mouth, but he found himself pushing back against her, strengthening the friction of their kiss. This time it lasted long enough for his lungs to burn by the time they pulled back from each other.

"I like you a lot, Karl. I... I just want you to know. You don't have to do anything about it."

His ears were ringing, and he couldn't fault the fireworks or their breathlessly passionate kiss. Still, he heard her clear as day.

She liked him.

And he loved her.

Most of all she wasn't trying to push him to act on what she'd said. True to her word, she gazed up at the fireworks, with a contented smile on her face, those tears still glistening in her eyes.

And then it clicked.

He was standing in his own way. He hadn't been able to save his relationship with Isaiah, but it didn't have to be like that with Lin now. Even as hope unfurled through him, he felt a hiccup of hesitation to act on this new and sudden drive to be with her.

To be *happy*, as Lin had put it a few nights ago.

"I like you too."

He knew she hadn't heard him when a particularly loud crack from the fireworks drowned out his confession. So he did the next best thing that ensured she understood him. He slipped his arm around her and swept her up into another kiss, breaking off quickly to murmur "I like you" against her mouth. She heard him now, her fingers clawing into his shirt, and her round eyes flitting over his face, possibly scouring it for signs that he was joking with her.

Her eyes begged for an explanation.

"It's true. I've been fighting it this whole time, thinking that it would be better if you didn't get caught up in my mess. I'm not…easy to be around. I get that."

He'd put his foot in his mouth a few times around her. In fact, it was how their relationship had begun, with him accusing her of stealing her own vase. Now she'd stolen his heart—

No. He'd given it to her freely, just unexpectedly.

"That's why I could never be upset with you. I like you too much."

She smiled slow and shyly, and he felt it because their lips were touching again.

"I need you to know that I'm willing to do anything to keep you with me, as long as you'll allow me."

"I have to go back home," she started.

"I know," he rasped out. "I can wait. Do long distance. I'm open to it." Losing her without putting in an effort wasn't an option. It would be far worse than risking heartache again.

"You'll wait for me," she repeated.

He nodded solemnly.

She draped her arms over his shoulders then, her hands massaging the back of his head, fingers teasing his crown. With another smile, she nodded too. "It's all I wanted. Well, that and *this*."

Lin kissed him, showing him exactly what else she desired besides being with him too.

EPILOGUE

Five months later

LIN WALKED DOWN the stairs of her second-floor studio
and through the floor space below that she'd leased and
converted into a shop to sell her three-dimensional designs. It was still early in the morning and a good two
hours before she opened the doors for business, but
she was there because the alarm had gone off. It had
sounded briefly before she heard the telltale noises of
someone punching in her code to silence the tripped
security system.

She clutched the vase in her hand and walked around
the corner into the store, preparing to clobber the intruder.

Lin shrieked when she ran into whoever it was and
they caught *her* by surprise.

"Lin." Her name came out huskily in a voice she'd
recognize anywhere.

She gawked up at her boyfriend. Karl took the vase
from her suddenly nerveless fingers as a little hysteri-
cal giggle emerged from her. Her reaction was understandable: she'd nearly sent him to the hospital or the
hereafter. A second later and she might have bashed his
head in, so she was shaken up a little.

Well, that and she hadn't been expecting to see him for another week. He'd booked off time to visit her as soon as his schedule permitted. He would've flown out sooner, but she had insisted that he focus on his business first. Just because they were dating didn't mean they had to sacrifice their other passions for their new-found love.

Setting aside the vase, Karl tugged her into an embrace that had her relaxing against him.

"I almost knocked you out," she pointed out.

His chuckle drifted through the shop. "Yeah, I saw that."

"I could've killed you." She glared up at him, but it was hard to maintain her annoyance when he pecked her lips and smirked.

"It would've been worth it just to see you."

She rolled her eyes and fought a smile. "What are you doing here? I thought you said next week. Also, you know there's a law about breaking and entering. Someone once mentioned it to me…"

His eyes twinkled at the shared memory. Their first meeting at Machelle's wedding venue felt like so long ago now. Lin would never have imagined they would be standing here, in her shop, his arms enveloping her, and his mouth descending down to hers.

She moaned around his kiss, a protest bubbling out and dying swiftly as his tongue swept hers up in a tangle.

By the time the kiss ended, she was breathless and blushing in full force. Especially when her phone sang out from the back pocket of her designer jeans. She answered without checking the caller ID and regretted it when her grandfather's voice came through the other end. She sounded out of breath, and he immediately noted it. With a heated face, she stammered through an excuse as to why she sounded like she'd run up and down the stairs, and she swatted Karl's chest when he laughed low. The last thing she wanted was her grandfather putting two and two together. He'd known about her dating Karl, and he had been asking to meet him more formally, but neither of them was expecting her boyfriend to arrive earlier than planned.

Once she was off the call, she yelped as Karl tugged her up against him again and stole a kiss while she was recovering.

"We should have dinner tonight. You, me and your grandfather."

"I don't think you know what you're getting yourself into. He's prepared to interrogate you."

"I survived my parents. Your grandfather should be far easier."

Unlike Cyrus, whom he had started to talk to along with his other siblings, Karl hadn't seen or spoken to his parents since Carrie's big event. It was better that way. He'd faced them and come out stronger for it. Just like she'd finally returned home and gotten her grandfather to accept that she didn't want to inherit his company. It had taken some work, and he was still skeptical, but contrary to her belief, he hadn't cut ties with her the way Karl's parents had. She'd been so convinced that she would lose her only family she didn't realize that she'd gained someone special along the way. Karl... but also his godmother and Miranda and Nadine—all three women kept in touch with her regularly, and Lin was making her own plans to visit Canada again soon.

For now, Karl had come to see her on her home turf.

"Are you going to give me a tour? Or do you want

to kiss some more?" He nibbled her lobe and dropped his head to do the same to her throat.

"Stop," she said and giggled but didn't try to push him away.

Eventually he lifted his head and gestured for her to show him around the shop. She complied, weak-kneed from the hickey he no doubt had given her. A love bite she'd have to mask with makeup before she saw her grandfather again.

He kept his hand looped around her the whole while. She pointed out the gold jewelry pieces she'd recently put up for sale. He was not surprised when she told him that the new pieces had been flying off the shelf.

With a knowing smile, he said, "Sounds like you've hit your stride."

She could say more than that. She was already ahead of her rent for the new space, and she'd used the extra revenue to buy another printer to help speed up production and stock. Her 3D designs were unique and coveted, and they might not stay like that forever, but she had plenty of time and drive to revitalize her business and keep it fresh for her customers.

"I see you were inspired," he said, pointing out African charm necklaces and bracelets and then glancing at the necklace he'd gifted her hanging around her neck.

"You could say that." She winked and tugged him along to finish the tour.

And when it was done, she prepared to open up shop. He insisted on staying with her while she worked, and she couldn't bring herself to shoo him out. Mostly because he kept to himself and, if anything, helped by bagging customers' purchases and wiping clean the glass displays. Karl was not only a model boyfriend but the perfect employee.

He stayed throughout the day, except for when he left for a moment but returned with lunch for them, for which she closed shop midday. Then she worked for another few hours before the last of her customers were rung through and she closed up after them. She'd usually finish up for the day by balancing the till, but she knew that she couldn't let Karl stand around any longer than he had already.

"Let's go," she said, grabbing her purse and swinging it over her shoulder.

He took her hand. "Are you sure? I don't mind sticking around longer."

"You've done enough for me. I just want to spend this first night with you *not* working."

They walked hand in hand out of her darkened shop and studio, and she was reminded of the night on New Year's Eve when they had both confessed to liking each other.

She jogged his memory and watched as a smile swept his face.

"I don't like you anymore," he told her, stopping, tucking her closer to his side and tipping up her chin. "Nowhere near as much as I love you."

Her chin trembled, and her responding smile felt wobbly. "I love you too." And she believed she always would.

* * * * *

COMING SOON!

We really hope you enjoyed reading this book.
If you're looking for more romance, be sure to
head to the shops when new books are
available on

Thursday 8th
December

To see which titles are coming soon, please visit
millsandboon.co.uk/nextmonth

MILLS & BOON

MILLS & BOON®

Coming next month

THEIR WILDEST SAFARI DREAM
Suzanne Merchant

She extended a slim hand towards him, her eyes fixed on his face. 'Hello, Jack,' she said, her voice as cool as her eyes.

'Anna?'

The word that came out of his throat was rough and harsh. It had lodged there, never to be spoken, for so long it sounded unreal, like some made up name. He tried it on his tongue again, as he closed his fingers around her hand.

'Anna.'

She left her hand in his for a moment, then withdrew it. He inhaled and tried to find some oxygen, but there didn't seem to be any in his vicinity. His head swam, and through a haze of shock he heard Dan's voice, again.

'Jack, this is Dr Kendall, who we've been expecting. Would you like me to show her to her suite?'

Jack pulled a hand over his eyes and shook his head. 'Thank you, Dan, no. I'll...I'll take it from here.'

'Okay.' Dan sounded doubtful. 'If you're sure?' He turned away then twisted round again. 'You were out of contact, Jack. The email only came in...'

Jack sent him a look and he shrugged and backed off, turning to take the steps down to the vehicle two at a time.

She…Anna…watched him with those frosty eyes. The last time he'd seen them they'd been sparkling like emeralds, with unshed tears. She'd jerked her head backwards, so the casual, farewell peck he'd steeled himself to drop on her cheek landed somewhere in the air between them. As he drove off he'd watched her in the rear view mirror and wondered if she'd let the tears fall once he'd gone. The set of her shoulders and her ramrod spine made him think otherwise. He'd breathed a sigh of relief, even though it felt as if a part of him had been ripped away.

He hauled his mind back to the present, to now, and how to handle this. His brain felt sluggish, as if he was watching a slow-motion movie of himself. He hated surprises. Most of the surprises he'd had in his life had been disasters dressed up by someone else to lessen the blow. Strangely, the only good one he could remember was Anna's first arrival at Themba, as a two-year old orphan. With the benefit of hindsight he'd realised that was the day some sort of purpose had begun to emerge from the random chaos of his childhood.

'It seems you aren't expecting me, Jack.' Her brow creased.

Continue reading
THEIR WILDEST SAFARI DREAM
Suzanne Merchant

Available next month
www.millsandboon.co.uk

Copyright © 2022 Suzanne Merchant

MILLS & BOON

THE HEART OF ROMANCE

A ROMANCE FOR EVERY READER

MODERN — Prepare to be swept off your feet by sophisticated, sexy and seductive heroes, in some of the world's most glamourous and romantic locations, where power and passion collide.

HISTORICAL — Escape with historical heroes from time gone by. Whether your passion is for wicked Regency Rakes, muscled Vikings or rugged Highlanders, awake the romance of the past.

MEDICAL — Set your pulse racing with dedicated, delectable doctors in the high-pressure world of medicine, where emotions run high and passion, comfort an love are the best medicine.

True Love — Celebrate true love with tender stories of heartfelt romance, from the rush of falling in love to the joy a new baby can bring, and a focus on the emotional heart of a relationship.

Desire — Indulge in secrets and scandal, intense drama and plenty of sizzling hot action with powerful and passionate heroes who have it all: wealth, status, good looks…everything but the right woman.

HEROES — Experience all the excitement of a gripping thriller, with an intense romance at its heart. Resourceful, true-to-life women and strong, fearless m face danger and desire - a killer combination!

To see which titles are coming soon, please visit

millsandboon.co.uk/nextmonth